MORE FROM JOSH GREEN

Dirtyville Rhapsodies

Secrets of Ash[*]

*Georgia Author of the Year nominee, 2024
*Winner, literary fiction: IndieReader Discovery Awards
*Runner up, fiction: Hollywood Book Festival, 2024
*Finalist, fiction: American Book Fest, Best Book Awards

PRAISE FOR JOSH GREEN

Secrets of Ash

"A fabulous book... These are great characters."   —*NPR*

"It's a propulsive suspense novel, with enough twists and turns to keep you reading until dawn."   —*Atlanta*

"A lyrical meditation on brotherhood and trauma. Green has a great observational eye and a talent for an unusual turn of phrase."   —*Kirkus Reviews*

"A compelling story of two brothers... whose fragile relationship is put to the ultimate test in the North Georgia mountains."   —*Atlanta-Journal Constitution*

"[A] finely written, intense, and powerful novel... Green unfolds [this] story with harrowing density and a raw-edged intimacy that is brutally compelling and deeply moving."   —*Indie Reader*

Dirtyville Rhapsodies

"These eighteen tightly plotted stories are a little unsettling and completely intoxicating, chock-full of dark, dark humor."   —Teresa Weaver, *Atlanta*

"In 'Dirtyville Rhapsodies,' the most unforgettable stories strike an improbable balance between sideshow, sermon, and war cry, leaving the reader to mull its idiosyncratic characters."
—Tray Butler, *Atlanta Journal-Constitution*

"This collection feels like a modern American neighborhood... Green reports from the literary homeland with a lion's heart and a steady hand. This fine book belongs on the shelf with any other collection published in recent years."
—Charles McNair, *Paste*

MORE FROM THE SAGER GROUP

The Swamp: Deceit and Corruption in the CIA
An Elizabeth Petrov Thriller (Book 1)
by Jeff Grant

Eat Wheaties: A Novel
by Michael Kun

#MeAsWell: A Novel
by Peter Melhlman

Death Came Swiftly: Novel About the Tay Bridge Disaster of 1879
by Bill Abrams

High Tolerance:
A Novel of Sex, Race, Celebrity, Murder... and Marijuana
by Mike Sager

Miss Havilland: A Novel
by Gay Daly

The Orphan's Daughter: A Novel
by Jan Cherubin

Lifeboat No. 8: Surviving the Titanic
by Elizabeth Kaye

Into the River of Angels: A Novel
by George R. Wolfe

See our entire library at TheSagerGroup.net

GOODBYE, SWEETBERRY PARK

A Novel of City Life, Creeping Gentrification, and Flesh-eating Snakes

Josh Green

Goodbye, Sweetberry Park: A Novel of City Life, Creeping Gentrification, and Flesh-eating Snakes

Copyright © 2025 Josh Green

Published in the United States of America.

Cover and interior designed by Siori Kitajima, PatternBased.com

Cataloging-in-publication data for this book is available from the Library of Congress

ISBN-13
eBook: 978-1-958861-51-6
Paperback: 978-1-958861-52-3

The Sager Group takes no responsibility for the interior content of this book. All editing was done personally by author at his request.

Published by The Sager Group LLC
(TheSagerGroup.net)

GOODBYE, SWEETBERRY PARK

Josh Green

For Rocco G. and Miss Anna

"They were proud of the place, proud of its growth, proud of themselves for making it grow. Let the older towns call Atlanta anything they pleased. Atlanta did not care."
— *Gone With the Wind*

"Scarlett looked about her for the little town she remembered so well. It was gone. The town she was now seeing was like a baby grown overnight into a busy, sprawling giant." — Same long book

"South of the North, yet north of the South, lies the City of a Hundred Hills, peering out from the shadows of the past into the promise of the future." — W.E.B. Du Bois

"Ain't a damn thing changed in Atlanta in a century and a half—except the whips and shackles is more discreet, and they usually involve a bulldozer!" — Squeaky

PART I

CHAPTER 1

Maybe it was the soupy summer—the soupiest I'd seen in Atlanta, as a matter of fact—that made the deranged zookeeper do what he did. Maybe "deranged" isn't precisely the word, but it's close. Because a man of sound mind wouldn't do such a thing to a city that'd really done nothing to him, as best we could tell. But he did. Oh, that bastard did. And because of what he did his name, Gerald McCaffrey, is forever mud. Maybe lower than mud. Certainly much lower than the belly of a snake. Gerald McCaffrey is the prehistoric bedrock of all tainted names. His reputation must be burning beside Lucifer, in the very lowest rung of hell. So yeah, Gerald McCaffrey: lousiest zookeeper that ever was. Gerald McCaffrey: worst son of Atlanta ever born.

Clearly, Gerald McCaffrey had gone mad. Like one possessed, shivering ant in a mound of six million. Looney Gerald. Batshit Gerald. Diabolically hurtful zookeeper Gerald. So probably deranged. And very much a product of our neurotic times. But maybe calling him the worst Atlantan ever born is too simplistic. This is a modern American metropolis, after all, which means it's a cesspool of bastards and worse. Or maybe I'm just being all indecisive again.

None of this is to say Gerald had always been a bad guy. Maybe not even a bastard, in the figurative sense. I would personally dig up the paperwork and report to the public that Mr. McCaffrey had thrice been honored as Atlanta Memorial Zoo's "Zookeeper of the Month." That's three times he bagged the *crème de la crème* of zoo-world attaboys— in the span of just two years, beating out the city's other eighty-five zookeepers. Gerald was, in fact, the Bill Russell and Meryl Streep of zookeepers. An icon. A standout. A stud. That was the good news, the bright side of Gerald, what any character witness would testify on the stand.

Now ask yourself how a person of such acclaim can become—within the span of just one year, since the last and certainly final trophy—the sort of asshole who'd steal seventeen of the world's deadliest snakes. Five snakes might've been permissible, possibly an accident. But *seven-damn-teen* snakes? That's basically four litters. And we're not talking about some idiot forgetting to lock the cages. Diabolical Gerald McCaffrey, per our reporting, transported this slithering cache into the night. Then he coaxed them from snake sacks and pointed them toward front-yard azalea bushes, myrtle branches, the beefy porches of proud Craftsmans, and street-side tricycles awaiting morning rides. He was the cruel piper no one saw coming, operating in reverse. All the while, amidst so much predawn steam, our city slept. We luxuriated in ignorance, beneath that merciful shade tree of night. The calm before the pandemonium.

At least there was a witness. Sort of.

These were the early facts: On Jackson Avenue, a woman who worked in the restaurant industry, age twenty-four, had stepped out for a menthol cigarette, her version of a lullaby on the front porch. She told police a man fitting McCaffrey's description—lanky, goofy, red-haired, leprechaun-White from a distance—was screaming in the meadow behind the zoo at maybe three-thirty a.m.

In the moonlight, per our smoker, the man was tossing empty beige sacks over his head and singing a tune she didn't recognize, though it may have been in the Yacht Rock or zydeco genre. He kept pointing toward the houses across the street, she said, all the pretty houses. He sounded upset, if not panicked. This strange man in the park wore a zoo uniform that incorporated every safari cliché; between his cackling, shouting, and pointing he appeared to comb the grass with his feet and holler voodoo nonsense downward, with the exception of the audible English word "basement." Then he slammed shut the gate of his old Ford, which had a homemade-looking cap over the bed made largely of wood. The truck roared north toward Midtown, per the smoker, the lone observer. Presuming that was indeed Mr. McCaffrey, it would be the last anyone saw of him, the snake sacks, or the zoo's roster of toxicology all-stars, for a while. With one very disconcerting exception.

My editor, Becky, rang me the next morning, just after daybreak. "*Johnson*," she said. "I've got one for you, man. You awake?"

"A bit," I said.

"You game to really chase something?" she said, her voice loud and caffeinated. "You got the time?"

"Time? What do you think?"

"I mean," Becky said, "you're not bogged down with other freelance writing this week?"

The longer I live, the more I'm convinced laziness is a virtue. I don't mean failing to put forth effort toward productivity or ignoring the needs of good people to instead take naps. I mean appreciating the little stuff, savoring the notion of life itself and not burning around in pursuit of dollars and impressive bullshit. I mean really *feeling* the couch against your back and the way that potted tulip in the window caresses Southern sunshine, which is honest sunshine. The capacity for not giving two shits is a tremendous luxury. But then the power lady calls and says three days and the lights go off and man that always gets me down.

"No, Becky, I'm ready," I said. "Let's do it."

I could hear her hands swiftly arranging papers, probably scrawled with her notes. "So you know that new snake habitat at the zoo? The one actually shaped like a glass python or alligator or whatever?"

"I can pretty much see it from my porch."

"Don't freak out, but there's been a jailbreak, so to speak," she said.

"Like a reptile mutiny?"

"No," she said. "An inside job. The work of a sadistic zookeeper."

"Ah, that makes sense."

"They think he'd come off his meds. And then, you know, unleashed his constituents."

"Unleashed?" I said. "Like they're roaming the sidewalks?"

"It's bad, Johnson."

At that point, my living room seemed to spin off its axis. I started to tear up a little. The zoo was maybe eight blocks up the hill. I shivered and looked out the window, expecting my windmill palms and Leyland cypress to be dripping with vipers. Or the ones that can spit venom—sniper vipers. I locked the dead bolt on my front door and collected myself. "How can you possibly know that detail already?" I said.

"The zoo's PR head called me himself," said Becky. "He trusts us, and he wants to preemptively take control, in every way possible. It's a problem. It's real. And it could get nuclear."

Sunlight from the front windows fell over me. I was shirtless in my underwear. I saw in the parlor mirror an age-induced slippage, from chin to knees, gravity's sick prank, a slow and sorry avalanche of complex ancestry.

"So the zoo wants to get this out there as methodically and safely as possible," she said. "The potential for panic is, obviously, huge. I need a steady hand. I need a pro."

"How many snakes?"

"They're counting."

"Is their black mamba among the missing?"

"Yes," said editor Becky. "They know that for sure."

"And that giant anaconda?"

"Oh, that too."

"This is terrible."

"It is."

"And one hell of a story. I'll leave now," I said, "and call you with an update at noon."

"That's my ace."

"This feels like a series of stories, Beck. It'll take some time to get to the bottom. Will you pay per story?"

"So long as the quality—and accuracy—is there. I need this all written in that calming, wry-grandfather voice. I think that'd come across best."

"This is new territory for me," I said. "I don't know snakes."

"Ditto, of course."

"But I'll try, ma'am."

"Stop *calling* me that," she said. "It sounds weird when you're twice my age. And it makes you sound so, like, rural."

"It only sounds weird to you transplants."

"Anyway," she said, "I'll email you all the contacts I have. Now go, go, *go!*"

"Thanks for the call," I said, swelling for a second with gratitude and rare pride in myself. My house was rickety and needed a new roof. A running story—and running income—could be a great help.

Doesn't matter if you're a blue-blooded Manhattanite or Nicaraguan sugar farmer, the notion of rampant exotic snakes does not jibe with your Monday plans. It's like an approaching hurricane, only sneaky as shit. Imagine the implications of a freewheeling green anaconda in your town, that slithering brontosaurus of up to thirty feet. That's a telephone pole of slick, gorgeous, silent, invincible muscle. Plus a head the size of a Ouija Board, and a hundred teeth like reapers' blades. Imagine this one beast's bearing on your consciousness as you walk your dog, retrieve kiddos from squealy day cares, or try to sleep. Our reptile phobia is deep as DNA, common as freckles. It's easily triggered, and it dominates the psyche. *Can anacondas pry open windows?* asks the paranoid brain at two a.m., coddled in a down pillow. *Can they worm through the ductwork and get me?* Now pretend that lout was ostensibly joined in god-awful emancipation by sixteen comrades infinitely more horrifying because they are smaller. So small, in fact, they're virtually invisible amid the chunky foliage of Deep South summers. Try to be productive. Try to smile. Try not to think—during every waking moment, and again in dreams—of their mouths aflame with kill juice, their brains without remorse, their bodies dropping from air-conditioning vents above your bed and getting you.

Let's say your town or city or village prides itself on getting along with itself. Imagine that harmony is a sort of local currency. Because around here, in what the Chamber of Commerce or something once coined the "New South," we've turned peace into profit. We've bandied the famous slogan "The City Too Busy to Hate" for decades, to largely positive effect. (Pessimists will say the slogan is half-truth at best and, at worst, a distraction from the historical reality: "Birmingham, Only More Monied, Way Bigger, and Less Blatantly Racist.") Still, in my sixty-nine years as a dues-paying member of society, I've learned that harmony is delicate. That a single foolish word can rile the masses, or shatter somebody's life. Classism, ageism, racism, the varied silly pressures of geography—these are the landmines. It's all a big, careful, American dance. And it doesn't take kindly to provocation.

As summer lay down upon us like a venom-sick horse, in the year 2018, in what'll probably be the penultimate decade of my life, our beloved urban cesspool was being gripped by remarkable change. The kettle had been bubbling for years, and right about the time McCaffrey did his thing, the boil was beginning to hiss. It was exactly what we had coming. But historians will probably just blame the damn snakes.

Gerald McCaffrey's selectivity said one thing for sure: His brain, however frazzled, wasn't total mush in the wee hours of May 22. The anaconda and a boa notwithstanding, he'd assiduously selected and stolen from the zoo's collection the fifteen snakes most capable of injecting lethal doses of venom. (Later, in his own captivity, McCaffrey would describe the picks as his "greatest hits," as if a liberated coastal taipan was an ear-wormy Motown ditty.) Growing up, I'd had two uncles and a cousin who'd survived—nay, *experienced*—bites from common copperheads. While traipsing around suburban woods, my clumsy ilk had been hit low, which was followed by the burning ankles, nausea, fuzzy vision, and sweats. Maybe they missed work a day or school for a while. That's about it. Point is, we know venomous snakes around here. Even city kids occasionally catch fangs. But copperheads, relatively speaking, give kisses. Flesh nibbles. Minimal tissue decay. Nothing a couple of frosty Buds and Motrin can't quell.

Unfortunately for inner-city Atlanta, or what the corporate developers by 2018 had coined "CenterTown®," the black mamba isn't much of a kisser. It's a family-wrecker, a widow-maker and wife-whacker, a sub-Saharan assassin. I'd studied this particular animal during zoo visits with my precocious niece. We marveled that something so seemingly benign (the small face almost smiles, with no sharp edges) could be the most dangerous thing on the premises, save maybe those understandably cranky Sumatran tigers. Worse yet, a black mamba in the shadows or leaves is no more conspicuous than a dark branch or bicycle inner-tube. The name is kind of a misnomer because they—or at least the prized one kept by our zoo—are really olive, or perhaps brown in some light. The black is in their mouths, behind the knives.

Think of a drop of red food coloring on a white dish. Now add one more little drop. That much venom from a black mamba (a fang's graze across your finger) can fry your nervous system and drop you dead within half an hour. Without antivenin, you have almost no chance; when it comes to mortality rates, these fuckers basically bite a thousand. Every year, as scientists would eventually explain for our stories, they kill hundreds of people in their wide-open native wilds, far from any Walmart or twenty-screen Cineplex or sculpted rose bushes like Miss Turner keeps around her dainty Victorian. They are incompatible with clueless Americans for all the reasons above, and because of this one, too: Black mambas, they say, are *faster* than most humans. And sometimes very long. Our particular renegade, per my recollection from zoo visits, stretched almost ten feet. When stumbled upon, or provoked in the slightest way, a specimen that big can rise several feet off the dirt—faking that it's a cobra, as evolution dictates—and not just stand its ground but *charge*. Which, of course, is the ultimate nightmare from hell.

After hanging up with my editor, I rang the zoo number she'd provided. A young, panting man answered. His pained tone and cracking throat suggested I'd interrupted his being tortured with battery probes, or the emotional equivalent of such. I wanted to catch him off guard, in hopes he'd spill an exclusive secret.

"It's God Johnson from *The Atlanta Beacon*," I said.

"Oh, God," he said.

People like that joke. They have for thirty years, since the kids in my formerly all-Black neighborhood cursed me with the nickname. Relative to them, I was White, the most honky thing around back then. When I spoke—and speak, I suppose—the dialect is more twangy Southern suburbia than the more interesting genetic component of me: rogue Nigerian. Add to that a silver mane and white beard atop a six-foot frame, and "God" I naturally became.

"Look, sir," the young PR employee said. "I pleaded with your Metro editor about this earlier. We're assessing the situation. I can't release much. I really shouldn't confirm anything yet. You understand the implications here, I'm sure."

"I'm just wondering something," I said. "How could a guy—just one guy, as I understand it—pull this off?"

"Look," he said again, with three times the aggravation. "I'm not confirming *anything* yet."

"Off the record?"

His sigh was loud, forceful. "Off the record," he said. "And it better *stay* off the record, God."

"Is that big black mamba among the missing?"

"There are many gone," he said.

"Come on," I said. "You know the answer."

"Yes, sir, that animal is the most disconcerting, as I understand it."

"What should we do?" I said. "I mean collectively, as a city?"

"Look, we're working on this, all hands on deck here." He was growling now, while issuing whispered directives to someone else. "We're devising a strategy for the dissemination of what we know, everything we've gathered so far—"

"Come *on*," I said. "That's bunk. Just give me something. Something small, even."

"It's unprecedented, as you can imagine. Call back in an hour, or come to the main zoo entrance."

"Ten-four."

"But, Mr. Johnson, listen," and he paused for a moment, as if hesitant to breach some professional barrier. "I know from your newspaper columns that you live in the neighborhood. I can't stress enough how careful you have to be if you walk here."

I spouted an inappropriate laugh; I wouldn't have walked a block for ten news stories.

"Goodbye, God. We have to get moving, OK?"

Loud background chatter. Ruffling papers. Someone shouting and another screeching in managerial tones. And then dial tone. Not one good fact for the record.

As it turned out, it wouldn't matter for long. The zoo never got to hold its calculated press conference that morning. Instead, the beginning of our self-inflicted summer from hell unfolded, unofficially, a few weeks before the actual equinox, at nine forty-three a.m. in the parking lot of Uncle Jimmy's Homerun Barbecue, down by the old baseball stadium. That's when a teacher en route to work downtown called the police. According to the 911 transcript, she said this:

"Yes, um, there's a *dragon* right here, in the parking lot, and it looks real dangerous. Just the wickedest thing. Like a fat, long, little dragon. That's the only way I can say it. But I think it's crushed, too. All the way dead. Obviously, it ain't from here. And it's scary, just bad looking. I hate to think what it might could do to some children."

Just as I'd started taping closed my doorjambs and windowsills, I heard the sirens headed west, and my gut said to follow them. I dressed and sprinted across my yard, jumped into my truck, and roared off. One broadcast station in town, Chanel 17 Action News, was right behind the cops in a white Action Van; they're a clever and nimble herd of enterprising scumbags who'd figured out how to circumvent encrypted police scanners, tapping the secret distress calls of police. Ample competition, in other words. I stuck close, and we went too fast through quiet neighborhoods. When our cavalcade arrived at the homicide scene, the crowd was already a squirming, sweaty mess. The dragon was indeed slain. But a dragon it technically was not.

Nobody could stand still, and from the crowd's chatter came an earnest question that, at that moment, at that scene, I alone held the answer to: *How the hell did a giant rattler end up smashed at Uncle Jimmy's Barbecue?*

Actually, it was an Australian death adder. A rattler's worst nightmare.

And maybe "smashed" isn't precisely the word. More like perforated. Understand that these particular snakes are short and extremely thick, with heads like shovels. It had twice been run over by different cars, near the tail and head, popping out its eyeballs and lending the body the appearance, from a few yards away, of arms and legs jutting off the girth. A dead dragon, basically.

Two cops shouted for the crowd to disperse. Nobody moved, so transfixed on the victim, the hit-and-run aftermath.

I could feel the beginnings of it, right then and there. Grace was exiting the city; decorum was boarding a one-way flight; placidity croaked atop sizzling pavement. The soupy season was upon us. And four months of historic ugliness— our summer of friction, tension, and death—had begun.

"Officer," a lady in orange shouted over the crowd, fanning herself with her hand. "I think you'd best call the National Guard."

CHAPTER 2

Two days before Gerald McCaffrey's mass kidnapping, in a musty basement meeting room at City Hall South, the city's most controversial, big shot real estate developer had come before the zoning board with what he called a historical land deal. I was there that night, too. Fishing for stories, working the low-pay hustle, enduring pre-snake mundanity.

The room, as always, was rank with governmental seriousness, its walls dotted with aerial maps and oil paintings. The paintings depicted historic decisions being argued by rigid men in tights and ponytails. All of the men were White—and extremely, SPF 100 White at that. The city's most powerful developer is not White. That sort of contrast in this town, I've always thought, is subversive and cool. The city's most powerful developer is not cool.

For me, seeing such a big fish flop into the zoning room that night was a cause for joy. It had been a slow spring on the freelance journalism front, and I was getting nervous. My pantry was loaded with hearty canned beans, jerky, and Pop-Tarts, but my cherished old gingerbread Victorian was failing again. Its upkeep had claimed nearly all of my savings.

Each hard rain sent fresh anxiety trickling down my upstairs bedroom walls. I knew I'd be powerless to fix the roof without landing a string of good work, which is why I was seated attentively in a metal folding chair that night, front row, scribbling down insufferable minutia about sidewalk widths and commercial storefront setbacks. Everything was boring. Until none other than Lawrence "Lotto" Livingston sauntered in, presenting his portly, haughty presence like a birthday cake. He stood over me and gave an unusually courteous nod. "Evening, God."

My white whiskers split into a smile. Story prospects and dollar signs whirled like pixies around my brain. "If it isn't Mr. Livingston, in the basement of zoning purgatory," I said. "Don't you have a team of underlings to handle something like this? A bunch of pissants?"

"Go easy, my brother."

I winced. Lotto had always been among the few dorks to play that "my brother" card with such a fair-skinned non-brother as me. My maternal grandmother, as the story goes, was a loose, freewheeling, but gorgeous gambler in early twentieth century Atlanta. The sort of low-grade hustler who thrived in the post-Reconstruction, prerecession boom. She had a downtown rendezvous one night with a visiting Nigerian academic at Georgia Tech. He vanished, and grandmother tried unsuccessfully to drink the shame of young, unwed pregnancy out of her. She was of Scots-Irish ancestry, and the combination made an exotic anomaly of my mother, who would never know her father's real name and then die, devastatingly, of a brain hemorrhage when I was just five. Further dilution of my melanin, courtesy of my father's Scandinavian blood, made me something like a bleached Brazilian as a kid, or in late summer, a sort of Bahamian rabbi beneath bushy, curly hair. A purebred American mutt—no big deal. That's how I'd always considered myself, basically. But at first, most people just thought I looked really strange.

"Wouldn't your wife do this chore for you?" I said to Lotto, still ribbing.

"Same old God Johnson," Lotto said, looking behind him. "Never short on quips. Always something to say." For a man of such means his teeth were a browning, busted-up disaster. And he'd developed an inexplicable affection for herringbone tweed sport coats, even at the cusp of summer. These lent him the air of an Edwardian detective or, when his jackets were older and threadbare, a homeless aristocrat.

"Seriously," I said. "Why are you down here, sir?"

Lotto reached over and clutched my shoulder. Whether it was an affectionate gesture or a silent, physical warning, I couldn't tell.

"I still like to get out of the office, to do things besides lunch with the mayor," Lotto said. "To face the people, the board members, you know. It's invigorating."

I flapped my arm, casting off his hand. "I guess that makes sense."

He leaned over again. "I've wondered," he said, more quietly. "You ever find a lady?"

"Sir?"

"I mean, *another* lady?"

I deflated. I crumbled.

"Oh, God," he said, grinning. "You can't still be celibate, right?"

Squirming, red-faced, and desperate to change the subject, I gave him my best confused-reporter expression, pointing to paperwork beside me. Lotto's name and that of his company, Pumpernickel Enterprises, were not mentioned on the evening's zoning agenda. The company name, as Lotto would brag to anyone, was not an homage to carbohydrates but a nod to our city's reputation as the brown mecca, a diverse and richly productive kingdom over which he ruled, he was convinced. I held up a copy of the agenda and shrugged. He winked.

"Just keep that pencil sharp," said Lotto. "We've got a story for you tonight."

His conniving smile was a confession: Lotto was operating under an obscure business LLC as a means of camouflage. The hairs on my neck danced. I dragged a big X across my other notes—all worthless scrawling, destined to bore editors. Something interesting and probably controversial was afoot. I guessed that Lotto was cooking up an even more detestable, dastardly plan than the uninspired schlock Pumpernickel Enterprises usually built. The stuff neighborhoods fight with yard signs. The *papier-mâché*-like apartments and office complexes that, when finished, look like lazy meditations on subpar building materials: all vinyl siding, asphalt parking lots, bargain windows, cheap stucco, and cloth awnings. Regardless, a well-connected, pedigreed titan of Atlanta development like Lotto could probably pass a condo stack of cow shit through zoning and permitting with his yellow eyes closed.

But these rooms, they change with Lotto in them. They reek of secrets, like bedrooms with a naked, trembling fling in the closet. Every set of shoulders on the eight-member zoning board—half women, equal parts Black and White, all tired from long days at jobs that actually paid them—visibly clenched as Lotto stepped up to the dais. His trick with the evening's agenda had apparently deceived them as well.

"Rest assured," Lotto began, his jagged teeth jutting from a forced smile, "I come in peace this time."

The board president, Kim Somethingerother (I had yet to confirm the spelling of her throaty Germanic surname), leaned forward. "The line item here says your LLC will seek council approval for a historic preservation project in the Sweetberry Park neighborhood."

"Yes, ma'am."

(I wrote "SHIT!" in my flip notebook.)

"I must say, Mr. Livingston," said Kim. "This seems out of character for you. Preservation? Really? From the king of clear-cutting and bulldozers? Anyhow, sorry—yes, please enlighten us."

"Gladly," Lotto said, grinning.

"As I'm sure you're aware," said another board member, Jerry Malone, a Spike Lee doppelgänger and retired history professor, "much of Sweetberry Park falls under historic protections."

"Indeed, sir," said Lotto.

"So," continued Jerry, "wiping slates of land clean for development just doesn't, and can't, happen over there. I'm not trying to be presumptive here—just diligent and forthright. And for the record, if you're not aware, Sweetberry Park happens to be the neighborhood of a certain well-known media member in the room." All eight faces turned to me; I blushed. "With God here, Mr. Livingston, any sort of municipal funny business won't be a secret for long."

Aglow with fake kindness, Lotto gave me a thumbs-up. "Relax, ladies and gentlemen," he said. "Sit back. Have a look." He nodded his immense, freckled head toward the audience, and three suited Pumpernickel Enterprises greenhorns (unpaid interns, doubtless) dutifully sprang up. They scurried toward briefcases and what looked like oversize satchels in a corner; he'd had reinforcements behind me all along.

"What I bring before y'all tonight is a win-win-win," Lotto said. "Or maybe a win times four. Goodness, maybe a *five-way* win!" He lifted his arms, inspired. "Now, just give us one minute to set up this short, compelling presentation..."

I'd first met Lotto in the late nineties, when he inherited his father's business and looked like the type of ambitious Morehouse College graduate who might affect lasting positive change in our city. They called him Lawrence back then.

With an army of contractors still loyal to his late father—Lionel Livingston, also a developer, and a sweet-hearted philanthropist to his golden core—the scion set to work rehabbing rec centers in destitute neighborhoods, of which there was no shortage back then. Despite those noble efforts, young Lawrence's first front-page headlines didn't come until he transformed a former tomato processing factory into an afterschool sports club for boys and girls who'd maintained B averages, or better. An analysis two years later showed substantial drops in petty crime in that district, and Lawrence was canonized. Scuttlebutt was that he might be angling for a shot at the mayor's seat, at age twenty-nine. And then this lucky scoundrel won the Georgia Lottery—$2.5 million, after taxes. After that, Lawrence nicknamed *himself* Lotto, and the name stuck. His wealth and head grew. He soon became national news, for a brief stint, in a freshly post-9/11 world starving for homegrown, earnest heroes who were lifting up cities. A national magazine editor (title now defunct) called me out of the blue; soon I was dispatched to the Livingston household in Evergreen Estates, the South's so-called Black Beverly Hills, a few miles southwest of downtown. Lotto knew of my previous journalism work within his community and granted me full access for some reason. I guess he figured I was either visually impaired or willing to gloss over a true domestic horror show, to which he'd gleefully flung open the front doors. The contrast between the guy in the papers and who Lotto actually was—and is, I suppose—all but punched me in the face.

For starters, I'd never seen a wife so robotically obedient. At breakfast, as I observed, Matilda Livingston nervously squeezed his grapefruit juice, halved a kiwi, poached his eggs, and whipped up an arrangement of tart sauces. She made Turkish coffee and buttered his wheat toast. All of this was done with the silent precision of an oppressed Russian seamstress. Upstairs in the primary bathroom, her man whistled optimistic tunes, a hodgepodge of early OutKast choruses, Marvin Gaye, and Sinatra. "You keep it warm, bay-bee," he'd called into the mezzanine; a melting pat of suburban Macon (his father's home turf) still buttered his dialect back then. "I'll need that nourishment today."

In a moment, Lotto sauntered downstairs and approached his wife with a wink and fast kiss, a gust of cologne. Back then, younger and more exacting, he wore Ted Baker London pinstripes and a precisely ruffled pocket square. The shoes, reflective as mirrors, were early John Varvatos. Without provocation—and I'm not making this up—he proceeded, in a sick and smiley way, to berate his wife for being "incapacitated by shyness" and "damn lazy." She merely nodded and said something inaudible about groceries. Beneath curly brown-blonde locks like nineties Janet Jackson's, she had big doe eyes that, I thought, telegraphed her breaking heart to me. It was history's saddest breakfast, and there I was, blatantly scribbling notes about sexism and galling ego. After just a taste of coffee, Lotto stood up and walked to a basket above the kitchen television. He shook out keys to the Jaguar, some kind of turbo, his favorite springtime ride, he said. And then he grabbed the back of Matilda's head and implanted a full tongue kiss, showing off. I nearly walked out the backdoor.

Instead I tagged along with Lotto to work, riding shotgun, and turned the old tape recorder on. We flew at ninety-five miles per hour to suburban Harton County, where Lotto was trying to sell commissioners on plans for a cheaply built subdivision. It would be obscenely dense for the allotted backcountry site, but he thought it was perfect. Nothing was particularly illuminating about that day, except for one telling detail that hung around Lotto's neck, which the editors thankfully kept in my lede paragraph for the magazine:

Lotto Livingston strolls through the Harton County Courthouse metal detector, pulling his tongue across big, jagged teeth, his briefcase swinging like an alligator-skin pendulum. He glides on leather soles across the ancient marble floor. Courthouse patrons nod in his direction but say nothing, which he considers reverence. He halts before the high oak doors of the Commissioners Quarters and digs the gold cross on his necklace from between two buttons of his Oxford, around the lemon-yellow tie. He studies the golden Jesus that he thinks is crying. His father, the beloved Atlanta developer Lionel Livingston, who died of bile duct cancer three years ago, had bought the necklace when he toiled as a law clerk in Macon, then handed it down to his prodigious, eldest son when he aced Morehouse. The successor has worn the piece at each government hearing for a decade, even though it's borderline macabre, an exaggeratedly tortured Jesus. Through land battles and zoning disputes and legal combat involving the angle of driveways, Livingston has never lost a decision. By the tally book he keeps in his Jaguar, he's one hundred seventy nine and zero when it comes to getting what he wants approved. He likes to think the Jesus heirloom has played a significant role, a deflector of bad luck and superior arguments. Then again, Lotto Livingston doesn't believe any arguments are better than his.

Lotto didn't take kindly to my dissing his Jesus in the story. And he isn't the type to let a grudge dissolve. I don't think he ever forgave me, honestly, which is why his concern for my well-being in the zoning basement was all the more peculiar.

As Lotto readied his presentation for zoning arbiters, I saw him snake his fingers through his shirt again, exhume the cross, and nervously rub it. An intern came forward and opened a briefcase, extracted a folded easel and a long white scroll. Lotto twisted and locked the easel until it stood erect before the board. He hooked the scroll and unraveled it the length of the easel, to the carpet. Now, displayed in bright reds and florescent greens, his vision beamed on white paper: a tight network of trees and cul-de-sac streets surrounded by long vertebrae of houses, all beneath the bold title, "Sweetberry Lanes: The Deluxe Urban Lifestyle You Know You've Earned." Lotto gave an elegant little cough.

"Ladies and gentlemen of the board, I don't have to remind y'all that we live in changing times, or what we might call a golden age of opportunity," he said, regally. "Our city, in more turbulent eras, was much too quick to bulldoze and throw away the wonderful, irreplace-able structures of our forefathers. Well, now, that's also changing." He reached into his pocket and dug out a laser-pointer, then threw a red dot on the easel. "You could say Sweetberry Park is perfect as it is. It's a showcase of diver-sity, in terms of demographics and architecture, that's for sure. But what I need you to see tonight, in the next two minutes, is how it can be *immeasurably better.* How it can be *more* diversified, and even more inviting. Especially for Atlantans who might not've hit their financial stride yet, but who are so hungry for a bite of the Big Peach. So long as they have good credit."

"You mean millennials?" said board leader Kim. "Isn't that the word these days?"

Lotto gave her a "bingo" point. "Not that we like to assign labels to potential buyers," he said. "But sure, the millen-nial generation. And upwardly trending young families. Late-wave urban pioneers. Budding zoomers. Downsizing boomers. Entrepreneurial hipsters. DINKs. You name it."

Kim cocked her head. "DINKS?"

"That's Double Income, No Kids households," Lotto said. "But we don't judge. We're inclusive at Pumpernickel, as the name implies."

That was so hilarious, and so stupid, I clenched every muscle in my face to not explode with laughter.

"Let's just cut to the chase," said Kim. "Where in the world are you planning to squeeze this in? I'm counting at least fifty houses up there on your board."

"Ah, yes," said Lotto. "Let's have a look."

I squinted to see the artist's rendering of the proposed subdivision: plastic-looking trees, ornate lampposts, generic three-story Monopoly houses so tightly packed you couldn't toss a beach ball between them, which is OK in a city, of course, just questionable in some historic settings. And everywhere in the rendering were giddy robots, the illustrated people. Each of these hypothetical buyers—my potential neighbors, all—had that daffy, the-weed-is-kicking-in facial expression, as they pedaled bicycles, tossed bocce balls, or drank from coffee cups with their like-minded friends in the streets. One looked vaguely Asian, but otherwise they all were White.

"Wait!" I piped up, breaking all protocol for zoning meetings. "This proposal here, it's shaped exactly like what we call The Flank, over by Sweetberry Park's railroad tracks. It's a historic district of shotgun houses that sprang up around the railroad, and there's no way—"

"Mr. Johnson!" scolded Kim. "Calm down, please. We'll save time for public commentary after the presentation, if we can. You know better, sir."

Lotto's glare burned hate-holes into my soul. He continued: "Our Lord and Savior here is trying to play spoiler, but yes, the shape of Sweetberry Lanes is no coincidence. And that speaks to the most innovative aspect of this entire idea: a preservation initiative like Atlanta has never seen."

"I'm confused," Kim said. "You need a blank slate of property to build this project that's on your easel, yet you're calling it preservation?"

"Fifteen homes," said Lotto. "That's the scope, in terms of what's on the site now. Just fifteen little houses. Shacks, really. And Mr. Johnson is correct; they're in the shotgun style. He's wrong, though, in thinking they're protected in any way. There's been talk for years of filing the paperwork for historic protections, but nobody ever followed through. Nothing can prevent another developer from displacing everyone who lives there, pulverizing The Sweetberry Flank, trucking it off to a landfill, wiping it away forever. Which is where I come in, but not how you're thinking…"

Lotto bent his knees, snapped fingers across his tongue for moisture, and flipped the big page back. "This might look like an ordinary, pole-supported structure to you, with its understated siding and metal roof," he said. "But ladies and gentlemen of the board, this is in fact a museum!"

"No," said a lady at the bench's end. "That there's a metal *barn.*"

"OK, yes, the exterior design is tentative," Lotto said, nodding. "It's what inside, as you see here in this illustration at the bottom, that counts. Every single home in The Sweetberry Flank will be meticulously deconstructed, and then rebuilt—*resurrected,* even—within this protective museum. The homes will stand for decades in here. Centuries, probably. Your grandchildren's grandchildren will marvel at the preserved, period architecture. And they'll barely have to travel to see this museum. I closed three weeks ago on the ideal site; it's a pastoral horse farm in Butler County, only thirty-five miles south of downtown—"

"Thirty-five miles!" the same lady shouted. "Hell, why not truck 'em to Florida?"

Silence from Lotto. He reached between his Oxford buttons and fiddled.

Kim intervened: "So what exactly are you seeking from the board, Mr. Livingston?"

"Nothing," he said. "The land is zoned multifamily residential already, from a similar plan that failed a decade ago. This won't fail. It's ready to go. Just add buyers. And on that note, the... uh, divine publicity from tonight won't hurt either."

Kim's eyes tightened. "I'm guessing you own The Sweetberry Flank now, correct?"

"I plan to, within about two months," Lotto said. "I'm under contract with every single homeowner, all fifteen houses."

I was writhing in my chair, biting my lip, but one vital point had to be made. "Those are very old folks, The Flank's owners, every single one of them, and they're not savvy to real estate markets," I said. "Where will they go? Where—"

"Mr. Johnson!" said Kim. "One more outburst, and you'll be removed!"

Lotto bowed his head and fiddled with the long-necked microphone. "Look, that's a discussion for another day," he said. "But suffice it to say, I've made very generous offers, all above market, and these folks were happy to accept. All of them. They'd never live to see a better offer."

Kim pointed a mauve-painted fingernail at the easel, nodding and happy. "Thanks for your presentation of—well—*all* of this, Mr. Livingston," said Kim. "Very courteous of you to keep each level of government in the loop. The city's changing, as you say, and there's a certain artistry to this project."

(Into my notebook I jotted, "KIM + LOTTO = FUKN EACH OTHER!!")

Lotto lifted a bejeweled finger. "One more point," he said. "Regarding the old folks... knowing that their homes will live on in perpetuity, in this sturdy museum, that really sealed the deal for them. Their blessings, I must say, were the proverbial cherries on my cake."

I slammed shut my little notebook, as if doing so was a powerful statement of protest. Then I saluted the board and stormed to my truck. I tore through the night to Sweetberry Park, to my street, to The Flank, and beat on the heart-pine door of bungalow No. 3. After several rounds of knocking I stopped, listened for a commotion inside, watched for a light. I saw nothing. But I knew she was there. I knew she heard me. And, because of her hiding, I knew she knew what I'd learned that night. I stepped back from her door, onto her little steps, and hollered, "How *could* you, lady?"

CHAPTER 3

The flattened Australian death adder forced the zoo's hand. Horrifying, inexplicable, slain creatures from the other side of the planet apparently do that.

In all my years covering crime, I'd never seen anything like the parking lot fiasco. Everyone there seemed sad, in a way, but nobody knew exactly what they were mourning. I watched as mortified police newbies were ordered to shovel the snake's remains into a sort of flimsy Tupperware coffin and then log them as evidence. Behind me, I heard an older man quip to his wide-eyed boy: "I'm thinkin' it's maybe from outer space."

Someone would have to come forward and offer an explanation, pronto. But no one from the zoo turned up at the death scene, as best I could tell. Nobody else had answers, and no cop would wager a guess on camera, so the news crews dispersed. The crowd at Uncle Jimmy's eventually trickled away, too, but on each sweaty face I saw the strain of percolating fear; the clenched foreheads and exacerbated crow's feet were speaking questions their mouths weren't: *How did that monster get here? And is it alone?*

Playing dumb and steering clear of bushes, I asked an elderly lady in a business dress for a moment of her time. She was hustling back to her car, obviously busy, but I wanted her input in case I'd need the man-on-the-street perspective when I broke the biggest story of my life. She whipped around, bothered by me, and Lord she was perfect. Her antique face was furrowed with parentheses, and her voice was coarse but strong: "Let me tell you somethin', and you can go ahead and quote me," she said, as I jotted notes. "The Bible say a snake came from Paul's burning sticks because of the heat. The *heat*. It couldn't take the heat and made a meal of Paul's hand. People in this city need to realize the fault of their ways. It's been boiling up, and now it's *here*, all the consequences. There's a hotness coming like nobody knows—a *reckoning* like ain't nobody seen before!"

The lady closed her eyes and prayed. Her comment had put paranoia where my professionalism was supposed to be, and I visibly shivered in her shadow. I scurried off, like some rookie, without asking her name.

By noon that day, zoo brass had emailed a very timid, vague, and corporate-sounding press release to every traditional media outlet, city blog, podcast studio, PTA LISTSERV, and significant neighborhood leadership group in town. It called for a two p.m. press conference in a building near the zoo entrance. The purpose was to discuss "a significant matter involving exotic animals and subsequent remediation," proving that even shit shows of Biblical proportions can be made to sound lame. Other media probably thought the gorillas were sick.

I grabbed a falafel and retreated to the newspaper's downtown offices. I waved my credentials badge to the security guard, Rick, and sequestered myself ten stories above the street, far beyond the climbing capabilities of any tree viper or red-tailed boa.

Without a position on the *Beacon*'s staff, I neither had nor wanted a desk in the building. So I beelined for my editor's office. It was a glassy corner space with perpetually clean windows but substandard views, mainly of dirty sky-rise roofs and dirtier alleyways. As expected, I found my editor pacing these windows like a caged momma jaguar, clicking a pen in one hand and thumbing a cell phone with the other. Becky Rodriguez, a Wyoming transplant with no discernible dialect and an aerial gymnast's physique, was half my age but the type of shoe-leather, no-bullshit journalist who gave me hope the industry might survive the Digital Apocalypse. She knew that, beneath my cynicism, I still lived to chase information the old-fashioned and righteous way: by jumping in the middle of volcanoes and describing the heat. She spotted me from twenty yards across the newsroom and waved me in. I clicked the office door closed and dropped my bagged falafel on the floor. I reached out and shook a tenacious, pretty little hand callused by the rocky knobs of indoor climbing facilities.

"You see the zoo's press release?" Becky asked. "Holy hell, how much you think they'll say?"

"I've seen a lot more than that."

"You need to be there, at the zoo," she said. "Two hours. I'm thinking about putting something short together, beforehand. Just a few paragraphs to show that we know. A preemptive thing that proves we're out ahead of this. But maybe that's immoral—"

"You hear me?" I said. "One's dead already, smashed by cars."

"What? *Where?*"

"At that barbecue shack between the expressway and the old Braves stadium. I followed a bunch of sirens over there and saw it all firsthand."

"Holy hell, Johnson."

"I can't tell you how sinister this bastard was," I said. "Body was like a long little tank. Like a swollen garden hose. Looked like Satan in the face, too, and I'm not exaggerating. But I don't think TV news knows the broader context yet. They didn't act like it."

"You get a photo?"

I slapped my forehead, which made my silver ponytail dance. "No. Forgot. Sorry."

Actually, I hadn't forgotten; I'd refused. Because I'm not a damn photographer. And I can't get accustomed to this whole internet shtick of wearing so many new hats, performing so many online monkey tricks that have nothing to do with our main job, which is reporting the news. All the constant updates and hot takes—it all gets in the way of the real duty. Not to mention all the whiny confessionals posted about various feelings and life passages, the begging for sanctification, the endless two-thumbed onanism of our cellphone-dominated lives. It just makes me want to vomit. Which, of course, is why I'm teetering on the edge of occupational extinction and total irrelevance.

"That's down by your neighborhood," she said. "Did they panic, in the parking lot?"

"I'd call it more stunned confusion. But Beck, I'm worried. My gut says this isn't going to be handled well, at any level. It's going to be big and ugly. It's going to make our city a viral joke."

She squinted her gray, serious eyes, the sort of non-listening contemplation that precedes bosses heaping a shit-load of work on you. "It's a crisis," she said. "And we can't keep it secret beyond two more hours. I don't care what the zoo says. Did you get anything from bystanders? Anything to work with right now, in the interim?"

"Yes. Well, a little. I tried to interview this voodoo church lady—"

"*Listen*," she interrupted. "I think we need to get a team down there. We need to pounce. We alone understand the severity of this, right?"

"Absolutely."

She paused a moment, wheels turning. "Maybe not a team. That's suspicious. We don't wanna tip our hand and have this whole thing stolen out from under us."

"Well," I ventured. "You could always OK more funds, let me ply my investigative shovel. Surge me into the story and let's see what I find."

She thought it over a beat. "Plus, it's probably best to not risk any staffer's lives."

"Damn!" I said. "So freelancers are expendable?"

Nothing I said was registering. "Don't you fish trout?" she said.

"Used to. Long time ago."

"You still have the wader-thingies?"

"Whoa," I said. "I'm not wearing rubber, trout-fishing pants to a press conference."

"Suit yourself."

"Maybe I will then, damn it!"

The next thing I knew, Becky was hugging me. It felt tremendous to be in the arms of a perfumed woman. Even a married one.

"Of course you're not expendable," she said, unhitching herself from the hug. "You're a civic treasure, God. And I want you to take care of yourself out there. Please head out, get established, and give me a call once you are." With a bounce she leapt, turned, and took a seat atop her desk. "I'm gonna position people at police headquarters, and with the school board. I'll plant reporters and photogs at a couple of fire stations, to get that angle, and at Atlanta Emergency Management headquarters. Everywhere. It'll be a full-court press, but not until you say go."

"I appreciate you trusting me, Beck."

"God bless," she said, hopping down to her feet again. "Now go, go, *go!*"

I kept standing there, and she looked puzzled. "Look, I know this might seem trivial on a day like this," I said, "but I was at this zoning meeting the other night…"

She cackled. "You're pitching a *zoning* story? At the dawn of Snakeocalypse! At the beginning of Snake Gate!"

"It's about Lotto Livingston," I said.

Becky perked up, intrigued. "Oh yeah?"

"Yeah," I said. "He's up to something again, on the development front. He wants to wipe out a whole section of historic shotgun bungalows. I know for a fact these homes have connections—well, rumored ties—to MLK's family. But he wants 'em gone, trucked off to a shoddy museum he's planning in the 'burbs."

"What's he want to build there instead?"

"That's the thing," I said. "A tract of workforce housing, or whatever they're calling it in CenterTown these days. Stuff that's relatively affordable because there's a whole lot of it, all packed together. A noble concept, in theory, but he's obviously not noble. He'll probably charge twice the going rate for the lowest quality. And those little old houses are irreplaceable jewels."

Becky deflected, turning her shoulders. "These things happen," she said. "It's Atlanta."

"But it's *different* this time," I said. "The old folks who live there never formally protected the district. They've been blindsided. They're going to lose their asses—I know it. And one of them, in particular, is a remarkable woman. She was a blues singer and the de facto mayor of Sweetberry Park, back in the blighted days. She's basically being extracted."

"You know her?" said Becky. "This lady?"

"Yes, well. But I can be objective."

"You'd better be."

"Long story," I said, "but back when you were in grade school, probably, she all but saved the lives of me and my friend. We'd be dead and buried without her, but she put up with our shit, and I mean that literally—"

"God, stop!" Becky cringed, but now she was really listening. "What's her name?"

"Genteel," I said. "Her name is Genteel Briggs."

Becky reached over, snatched my lunch bag off the floor for me, and flung open her office door. "I promise to keep her, and that dirtbag Lotto, in mind," she said. "Now get to the zoo!"

With a spring in my step and revived sense of self-worth, I hustled down to the parking lot and woofed the falafel, smearing my beard in sour tzatziki. I tossed the waste in a basket, eyed the sidewalk for slithers, and hoofed out into the lot. And there gleamed my old truck in unrelenting sunshine, like a tired promise nobody believes but me.

Maybe "gleamed" isn't precisely the word. The truck is a Ford SuperCab from 1982, a long solid beast, fattened with a cab that fits three. It's a vehicle caught in stylistic limbo between vintage cool and Reagan-era hideous. I call her Great White, because she's white and great and has bitten the fucking head off my savings account several times. I've poured twice as much into upkeep as I did the original sticker price. The wheel wells are rusting out and the exhaust pipes sound like metal in a meat grinder sometimes. If Matisse worked in duct tape instead of oils—that's basically what her seats look like. She'll soon achieve a quarter-million miles, but I plan to ride her 'til the day I drop, or her chassis combusts. A neurotic sort of attachment thing, I guess.

I cut south in Great White toward home. The city was bathed in that uplifting, midday sunlight of May, the kind that doesn't yet oppress but confidently declares the chill of spring to be gone. I watched the busy corporate stiffs shuffle between skyscrapers, blissful in their last hours of ignorance. Down on DeKalb Lane, just before I caught the interstate, I saw a little boy standing with his mother. He held her hand and studied the contours of an immense bronze sculpture. Things like that destroy me.

I cranked down the window and let the exhaust-tinged wind swirl around in my whiskers. In the rearview I glimpsed the wide back seat and thought of bygone times, three decades behind me now, when my own little family had sat back there. I'll never forget the pride of bringing home a new truck I'd bought with cash. Not because it made me some hotshot, but because I felt I'd screwed over the banks and escaped their indenturing interest rates. (No one had to know my loot had dropped out of the sky—an unexpected inheritance from my paternal, non-racist grandmother, a cool $25,000 for nothing, the real damn American Dream.) That day, way back when, the truck looked perfect in my driveway. Like it was designed to complement an oversize, vinyl-sided, shamelessly replicated house on a cul-de-sac, all recently carved from dense forests of Georgia pine. But if I'm being honest, I resented the truck and house, in a way. Or at least I didn't fully love the implications of them. They made me feel happy and satisfied, which in my head also meant sedentary. Barely past my mid-thirties, I'd hit that point where your biggest, stupidest dreams start to show cracks, the midlife wake-up call. Except for those blessed star-bound few, I think, every exceptionally ambitious person eventually has to accept the same morose plateau. It's the junction at which we stare down reality—crushing, heinous reality—and make peace with it. And it's best to do this before age forty, I think. Because the alternative isn't pretty: thrashing at your cheeks in the dark, bemoaning the curse of your creative frustrations, the sound of your potential sputtering out, the wheeze of your allotted time starting to end. But I'm not talking about unreasonable things. Not the baseless, dumbass expectations of making an NBA roster that afflict every boy who's ever dribbled a basketball. Or the delusion I once had of becoming a poppier version of Otis Redding meets Axl Rose. I mean things that, in an alternate reality, could have happened for me, and for us.

I'd toiled at small-town daily newspapers around North Georgia throughout my twenties, convinced my big-ticket nonfiction book subject was just around the corner. I felt confident—and more than one well-meaning editor assured me it was true—that I was capable of bleeding out a best-selling book, either long-form reporting or memoir. My *Notes of a Native Sun*. My *In Cold Blood*. My *A Moveable Feast*. One day it would happen because, well, some people said that maybe it could. Instead, the years melted away like lard on a campfire log. I tackled daily assignments in superior court, county commissioners quarters, and at the fringes of police cordoning tape that kept the bleeding cadavers at peace. Once or twice in my twenties I sat down, drank buckets of coffee, and ripped off thirty or fifty pages of unreadable novels. Other years I tried to make books of subjects (an exposé on filthy 4-H fairs; the art of cutting grass; a memoir about losing in general) that didn't deserve ten column inches in the *Ash County Gazette*. Then I met my wife; she had a thing for lush long hair, atypical facial structure, and wild, baseless talk of dreams. And then we made a boy. Naturally at that point I stopped chasing the nonessentials. I held tight to the mundane fortunes we had, the tangibles like furniture and functioning automobiles; and the less-tangibles, too, like a good school district, bouts of laughing at dinnertime, and a meager savings account that could cushion a young family's future. I let the fool's paradise in my head drift away. Took my foot off the gas. Forgot the books and focused on my newspapering and awesomeness at being daddy. I convinced myself the best blessings are small, and that being a hotshot bestseller asshole would've actually been cumbersome and annoying. That ascending, expectant, youthful naivete simply flickered out. I'd found terra firma. I was intent to stand up, accept my place, and be a good man, whatever that is. Back then I had a big mess of bourbon-brown hair and a clean-shaven face. And everyone called me by my unfortunate, white-bread birth name: Archibald.

Nearing my house, I roared past the zoo. Nothing yet. No crowds. No high-perched satellites from news trucks, either. The only sign that it wasn't a humdrum late-spring Monday was a golf cart on the sidewalk, manned by three zoo employees. They shuffled a jogging man back into the street and pointed him home, despite his entitled yuppie protestations. They were keeping the park clear of visitors, which was nice of them. The zoo guy on the back of the cart was searching bushes at a distance, via high-tech binoculars.

At home I pulled my old trout-fishing waders out of the attic and dusted them off, shaking out the attached booties in fear of black widows. I'd forgotten they were fluorescent blue. And two sizes too big. But those were minor inconveniences for being fang-proof, I thought. The waders were no shield against anacondas, of course, so I tucked a folding hunting knife into my jeans. Which meant I'd be going armed to a press conference. I slipped on this massively hot, clownish garment and scurried back into the truck.

At the zoo parking lot entrance, a security guard on a ladder was blocking people from entering, informing them of an emergency closure. He recognized my face, waved me in, and said, "Please don't leave the truck, Mr. Johnson. Or open the door. Not until we come get yuh."

As I parked it dawned on me that, in the glove box, I had an old zoo program from visits with my niece. I still had an hour to kill, so I locked the doors, blasted the wheezy air conditioner, and studied the pamphlets. The snakes from the modernized reptile habitat were all showcased on the pages like Broadway stars in a playbill. Their up-close headshots were bathed in fuzzy lighting so that each snake seemed approachable, almost cute. The blurbs beside each head were laughably sanitized—intel about rat diets and tongue length. I wanted the truth. So I rang up the University of Georgia's zoology department and asked to speak, on the record, with a snake expert, the preeminent herpetologist. With pen and notepad ready, I waited for fifteen minutes, until a public relations flak looped me in with Professor Steve Ralston, snake wizard. Meanwhile, the news vans were all filing into the zoo property and parking, but nobody was getting out.

"Just for background purposes, professor," I said on the phone. "Can you help me understand what a human who's bitten by a..." I reached for the pamphlet again, flung it open, and picked a snake at random: the fer-de-lance of Central America. It looked to me like a sizable rattler, sans rattle. "A human who's bitten by a fur-day-lance snake. What's that mean?"

"Huh, huh, *huh*!"

"Come again?" I said.

"Sir," said the professor. "There's no need to worry about that in Georgia."

"Just hypothetically," I begged. "The internet's full of horror. But what's the truth?"

The professor paused for a moment. "It's a fascinating animal, but you don't want to cross it. Ever," he said. "It's very defensive, and its strike radius is wide. The bites on people are almost never dry. And in some cases, it can paralyze you within the span of a minute—literally buckle your knees and trigger paralysis." He waited for a reaction; he couldn't hear my quivering. "Tissue begins to necrose immediately," he continued. "It's the snake's way of predigesting prey. And as you're sucking small breaths on the ground, you're actually rotting from the inside out—"

"*Jesus.*"

"What's this for again?" said the professor. "The Atlanta paper, but what's the story?"

The broadcast news folks were unloading from their vans and hustling to the zoo entrance. A crouched man in safari gear was frantically waving them in, as if Godzilla was raging around the corner.

"Sorry, professor," I said. "Late for a meeting. Appreciate the time. I'll keep your number handy. I promise you'll hear from me soon, and you'll know why."

I leapt out of the truck running, fumbling. The man at the gates called me by name; I could tell it was the same cagey zoo official who'd begged me on the phone earlier to keep the story quiet for a while. He eyed my trout pants in disgust. "Seriously?" he said, pointing. "Real subtle, God."

He locked the gate, spelled his name for me (Adam Evans), and ushered me to a meeting room where a crescent of media was readying camera tripods and microphones. None of them seemed too excited about the zoo story's potential, but they all looked eager to film a three-hour documentary about my pants. "The bass bitin' today?" quipped one camera-toting slacker in a faded golf polo. From another: "Baby blue's in vogue in heaven, eh?"

"Just wait," I said. "You jokers are gonna regret showing ankle."

Tabitha Jones, a recently demoted veteran of Channel 8's evening anchor desk, gave me a quick fist-bump. She fluttered blue-shaded eyelids. "You got a clue what this is, God?" said Tabitha. "I was thinking they dragged us down here to say a gorilla's sick or something. But then we get sequestered in our vehicles and ushered in here like the world's about to end. What the hell, you know?"

"I know."

"You *know*?"

"I mean, I agree."

Adam the PR point person stepped to a little podium crowded with microphones and thanked everyone for being there. He launched into a nap-inducing spiel about the zoo's flawless safety record and high marks for visitor satisfaction, and nobody took notes. But then he went quiet, intensely silent, for maybe a full minute. That was unprecedented. The media intrigue suddenly was palpable.

"In an act of what we believe is retaliation," a somber, deep-voiced Adam began, sounding like a president at the outset of war, "an employee—*former* employee—of Atlanta Memorial Zoo committed crimes this morning we believe are of significant public interest. The result is a possible hazard to the public, as we speak, at this hour." He gulped from a water bottle. "Fourteen venomous snakes and two large constrictor animals are presently unaccounted for at the zoo—" a gasp from the gallery—"and frankly, we're unsure of their whereabouts at this time. One animal, an Australian snake that is also venomous, was recovered this morning in a restaurant parking lot, approximately three blocks from here. It is deceased. We're actively working with police, firefighters, and city officials to develop an emergency plan, but we can't withhold this information a minute longer. The public needs to be aware of this, right now."

As he paused and I scribbled, wide-eyed Tabitha whispered to me, her breath sweet with mint: "They're gonna close schools. And businesses. Shit, city *government* will shut down."

Adam saw us talking and was perturbed. "We don't dictate how the news is disseminated, obviously," he continued. "But with your capabilities for special program alerts and social media channels and whatnot, we just ask that you please help us send word to Atlanta as soon as possible, but also as civilly as possible. And we do have some tips." He shuffled papers and lifted a sheet above the podium, his hands shaking like a late-stage wino's. "For anyone living on the eastside especially, we ask that you stay home. Shelter in place. Close doors and windows. Avoid woodsy areas and even thick yard bushes and trees. Please, remain vigilant—"

"What kind of snakes are we dealin' with, sir?" Tabitha interrupted. She exuded actual *fear*, not the showbiz, self-righteous, press-conference concern that's so typical of our ilk. "These don't sound like little backwoods copperheads. Are we talkin', like, king cobras?"

Adam flinched and nodded. "So I won't belabor the point and try to discuss each animal. We've prepared a fact sheet here for each of you, with all the species details you should need. We also have photos of each animal so that people can be aware. But I can't stress enough that if you're close enough to *see* any of them, you need to slowly turn and flee."

I raised my hand and had the floor: "Is the suspect you mentioned in custody?"

"He is not," said Adam.

"Why not?"

"We're actively searching for him, Mr. Johnson. We have no reason to believe he's left the city."

"As I asked you earlier," I said, trying to prove my integrity and establish the provenance of my scoop, albeit unreported, "could you give an indication as to how a single, unhappy employee was able to pull this off? Doesn't the zoo have protocols to stop someone with this sort of bad intention?"

"Listen," said Adam, a vein like lightning in his forehead, "we won't discuss personnel at this time. Suffice it to say the employee had special permissions, because at one point he was an exception. And by that I mean he was exemplary, an award-winning zookeeper three times over, in fact. But that's not what's critical right now—"

"With all due respect," I cut in. "The first question readers will ask is *how*. So, again, how could this happen last night?"

"What we need people to know," Adam said, ignoring me, "is that the chances of something bad occurring are very small. These animals rarely hurt humans in the jungles and arid places they come from. And there's typically a lot more of these animals there."

"But," someone else piped up, "they're right in the middle of *six million people* right now."

"Let's not panic," said Adam. "Again, mind all bushes and trees."

"Isn't that going to be difficult, sir?" Tabitha said flatly. "This is technically an urban forest, correct? How should anyone expect to be mindful of all these trees? How do you expect people to go about their *lives*, sir? Is that possible?"

Whatever poor Adam said in response was not coherent English, but I'd had my fill of noninformation. Weaving through live cameras, a frantic chorus of shutter clicks, and tense scribblers, I said, "Welcome to the jungle!" louder than I should have. I hustled out the door to a concrete courtyard with clear phone reception and very few trees. I called Becky.

"It's time," I said. "Can I dictate a story to you, over the phone? With the notes I have and what we both know from earlier?"

I could hear her shuffling to her desk computer. "That's old school."

"It is," I said, "and I am."

"Fire away," she said. "I'm ready."

The immensity of the situation stunned me for a second. Behind me was a lifetime of covering high- and low-profile homicides, government corruption, and one award-winning exposé on puppy mills. But this had all the makings of the most important work of my life—bona fide *global news*. And in the deep, weird annals of Atlanta history, we'd forever be the ones who had the story first.

"Alright, *damn*," I said. "Here we go, Beck. Here it comes..."

CHAPTER 4

The morning after Lotto Livingston had made his development plans public in the zoning department basement, I awoke and paid an emergency visit to my Cubby of Misdeeds, a lacquered, freestanding bar cabinet. I was off work for the whole morning but way down in spirit.

My alternate editor at the *Beacon*, a second-shifter named Sam Hunt who I'd never met in person, had little interest in my "major news" about such a small residential development as Lotto's Sweetberry Lanes, despite its potential ramifications on neighborhood history. More concerned with scoops about skyscrapers, editor Sam requested a hundred-word blurb on the subject, which paid me $60. That's for five hours of meeting coverage combined with writing and revision time at home. Not even minimum wage. Chicken feed, basically. The light bill, almost. For these reasons I'd gone to the liquor cabinet and pulled my trusted, liquid fire alarm in times of occupational crisis. It's a drink I call Bloody Marnie, for when I can't justify the cost of using real vodka, not even the kind in plastic. Bloody Marnie is canned tomato juice with a few olives, ice, pepper, maybe a pickle, and a long pour of illegal moonshine distilled by a dead neighbor who had no idea what he was doing.

I was peeved about the $60 insult, but I exercised discipline, because I did have some business. I downed just one Bloody Marnie and took a walk up my street to The Sweetberry Flank. It was a nice day, all songbirds and blue sky.

This, it should be stressed, was one day before zookeeper McCaffrey's ophidian discharge. So we still had our normalcy, our cool. Subtropical humidity had yet to unfurl upon us like a steamed wool blanket, too. The long delicious spring of the South was still in town that morning. It made me feel great, energized, and more inquisitive than usual.

I went up the steps of bungalow No. 3 and struck the door with three authoritative knocks. "I know you're in there, Genteel. Open up." All fifteen homes in The Flank, arranged in two neat rows with pretty myrtles out front, were exactly the same, and the epitome of utilitarian residential architecture. From the two-chair porches to the brick nubs of chimneys, nothing about them varied except the exterior colors, which ranged wonderfully from avocado to loud purple to a blushing sort of amber. Maybe a dozen feet wide and five rooms deep, the housing style was called shotgun because—legend has it—a flurry of bullets fired through the front door would zip right out the back. The layout had also allowed for great airflow in those abhorrently primitive times before air-conditioning. Which must have lent the White textile workers comfort, as mill bosses kept building these shotguns for them here. The original denizens of The Flank, in fact, were nothing but White factory men for two decades, likely the descendants of kilt-wearing pugilists. Then came the Uprising of 1918, exactly a century ago, when a lynching downtown spurred riots in districts all around Sweetberry. The mill workers scatted like water bugs, off to logging and pig-farming jobs in the country, a precursor to their grandchildren's mass White exodus from Sweetberry fifty years later. "I'll knock once more," I said, "then I'm calling the fire department and reporting a missing blues singer."

A voice piped up deep within the house, probably from behind a second door: "Wrong number!"

I knew she was lying, but I stepped back to see the door number anyway. It was, as she called it, Shotgun Three. Each resident of The Flank for three decades—many of them the same folks here today, watching their console televisions, wearing slippers—referred to their home not by its official address but by the word Shotgun and its numbered distance from the entrance. In bygone days, they'd say these numbers with pride—"I stay at Shotgun Eleven, damn right!"—as if each number was its own little province under benevolent rule.

"Whups, sorry, ma'am," I said into the door, and apparently through it. "Guess I'll have to take this bottle of brandy a few doors down."

"What you want, Johnson?" and she was hollering now.

She called me Johnson, or the awkwardly formal Mr. Johnson, because within the sacred purview of Her Creator, she'd never risk using my blasphemous nickname like everyone else.

"Why didn't you answer the door last night?"

"Wasn't here."

That made me chuckle. "You haven't left the house in a year, but you stepped out? After dark? You got a new boyfriend? You guys go clubbin' in Midtown last night?"

"Go on back home, you gnat!" It was the same tone she used for wild grandchildren, when she'd warn the kids she was bilingual: *I speak two languages—English and belt!*

"No, Genteel, you come out."

The door inched halfway open, and there she was, hobbled in posture but still a supernova of sass. "The *heck* you want, honey?"

"I want answers."

"For the paper?"

"No."

"You lyin'?"

"Not for the paper yet. I'm just a curious neighbor. We deserve to know."

"Where that brandy?"

"You don't need it. Plus, I was lying."

"Just go on, Johnson."

"I hear you made a deal with the devil."

She knew she was busted, and that softened her. "Fine," she said. "I guess we do owe explanations." Her nightgown was a great pink sail, shivering in the agreeable breeze. She tipped back her head as an invitation to enter.

I followed into the front room, which was thick with the aroma of fresh molasses cookies, a fragrance of country stores and doting grandmas. "Hungry?" she said, but I was lost in a menagerie of photos on her credenza. The pictures were a paean to her singing days, when she fronted Sweet Genteel and the Gnat Line Players in blues shacks from Valdosta to Lake Lanier. Her big ebullient face had changed very little since then; it was a smiling Fats Domino face with the spunk, fire, and sculpted hair of prime Aretha Franklin. Her body, as always, was broad and strong, bursting from gowns striped like candy canes and sequined tops in ways that would have bothered other women. But Genteel never cared. She wore her bigness like a declaration that fried catfish, salty greens, and tea sweet as cake could not weigh down her spirit; her heft, after all, served as one great gyrating platform for that down-home earthquake of a voice—back when she sang, that is. She'd convinced herself in recent years her voice had diminished, that she was "croakin' out," but that was an excuse. Saying her instrument was broken was a means of justifying her reclusion, for keeping off the road on tour, which her immense body couldn't really handle anymore, not after seven decades. I was convinced that her voice, though, was still in there, caged. In the course of any mundane sentence, her cadence would climb dramatic peaks and swoosh back down into the syrup; even in her waning years, while simply talking, Genteel's natural song would not die. Her voice moved a listener by accident. It had a very specific *feel*, visceral and rapturous, all bright spirit and real comfort, a red-velvet tsunami.

"Look the same, don't I?" Genteel said, handing over a warm cookie. She pointed to a color photo of her onstage, moving so wildly the microphone's cord looked like an electrified sea snake. "Been big all my life. My daddy, like my uncles, was a big man. Big, *big* man. I still look just like him, and the same as I always did, since girly-hood. A lot of people my age is pruned up. All nasty. But not me, honey."

"Is your band still kicking? All these guys here?"

"Not a one of them."

"That's too bad."

"They all gone."

I could see her starting to slink into one of those elderly, woeful cocoons that kept her sequestered indoors, watching talk shows and grainy reruns, biding time until the light went out, until the sweet day she could dance on tables with her Charles again.

"What's the number on the contract?" I said. "What's he say this house is worth?"

"*Who?*"

"Don't do that. I saw Lotto Livingston at a zoning meeting, licking his buttery lips. I know the deal, Genteel."

"One twenty."

I paused to swallow the delicious cookie. "OK, then," I said. "And where do you plan to go with your one twenty?"

"The country."

"Ah, that's nice. Where?"

"Alabama. South Care-o-line, maybe. I have cousins, both places. And I'm ready to go."

"Do you know what one twenty gets you there?"

"He said three bedrooms, probably. Some land. With change to spare, enough to keep me upright awhile and get the yard mowed."

"That's not true, Genteel. One twenty doesn't buy a country smokehouse anymore. You're being scammed."

"He wouldn't. I knew his daddy."

"It's his forte," I said, "and he would."

"Now look here, Johnson," she said. "Who you think you is, bargin' in being critical? This ain't my city. Not anymore. My city gone. My friends gone. And soon, so am I!"

"All of your neighbors here," I said, "they're under contract with Lotto, too?"

"Yup."

"I thought maybe he was exaggerating. That's disheartening."

"We only fifteen homes big."

"It's deeper than that." I went for another cookie and came back, feigning an experience of mediocrity; it was no time for compliments. "All of this presents three problems."

She dropped a big foot on the heart-pine floor. "Only problem is with you."

"No, it's bigger than me, or us," I said. "There's history and character under these roofs that can't be replicated. Never again. And maybe I'm being sentimental, but Sweetberry wouldn't be right without you in it, and I don't think you'd feel right being gone. Lastly, and this might sound wonky, but beyond the architecture here, The Flank has soul the city, at large, can't afford to lose. Not in times like this. It's real, and there's a shortage of real around here."

"Mmmrr-hrrm."

"That's all you're gonna say?"

A nod.

"Why do you sound suspicious?"

A shrug.

"What about that Flank history from the 1930s?" I said, sounding more conspiratorial than I'd meant to. "Can we prove that story about MLK having ties to any of these addresses? What was the connection?"

"His nanny stayed over here. And he stayed with her."

"Is that written down somewhere?"

"Get me that pen, Johnson—I'll write it out now."

"I mean is that hearsay, or documented?"

"Doubt you can prove it. But everybody know it's fact, honey."

I plucked at my beard, a habit of nervous frustration. "So you're cool with all of this being flattened? For some corporate-looking thing called Sweetberry Lanes? You think a hundred or however many tall, skinny homes would be an upgrade over irreplaceable history?"

"Did Lotto speak to his plans 'bout me? To his homage?"

"*Homage?*"

She clutched the small of her back, her face pinched with pain. "It'll be part of the new homes forever, he said. And he'll be lettin' all the new folks know who I was at one time. How I was the mayor, more a less, of Sweetberry Park."

"You're getting a statue?"

My floral button-up reverberated with her belly laugh.

"Naw," she said, "it's the names of the biggest homes. They'll have my name. He's calling them 'The Genteel.'"

"Ghaw!" I spat tiny bits of chewed molasses across the couch. "That's no homage," I said. "He wants to name a *floor plan* after you. The man has no shame."

"Look," she said, now jabbing her index finger. "What're you gettin' out of this?"

"Who says I'm getting something?"

"Be straight with me, Johnson."

"Hell, that's offensive."

"These old shacks, they're not doin' your property values no good."

"You think this is about property values?"

"And why you care about a bunch of old Black folks when you Mexican?"

"You know I'm not Mexican."

"Well, then, you ain't but a teaspoon Black."

"One-fifth, or something, I'm told," I said. "But it's not about that."

"It's *always* about that."

"Fine," I said. "If that's the case, it's about y'all gettin' played—by a wealthy Black man no less."

"Go on down the road, Johnson!"

I dropped my hands and squinted. "Look, I'm not aiming for sainthood or some kind of salvation here. And this has nothing to do with bullshit guilt." At that, she hollered to never curse in her house again; then she dropped her accusatory finger, easing off. "I really don't want to get in the way of your country bumpkin dreams, if that's what you want," I said. "But I think this is wrong, on several levels, and I think you should know why."

"Go on—get *out!*"

"Plus," I said, pointing back at her. "Not to sound sappy, but I'm a man who returns favors."

"*Favors?*"

"There's a debt I feel I've owed you for thirty years."

"Nonsense," she said, turning away. "I respect where your heart is at, though, I suppose. But that ink is dry on them contract papers. I signed. And I think we all did, or we will."

I patted her shoulder and made my way to the door. "I'll get out of your hair," I said. "I have some more digging to do, but I think there's wiggle room, if you see the light and want out of these bad deals. You could make a lot more money soon, if y'all really want to sell out."

"I *knew* you was up to something," she said, retreating to the kitchen. "Sounds like you huntin' for commission!"

"Now *you* look here," I said. "Georgia code has a clause that says, basically, real estate contracts can be null and void if either party was on medication at the time of signing. If a single one of you *wasn't* popping pills before signing with Lotto, I'll eat my sandal."

She tossed her hand in a dismissive wave. "It's prayer time, Johnson. I just wanna see what the Lord's gonna say. I'll let ya know."

I stepped outside, but quickly poked my head back in. "The Lord's word is one thing, Genteel," I said. "But the city's about to issue demolition permits. Make up your mind, or kiss these old walls, and this life, goodbye."

Hustling back down the street, feeling late for my self-imposed, four-hour, half-pointless daily work schedule at home, I came over a hill and saw the most repulsive thing: Lotto Livingston, donned in herringbone tweed up to his neck, sat behind the big wheel of a mid-eighties Lincoln Town Car, grinning like a gangster.

This angular titanic of an automobile, painted sandalwood with a vinyl top to match, gleamed in the sunshine, from its grill, shiny emblem, and hood the size of a queen mattress, down to the spoked chrome wheels. It made me want to scream. I stepped in front of the car and held up my arms, palms out. His window was halfway down, and I rushed over to it.

"Quite a coincidence, Lotto."

"Well, now, if isn't our Lord, the savior of Sweetberry!"

"This is low," I said. "Even for you. You're a sick man."

"Calm down."

"I have every right, right now, to punch you in the mouth."

"Go easy, God."

"I can't *believe* you. Look at this shit!" I balled my right fist, bluffing, knowing damn well I hadn't punched anybody since about fourth grade. "Have you been cruising around in this thing, in *my* neighborhood, trying to let me see you?" No answer; I could tell by the quiver of his cheek he was nervous, bracing for assault and battery, for lawsuit fodder. "Look, if it wouldn't kill my income, I'd do my best right now to break your goddam nose—"

"I don't know what you *mean*," he said, leaning away, across tan leather. A slow smile lifted icky little moustache hairs into his nostrils. "I've owned this car for years, God. Maybe a decade. I think you've gotten a little too wound up, maybe, over your real estate scoops."

I dug my hands into the pockets of my beach khakis, unfolding the fists. "If this is some sort of intimidation tactic," I said, "driving around my neighborhood in this damn car... you're just despicable, to the lowest degree."

Lotto clutched the massive steering wheel, smirking again. He was a cocky cruise ship captain successfully arriving at his sordid destination. "Got nothing to do with you," he said. "We're basically gonna be neighbors, God. Last thing I want is to piss off my neighborhood. Whatever's got your goat about this car, as you said, is just a coincidence."

As much as it pains me, I think we've reached the point where I'd best discuss The Juncture, as I call it. It's time to talk about the sour years, my charred era, how my cushy old cul-de-sac life ended; and how my weird world began here, in Sweetberry Park, long before the yuppie invasion and Lotto's high-dollar displacement fetish. I was led here by tragedy. And/or fate. And/or God. And/or coincidence. Or whatever happened when my wife and little boy were crushed beneath the weight of a mid-eighties Lincoln Town Car.

If you can believe it, my wife and boy had gone out to buy a quart of milk. I was home. But I wasn't really anticipating their return as much as trying to capitalize on the quietude of their absence, pecking out the prologue of a never-finished book about the lighter side of Reconstruction. It was Saturday afternoon. Just before football weekends. Just before glorious Sunbelt autumn. If it would have been the state patrol at the door, I would have seen his brimmed hat and had some warning, a moment of fortification. Instead I heard the doorbell and saw only the tidy black hair of a young man, bobbing nervously beyond the door's little oval of glass. I pulled back the knob, telling myself to be polite in rejecting whatever he was peddling, but instead of that, I was sucked headlong into a vacuum of absolute pain.

At the scene, my wife was unconscious but still breathing, which lasted maybe five minutes. The end of us didn't come until I was actually there. I'd met Sage during sophomore year in the University of Georgia's journalism school. We shared a lunch of cheese pizza and half-dollar beers one September day, and I knew our boy would be named Wyatt and that, after a few decades of sensible living, we'd retire to a cabin on Lake Rabun with maybe a modest condo on Tybee Island (assuming, at the time, those places would allow mixed couples), the rigors of our sprawling native metropolis in the rearview. With her serious posture and crystalline eyes, she would have made a great TV news anchor, after cutting her teeth with field reporting. With her intelligence and doting heart, she'd have been a terrific mother, too, throughout the tough adolescence of our wild child in the collapsed back seat that terrible day; and throughout whatever was to come with our tiny child in her womb, no larger than a potato, whose gender I would never ask to know.

The Lincoln's driver, a furniture salesman who specialized in leather couches, had been at a pool party all day, my friends at the local paper reported. He liked martinis. He'd run out of vermouth. He missed the stop sign at the highway's hilly bend. Milk and vermouth.

Instead of Piggly Wiggly's dairy section, he sent my family ricocheting into the path of a westbound trucker pulling rebar to Memphis, completing three doomed trajectories. Our Toyota essentially bounced against the semi's weight and hurtled back upside-down into the Lincoln, moving at an estimated seventy miles per hour and crushing the roof. Barely a chance to flinch.

Immediately I missed the usual, domestic things about my wife. But I missed them with a quaking sort of urgency. The way she fumbled out of bed, decaffeinated at dawn, angry at the world and life, but adorably so. The way her pumpkin chili made our noses run in autumn. The way she'd vent about her egotistical on-air coworkers and flirty male bosses—and the way I trusted her so much not a single thought of infidelity ever stabbed at me. I missed the way she killed plants—including pricey, potted palms—by neglecting to water them, because that was so patently her. The way she welled up and bawled at ridiculous plot twists in television programs so unworthy of crying as *The Cosby Show*, *Cagney & Lacey*, and *Punky Brewster*. But mostly I missed her prowess at being a mother hen, to both me and the boy. She'd rant about my weekend talents for Budweiser consumption, or the rare occasions we'd drink enough bourbon that I'd forget my little wooden weed pipe on the living room couch. When raging, she'd use my full birth name for maximum syllabic shrapnel—"*Archibald Wesley Johnson!*"—instead of the softer "Archie." Sage was a pro at implanting slow-burn guilt when my wild side took off. In that sense, she was an anchor, and without her I felt unmoored, set adrift in poisoned seas. I think "unmoored" is precisely the word, because everything I'd grown accustomed to holding was gone. Instead of sturdiness I felt a kind of gravitational distress, pulling left, right, and especially down. But not in a way that seemed particularly consequential, because I couldn't bring myself to care about me or the world anymore. I was too numb to give a damn. For a week. And then a month. And then two months, and three. The deadest autumn a man ever survived.

I never told Sage this, but while hovering over his tiny cot of a bed, I used to imagine my boy's name stitched into the fire suit of a debonair race car driver, dominator of some exotic road circuit. Wyatt H. Johnson, holder of all *Le Mans* records, or whatever. I didn't even like racing, just the thought him being faster than everyone else. At one point, maybe age three, I was convinced he could sing like Pavarotti. A butterball baby, he'd slimmed down in toddlerhood and seemed leading-man charming, too. These were normal fatherly delusions. The death of those fantasies didn't eviscerate me so much as the silence in his bedroom. It'd been our little place, a soft realm once filled by his squeals and amazing, terrible grammar. Wyatt used peculiar sentence structure from his first words on—so hilarious his day care teachers had refused to correct him. He didn't ask to be picked up, but said, "Hold you me." He didn't inquire about where I'd been, but said, "Where's that you just did go?" I relished how "yours" was always plural—"Was that yours friend, daddy?"—and how any amount of time in the past was always yesterday: "Yesterday where's yours friend did go?" Each night, after the bedtime story, he insisted on wrapping my neck with a choking wrestling procedure he called "leg hugs." Sometimes I'd wrestle back, lifting him Emperor Palpatine-style over my head in a move he liked to call "Yours Darf Vader."

I'd written down my boy's idiosyncrasies and tried to speak the whole list aloud on the witness stand, following the guilty plea. But I felt seasick. I managed only to mumble something about mistakes, forgiveness, and the uselessness of craving revenge. The son of a bitch had been weeping at the defense table for two days straight, absolutely disheveled in his shiny suit. All I could think about is how easily I could have been him. Everyone had urged me to destroy him in my victim impact testimony. Sage's parents, my older brother Tommy, strangers from the subdivision. But I couldn't help imagining the tables turned. He had a young boy, too, I'd learned. He would get to keep his boy, and knowing that was probably, in a way, killing him. We never directly spoke, but I like to think survivor's guilt was driving his courtroom fits. I like to think that maybe he'd go on to be a better father—once his state-sanctioned penance was paid—to his kids, and that my boy's life helped serve that purpose.

Looking back, though, I realize those days were merely the prelude to The Juncture. Not a time of decisiveness. Not of doing, or not doing.

The Juncture came the following spring, after I'd gone back to work covering suburban governments. After the hair at my temples and the scruff of my chin had quickly bled out from rich brown to gray. I'd aged, friends said, a decade and a half that winter.

I remember the moment exactly. I was standing in my street, beside Great White, and the fraudulence of my existence became too real. The predictability of my buffered-away cul-de-sac was suddenly appalling. The ghosts of family happenings inside those two stories were too much. And the materialistic competition among my neighbors, albeit unspoken and friendly, had never been more apparent; I could see in their faces, both Black and White, that I wasn't their friend now so much as a limping survivor who needed coddling, if not monitoring. The calculations behind all of it—their careful waving, our primped streets, and the covenant-dictated dormers of our roofs—made my hands tremble. Suddenly, it was all a prison. But I wasn't sentenced to life.

As luck would have it, just before I put that house up for sale, my grandfather died. He was a drunk, meanspirited, racist prick. Which is why, back in 1963, he'd abandoned a beautiful Queen Anne Victorian home when the first Black family moved in down the block. But unlike his pals, grandpa didn't sell low to predatory real estate agents; he just up and left, hightailing for the semirural eastern suburbs of Atlanta. My father, his son, thought he secretly hoped to return to the city one day, to his boyhood stomping ground and once-cherished neighborhood of Sweetberry Park, whenever the demographical tide shifted back to his liking.

Imagine my surprise to learn, at age thirty-six and distraught, that in grandfather's will there existed not a nickel of his substantial savings for me. Instead, I got an abandoned house in what his document described as "the inner-city ghetto." It made sense, though. Grandpa had forgiven his son for the accidental pregnancy with my mixed-race mom, but he never got over the non-Anglo impurity of me. Growing up, I didn't view him as a mentor or ally but rather a bully. He was a taunting, mean presence who addressed me with squinted, drunken eyes only as, "Yeww! *Yeww!*" He'd left me the house and its tax commitments, I'm convinced, not as a favor but as revenge—or, at best, an insulting challenge. At worst, a curse.

Grandfather's gift came two days after my cul-de-sac home had gone under contract, and about two hours after I realized I would need a place to sleep within a few weeks. So dead bigot grandpa inadvertently did me a favor, at least at the outset. Fate, man.

I drove down to Sweetberry Park, where I'd never been, and followed the street address to what looked like a melting gingerbread house amid waist-high weeds. This was the crack-cocaine eighties, the AIDS eighties, the economic nadir of most American city centers. For parts of Atlanta, those were the least populated, most desperate years of the twentieth century, arguably worse than being on fire the century before. Yet standing there in that street, at the house where my father had taken his first steps and given his own choking leg hugs, I felt, in a way, reborn. I clutched my face.

Amidst so much blight and misery, so much societal immobility, racist suppression, chemical dependency, and the ubiquitous, laudable stubbornness of people to simply stay alive, I'd never felt more at home.

"You think I'm-a dummy, right?" Lotto was saying now, revving the Lincoln. "I can *sense* you're devising some sort of interference. Aren't you, God?"

My mind adrift, I said only, "Huh?"

"I've got a feeling you want to get in my way."

I snapped back to the present, to anger. "You're low-balling all those old people. Those properties are worth twice what you're giving. You're fuckin' shameless."

"See?" he said. "There it is. Here it comes. God Johnson and his one-man crusade!"

Ignoring him, I waved my hand, pointing a finger from bumper to bumper. "I really can't believe this car."

Lotto's face relaxed. "You're saying, I guess, she's too beautiful for belief?"

"I haven't written a column about my wife and boy in ages," I said. "But *this* is where your mind goes when you sense a fight coming? What kind of human being does this?"

Lotto kicked the gas, and the Lincoln roared down Praytor Boulevard, its paper license plate flapping, shivering, taunting.

CHAPTER 5

Americana Mama, to no one's surprise, was the first Sweetberry Parker to lose her shit about the missing snakes.

Yes, Sweetberry Parkers. That's what monied newcomers had started calling themselves in post-Great Recession economic boom times. It was an effort to sanitize and sweep out the last bits of real urban grit with insufferable, cliquey cuteness. It was also like rebranding a cereal from something respectable like "Fruit Loops" to "Explosive Mouth Orgy" to make it sell better. It was the product of people without real pain having too much time to gossip and plot. And when it came to Sweetberry Parker gossip, Americana Mama was the unchallenged monarch.

I didn't know anyone who knew her real name—or anyone who wanted to. But her alarmist, unyielding bitching was one of the first indicators, for me, that this neighborhood had gone so vanilla it was headed straight to hell. Americana Mama had made a part-time job of fretting (boldly, on the internet) over such travesties as crooked on-street parking, leaf piles as litter, "obnoxiously loud" bicycles, exterior Christmas decorations still blinking in January, and the occasional unscooped nugget of labradoodle crap. There was seemingly no aspect of modern Sweetberry life that didn't irk her. She'd get hopped up on peach-apple tea, or whatever, and unleash rage on our private online forum for neighbors. Her frequent targets were the latest "scourge" of dented communal trashcans, roughhousing preteens in a park (actually, in three cases, organized flag football games), and too-loud Weedwackers. She was nearly banned once for extolling the virtues of "more gates everywhere" to ward off "invasive, odorous bums" while poking fun at the paint schemes (with photos) of ten different new-construction homes. Once a harmless depository of yard sale news and real crime alerts, the webpage had devolved into a tarpit of biased and asinine rushes to judgement—Americana Mama's natural habitat. The threat of rampant cobras, as one might imagine, doesn't exactly soothe such a frazzled psyche.

Her nickname, which I'd created but never shared with her, was born a few years ago. I think it was a Sunday. I'd had a quick waltz with Bloody Marnie and was taking my buzzed morning walking laps around Sweetberry. Down the block, I spotted this loud, fantastic argument underway between a woman wearing business slacks and a man in work boots and jeans. I moved stealthily toward the spat, which happened to be at a construction site, and I ducked into a porta potty. This position, although not without drawbacks, allowed me to listen undetected. What I heard was baffling, amusing, horrifying. She'd kept hollering "Americana!" and "You missed the mark on Americana!" and "No, no— *Americana!*" because, it turns out, she was buying the home the man, a builder, was constructing. This poor dude's interpretation of dormers and wainscoting and throwback exterior paint schemes wasn't remotely Americana enough, per Americana Mama, and she started belittling him about being both "inept" and "blind." She noted with added vitriol and no sarcasm: "My young children will have to *live* with what you've done!" Meanwhile, I was fighting the urge to either burst out cackling or sob. Against his client's insults, all the guy could counter with is "of course, ma'am" and "that's exactly right" and "we'll make a few tweaks and adjustments" until he couldn't stomach another word of it. "Americana?" he finally snapped. "Lady, where did you even get that? I don't know what the hell it *means!*"

Thus, "Americana Mama" was born—in a foul portable shitter.

At the very dawn of Snakeocalypse, after I'd called in the breaking news story to my editor and it went live online, I fled home for lunch, and who should appear but Americana Mama, hanging out the window of her moving minivan.

"Stay indoors!" she was hollering from the middle of the street, driving at ice-cream-truck pace. She was using an inverted cone made for soccer boundaries as a bullhorn. Her sweaty face had all the composure of a geeked-out meth smuggler being probed by airport security. "Run inside your house! Don't walk! Warn the children!"

I rolled down Great White's window and peeked out. "Hey, there," I said. "Let's not go berserk, OK."

"You don't understand, Mr. Johnson. It's life and death out here!"

"I *do* understand," I shouted, struck by the ridiculousness of our loud public interaction. "The story you read was ours, at *The Atlanta Beacon*. But let's not incite panic. Let's be vigilant but, you know, *sane*." Her face kept darting back and forth, yard to yard, bush to bush. "At the very least, don't go hollerin' down by the school, please." I killed the engine, checked the sidewalk, and hustled into the yard, where the grass was low and bereft of mysteries. "If you can," I shouted back, "you might head around to Sweetberry's smaller parks. Some people might not have heard yet, if they've been outside."

"Those fishing pants are brilliant," she boomed, through the bullhorn. "Is that what we all need?"

"Stop talking at me through that thing."

"Sorry." (Still with bullhorn).

"Please, just inform the parents," I said. "Especially at that little triangular park by the municipal woods. But let's do it calmly. This isn't a natural disaster, OK? We can take control. Now I have to get back to work."

"Ten-four, Mr. Johnson."

Like a slow, dying gazelle, I reached the porch in four weak hops, skirting my bushes and then darting to the ornate front door. I fumbled with my keys, my neck hairs dancing with imagined anaconda breath, my pulse wild. *Calm. Breathe. Be the key. Insert yourself.* That worked, and once inside, I collected old shirts and towels, twirled them tightly into long rods, and spent two rolls of duct tape securing these makeshift plugs into crevasses beneath each door and atop my wobbly stained-glass windows. Starving, but still nervous, I devoured a half-sandwich and glass of tomato juice and was overcome with what seemed like a brilliant idea. I fetched a ladder and scurried to my bedroom, to the first-floor roof, and then via the ladder to the gothic apex of my old Victorian, where the wicked, fanciful peak and weather vane looked almost medieval. For a moment I enjoyed this breezy, lordly new vantage over Sweetberry—until my heart sank. I could see over to the elementary school, three blocks away, where a squirming, panicked wave of children and their parents was screaming toward the school parking lot. A few mothers who'd come without cars were sprinting down the sidewalks, flailing their arms, shouting to boys in front of them on bicycles: "Go, go, move!"

Down on the street, in front of my house, I heard clanging and the rustle of my big boxwoods. There were two boys, one preteen and the other a little older, wielding metal rakes, stabbing the teeth into bushes and bashing trashcans with the wooden ends. I recognized them as the grandchildren of Genteel's poker-playing friends, a reclusive, ancient couple who lived a few doors down from her, former purveyors of a Sweetberry hardware store.

"Hey, boys," I yelled. "Go on. Get home."

In unison: "Naw." The older one flipped me off.

"Get home *now*," I shouted, and then came an echo, but it wasn't my voice.

"*Now!*"

The boys stiffened, spun around, looked down the street, and bolted toward The Flank. I leaned over farther to learn the identity of my assistant: It was Carlito, the charmingly neurotic clerk who worked at Sweetberry's lone gas station. This hulking man had come to hyperlocal prominence, or maybe infamy, by refusing to remove the Pope-grade bullet shield from around his cash register. He stood his ground and kept the glass in place despite 1) a track record of zero armed robberies in our district for five years; 2) the outcry from Sweetberry moms, who argued that such protection sent "bad messages" about "the wrong element" still being present around here; 3) his own behind-the-counter arsenal of guns and knives, which was always within reach of his gigantic, nervous hands.

"Mr. God!" Carlito shouted. "What's the latest, man?"

As he scatted away from the sidewalk, opting for the refuge of the open street, I saw a handgun tucked above his butt and a long, glistening blade in his right hand. In his left hand, pointed downward in serial killer position, was clearly a huge, tactical Rambo knife. "Is that where we should be?" he said. "Up on our roofs? Is that the safe place now?" He spun around again, patrolling. "Should I go get my kids and climb up on my business? I mean, *what the fuck*, man?"

"Is that a Rambo blade—and a machete?"

"Goddamn yes it's a machete."

"Well played, Carlito."

"Are we safe on roofs? But not down here?"

"Man, I don't know." I shrugged and tilted my head, a physical apology. "You got a spare machete, by chance?"

He spun in a faster circle, face to the ground, quick surveillance. "Sorry, sir, it's my only blade this size. I have guns and a sharp-ass shovel, but not on me. You got any more fish pants?"

I shook my head, frowned.

"It's all over the news, God," he said. "People's going nuts at Happy's Pit Stop, just flooding in. They're gassing up to flee the city, man. Others is talking about forming a *hunt*. Like a snake safari, with guns and shit. They said you know what's going on."

It was inappropriate, but I swelled up with a bit of pride right then. "I mean, I'll be honest," I said. "We're really close to the zoo. All these neighborhoods are too close to be safe, based on intelligence—or what passes for it now—at a press conference I just left. I'd say you should button up the gas station, and your house, as best you can." His deflating shoulders suggested my intel wasn't impressive. "The authorities must be planning a mass roundup soon," I said. "I'd imagine we'll all be safe by the weekend."

Now Carlito looked twice as agitated. "Seriously, though, be real," he said. "How bad is it? What are we dealing with?"

No point in sugarcoating it, I reasoned, if sugarcoating it could get a man or his kid killed. "Between us," I said, "it's bad. Crazy bad. These are the worst in the world, the most venomous there is—"

"Ah, *hell!*" someone piped up, a voyeur who'd been listening from an unseen, screened-in porch. Everyone was starving for intel, for instructions, for the word of God.

When I looked back to the street, Carlito was sprinting away, toward Sweetberry's commercial village, utterly spooked and unstoppable, his glistening half-swords like Olympic batons. I pulled out my phone and dialed editor

Becky. She answered midway through the first ring and demanded the latest.

"Pandemonium," I said.

"Alright!"

"That's the right word, I think. That's the scene in Sweetberry right now. I can't believe what I'm watching."

"Channel 17 is using B-roll footage from that barbecue shack's parking lot this morning, because everything is suddenly relevant now. Damn, I wish you gave me some photos. I can't believe the size of that thing!"

"Anyway," I said. "I'm told that people are fleeing town. Others are forming militias. What's our next step?"

"*Militias?*"

"To fight back. To hunt."

"We need to report how *ignorant* that is," said Becky. "Will the cops go on record saying that? You have your laptop with you? Go find some cops. Bang me out an update, with a service-y angle. Let's enlighten these fools as to what they're up against."

"Any news about the zookeeper?" I said.

"None. Unfortunately."

"He vanished?"

"So far, yep."

"What about the rest of the city? What's going on out there?"

"Madness," said Becky. "City offices are closing. Every school anywhere near you should be dismissed and emptied by now. Fire trucks are roving streets within a mile of the zoo, ordering people to stay inside. Other city officials— maybe the watershed department, I think—are concerned about sewers."

"Sewers?"

"Yeah. We heard they're deploying teams down there. Not to freak you out, but they're saying sewers would be a natural habitat for these scared, disoriented little demons."

"They don't think—"

"Don't even say it, God. I don't need you up all night, tossing in bed."

"Did they mention the possibility of toilets? Like, residential *toilets*?"

"Just stop, God. You're cracking. You're better than this."

Feeling clammy, I took a seat on my hot roof tiles. "This is the worst nightmare possible."

"Calm down, man."

"I'm gonna have to tape my toilets shut. With duct tape or something stronger. Maybe chains. We all are. This is horrible!"

"Look," said Becky, losing patience, "you're at ground zero, and we need you. The snakes have gotten a twelve-hour head start on authorities, they estimate. The quicker ones can be damn near the City of Praytor by now."

"You know what?" I said. "I bet every redneck, swamp-snake trapper from South Carolina to Texas is heading *into* the city right now. I bet a lot of people are eager to help, and hungry for glory."

Becky replied with her mouth full, likely with protein: "That's an angle to explore. Get me an update within two hours. Keep your laptop on you. Stick near internet. I don't have time to transcribe another of your phone calls."

"The militias," I said. "I'll find one around here, talk to them, and get that angle, too?"

"Sounds good. Be careful. Godspeed!"

"*Wait*," I said. "Just real quick: the story I'd mentioned about the zoning situation over here. Well, I've been thinking about it, after having talked to neighbors, and it's big—"

"Get the hell out in the street!"

"Sorry, but listen," I said. "Some points I didn't make earlier to you: Lotto Livingston is out of bounds with this one. And he knows that I know it. So he wants to keep me quiet, by way of absolutely despicable intimidation, so far.

But I think we're dealing with violations of elderly protection laws here. When things settle a bit, I'll be getting back to pursuing that story, just so you know…"

Aggravated lioness sounds. I said goodbye and hung up. I circled the roof twice, surveying the neighborhood, timidly inspecting the trees and neighboring streets, trying to find the first signs of an oncoming, angry, metastasizing mob. I scanned the few streets visible through such a thick canopy and didn't see anything suspicious near sewer drains; no city inspectors braving the rank depths or manhole covers bobbing with python heads. Instead, the sparkle of Carlito's great knives again caught my eye. He was barreling back toward my house.

"Mr. God! Mr. God!" he was shouting. "Come, come on! They've got one cornered!"

"Holy hell," I screamed. "Where?"

"In a backyard," Carlito said, now panting in front of my place. "It's by a creek and the school's bamboo forest. Grab your camera, man. Big news. Get down. Let's go!"

CHAPTER 6

I instructed Carlito to take cover in the back of Great White while I hustled down the ladder and went ripping through boxes to find my old Canon thirty-five millimeter, a beautiful little artifact I hadn't deployed for duty in a couple of years.

I scurried to the upstairs hallway, and then up the dusty attic ladder, where I grabbed the first box at hand and found, by accident, a distraction that cost me four minutes: It was my son's Halloween costume from maybe 1985, when he went dancing around the cul-de-sac as a California Raisin, his legs in black tights, face painted purple, and the rest of the goofy getup bought from Kmart. I'd had some special-occasion bourbon that night, as is parental trick-or-treat protocol in Southern suburbia, and I remember teaching Wyatt to say, when his mother was out of earshot, "I'm Raisin hell!" to the amusement of equally tipsy parents. The boy was too young to realize the profaneness of his blurts, which made them all the more hilarious. I recall that night vividly, but I have no inkling why I kept something so specific and devastatingly tactile as the costume, when I couldn't bear to squirrel away a single one of Wyatt's T-shirts or finger-paintings from kindergarten. It's strange the way grieving animals behave. Like our dog who quit eating after we'd put our older Beagle to sleep. Or the mom I would come to know, through newspaper assignments in the late nineties, who'd crystalized her teen daughter's room—the bubblegum wrappers on a nightstand, the scrunchies on doorknobs, the piled clothes hangers in a closet, all sacred—after the leukemia. I closed the old box and tossed it in a corner. The attic had never felt hotter.

The camera, turns out, was downstairs in the foyer closet. Carlito, a ball of hair-trigger nerves on good days, didn't take kindly to being left outside for five minutes.

"You want me to *die* out here, fucker?" he shouted from the truck bed.

I held up the old camera and opened the driver's side door. "Had a little trouble finding this. Sorry. Ride shotgun. Let's go." He hopped into the street, pushed me out of the way, and crawled across my seat to the other side. I ignited the truck and turned toward Sweetberry's commercial core.

"Does that camera even work?" he said. "For sure? I want this on film. I want documentation. I'm going to cut their heads off! Or shoot them in their little brains!"

"You're gonna get bit, that's what," I said. "But yeah, this thing still makes killer, precise images, if you know how to work the aperture. Those little digitals are cheating."

I took a left down West End Place. The streets were deserted, which looked strange beneath such crisply beautiful skies. It felt like those utterly normal, abandoned places depicted in movies as zombie hordes approached. A day like this, Sweetberry would normally be teeming with pram-pushers gulping kale-coconut smoothies, for which they'd happily forked over one dollar and twenty-five cents per ounce.

In a minute we arrived at the rear entry of the elementary school, where the bamboo cluster grew. It was here that college-age protesters from Georgia State University had assembled the previous summer and decried the "transitioning" school as a "GENTRIFICATION ASSEMBLY PLANT" with their well-meaning but hyperbolic signs, all pumping in unison. I got two stories out of that saga, but the peeved college kids got nowhere, obviously, in their quest to squash the bougie influx. Today, the grounds were eerie, sad, and quiet, with swings on chains gently rocking in the pollen-tinged breeze.

"This is where they were headed," said Carlito. "It has to be. They said the bamboo, at Sweetberry Elementary, which would make sense, yes? I think a teacher saw it back here first."

"Let's head closer, to the bamboo's edge," I said, sounding more anxious than brave. "Get your weapon ready. I'll hang beside you to document it. But let's hustle—I got another story due in about ninety minutes."

We cautiously exited the truck, hopped a chain-link fence, and ran crouched like soldiers across the playground, before taking positions on all fours in low, primped Bermuda grass. From there we could see them: a cluster of men maybe fifty yards into the bamboo. Each of them was crouched, too. Carlito squeezed my arm, his dark eyes big as pecans: "I *told* you, man. Look at them hunting!"

"What can you see, exactly?

"*Look.*"

"My eyesight's crap," I said. "Is it the police?"

"I recognize them all from the neighborhood," he said. "All amateur hunters. Not the cops, not the zoo people. It looks like Squeaky is the leader."

"Oh hell, *Squeaky*? You sure?"

Carlito grimaced. "Yep. You know that crazy fool."

I stood up and spoke loudly, confident some element of this situation was harebrained. "Squeaky doesn't know what day it is, let alone a snake from a damn jumper cable," I said. "Come on, let's move in."

A few steps closer I could tell it was Squeaky indeed, plus what looked like a petrified band of a half-dozen boxed-wine addicts, the type of loafing clowns Squeaky ran with. I called his name; they all flinched, turned, and waved us in. We tiptoed into the tall long shadows of soaring bamboo stalks and found the first acquaintance I'd ever made in Sweetberry Park: the affable, irascible Squeaky, or Reginald Antoine Jackson, as his momma called him before she passed. The nickname didn't stem from his voice or anything anatomical but from the old, squeaking, banana-seat bike he'd pedaled around Sweetberry as a penniless boy. He stood there wearing a faded T-shirt depicting the rock band Poison (poor choice on several levels) he'd probably won in some dart game at the Fulton County Fair in 1989. Despite our harrowing predicament in the woods, this image of eighties hair-metal rockers in heavy makeup on an old Black man's chest made me crack up. "The hell you doin', Squeaks?" I said.

Even in his thirties, way back when, Squeaky's happy face had hung off his skull like it was slowly melting. Now, in his sixties like me, his face was still capable—miraculously—of lifting up, like a gleeful puppet's, into a buoyant, smiley, disarming explosion of sunshine. He reached down and unsheathed something legitimately terrifying in such incapable hands: a long, gleaming Samurai sword.

"Get that camera ready, God," Squeaky said in his rich, ironic baritone. "He's trapped under this log."

My back and neck devolved into a heebie-jeebies earthquake, a spasm of loose flesh. My heart kicked, my feet oozed sweat, and I whispered: "Is that right, Squeaks?"

"I'm real sure," Squeaky said. "We ran him under there and got him surrounded. Nowhere to go. It's a cobra, I think.

We gotta take him down, for the community. And to be on the news tonight."

"Just go easy," I said. "Could be that fast-ass black mamba under there."

Several of them looked confused, terrified.

"From the same continent as cobras," I said, stepping back twice. "I mean, a cobra's bad enough. But you have any clue what a mamba will do to your nervous system?"

"*You* have any idea," said Squeaky, "what this sword will do to his *life*?"

"Come on!" Carlito spouted. "King cobra or mumbo jumbo or whatever—who cares? Let's get this son of a bitch!" He lifted the revolver from his waistline and pulled back the hammer. "Kick the log, boys. Someone kick the log!"

Squeaky took a sword-raised, butt-down ninja stance, but otherwise nobody moved. I clutched Carlito's shoulder and said that maybe we should all just slowly back out, get to the parking lot, and call the authorities. "Listen, guys," I said. "These bastards can launch off the ground like arrows."

But Carlito, swept up in macho glory lust, was ignoring me. "Fine then, you little *bichanos*," he said, shaking his head. He held the gun at arm's length and fired a booming round into the log—and then a second one. We all shrieked.

"Idiot!" I said. "You know how close that school is right there? That's a federal offense, what you just did—"

"Shut up, God," he said. "The camera—get it in focus. And watch *this*!"

Carlito shot forward, leading with a white Adidas, and he basically speared the thickest section of the log with his leg, so that it teetered away once, then back toward us, hard enough to roll out of its groove. As we darted away, back toward the school, Carlito's momentum carried him in the apocalyptic other direction, and he fell into the earthen place the log had been. I glanced back and saw the machete raise up and swoop down like a reaper's scythe. And then came disappointed laughter.

"You putzes," Carlito said. "Are you kidding me?"

In unison, our cowardly platoon stopped and turned back. We found Carlito sitting cross-legged in the log's little ravine, next to the halved, curled carcass of a common garden snake. The poor thing had vaguely copperhead-y coloring, and the same triangular scale patterns, but a docile, rounded face no more menacing than an earthworm's.

"You're a hero," said Squeaky. "Bravest clerk in Atlanta."

Carlito plunged his knife into the soil. "I thought they got rid of crack rocks around here?" he said, seething. "Anyone who mistakes this for a cobra is clearly cracked out. It's what, two feet long?"

Click. Click.

"Do *not* publish that photo," Carlito said.

"But it's news," I pleaded, half-joking.

"Fine, Mr. God. But crop me out of it."

"It's so honest," I said. "And hilarious."

"Here's some honesty," Carlito said: "If you publish that, with me in it, I'll come by and shoot out those stained-glass windows you love so much."

I latched ahold of his elbow, hoisted him up, and pointed Squeaky and his scalawags toward the truck.

"Let's get the hell out of these woods," I said. "I'll take you all where you need to go, but I need to get back to work, pronto." We all tromped back into the grass. "But first, Squeaky, you're coming with me, down to The Flank. Let's make sure the old farts without cable or the web realize what's going on."

Squeaky gave two thumbs up and a sunny smile. "Down over there," he said, "they probably got no clue."

On the eastern fringes of Sweetberry, the tucked-away side farthest from the zoo, we dropped off Squeaky's pals at one of the neighborhood's few remaining Houses of Dubious

Purpose. It was a leaning, brownish-avocado American Foursquare where grown men lounged all day on desperate couches, beside a vintage, broken Coke machine, as a menagerie of shifty people quickly filtered in and out. What we used to call a drug palace, basically, and a constant source of bitching on the top-secret neighborhood members-only web hole. All six guys bounded from my truck bed, scurried across the yard, and shot inside. I didn't ask. I didn't honestly care; to each his own, and I'm no hypocrite to knock a man's hustle. Nobody said anything, until Squeaky conceded: "What? I needed a crew, and that tall dude's my cousin. I didn't *buy* nothin' from them."

We turned back westward. The midafternoon sun blinded us as we tried to deliver Carlito to his shift at Happy's Pit Stop. When tall merciful shadows from old commercial buildings spared our eyes, the scene in downtown Sweetberry came into focus, and we all three gasped. From each gas pump, lines of maybe ten vehicles wormed out into the village, blocking traffic on all arterial roads and relegating a few drivers of large vehicles to park on the sidewalks, where they angled for position. Moms and police and off-duty nurses and the grill man at Dawgs Hot Dogs had exited their seats and were standing on their hoods and roofs, shouting at each other. Riding shotgun, Carlito was so angry he quaked. He rolled down his window and said to the first rooftop paranoiac he saw: "What are you *doing*, lady? There are other gas stations within ten blocks."

"Not today," said the lady, a thirty-something brunette in a Panama Jack hat. "This side of town, gas stations are either closed, or they look like this right now. Don't even bother trying."

"*What!*"

"Every CenterTown neighborhood has gone bananas," she said. "People want *out*. They want to go far. And they wanted to hit the road an hour ago."

Squeaky erupted in hysterical giggling, and Carlito jabbed an elbow into his chest.

"Look, I'm part-owner of this gas station, so I don't actually mind the business," Carlito told the woman, loudly enough that other car-top bystanders could hear. "But you do realize we're talking about *snakes* here, right? These aren't, you know, poisonous birds or something. They're slow-as-shit snakes. You don't need to drive fifty miles to get away."

"Yeah, but," she said, lifting her arms, "ana-fuckin'-conda!"

Carlito rolled the window back up, huffing in disgust, sweat catching in his short black beard. He closed his eyes and mouthed a silent something in Portuguese. "Throw it in reverse, fellas, get out of here while you can," he said, clutching his knife, looking psychotic. "Thanks for the ride. I'm out. Take care of yourselves. Don't let the bushes bite."

Squeaky hopped into copilot position as we backed out and tore away, down Oakhurst Drive, headed for The Flank. He offered $75 he surely didn't have for my pants. After declining, I suggested that he might turn his ridiculous Poison T-shirt inside out. He looked down at his chest: four White dudes with flamboyant frocks and rogued cheeks. He gasped and swore he hadn't realized those *weren't girls*. We laughed for a while, which felt foreign but good, a fleeting elixir.

"You think Genteel knows yet?" I said. "About the zoo break?"

"She ain't called you?"

"Nope."

"Then probably not. Unless she's locked herself in her bedroom, in fright."

"I have duct tape in here," I said. "We'll make her bungalow slither-proof real quick, then I have to go pound out another story. About something. Damn, I should have quoted that girl on the car—"

"You know what I heard?" Squeaky interrupted, cracking the window for fresh air. "Word on the street is some big-money company wants to knock down The Flank. Just bull-doze all them old shotguns. And then they'd put up, I guess, a bunch of brownstones or somethin'."

As he spoke I could see my potential Lotto story scoop, like a gorgeous virgin dove, fluttering out the window, disappearing forever. "Damn," I said. "Where'd you hear that?"

"You know Tall Walt? He's the grandson of somebody who stays at The Flank, one of Genteel's neighbors," he said. "You really don't know Tall Walt? Well, man, he don't mess around. And he's pissed off about his grandpa gettin' short-changed in this land deal." Squeaky paused to lean out of his seat, shade his squinted eyes with an open hand, and inspect a tangle of young palms outside a postwar bungalow, spot-ting nothing suspicious as we zipped by. "I saw him at the park, playing basketball. Walt got his hands on some plans, some blueprints or whatnot. Looks like they want to pack in about 600 people over there, give or take a few hundred. I'm talkin' about new residents. Fresh blood. Probably caw-kay-zyin blood, too, you know. Type of folks who like long breakfasts."

"So what's this Tall Walt gonna do about it?"

"I don't know," said Squeaky. "He's thinking about it, I heard. Thinkin' hard. And the outcome of his thoughts usually ain't gentle, at least from what I heard."

We passed my corner-lot Victorian, which tends to glow, behind her iron gates, in the western light of after-noon. I couldn't help but grin a little. "She's lookin' good, God," Squeaky said, in a reverent, honest way. "Proud of you, man." I thought of how the home looked the day I met Squeaky—the same week I'd become an ex-suburbanite—when he introduced himself on my sidewalk and asked me if I needed weapons or "smoke." I said yes, on both accounts. He also asked, "What is you, Greek or somethin'?" and I said no without expounding. We did discuss his personal history (honorable discharge from the Navy; dishonorable decade thereafter) and the history of my property. My grandfather had commissioned architectural plans for the home after brokering some deal involving the transportation of grain; he requested that she echo the grand Victorian spreads of Savannah, and with gas lamps beside the entry, a gorgeous slate roof, bay windows, and gingerbread porch detailing, she certainly did. By the time of my 1986 arrival here, however, a rain-soaked, mold-eaten wall or two was flirting with collapse inside; as such, I felt a kinship with the Victorian immediately. At first, I slept in a tent in the kitchen. I would clang pots to scare off squatters. I would boil water, always slightly tan, and bathe in a claw-foot tub that I feared would crack and flood the downstairs. I replaced the gutters, installed a working mailbox, and planted a Japanese Maple—and all that shit was promptly stolen. The scourge of theft did little to calm my nerves and toxic grief levels back then, or to maintain the remaining brownness of my beard and hair. Within a few months, deep into my second winter alone, as I squirmed all night with morbid dreams and barely ate anything, my hair went fully silver. My beard switched directly to white. All of this at age thirty-six. Squeaky bore witness to my transformation, which he likened to a dying Greek werewolf. It all contributed to his amazement of me, this moping enigma who'd suddenly shown up to live in his beloved, forgotten community. He started calling me "Gramps" at first. But that seemed trite and easy. So one evening, while we both were smoking crack on my rickety porch, Squeaky had an epiphany: "I'm-a call you God! I like the sound of that. God Johnson!" I laughed it off, but then everybody started calling me God. The mailwoman. The barber who trimmed my mop. And especially the little neighborhood kids. They were awed that a young, old man from prestigious Gwinnett County would not only plant roots in their section of Atlanta but dump all his money into resuscitating a "haunted" Victorian, spending each weekend painting the scalloped shingles or nearly falling off its steep, sagging roof. I wondered if one of those kids hadn't grown up to become this agitated Tall Walt character. It was possible, if not likely.

"She needs a fresh roof, but thanks for noticing," I said. "We'll find you some fang-proof trousers in due time."

Not a slow-moving soul was stirring outside at The Flank. I parked the truck beside Shotgun Three, and we knocked gently on the door and windows. Nothing, nobody. Squeaky preemptively jabbed his sword into the boxwoods around Genteel's porch, and we moved cautiously down the dusty lane, like a couple of clueless Tombstone gunslingers. The grounds around the bungalows were pristine. I peeked beneath them; all clear. As always, the colorful, modest, pretty facades all but radiated in fading sunshine. I took a few pictures, for posterity's sake, I thought, should it all be trucked off to pole-barn purgatory.

At The Flank's flank nearest the railroad tracks, we heard faint singing. We moved closer, toward the old preacher's home, and soon we could decipher the words of a soaring hymn, sung by many, praising something about a "divine light" in the "unknown distress" of the "waiting darkness." We timidly stepped to the porch, waved into the window, and were welcomed inside by Genteel, who pointed to the sword and smiled. Each resident of The Flank, as best I could tell, had sought refuge in the preacher's bungalow, and they gathered around Reverend Maynard Terrance now, perfectly circling him, hymnal books open on laps. The white-haired preacher, eyes closed, lifted his open hands, as if beneath a cleansing waterfall. He sung so forcefully I thought the two handguns would surely shake off his lap.

As the singing ebbed, the crowd acknowledged us, and Genteel asked Squeaky, who lived in a different American

Foursquare near Happy's Pit Stop, how rent was going on his side of the neighborhood.

"Up," Squeaky said, triggering a chorus of knowing *mrrrm-hrrrrms.*

"The city's on edge," I said, trying to sound authoritative but reassuring. "We just saw as much down in the village, all around Happy's. People are going crazy for gas, just panicking to get out of town. But honestly, y'all, I think we need to keep our heads. If we be careful and button our homes up tight, we're all going to be A-OK."

"You know what Miss Prissy told me? The lady from Oakhurst Drive in the blue house?" said Genteel, to nobody in particular. "She said, down at the village, she see people go in shoppin' and leave their cars runnin' nowadays. *Runnin'!* Can you imagine seein' that in the old times, the way things was?"

This prompted a loud, impassioned discussion about shopping and the price of gas in the village and the questionable hues of forthcoming tomatoes. They were clinging to distractions. They were clutching for the unthreatening normalcy they'd always known. I could tell nobody wanted details about the fire-mouthed fer-de-lance of Central America or the striking capabilities of coastal taipans. They wanted the ointment of their neighbors' company and the coziness of their nook, the travails of our berserk metropolis be damned. Nonetheless, I saw an opportunity to hammer in a spike of guilt.

"Folks, I have to get back to work," I said. "I'll leave my rolls of duct tape. Squeaky, could you be so kind as to assist with plugging and sealing doorjambs and windowsills—any little cracks to the outside?" I turned toward the door but then whipped my head back around. "They say you can see what people mean to each other in times of crisis," I said. "Shame y'all are throwing this away for a quick profit, for the easy out." I tried to grab the door and flee in a dramatic, poignant, remorse-inducing exit, but the armed preacher spoke in such a thunderous rebuttal his words were magnetic.

"We've changed our minds, if it isn't too late," Reverend Terrance said. "Genteel tells us you're serious about helping, Mr. Johnson."

I crossed my arms, had a quick think. "Frankly," I said. "It's really not my business."

"Oh, phwoo!" Genteel exploded. "No time to get cold feet now, is it? You was nothing but ideas yesterday, and now The Flank ain't *your* business? Come on!"

Every weathered face in the room scalded me with expressions of rage and disgust; Genteel had clearly won the jury in advance.

"I said it'd be a shame to see y'all get bulldozed out," I said. "This town's way too obsessed with destroying the best parts of itself, and it always has been. You know what I mean?" All around me, the vitriol lifted. "Maybe I'm too sentimental. But that's my stance."

Genteel folded her big arms, cocked her jaw sideways. "OK then," she said. "That sounds better, but—"

"Maybe it *is* your business," the Reverend said, smiling in the warmth of what looked like epiphany. He stood up and holstered his weapons in svelte little pockets secured by Velcro to his cowboy belt. The ingenuity of these modern holsters, and the Reverend's ease with operating them, reminded me how much maniacal church rampages had unfortunately become reality in our era. "I mean that literally," he continued. "Because I think we have a real story here, about this dirty deal we're caught up in."

"Exactly!" I said.

"Yes," he said. "But exactly how?"

"Does this involve elderly exploitation laws?" I said rhetorically. "Is that what you're asking? Because that was my thought. But with this other, uh, slithery issue, you know, I haven't had time to dig in."

The Reverend dragged a palm across his fluffy head, down a hook nose, over his salty chin. "I'm not sure, either," he said. "But I know one thing: I was shown some paperwork that the developer, Lotto, had fudged on me. Like a trick. I'm sure of it. Pictures and paperwork."

"Be more specific."

"Well," said the Reverend, "Lotto showed me photos of housing stock in the suburbs. Stuff I could buy for cash with profits from selling this house. But it's stuff that doesn't exist. They were ghost houses. Maybe from some other town, but it looked like Gwinnett County to me. Real nice one-level ranches with decks and Jacuzzis. Tell you what, I trusted him too much. I should have used an agent, I guess. Or at least called around. He lied to me, flat out."

Electrified by this slam-dunk evidence, this proof, I said: "That's lowdown! And it sounds like something we could print without worrying about libel."

Revered Terrance took a long pull from a glass of milk. "Look, I'm calling a community meeting, a week from today, when all this serpent hype has hopefully calmed down," he said. "I want all of us there, all the other Sweetberry community, plus pertinent city officials, and Mr. Lotto Livingston and his crew, too. If he try to say we can't back out, we'll make a fuss in the most public way."

"Bravo," I said. "I'll mark the date."

"I was hoping you would."

"Is this Tall Walt gonna be there?" I said, careful not to come across as too informed and clever. "Squeaky tells me he's sideways over this deal, just roaring. He's one of y'all's grandson, correct?"

Not a peep from the crowd. Fifteen blank, stoic faces.

"No matter," I said, slowly opening the door, surveilling the porch. "A week from today it is. Now, excuse me, the *Beacon*'s paying me by the word, so it's time for work."

I heard Genteel quip to her friends about my "backwoods clown suit" as I bounded back to the truck, went home, taped my three toilets shut, and pounded out 850 words of stream-of-consciousness, half-paranoid, first-person, Lord-save-us gibberish that I emailed away in a hurry. Becky rejected the story within five minutes. Her email's subject line read "I said a REPORT OF SERVICE to readers!" and the body was hollow. White. Barren. Bereft of money talk. No potential for food. And that capped a day of true misery. The biggest story ever and I'd managed to produce a dinky web blurb dictated by phone. Naturally I asked Marnie for a dance, and we moved to the darkening porch windows, my community scared and silent just beyond. In the fibers of my deepest human self I just wanted someone there with me, a sounding board for my complaints, an ally in my panic, a landing spot for my love. Instead my only partner was the darkness, that deep and wicked darkness.

CHAPTER 7

Five days passed with no snakes. And no trace of zookeeper McCaffrey. Working in concert with frustrated zoo officials, city leaders astutely lessened the "Ultra High Alert" status on the first Sunday to "Ultra Alert" and declared that city services would have to resume by late morning Monday. People's homes were becoming choked with their own detritus. Trash trucks were coming—but only for receptacles placed at least three feet from bushes and trees.

Starving, I was forced to produce some puffy reportage about the city's shortage of anti-snake essentials, such as snake repellent (useless), knee-high snakebite socks (they exist, but also useless), and yes trout pants (Mozartian genius). Tabitha Jones, that snazzy Channel 8 story poacher, had shown a B-roll clip of my attire at the initial press conference and advised that "rain gear" and "fishing trousers" might thwart fangs. And then outfitters from Buckhead to Douglasville promptly ran out of waders, with no kickback to *moi*. I visited a couple of grocers and reported on the scarcity of bread and milk, which normally happens around Atlanta when seven snowflakes are forecasted. Then I wrote some more serious stuff about the slow trickle of Sweetberry

Parkers—God I hate to say it like that, but they all do—who were deeming it safe enough to leave exurban hotels and come back home, into the city. Everyone had theories, but nothing made sense. *The sewers! The sewers!* said the few FEMA flaks who would actually take the time to speak with me. They basically posited this: *We think they became very scared, slipped into the sewer systems, and if they haven't instinctually found their way back to jungles, you know, they're probably just happier down there.*

Like my neighbors, I began to feel comfortable enough to venture onto my rocking-chair porch to catch fresh air while wearing regular cloth. Except the air was suddenly short on freshness. It was heavy. Thick. Terrible. Like stepping into a citywide bathroom of blow-dryers on high. It was the inevitable, uninvited skin molasses—and maybe the heat of Paul's burning sticks, harbinger of snakes. The Deep South swelter had come early, the last thing a tense city needed. Even worse, my window air conditioner sputtered, and I conspired to slip out, hop the fence, and splash into the backyard pools of the new $840,000 Craftsman-style, five-bedroom behemoths down the street. But those pools seemed likely hangouts for overheated pythons, too. So I sat. We sat. And we sweated. And we waited. For something. For anything. All of us now uncomfortable in our ignorance. All of us clueless that the summer from hell had but barely dawned.

Then I broke the news about the first real snake catch.

As predicted, glory-hounding reptile trappers had descended upon Atlanta from a vast crescent of backwoods nowheres around the Southeast, which was mighty-right nice of them. They fingered out into bamboo backyards and urban forests and even manicured greenspaces like Piedmont Park. But the first real champions among them were some back-slapping swamp boys from Buck Nards, Alabama, or thereabouts.

Five blocks from the zoo, near a kudzu-engulfed power station, they'd pulled a hulking canebrake rattlesnake from the underbrush. I caught wind of this when my police scanner erupted with the loud, jubilant, unencrypted chatter of first-responders: "We got one! We got one!" I flew to the scene in my truck and joined the waves of cops, medics, and what looked like safari guides from the zoo, all of them clearly exhausted after five wild days. As luck would have it, I was standing next to the lead hero trapper, where I was not credentialed to be, when the predominate safari man called that big fat snake a fraud. His exact words—*a fraud!* I pulled the Canon from beneath my shirt and snapped as many photos as possible.

"The hail y'all main uh fruhd?" protested this camou-flaged genius. "Sumbitch dang beeg as this don't bee-long in no damn setay!"

With two pinched fingers, he squeezed the head, raised his muddied boot off the body, and lifted the animal to chest-height; festooned with rings of autumn colors, in shapes that reminded me of pueblo wallpaper in Tucson, the great snake was beautiful in its awfulness. Its big mouth yawned into an aggravated, blossoming death flower. Two semi-clear daggers jutted forth, and a dozen grown men around me stepped back in gasping retreat. But the safari man stood his ground, jabbing his finger. He pointed so close to the fangs I thought he might try to kill the snake by gagging it.

"You boys should be ashamed of yourselves," declared the zoo man.

Them boys was stunned.

"Ain't no shame in this right here, main," the trapper replied, mouth agape. "It's caught fair un square. Now who dwee see 'bout about dat ree-ward?"

The zoo official, now sweating and angry, waved in the Atlanta police officers who'd stepped back toward the road.

"There is no *reward*," he said. "Last thing we want is encouraging the public to try bagging snakes like this." He turned to the officers. "This animal isn't on the roster of missing snakes," he said. "And it's not native to this region at all. It's more a Louisiana species, in fact. So it's obvious these fellas have *imported* this animal in an attempt to make themselves heroes—and to cash in on a reward that doesn't even exist."

The enterprising out-of-towners said nothing. Their fallen faces all but admitted guilt. They were charged with making false statements and booked. When I'd finished laughing I banged out a 300-word blurb (Headline: "South of zoo, five Louisiana 'hunters' charged by police in snaky scheme") that Becky readily accepted. I got an extra $44 for the photo I'd quickly developed in my basement darkroom, scanned, and emailed away. But the value in this little sidebar was greater than that paycheck. It restored Becky's confidence in my news judgement. And she asked me to swing by her office the following morning, at the dawn of Day 6, which I eagerly did, more or less on time.

"Let's talk strategy," Becky said, sitting atop her smart midcentury desk, which she'd pained flamboyant fuchsia, a middle finger to the chauvinist editor who'd owned the desk before his firing. Behind Becky, a few blocks to the west, stood the angular framework of the new Falcons stadium, rising out of the clay like a deep-sea crustacean from the future.

"Permission to speak freely?" I said.

"Shoot."

"You look a bit strung out," I said, doting. "Don't think I've seen ya without makeup before. Or wearing a ponytail like that. Or with your clothing all crumpled up. You doin' OK?"

"You're a sly one, God," she said.

"Seriously, Beck."

"OK, so, you're right. I'm busted. I'm frazzled. Congratulations."

A few years ago, I'd accepted Becky's offer to be a salaried reporter here. I relished the stability but couldn't stomach the confinement of a cubicle. And it hurts my heart to say this, but reporting to work each day at a newspaper office felt like saddling an arthritic dinosaur. The worst part was knowing that the dinosaur, for all its creaky joints and slothfulness, was still the most indispensable wellspring of information in this town, like every town. An invaluable monitor and oracle within its wrinkled skin. A societal treasure less appreciated by the day. Anyhow, I quit after a week. And Becky didn't respond to my freelance pitches for a month.

"This situation, man," Becky wheezed. "It's making me sick, I think." She lay back flat on her desk and sighed toward the ceiling, hands behind her head. Apparently, I'd assumed the role of therapist. "Every minute I'm sitting here expecting that damn phone to ring. I expect one of my reporters to be screaming on the other end, telling me some kid's been bitten and is convulsing in a park. Or on a porch. Or in the street. I mean, are we doing *enough*, as a city? FEMA officials and who *knows* who else is here, for heaven's sakes. Atlanta is literally crawling with searchers. Yet here we are, nearly a week later, without a single fucking snake to show for it. We're got nothing but fear. And it's all the more crippling when you don't really understand what you're afraid of."

"I haven't really slept yet, either," I said. "Not since the poor Australian death adder. So I can relate. You're not alone."

Becky closed her eyes, and for a minute I thought she'd dozed off.

"Permission to speak freely," she said this time, softly

"Shoot."

She gritted her teeth, and underneath freckled cheeks the mandibles bulged. Her face was the epitome of health;

her spirit was not. "I've slept here the past three nights." She moaned at the thought, the admission.

"I'm not surprised," I said. "You're tenacious like that."

"It's because the hotel was killing me, financially."

"I can imagine."

"I haven't been home in three weeks."

"*Huh?*"

She sat up, but her shoulders dropped. "Timothy and I are divorcing," she said. "He says I'm married to here. To this. To a dozen people like you, God."

"If you're proposing, I'll have to decline—"

"Stop," she snapped. "No jokes at a goddamn time like this."

I tugged my ponytail and slapped my ear with it, an obnoxious, nervous, equine habit. "Apologies, ma'am. I'm really sorry to hear."

"Listen, I've wanted to ask you something," she said. "I want you to be real with me. So can I now?" I smiled, nodded. "So, you lived through worse than this, much worse than an acrimonious divorce," she said. "Worse than most people. Worse than anyone deserves, I'd say."

She turned toward me with big wet eyes, and I fidgeted without meaning to. The pitch meeting had devolved weirdly into something else. "That'd be accurate," I said. "I don't think, you know, that it gets much worse than where I went."

Becky's face tightened, a vulnerable hurt I'd never seen. "Tell me, then, please," she said. "Tell me that anyone who keeps pushing will eventually push out of something like this. This hollow sort of feeling. This aloneness. This hole."

"That's right."

"Tell me I can do it."

"You're strong, Beck. The strongest I've known. And I'm not talking about pull-ups or biathlons—"

"Thanks," she said, cutting me off, and then scooting across the desk and plopping into her office chair. She was boss again, and the anguish slid right off her. "You're a good, honorable man, deep down," she said. "Must be the Navajo in you."

"I'm not Navajo."

"Then Cherokee? It's American Indian, right? The heritage?"

"I'm just a guy," I said. "Just another American mixed-drink."

"Sorry to prod," said Becky. "I think it's cool, though, and always have. A mysterious look."

"The story goes," I said, sighing, "my grandma was what they called a 'fancy lady' in post-Reconstruction times, if you must know. Not technically a ho—but pretty close. She met an engineer from Nigeria, who was also a failed essayist, at a tavern near Georgia Tech. They knew each other for four hours, but that's all it took."

"So you're a smidgen Nigerian?"

"And a whole lotta cracker-cornbread," I said. "For better or worse. It's not the most comfortable subject for me; growing up in the 'burbs, I was the outlier, always pissed off it mattered so much."

"Anyhow," she said. "Thanks again, man. I owe you."

"Just keep me fed with assignments. That's all I ask."

"Speaking of," she said. "Anything new with that scandalous development deal in Sweetberry Park?"

"There is, in fact," I said, my heart leaping. "So the gullible victims in question, the old folks, are building a case that they've been scammed. A strong case, I think."

"Oh yeah?"

"Yep. And don't laugh when I say this, but a few college-age guys around Sweetberry formed a militia to fight the snakes, like I was saying, and when they caught wind of

Lotto Livingston's scheme, they also were pissed. Super pissed. And now, according to my sources, a *splinter militia* has formed to fight Lotto, to keep his bulldozers at bay. Their leader calls himself Tall Walt."

"Tall Walt and splinter militias?" she said. "You can't make this shit up."

"Anyway," I said, "this Walt, from what I've been hearing late this week, is the grandson of one of the old folks. But none of them will even claim him. I don't know why, but it speaks to his reputation. And what he might be planning for the likes of our boy Lotto."

She clasped a hand tightly over her forehead, above her tired eyes, thinking. "Sounds juicy," she said. "What's next?"

"What's next is, tomorrow night, at this church down the street from me, it's all going down," I said, grinning. "A preacher everyone knows has called a community meeting. A civil sort of powwow, he's calling it, but we'll see. Every key player is supposed to be there. The victims from The Flank. The asshole developer and his disciples. These hyperactive yuppie nitwits who're buying the big new homes. The old-timers like me. And this splinter militia. Happens at eight p.m. sharp. Make sense?"

"It does."

"You have interest?"

"I do."

"To what extent?"

"Eight-hundred words," she said. "By eleven p.m. deadline tomorrow. Not a minute later. Can you get me that?"

"Yes, ma'am."

"Don't be cute with it. Just facts"

"Fine—eleven p.m. it is."

"Good," she said. "We need something fresh on the Metro page, if not the front, instead of all this madness. So good luck. And if you mention a word about my little breakdown here, you'll never be assigned another paragraph from this desk."

I stood up and saluted Becky, and I started to walk out. But the dormant Southern gent in me, the one good thing implanted by my grandad, awoke; I realized it'd be prudent to offer Becky a few words of comfort, some balm for her chaffed soul.

"Speaking from experience, I wouldn't listen to sad music for a while," I said. "Keep busy. Keep pushing. Stay creative. If he doesn't like your ambition, it'll be for the best, eventually, and it definitely means you deserve better."

She cocked her pretty head and frowned. "Why'd you never get married again?"

"The way I see it," I said, opening the office door, stepping out, "I still am."

CHAPTER 8

The following evening, from within my screened back porch, I watched the sun slip into a denouement so gloriously pink it was somber, because I knew the sunset, like every blessed thing allowed to be, would end too soon. The orb bowed between wax myrtles, pulling with it a brilliant ruby cascade, until there was nothing left but gray horizon. Even in the dark, though, the heat wave's woolen humidity did not relent. To air out, I wanted to walk the two blocks to the church meeting but, like everyone else, I elected to drive. The darkened sidewalks, in my estimation, were just too bushy.

Driving up, toward the commercial village and church, I realized I'd forgotten how majestic the old prayer house was, having been numbed by the familiarity of passing it daily. The Holiness Church of Our Savior, a towering Greek Revival structure made of stone pillars and brick, was alive with patronage that Tuesday evening, its stained-glass glowing like sunlit kaleidoscopes. The church was flanked by two parking lots, but with night coming on, nobody used the one nearest the stand of oaks and privet bushes. I parked as close as possible and joined a stream of folks using the back entrance. To my surprise, I felt no fearful tension in the air yet, and no hunger for uprising in so many polite faces.

Ushers pointed us to the basement, a low dingy space with suspended ceiling tiles and neat rows of standard folding chairs. They'd left a wide aisle clear of chairs in the middle. Maybe a hundred people were there, with room for twenty more. Squeaky spotted me and waved me over in a weirdly formal but gyrating way, like a demented prom king. I took the seat he'd reserved next to him and unfolded my notebook, checking with nonsensical loops the ink reserves in my pen. I was ready.

"On the clock tonight, huh?" said Squeaky.

"Where the hell's Lotto?" I said. "He better show."

"They waitin' outside," Squeaky said. "I saw 'em wearing suits, his whole crew, in a fine-ass old Lincoln."

That made me want to bound to my feet and kick a chair. "He's the diseased rat of Atlanta development, man."

"God, *damn*."

"Sorry," I said. "Long story. You seen Genteel and her gang?"

"No," he said, "but that's Tall Walt, right over there."

Squeaky nodded to the second row, at left, where maybe a dozen younger Black men wore T-shirts in the same blue hue. Standing over them all, near the radiator, was maybe six feet, five inches of hefty twenty-something ringleader, his precisely trimmed hair leading down to a thin, chin-strap beard. I could see half the bold front of his T-shirt, and it said something about Preserve The Flank. It was obvious this splinter militia wasn't the mindless, brutish counter-force Squeaky had portended, but an organized movement.

"Save my seat," I said.

I hustled over to shake Tall Walt's hand. Skeptically, he accepted, and his great palm and digits devoured mine up to the wrist, a Burmese python to my swamp rat. Above the whiskey barrel of a chest his eyes were red and tired. I introduced myself and he nodded, not offering his name in return.

"You grow up around here?" I said. "You look familiar."

"Yes sir, a little," he said. "My granddad lives down the street. Grandmom used to, too, but she's passed."

"Does he know Genteel?"

"Of course."

I scribbled something down, and his facial expression shifted from staid courteousness to stung annoyance. "The T-shirt uniforms are nice," I said, scrounging for compliments. "Has your group had any luck finding snakes yet?"

"Nothing that wasn't here naturally. A few copperheads in the creeks. But we're looking. We're bigger than what's represented here tonight."

"I've heard that," I said. "Does your militia, or this splinter group, have an official name?"

He looked over my shoulder for eavesdroppers. "Off the record?"

"No."

"Then no," he said. "We don't."

"You've secretive," I said.

"You're nosy."

This Walt, obviously, was a hard-shelled nut.

"Can you just tell me, quickly, what your motivation is here tonight? Beyond the fact that Lotto Livingston is what he is?"

"What do you think he is?"

"Good question," I said. "He's complex, for sure. I think he's the most reviled developer in Atlanta right now. Or at least top three. But he's also tremendously good at what he does."

Walt inhaled—in the long deep way of a bothered man—and then exhaled for roughly three minutes. "You been in Sweetberry forever, right?" he said. "Living in that house we thought was haunted as kids?" I nodded. "Well then, sir, you know how The Flank is. What it means. How there will never be another Flank. We've got no formal name, Mr. Johnson. We're just standing up for what's right."

"I see," I said. "So you're sort of activist history buffs?"

"You know what I mean," he said. "Don't trivialize it." He glanced at his watch and started to sit down.

"One other quick thing, Walt," I said. "When somebody says 'militia,' I think a bunch of reckless, aggressive fools. But you guys are polished. Organized. What's your background?"

"Checkered," he said.

I laughed. Hard. He didn't.

"Mine too," I said. "But can you expound?"

"Why?"

"Just for context, in the story?"

"Go on back to your seat, sir. Show's about to start."

I followed his directive and noticed, for the first time, Genteel and her gardening clique seated on a riser in the back. She looked tremendously nervous to be in public.

The last neighborhood representative to arrive was none other than Americana Mama, Sweetberry's queen critic and omniscient arbiter of other people's business. She looked especially anal and ferocious in a pressed, houndstooth business suit. Her black hair hung straight and smooth—not a strand out of place—to her chin, framing her pink cheeks and sweat-speckled forehead. As usual, she looked ready, militant, poked.

I leaned up over heads to see who was sitting with Americana Mama at the front of the room, facing the crowd, and immediately my respect for her grew tenfold: at her side, in an elaborate motorized wheelchair, was a young boy, maybe seven years old, contorted by some terrible muscular disorder. He wore a thick, soft seatbelt that made an X across this abdomen. His arms, skinny as sticks, were frozen in mid-reach away from his body, one wrist turned down and the other toward his head. His close-cropped hair, black as his mother's, framed a face that was slightly disproportionate but otherwise normal, fixed in an open-mouthed smile. Despite his predicament, the boy's ice-blue eyes projected happiness, as if he were delighted to be among so many people, so much stimuli. From socks to shirt he wore the red-yellow-black attire of the Atlanta Hawks, a team showing itself the door, as usual, in the pro basketball playoffs that week.

Americana Mama—an honorable mom, clearly, of the highest order—was stroking the boy's arm and speaking softly into his ear as Lotto and company entered the room, lugging a convoy of briefcases, boxes, and luggage on wheels. As he passed the boy, Lotto leaned over, reached out a fist, and bumped the kid's dangling knuckles in greeting. Mama looked none too pleased about that.

Preacher Maynard Terrance from The Flank rose up to meet Lotto and shake his hand. Then Lotto turned toward the audience, and up went his hands: "*Lord*, what a crowd tonight!"

Lotto was dressed less formally than I'd seen him in years—a simple red Oxford and slacks—and his complexion had gone pink. Maybe it was the shirt, reflecting. Or the heat. Or embarrassment. Or simmering rage. I flipped to a blank page in my notebook and started scribbling fast enough to make smoke.

"Good evening, Sweetberry Park," said the preacher, before introducing himself, Lotto, and Lotto's three suit-wearing assistants, all straight-lipped and nervous. Not a single grumble, shout, or declaration of imminent homicide sprang from the crowd. "We're in the midst of one hot, tumultuous summer," the preacher continued, "the likes of which I've never seen. None of us have. Probably no city ever has before, thank the Lord. I've spent all my summers right here in Sweetberry, and like you, I love my city and neighborhood deeply." He paused for proper golf claps. "Now, my purpose for calling this meeting, if it isn't obvious, is to lend our community what we need most right now: togetherness. I realize we're all still on edge about the zoo mishap. Being out past dark, I know, is inadvisable. But we need to reach common ground here before it complicates our other problems. Before it exacerbates these snake-related tensions. Now, at the risk of exciting folks, I'm just going to put this out there, for the record, from the beginning…" The preacher turned to the developer and spoke with booming conviction: "Mr. Livingston, residents of The Flank, as well as I, believe you misrepresented certain realities in our real estate deal. You personally showed me comp properties that don't exist in metro Atlanta, I don't believe. You made promises to others about country homes and beach bungalows that can't come real. We don't feel we got a fair shake. And for those reasons, we want out!"

Attendees leapt up in applause, roaring. The holy concrete beneath our feet shimmied. Lotto looked flabbergasted and sabotaged, even more than his young colleagues, for a moment; but his quickness in composing himself made me suspicious he hadn't been planning for such pushback all along.

"Please, team, erect the easels," Lotto said. "We can discuss numbers later. For now, folks, give me two minutes. Please. That's all. Just a couple minutes to outline my proposal for your—"

"No need, sir!" shouted Tall Walt from the corner. "Not interested!"

This assertion garnered more applause—a passive-aggressive, loud-mean clapping—and Walt was instantly exalted to local warrior status. Strange, because nobody except Squeaky and The Flank folks seemed to know this deep-voiced stranger.

"I appreciate your passion, and these cute T-shirts you're all wearing, but I'm entitled to the floor, too," Lotto said.

"Now, please, direct your attention here…" He swung back his arm like some vintage carnie and ta-da'ed the introductory panel with its fluorescent home renderings and bold declaration: "Sweetberry Lanes: The Deluxe Urban Lifestyle You Know You've Earned."

"But first, folks," said Lotto, "before we discuss the future… and the future of eastside Atlanta *is* affordable, workforce housing in this contemporary-rustic home context… let me tell you about right now." For the next minute he danced through a saccharine, forced spiel about The Flank's inimitable architecture and how each plank would be masterfully deconstructed and built "with newfound pep" in its suburban museum home. Meanwhile, Lotto's flunkies flipped through panels showing his proposal from different angles. Each building and multipurpose mini-lawn teemed with stylish, uppity-looking young people who had yet to be crushed by life's realities.

"Hold the hell up!" shouted Walt. "In every one of those drawings you're showing, there ain't a single non-White person."

The pinkish orb atop Lotto's shoulders went full purple. "Don't fret that," he said. "It's just industry standard."

"I'm sorry, but *naw*," said Walt, now standing and pointing. "That's a one-eighty, man, ethnically speaking. That's wrong. Not a single resident of The Flank isn't Black now."

"I'm aware, sir, because I inked deals with them all," said Lotto, nodding toward Genteel and company. "Cities change, though. We have to keep that broader context in mind. OK? This isn't rural Iowa. This isn't North Korea. This is the A-town, baby, as the rappers used to say, and it's always moving. It evolves and evolves. If you want a static town, Mississippi has plenty—"

"Hold up," Walt interjected again. "Look, I'm not here to make this a race thing, because I know it isn't that simple.

But, brother, for real: *Look* at these images. Look at what you're saying here. How is what you're showing us any different than Nazi propaganda?"

The question was so provocative—so *atomic*—I lost the ability to write, momentarily. My tactile functions simply shuttered. I don't think anyone else could really breathe. I saw Lotto reach between buttons of his shirt, his fingers scrambling for the lucky charm, his overly glum savior.

"You're gonna come at *me*, with an accusation like *that*?" Lotto was breathing heavy now, in the manner of a scorned, contested rich kid. He was also trying to sound urban. "You know who my daddy was? You know how much he did for this city? For this *neighborhood*?"

"Man," Walt shot back, "I could give two damn shits—"

"Enough!" Reverend Terrance interrupted. "This won't devolve into a shouting match, gentlemen."

Americana Mama very politely raised her hand. The preacher called on her, pointing.

"So, Mr. Livingston," she said, "can we talk numbers for a minute? Just, like, facts? What is that you have there— about fifty units, each with garages? OK, thought so. Who approved this mess, and what were they thinking?"

"It's been approved, don't worry," Lotto said, regaining corporate dialect. "This meeting is a formality, a favor to y'all." He straightened his casual collar. "And the contracts with *you* all"—he pointed to Genteel in the gallery—"are absolutely valid. Each one of them. I won't bore you with minutia, but don't even try to go there."

"Look," Americana Mama said, "I'm all for density in the city, and a tight-knit community. But what about traffic, Mr. Livingston? The vehicle dangers your project poses to kids? You study that?"

Rocking from heel to toe, Lotto was boiling now. "All of that, I assure you, has been systematically vetted by the city, and every bit of Sweetberry Lanes complies." Lotto exhumed the cross from his shirt. He shamelessly, blatantly kissed the piece and rubbed it across his lips and nose, as toddlers do the frayed ends of blankets.

"Lastly, sir," she said, "as that gentleman was alluding to... what about the elimination of diversity? You in compliance with that?" There was clapping, again, and Mama was inspired. "I want my little boy here to grow up in a place open to young and old, all colors, all creeds. From what I'm seeing, it looks like you're selling to nothing but disposable-income types. I bet all your robot people, there on those marketing materials, have IT jobs."

"It's Shirley, right?" said Lotto. "Don't you live in a six-bedroom, custom home on Ponce Terrace? Of course you do. Your land was Section 8 apartments before. Seven families moved out. I know you already know that. Which begs the question: Who the hell are *you* to talk? Where did your home put those families? You're Sweetberry's biggest hypocrite right now."

The crowd's thunderous, chaotic rebuttal was too animalistic to quote from, so I jotted: "FUKR MIGHT HAVE POINT." Red-faced Americana Mama shot to her feet, but then crouched and said nothing. The preacher stepped between Lotto and his pant-suited adversary and shouted to calm down. As people complied, the preacher called on a young White man, hand raised, with a checkered Oxford tucked into his pleated, frat-boy khakis. Before speaking, the dude used four fingers to comb aside his stylized, Kentucky Waterfall bangs.

"We, like, *paid* for diversity!" said the guy. "Seriously. Literally. Like seriously literally!"

"OK, son," said Reverend Terrance. "We've covered that for now, but thank you."

Lotto tucked his necklace away. "Tell me," he said, fixing tiger eyes on Alpha Kappa Sigma Ki Lambda. "Why, exactly, do you covet this diversity? I'm curious. Because it sounds like a buzzword—like a commercial—coming out your mouth. You're talking, but you're not feeling a thing. Are you? You're saying what you think you should. You like diversity so you don't have to experience the guilt of your kind extracting the old Blacks who kept this place alive for decades. I'm rewarding them, to the tune of *five percent* over market value, per our estimates, for their hard work. These old shotgun homes are leaking. They're failing. Foundations breaking apart. Rat nests and termites under the porches. Did you know *that*? Of course you didn't. You have to understand I'm offering a cash escape, a reprieve from serious repair costs, the damn lottery. Heck, it's another reason, really, to call me Lotto. And it's just capitalism, boy. It works. Now either shut up, step up, or *wake up* to the simple math of it all."

My writing hand was exhausted and quaking. I could keep no more notes, but every word was too important. So I cheated. I pressed "Audio Record" on my smart phone, that digital shortcut I usually shun. This allowed me the flexibility to stand up, nod at Genteel, and raise my hand. The preacher blessed me with a point.

"Full disclosure, for the record," I said. "I'm here as a Sweetberry resident and member of the news media. I'll be doing a write-up about whatever transpires tonight, so I don't want to interfere. But again, for the record, I think a very specific piece of The Flank's history should be taken into account here. It involves Martin Luther King Jr.—and diapers!" I scanned the room for laughter; it was no damn time for that. "Anyhow, Miss Genteel Briggs, could you please expound?"

With the help of an old neighbor beside her, Genteel lumbered to her feet in the back and held up her open right palm, as if taking an oath. "MLK, I know for fact," she said, "was babysat over there in The Flank, where I stay. Where I've stayed since forever. My auntie told me about Martin, and she ain't never lie!"

Lotto tossed his hands into the air. "Good one, God," he said. "It's really ironclad, isn't it? That'll stand up before the Georgia Historical Structures Review Committee."

Now my heart was a kicked, caged rodent. "Just a question, now for the paper, on the record," I said. "When you signed these contracts with each and every resident of The Flank, did you verify that none of them were on medication?"

Lotto's head went burnt amber. "Not one of them was intoxicated, God," Lotto said. "Don't even try that—"

"Because if they were," I continued, "per Georgia code, there's a chance each document is void. And that's to say nothing of fraud, if you indeed gave information, as the preacher alleges, about irrelevant or out-of-state comp homes."

"This doesn't sound very objective," Lotto said. "Did you have a question? No? Does anyone else have legitimate questions, without baseless accusations that paint me as the boogeyman? No? *No?* Nobody? Then I think I'm done here, and we're going to pack up. Last chance..."

Lotto cast his eyes to the back of the room, to the gaggle of elevated fogies, and I watched his face drop with a mix of wonder, indignation, and fear. I turned around, and there was wobbly Genteel, standing on her folding metal chair, lifting her tremendous arm and inhaling the oxygen required for a heartfelt blues chorus: "I'll tell ya now," she started to sing, in a deep, punchy register between dirty roadhouse grit and opera house vibrato. But then she stopped herself, as if embarrassed, and spoke the rest: "This ain't the last you've seen-a me, and us. We ain't goin' down quiet!"

For a second Lotto smiled. He waved a hand dismissively, turned to his minions, and hissed more loudly than he'd meant to: "Oh, bitch, sit down." And that was Sweetberry noprivilege.

Americana Mama burst up from her seat, as did Squeaky and the rest of my row. The splinter militia started shouting in the corner, as did Reverend Terrance; clearly fearful of a riot, the preacher hollered, "Out, out, *out now!*" to the development posse. Before the easels were deconstructed and renderings packed, the entire room was standing and shouting, and as someone made a break for the front, someone else tried to hold them back, and when they both toppled into a mess of chairs and shorts and skirts, the neat rows began to break apart, and the crowd became a screaming amoeba of angst.

A man toward the front put a finger in Lotto's face, and when Lotto slapped it away, a new charge of folks went toward him, while others fell back to avoid conflict, and the room had no uniformity at all, only chaos, only madness, only desperation to get out—until a thundercrack of gunfire sent everyone diving onto the floor.

I lay on the coarse, cold concrete, face down, palms clasping the back of my skull, silently praying for help so that we might not die in church. What caused me to tepidly lift my head and peek toward the preacher was a sound I can only describe as the guttural wailing of a frantic cat—a big cat, like a mountain lion, in utmost agony. It was a wet, terrible screech.

At the front of the room, still seated in his elaborate wheelchair, Americana Mama's son was writhing; he jolted and shook as if his seat was the electric chair, as if the switch had just dropped. He was wearing a yellow Hawks T-shirt. And in the middle of it, just below his sternum, I watched a red rose slowly bloom.

"The boy's hit!" I screamed, struggling to all fours, and then upright. "Her boy's been shot!"

I nearly stepped on the weapon. It was still in motion, spinning, shinning, and scratching across the floor, kicked or dropped from somewhere near the front, headed in Lotto's direction. As it stopped, I could see it was a rickety cowboy pistol, almost comically old. The air smelled as if some burning industrial thing had just flamed out.

Lotto, hunched with forearms over his scalp, burst upright and flew out the double entrance doors with a panicked stampede behind him. I ran to the confused boy and clasped his hand, alongside a woman who shouted about being a nurse. The boy's shrieks were piercing, nightmarish, and unjust, his face a geyser of pinkish saliva. His mother, shocked and trembling, clutched his forehead, crying so forcefully she could not breathe. In a moment she composed herself slightly and moaned, "Joey, Joey, Joey, *Joey*..." Squeaky appeared behind the boy's back, over his head, and with the nurse, we three lifted the wheelchair and darted out into the night.

As mother and son boarded an ambulance, engulfed by a blue-uniformed frenzy of first-responders, I tried to give one last reassuring wave, but I noticed then my hands, forearms, and shirt were smeared with blood. I walked home slowly without a worry for the bushes or trees. I watched the eleven p.m. deadline roll by on my wall clock but couldn't bring myself to sit down and type. For some reason I could not stop looking at my arms, appalled by the cracking red riverbeds in my palms, unable to walk to my sink and remove the evidence, the coppery stench. I wished in every way the blood had spilled from me instead, from my aged veins. I felt a deeply sad suck, a strange gravity in my heart, a familiar sting, and above all a diminishing hope for the human condition.

PART II

CHAPTER 9

The antique rotary phone I kept in my foyer rang at seven the next morning. I'd fallen asleep with a whiskey glass of Marnie, which had tipped, spilled, and now coated my lap redly. On my skin the pink tinge of scrubbed-off last night was still there, and the sight of it almost made me vomit. I scurried over and picked up the phone.

"Were you there?" editor Becky shouted into the line.

I leaned back my head and massaged the acid from my eyes.

"Were you *there*?"

"I was."

"Did you see?"

I clenched my jaws. For a moment I couldn't say anything, in fear of being sick.

"God, did you *see*?"

"I did," I said. "Unfortunately, I did."

"Who shot the boy?"

I took a big cool gulp of breath as my thoughts dragged back to the church basement. "Like I told the cops, it was chaos. A riot in the making. I don't know. I couldn't tell. Just screaming, people falling, a mob scene in my neighborhood, the worst."

"Holy hell."

"Any suspects?"

"Not yet," Becky said. "But an APD sergeant did release the basic details, at about three a.m. So we have that, at least."

"Sorry about the deadline."

"I understand."

"I was in no shape—"

"We've got the basics covered," she said. "What I need from you is something deeper."

"I don't know if I'm in any condition—"

"Yes you are, God. Go sit your ass down and start venting on the page. Tell us what you saw. And tell us what the neighborhood means to you, too. Tell us what's really going on, and how it got there. *Capiche?*"

"You sure that's the angle you want?"

"Yes."

"I could go on for two or three thousand words."

"That's fine," she said. "We'll buy it. Between the snakes and this horrible shit last night, the entire state of Georgia, as I understand it, is talking about Sweetberry Park right now. Probably the whole Southeast. It's your moment, God. Get it together."

"OK, then. How deep you want me to mine myself for this?"

"Whatever. Just move. Write. Give context. Start from the beginning, I don't know. I'll need it by five p.m. Can I count on that?"

"Beck, I have this kid Joey's blood literally on me, on my sleeves—"

"That's the sort of detail I'm talking about!"

"Don't be morbid."

"Look," she said. "This is when we need you. Your voice. You know the deal, God."

I thanked her, hung up, and took a shower to whip up positive ions. That's an old trick for when I'm lacking inspiration. Or faced with confronting topics that hurt.

I've never spoken much about my addiction, because when I have, dumfounded listeners have taken in the story with the same bemused, offensive facial expression, as if they're eager for a punchline. Talk of crack does that. The conspiracy goes that shadowy Reagan minions fed this garbage into the ghettoes of eighties America. It's possible, I guess, but who knows. I think of crack as America's original painkiller epidemic. Which is exactly how I got snared, back when "crack capitalism" was crippling Sweetberry Park more than White flight, violent police, and a brief heroin scourge of the very early eighties combined. I'm not claiming to be a casualty of the ghetto, obviously, so much as my own stupidity, and vulnerability. To say I smoked crack and understand, to a degree, the demons in those chemicals—maybe that sounds contrived, but it's true. I'm sure as hell not proud of getting pulled into addiction and then surviving what so many did not. But before you judge me, let me describe for a moment my dead son's elephant blanket.

Wyatt was born a few weeks before Christmas. He was my likeness, if a little lighter. As with most new fathers, I felt a great religious warmth in watching his mouth twist open to produce his first cries. All pleasure, of course, was quickly trounced by a seismic punch of sleeplessness. Complicating matters was my paranoiac assuredness that his life was always at risk. I worried he'd suddenly stop breathing—or that our house might topple over for no reason but poor construction and kill us all. I fretted over the possibility that rats—yes, suburban rats—might burrow under his locked window and nibble away his face. My mind was frantic, and I longed for the liberties of childless existence. We don't realize how selfish our lives have been until eight pounds of fury demands so much selflessness of us.

Anyhow, the blanket. For Christmas, my grandmother—the open-minded one who would die in a couple of years and bequeath to me an unexpected $25,000—bought this tiny square of a blanket for Wyatt. And to this square Grandma Josephine sewed a blue elephant of the softest, most wonderful material. It was like felt and velvet, woven with the freshly bathed coats of Labrador puppies. Amazing stuff. And Wyatt agreed. Basically from his first touch, the boy and blanket were inseparable. As his muscles developed he would rub the thing across his face and bald head or twiddle it between his thumb and forefingers like a fat cat feeling money. It was the world's cutest addiction. And then one morning, when he was two, I peered over his crib and succumbed to the most gutting realization: Draped across Wyatt's chest, illuminated by harsh early light, was the blanket; but the soft material of his elephant had all but worn away, down to an unsightly, brownish layer that looked like burlap. Maybe this sounds melodramatic, but it almost buckled me in half, this elephant epiphany, right there in the bedroom. I realized in that moment how temporary my boy really was. How one day he and I would die and break apart, no more consequential to history than remote forest pines, felled by wind, that nobody ever saw. I snatched the scratchy, abused pachyderm and rubbed it across my face and forehead. And I vowed in that moment to savor, embrace, and maximize each day I'd been given with Wyatt, and with any sibling who'd follow him. I promised, as cheesy as this sounds, to be Super Dad. I'd been committed, naturally, to molding Wyatt into a decent man, ushering him toward his preferred activities and talents. But on that morning, I took a silent, serious oath. I'd never get in my own way again. I'd relinquish my fantastical dreams of literary success in pursuit of real work that might quickly make a better life for my wife and child.

And for two more sweet years, until the Lord's taketh-away roulette wheel determined it was our turn, I honored that oath.

When I came to The Juncture, leaving the cushiness of suburban insularity for Sweetberry Park, I felt I was carrying all the cracked bits of a broken promise to my son. I felt I'd let Wyatt down—that I'd somehow *lied*—by not dying in a twisted Toyota instead of him and Sage. That's a lot to bear on its own. Combine that with the actual loss, the void of their gone voices, and it's a weight that most would find intolerable. My new reality was a boulder, chained to my ankle, as I tried to tread water, far from shore in a dark lake.

During my first Sweetberry weeks, I busied my mind with visions of grand Victorian restoration victories. It was healthy. After all, for the first time in my life, I was loaded with cash, having scored grandma's inheritance and $12,000 in equity from the sale of my well-kept cul-de-sac residence. Then I met Squeaky, the Sweetberry jester. Jittery and malnourished, he'd fallen far from his puff-chested, white-uniformed service days on naval warships. He was lost at the time, like most of his family, in dependency's howling wilderness. He sensed, I guess, a kindred brokenness in me.

A few days after I'd met him, Squeaky wanted to share that numb euphoria he couldn't live without. That speaks to his big heart, because sharing is not the strong suit of crack-addled people. One day, as I raked out decades of weeds, leaves, and garbage, he offered this long, thin glass pipe over my fence. I'd read the warnings in headlines and heard Peter Jennings on the news condemn crack as a one-puff ticket to lifelong cocaine dependency. I'd seen the magazine stories with bare-gummed fiends in Los Angeles and Brooklyn, their ghoulish cheekbones a testament to the strength of need. But I could've given two shits, honestly. Because addiction couldn't happen to me, and if it did, at least I'd be living for something.

I took my first soft-smoke pull from a crack rock in broad daylight. I winced, exhaled, smiled. In two seconds, I dropped the rake. The next twenty-two minutes were a phantasmagorical ride on the airborne love boat of sensual dopamine nonreality. The leaves of dogwoods and magnolias pulsed at me in yellow waves. Passing cars were symphonies. For the first time in months, I felt energetic and excited about the prospects of absolutely anything—a drink of Coke, a Michael Jackson hip thrust, a whiff of fresh air—yet with the spacey, pleasurable detachment of weed highs. I reached across the fence and high-fived Squeaky: "Well hell yes, maaaaaan!"

He chuckled in that sneaky way of addicts. The more we talked in that moment the more I came to adore my fractured life, because being alive was so splendid. Problems were inconsequential, even funny. With Squeaky's help I had triumphed, I thought. There was no death, no poverty. We had graduated, via crack, into instant emotional aristocracy. Together we'd rule over Sweetberry, our woebegone urban province.

Then, the drain.

Within a few minutes, my spit tasted like gasoline. My brain filled with a desperate wanting to be lifted again. I longed to revisit that virgin dopamine glory that only the first high will ever provide.

"You have money?" Squeaky had said that day, as we came down like shot birds.

"You gonna rob me?"

"Naw."

"Good. You have more of that shit?"

"I do. Yessir. But I'm gonna need cash to get more when we run through this here." He dipped into his flannel pocket and fished out a twisted baggie with what looked like a few busted human teeth.

"None of my business," I said. "But how'd you get the money for that much?"

"Straight stealin'."

"Stealin' what?"

"Everything."

"Around here?"

"Hell naw. Everything been took 'round here. All Sweetberry's good for is dog ransoms."

"The fuck are dog ransoms?"

"It's easy." Squeaky smiled, and I took comfort in seeing so many teeth still fastened in there. "You just snatch up a dog from the nice yards, from the nice houses, and leave a note where they can get it back... if they bring a hundred or fifty or whatnot."

"And they don't call the cops?"

"*Sheeeeeeet!*" he laughed. "APD won't come over here unless somebody's shot. Even then they sometimes don't. Ain't no pig drivin' through here for no took dog."

"That's some lowdown shit, man."

"It is. I know it, too. It's why it's so quiet around here at night. People keep them puppies inside now." He wheezily laughed for a second. "And it ain't no use trying to get in, not with all these burglar bars they got now, cagin' every window."

I turned around to examine my rotting house, so easily penetrable back then; the original chandeliers, light-switch covers, even the gilded wallpaper had been thieved. "So where's your cash flow come from now, if not here?"

"Malls," he said.

"Which malls?"

"Different one around Atlanta every week," he said. "I ran track in school, and ain't no mall cop stand a chance. Clothes, shoes, a microwave from Sears, necklaces, watches, any damn thing that say Nintendo. I'm out the door, and I can sell it within about an hour. But, man, this can't go on forever…"

"Listen," I said, patting his bony shoulder. "You don't have to do that anymore. If you have the connection, I'll have the means. Just keep it coming. But if I get robbed, I'll know exactly who ratted me out."

We went to my porch with Squeaky's sordid baggie, and we didn't really emerge for several days, and then a few weeks, and then late winter breathed out that yellowy pollen air and the luscious green spring of Ireland hills was there. I dropped twenty pounds. My burned lips, like Squeaky's, split and bled. I stopped answering calls from editors and family who were trying to find some hellhole called Sweetberry Park and lend a hand, casserole, or any other help. Sometimes Squeaky's pals joined us, and we told rambling nonsensical tales about police raids and dog kidnappings and MTV videos as prostitutes ambled by my gate and flashed untidy crotches for a puff. When we denied them, they'd walk by in predawn hours and toss heavy condoms on my brick walkway. All of it was lunacy. All of it tragic. Some bits, though, were almost comical. The nature of the drug, I guess.

In the wee hours, our brains sizzled with bad ideas. Squeaky and I would sometimes wander mischievously into the overgrown Confederate cemetery out of boredom. Back then, the little graveyard was Sweetberry's only surefire robbery-free zone; nobody but us dared to traipse in there, messing with such bigoted ghosts. With a flashlight we'd study obelisks carved with phrases like "Fine Subsistence Farmer" and "Loved His Mama" and others that specified rank in the gray Army. "Got me a first lieutenant here, and a first major right there," Squeaky would say, before unzipping and pissing all over the dirt. Though I could understand, to a degree, the deep-rooted vitriol driving such behavior, I'd usually push Squeaky away mid-piss, because almost nobody deserves a golden shower in death. But then, one cold night, he went a step further—*way* over the line. I put an end to the cemetery wandering, under a full moon, when Squeaky found a decayed headstone belonging to the wife of a captain. I turned away for one minute to fiddle with the pipe, heard something weird on the ground, and I'll be damned if Squeaky's bare butt wasn't bouncing like two salad bowls. With dirty briefs around his knees, he was screwing the grassy grave of a Confederate's lady.

"You fucking *animal!*" I shouted. "When you're done, pass over that lighter!"

Occasionally we'd flip out about invisible fleas on our skin and accuse every scalawag on the porch of putting them on us. Typically, that prompted my kicking everyone out, and then begging them back the same night. We all digressed into zombies. Or maybe "zombies" isn't precisely the word, because the crack-addled aren't so blatant; we were sneaky, rather, a cast of motivated liars. And we were never wanting. The pleasure centers of my brain were so disoriented, for so many months, I don't think I ever properly grieved.

By deep summer, though, as much as it doesn't sound possible, everything had begun to take a much darker turn. I was down to my last $7,000 with absolutely no writing prospects. Squeaky's besieged upper gum relinquished his four front teeth, which alarmed us all. And then one of Squeaky's compadres tried to hot-wire and steal Great White in the middle of the night; he failed to connect the right wires and make off with her, but the damage to the driveshaft rendered her (and me) immobile. I was in no shape to read a repair manual or haggle with crooked eastside mechanics. I was stuck on the porch—stewing, smoking, dying.

One blazing morning in June or July, I rocked feverishly on the porch and stared into a tiny makeup mirror Squeaky had lifted from a Buckhead Mercedes. I hadn't really seen myself in weeks. And all I saw was failure. A cop-out, a quitter, a sickened man. The wilting flesh of my face previewed a slow, morose death. It all suddenly made me furious. I dropped the mirror and stomped it to shards. A bizarrely warm energy welled up in me, lifting my decaying lungs, and then put the rest of me onto my feet. I stepped into the glimmering grass and tossed my pipe into the street, where it shattered. And I walked, but not my usual route, which was right, toward the dodgy gas station, with its Budweiser and Doritos. I went left, toward the little old shotguns by the railroad tracks.

Down there, on her porch, cleaning carrots, was younger Genteel, singing Robert Johnson's sorrows to herself. She wore a pink sash around her neck, which she lifted up to dab sweat from her forehead. Her hair back then was a perfect, curly orb, fashioned in a way that reminded me of fifties doo-wop backup singers. But you could tell that nothing about the woman was backup; she was the star, the beaming marquee attraction. Though no longer young, she exuded fiery health, and her smile could sell a broken furnace in Georgia July.

"You lost, baby?"

"I am."

I plunged my quivering hands into jean pockets. It'd been several hours since Squeaky had scatted off into the dawn, abandoning me, and I was beginning to need his cache.

"Squeaky and them's callin' you God, ain't they?"

"Yeah, ma'am, they are."

"Mrrrmmm-hrrmm."

I could tell she was upset.

"It's the white hair," I said. "And beard."

"I've told 'em not to, honey. Them fools. That's blass-fuh-*me*!"

"It's cool, really."

"You want some water?"

"No."

"You lookin' for likuh drinks?"

"No."

"Well, then, whacho want?"

"I don't know. I just wanted to walk around."

"You *real* lost, ain't you?"

"I'm in trouble."

She stopped cleaning the carrot and analyzed me for a moment. "You gonna fix up that old spooky house down there?"

"I was fixin' to."

"I remember, back as a girl, your granddaddy leavin' it. Movin' out, all scared. His kids must be your folks, right? They was older back then, out of school, but I remember that man hollerin' at them. And he didn't like my folks movin' in around here. Not one bit."

"He's family," I said, "but he's a jerk."

"Is you like him?"

"No, ma'am."

"You sure?"

"He's hateful. And now he's dead."

"Then who are you?"

"I'm lost."

"Lost how?"

"Lost in the worst way. I'm a lost man."

"You been in them drugs, ain't you?"

"Yes, ma'am."

"Like all the others, I can see it suckin' the life out, takin' your light."

"My wife and boy died last year."

She froze. "Oh, baby. No…"

"I'm alone here," I said. "The drugs, they seemed like medicine, at first. But now they've really got me."

Genteel clasped her shiny face, closed her eyes, and fell into silent invocation. I wondered if she was praying for me, my departed kin, or maybe Sweetberry's lost-souls collective. I didn't ask. But I knew she emitted a soft, motherly sweetness, antithetical to my catacomb life down the street. I stepped toward the porch twice before she told me to back the heck up, the carrot outstretched like a switchblade. At that point, dejected, I fell on my knees, down into the dusty red dirt. The sun cooked me. I stunk. I sunk. And I wept.

"I've lost my way," I moaned. "I've *lost my way*."

Genteel lifted a glass of water, took a sip, and tossed the cool contents across the top of my head. She harrumphed, stomped inside Shotgun Three, and locked her door.

By three p.m. I'd pounded out the strangest, most rambling newspaper report of my career, under a preachy headline I knew would be instantly deleted: "How Today's Urban America Might Cost Atlanta Boy His Life."

The writing was a pastiche of recollections, more than a quarter-century's worth, ending with the moment the gun went off. The lede sentence (it was a draft, don't cringe) went: "They used to call my neighborhood Sh*tberry Park. Little kids who couldn't cuss would use the alternative: Sweetscary Park. This was back in the crack eighties. This was back when I moved in and—pummeled by grief and desperate for friendship—walked into the jaws of poverty, crime, and deprivation. That was the Atlanta you either never knew or are still straining to forget. And that, most people would argue, was my neighborhood's low-point, the nadir. I'd argue otherwise. Because I think I saw the low-point last night."

The story was open-ended. Becky would need a second installment, hopefully. And maybe a third. Groceries for weeks. But then I clicked "Send" and fell to the floor. Something in me was incredibly heavy, a mass of guilt and regret. And I was oddly freezing. I shivered and shrank into a fetal ball.

Wallowing on the dirty hardwoods, it dawned on me that any respectable person would swing through the nearest toy store and pay the hospital a visit, pronto. It's the least we could do to lift the spirits of a critically injured boy. I sat up. In a moment I lumbered to the kitchen and made a coffee for warmth. The panic passed. My strength returned. On my way out the door, I grabbed my trout-waders and police scanner, in case it would be a long night.

CHAPTER 10

My trip to the hospital to see Joey was impeded by the hours-long sludge that is afternoon traffic on The Connector, Atlanta's roughly fifty-lane freeway monster of perpetual immobility, our city's source of constant constipation.

I recall the days, as a suburban boy, when this highway was but three docile lanes in each direction. We laughed at its unbridled fattening and the notion that people from exotic places like Jersey City, Portland, and Topeka would ever consider migrating to our baby metropolis. But they came, and they kept coming, these snowbird droves. The gridlock we've created, on such a wretched day, made my face tremble. And then my truck's AC quit working. I drove knuckles deep into the horn and bashed the headliner. "Here we are!" I hollered, rolling my window down. "All stuck together, just like we wanted! Go back to Cleveland!"

A mile later, under the forgiving shadow of Courtland Street's overpass, I anxiously twisted radio dials to each afternoon news broadcast and caught a few factoids about the Braves' recent slide in the Major League Baseball standings. I heard the latest sensational tidbits about Southside homicides and how a Doberman pincher had died down there from nosing into a closet stash and scarfing heroin baggies. It was a depressing news day, for sure, like most on the metro beat. No updates on Joey or snake captures, though.

At the top of the four o' clock hour, however, a briefing broke through: The Atlanta Police Department chief herself was expected to host a morning City Hall press conference the next day to update the public on the summer's two biggest stories thus far: the ongoing serpent rodeo and the shooting of a DeKalb County prosecutor's handicapped son. "*What?*" I screamed at the radio. "Americana Mama works for the D.A.? How'd I not know that?" I took solace in hearing that her boy was still alive, though. If he'd died overnight, the updater would have called "shooting" something graver, like "slaying." I felt buoyed by the boy's toughness. He deserved a damn good toy.

I exited the interstate near the hospital and popped into the nearest big-box store to buy Joey the most expensive action figure possible. Given the lightness of my wallet, I knew the possibilities were limited. Walking through the parking lot and into cool corporate air that smelled of popcorn and slushies, I underwent one aha Americana Mama moment after the next. I'd had no idea what she did for a living, but everything from her stern demeanor to her pressed pantsuits and the massive, nondescript, tanklike Sport Utility Vehicle she drove for work now made sense. She spent her days sending people to prison. The more I thought about it, the more she seemed born to do that. And in a prosecutorial role, she'd have been seasoned at dealing with scenarios of violence and death, which I hoped had thickened her skin. I hustled past the electronics department and kitchenware aisles and felt that quicksand ooze in my guts upon finding the toy department. I hadn't dared enter one of these aisles in thirty years—and I physically couldn't bear to now. With feet planted in the main aisle, I stretched toward the top shelf and snagged what looked like a mean, delusional cowboy robot. Perfect.

I parked at the towering midcentury edifice that is Peachtree Medical and realized—to my horror—that I would never gain entry without knowing Joey and his mother's last name. I paced around the front awning, sweat darkening the pits of my Oxford, until I heard a familiar, droning tone of complaint from within. The automatic doors parted, and there was Americana Mama in a wrinkled pink T-shirt. She looked like she'd been dragged through a hellscape of sleepless misery. She was talking to a police officer while, behind her, a dead-ringer older version of herself, presumably her mother, kneaded her hunched shoulders. She spotted me standing awkwardly outside with an unwrapped toy. She hugged the officer, dropped her head, and trudged in my direction.

"Oh, no, sorry," I said. "Didn't mean to interrupt. Just wanted to drop this off. Maybe wish the boy luck in person, if he's stable enough for that."

She nodded but didn't smile.

"But now, you know, being here," I said. "It's just kind of heavy, and maybe I'm not up for doing that. I see you're busy, so I'll just get moving."

She latched onto my wrist. "What'd you *see*, God?" Her breath smelled of coffee, and her dark eyes blazed, the corneas somewhere between pink and mauve, the sockets a tired brown. "From your seat, you had a different angle. Did you see something material? Anything?"

"I assume they have the gun, right?"

"Yes."

"That's all I really saw, in terms of the shot. But it was already on the ground."

She let go, tossing aside my wrist. "It's a fucking joke weapon. A five-chamber antique. Who'd have thought it could so much damage? Who even owns those things anymore?"

"Old Southern White men," I said. "And pawn shops."

"Right," she said, drifting into contemplative silence.

"Probably nothing you don't know, but I've covered a few cases where people have dropped these things while cleaning 'em and killed friends. Or themselves. They go off sometimes. I'm not saying it was totally accidental—and certainly not legal—but you saw the room. That was chaos."

More dazed silence.

"Anyway, I heard them say on the radio news what you do for work. I had no idea. It's Shirley, right? Is that what I heard Lotto call you last night?"

At the sound of her name she snapped back. Her face brightened, loosened. "I've liked your reporting, your style, for years," she said. "Are you here today working?"

"No, no," I said. "I'm here as a neighbor. How's the boy?"

Her face twisted.

"Another long surgery, right now," she said. "I was about to lose my mind, up there on the eighth floor. My sister's in the room, just wailing. Joey's older brother hasn't slept. There's a lot of blood loss for such a little body. I forget how many pints they said. A few organs were damaged, but nothing is failing, thank Jesus. Sorry to be so specific, but I can't stop thinking of details."

I handed over the robot; at last she smiled. "I know," I said.

"You know?"

"Yes."

"You know what?"

"I know you're lucky," I said. "One-tenth of an inch, one way or the other."

She laughed in a tired wheeze of surprise, sounding like she'd either taken offense or was charmed. "His father's on a mission trip with our oldest in Honduras," she said. "They're still trying to contact him. This is such a nightmare."

"How can I help?"

"I just want to snap out of it," she said, ignoring me. "A waking, awful nightmare."

"You'll wake up, eventually," I said. "I bet you'll wake right up when Joey does."

"Hold on!" she perked. "You helped carry Joey out of the church, didn't you? That's just coming back to me. Shock, you know. I'm definitely in shock." The admission of weakness embarrassed her, and she blushed a little. "Thank you for that, and for this toy. He'll love this. He loves your house." She hugged me, and I bowed my head. "I was just up there thinking of how simple yesterday was, relatively speaking," she said. "I was only worried about property taxes yesterday. And neighborhood traffic. And my boy's muscular dystrophy. And those damn pythons or whatever."

Beneath the awning we laughed deliriously, until she clasped her mouth and forced the laughter to stop.

"There's a big press conference in the morning," I said.

She nodded. "I just heard."

"Police Chief Montgomery herself is coming."

"Yeah?"

"Yep. And when that happens, you law folks usually have something of substance to say. Right?"

"Whoever did it will get what's coming."

"Yep," I said. "Let's hope."

"Atlanta PD is on it full force."

"That's great."

Itching to change the subject, and maybe lighten the mood, I cracked a grin. "I hate to admit this now, but maybe it's worth another laugh," I said. "Some guys and I, having never really met you, have always referred to you as 'Americana Mama.' I started it, to be honest, after I heard you eviscerating some homebuilder about your roof shingles or something—"

"I know, God," she said. "I know the nickname, and I probably deserve it."

This candid, compassionate side of her was growing on me. "We all could be a little more self-effacing, I think," I said. "Especially in these times."

"What's wrong with us?" she said, swinging the toy beside her, rubbing her tired eyes. "I mean, I used to *berate* that poor builder. I was about to rip his head off a few times. I'd read about Americana facades in magazines, something about folksy dormers and postwar paint schemes. I became, I guess, obsessed with the idea. I lost perspective. My daddy spent forty-five years in a steel mill, and we grew up in 1,200 square feet!"

She turned back toward the lobby, tucking with a sweep of fingertips her black hair behind her ears. "But wake up, man," she said, in parting. "There are no secrets in that neighborhood."

The hospital doors consumed her, and she was gone. I went home, flopped on the parlor couch, and slept for twelve hours.

In the morning, with two hours to spare before the ten a.m. presser, I finalized via email my biggest writing deal in eons. After some heavy edits, editor Becky bought every word of my introspective gentrification manifesto, part one. It would publish tomorrow. And the fee put me 1,375 dollars closer to a new roof.

Beyond the first story, she requested a periodic "deep-dive series" on the plight of Sweetberry Park, pronto, with commentary from academics, young-couple new buyers, and my fellow fossils. Up to five installments until the summer ended, or until the last snake was apprehended, whichever came first. She could allot a budget of up to $11,000, so long as I kept the series compelling and accurate. I couldn't believe the number—and my luck.

But first, Becky wanted a thorough update from the police presser. "Yes, ma'am," I typed, before closing my laptop and slinking, unexpectedly, into a tarpit of depression.

I couldn't stop thinking that Joey's health had taken a turn for the worse overnight. I guess it was intuition born of experience. I yearned to call the hospital but didn't want to interfere. Instead I sat at home and watched the clock, waiting. And then I eyed my bad cubby. I could not extricate myself from morose thoughts of another dying boy; my brain rang with echoes of the gunshot and Joey's terrible shrieks. Then I had an idea: Having just a quick libation, maybe two at most, would shepherd me through this most difficult morning, lightening my mood so that I might better cover an extremely important news event.

While pacing the living room, I sipped two wee, potent Bloody Marnies until it was time to go. I gargled mouthwash, packed my mouth with chewing gum, and set out toward City Hall, feeling so much better.

At the press conference, I was shuffled along with every broadcaster, blogger, sportscaster, and poet in metro Atlanta into a long clinical boardroom. I could tell everyone but me was nervous, with so much on the line. And then, exactly one minute before ten a.m., in sauntered Tabitha Jones from Channel 8 in a pink business jacket—and trout-waders! They were tight-fitting, pink-and-black, *fashionable* trout pants with glistening little zippers. I emerged from a pocket of print media, pinched her elbow, and yanked.

"You gave me no credit, Tabitha. I saw the report."

"'*scuse* me, God?"

"Don't play dumb."

"I had these made in Buckhead."

"You plagiarized those pants!"

She said something to her camera guy, snagged my Oxford, and pulled me close. She leaned over and whispered into my right ear: "Settle down. It's obvious you've been sippin' on somethin', man."

My jaw fell. "Huh?"

"I smell it," said Tabitha, a bit too loud. "You reek of toothpaste and grain liquor."

That caught the attention of several seated newspaper scribes, including this twitchy dude who covered the Falcons for the *Beacon*. I'd met him once or twice but drew a blank on his name. I held a finger to my lips and said to him, "It's been a rough week, man. Just don't tell Becky on the Metro desk, OK?"

I was spared from giving a stuttering explanation by the entrance of Police Chief Candice Montgomery, a tall, stout woman with bluish eye shadow, arrow-straight eyebrows, and closely shorn hair. Installed five years ago, Montgomery was a seasoned police-beat bruiser who'd look totally natural winning a men's karate tournament. She gave no verbal salutation whatsoever, only nodded. She was sitting on big news, I could tell.

"Three primary updates this morning," the chief said behind an ornate podium. "Please let me finish these brief statements before asking questions. I'll take a few. But as you know, we have a lot on our plates already this summer, and I'm needed in the field. Now..."

Camera shutters started flapping, and the room tensed up.

"First off," said Chief Montgomery, "our efforts involving the exotic zoo snakes are ongoing. We haven't captured more animals or hard evidence, frankly, but experts and officers in the field are certain they spotted a particularly dangerous species in a wooded area on the eastside yesterday. It's native to Central America. It looks similar to a rattlesnake, only larger—"

"Chief!" I blurted, hand raised. "Was this in the Sweetberry district?"

"Again," she said, "hold your questions. But for now, to avoid any sort of panic again, we're not releasing the specific neighborhood. Rest assured that officers are there, monitoring these woods. My lieutenant will distribute photos of similar animals, so that people are aware of what *not* to approach. This animal, in particular, is very hard to see in Georgia's foliage."

The reporting contingent grumbled, speculated, worried.

The chief went on: "On the same topic, we do have new information on the suspect we believe to have intentionally endangered Atlantans by stealing these snakes. Gerald McCaffrey, the former zookeeper, is known to moonlight as a landlord. He owns and manages numerous homes throughout the city. He's fallen behind on several mortgages, and we have reason to believe he hasn't been following a medication regimen required for a mental health condition we aren't at liberty to specify now. Mr. McCaffrey's family and friends are cooperating, and we have no reason to believe he has left Georgia—or even Atlanta. But we ask him, if he's watching, to please turn himself in. Immediately. Short of that, we ask him to submit, via *any* means, information regarding the whereabouts of the animals he stole from his employer."

The chief flipped a stack of papers to a separate case, and her cheeks dropped.

"Lastly," said the chief, her voice dipping into dour, tepid tones. "I have some new information about this week's shooting at the Sweetberry Park church..." she lifted the stack of papers twice and laid it down neatly, an act of nervousness. "We have made an arrest in the shooting. Walter James, age twenty-four, of Atlanta, is in custody. Officers executed search warrants at Mr. James' mother's home last night, where he was ultimately tracked to. At approximately midnight, Mr. James was charged with aggravated assault."

"It won't stick," I said to myself, although Tabitha heard.

"What?" she whispered.

"That's Georgia's equivalent of attempted murder. They'll never be able to prove Tall Walt meant to shoot anyone. If they can even prove he was carrying an antique pistol for some reason—"

"Tall Walt?"

"That's right," I whispered. "Not surprising they picked him. It's a cliché move, picking the most vocal Black guy in the room and putting the gun in his hand."

"Who's *he*?"

We were being too loud, disruptive kids in class. The chief was so irritated I thought she was going to toss us out. Instead she bowed her head.

"The latest I have for you is that Mr. James' charges, as of this morning, have been upgraded to murder," said the chief. "At approximately eight a.m. this morning, at Peachtree Medical Center, the victim, Joseph Kline, age seven, succumbed to internal wounds and passed away. Our thoughts and prayers—"

Before she could finish, I lay my head on the boardroom table, and in the most unprofessional way, moaned, "Joey!" until each camera had swiveled around to me, collecting B-roll footage. Nobly ruining her own shot to help me, Tabitha reached down, hummed words of consolation, and patted my tremoring back. She knew.

I wept for a boy cursed at birth and now slighted by fate, for his mother, and for the pain she would feel in her quest to exact revenge, quite possibly on an innocent man. I'd never even properly met the boy, but for five minutes I couldn't think of standing up, let alone stringing together just-the-facts copy about Walt's charges and Joey's demise. No one bothered the chief with a follow-up question, so she walked out, seeming almost disappointed. We were all overwhelmed, stunned, morose, sickened. There were so many directions to take the information and run, but the only viable, humane reaction was, for the moment, reverent paralysis. Every head in the room hung.

To break the silence, after a couple of minutes, Tabitha took an awkward but informative stab at small talk in her warm, sugary way. "Y'all see the weather coming this week?" she said. "They're saying four record highs, right in a row. And it's still damn May!"

CHAPTER 11

I barreled away from the presser, grabbed a jug of gas station coffee, and set to work. As my desktop Apple warmed up, I called Becky and asked what she wanted of me. Nuts-and-bolts, for now, she said. Something quick for the internet. I felt, to be honest, slighted.

"You sure you don't want me down at Superior Court?" I asked the boss.

"Nope."

"Or I could detour into a sort of deeper dive with this angle of the snakes and sewers. The cops sound confident there's a really nasty one from Central America, right around here. I know folks at Watershed Management, and there's this herpetologist in Athens who's really terrific—"

"Just keep it simple, and quick," Becky said. "I've got people working the cops angle, the murder charges, even the sewers. I know you know the boy's family, so I want to be careful to avoid any bias; I've got someone who's up to speed on hospital PR contacts heading to Peachtree Medical. Hopefully she'll speak with the boy's mother and the rest of those poor folks. The snake expert sounds intriguing. I might have someone call him."

Her suggesting that someone else would bully in on my turf was offensive. Something was amiss. But the work was in hand. I copped out and chirped: "Sure thing, Beck. Just keep me posted!"

She lay down the phone, and I could hear her office door click closed, firm and ominous. "Listen, Johnson, I've got some troubling information here. I got a message from the press conference this morning, from a source I would trust, telling me a freelancer for the *Beacon* showed up intoxicated and made a weeping ass of himself. Know anything about that?"

"No, ma'am."

"That's funny," she said. "We had only one freelancer there."

"I've never done anything *that* stupid," I said. "But I'll tell you that, in a very horrible way, I knew the boy had died this morning. I felt his exit from the earth, somehow. I mean, honestly, it just suddenly became the morning from hell—"

"Are you admitting to what I'm asking, Johnson?"

"Again, it's not like me, but I felt like I couldn't even walk outside without being a little numb today."

"You drank before a press conference? With a credential from *this* company?"

I breathed deep, steadied my hands. "What are the implications of, you know, answering in the affirmative right now?"

"Answer me straight, God!"

"I'll get you three-hundred words—one hundred for each catastrophe, per the chief's statements—within forty-five minutes. You'll have two-sentence updates for internet teasers within three minutes."

"Fine. Get moving."

"And I'll touch base later about my Sweetberry Park series."

"This is a hell of a time for you to bring that up!"

"So, wait... are you cancelling the series?"

"We'll take this up later," she said, before hanging up.

The coffee lifted me through the menial writings, the journalistic chores for a paycheck. Instead of stewing inside, suffering amongst so much humidity and dust, fearing another collapse on the floor, I fetched my umbrella for shade, hustled down to The Flank, and rapped on Genteel's door. The heat came at me sideways. It had to be a noontime ninety-five degrees and climbing. Tiny perspiration waterfalls slid down my legs.

Genteel ripped open her door, and without even a nod of greeting, she said, "How that boy doin'?"

I flinched and asked to come in. She grabbed my shirt at the shoulder, balled it in her fist, and demanded an immediate update. I shook my head no. The sort of no that says it's over. She let go. I went inside.

I sat on a paisley love seat protected by a clear plastic membrane. Genteel scurried across the room for a plate of cookies. When I declined, she tipped over the ornate dish, and a cascade of beige saucers went flowing into an open trashcan—followed by the plate itself. Then she swatted at thin air and chomped down on her voluptuous lips, humming. It was her protest against the news, against what she'd witnessed in the church basement, the awful truth. I'd never seen the woman have a fit like that.

"Of all the crazy stuff we seen around here," said Genteel, "I'm thinkin' that last night was the worst. Whacho think?"

I nodded. "Lot of sadness and death around here, over the years," I said. "But you're probably right."

Genteel ambled over to her window, looked out across the porch and street, and hung her head. She began to rumble and hum.

"Have police questioned you yet?" I said. "You see anything I didn't? Anything at all before that thing went off?"

No reply. Only humming. Louder humming.

"Don't suppose you heard the news about Tall Walt, did you?" I said. "He's in bad trouble. But I just can't picture him dropping a dang John Wayne pistol. Especially not in a meeting he'd attended in the most organized way."

Now she swayed, her head and thick bush of hair fluid in her movements.

"This summer's really got me low," I said.

She raised up her hands and touched her cheeks.

"I don't wanna alarm you, to give an indication that I'm backsliding or anything, but I'm *really* craving drinks lately. To the point I'm worried it'll make me crave stronger things. And it may have really cost me with the *Beacon*, my main client."

Nothing I said was registering with Genteel. She looked a little possessed, but in a powerful, benign way.

"You OK over there?"

She spun around and shot a glare right through me, her face pained, serious, inspired. "I'm-a come out retirement for this," she said, chest heaving. "I'm-a sing at that boy's funeral!"

Flabbergasted, I fell back into the couch, landing in a soft crunch of plastic, rendered immobile.

The first time I'd seen Genteel really sing, I knew her talent was volcanic. I'd come to her porch for help in the stupor of addiction, which thoroughly spooked her, as it should have. That was the summer. By December I'd dropped another fifteen pounds and had excommunicated my entire family. Squeaky, freshly evicted, had moved into my home with little more than a pup tent and glass pipe. Then our primary connection got busted in Midtown. Another guy stole $380 from us for four baggies he never produced. At a crack den where Squeaky had once lived, a dope-sick Army soldier who'd absconded from Albany put an M-16 in Squeaky's mouth, robbed the rest of the home, and shot a customer in the leg on the way out. Word got around Sweetberry that you could rob us, and we were powerless to retaliate. Some nights I slept on the roof with an arsenal of knives and creek rocks.

One night, we paced my porch, brainstorming. The best tactic, we decided, would be to head out on foot and ask around about either more drugs or recommendations for not dying from withdrawal. I remember it was a bitterly cold night, ominous in its silence, the kind where clouds slide by in angry Zeusian layers. Virtually all of the holiday lights and decor on my street had been stolen. But somehow, as I stepped with Squeaky beyond my leaning iron gates, into the gasping urban blight, I could feel that it was Christmas Night.

Maybe a block into our quest we stopped dead. We'd both heard it at the same time: a choir of angels. We went slowly toward the singing, drawn to benevolence we so needed. Block by block the angel songs were more pronounced. Block by block I was getting stronger. We felt we were trekking toward righteous healing, a metaphysical bath. The singing led us to The Holiness Church of Our Savior, the later scene of Joey's mortal wounds.

Cast aglow by up-pointed spotlights in the bushes, the church's stone columns and sacred steeple were gorgeous amid skies gone wintry pink. I looked at Squeaky. He nodded. Without an invitation we moseyed inside, filthy and maniacal, and I can hardly describe the immensity of the enveloping warmth within. The sanctuary, bedecked with hollies and bows, swayed with a standing congregation. On the stage, three rows of white-robed choir singers with red scarves belted from songbooks in a way that convinced me, immediately, that no human is alive so much as one who is singing. A hundred gyrating hands jutted up from the congregational frenzy. Then the chorus quieted, dipping into a murmur. And from within its swaying mass, Genteel Briggs confidently stepped forward, into the maternal cavern, wearing the spotlight and giving it back like Swarovski crystals. She smiled. She glowed. She swelled. She was glory incarnate—and when she sang "Holy Night" solo, I could feel the desperation begin to melt from every tired fiber of me. I could sense the need extracting its claws. A new era opened in an instant, like the night my boy was born. Beside me, Squeaky was equally annihilated by a feeling of love, and all he said was, "God, *damn*."

About halfway through Genteel's solo, Squeaky latched ahold of my wrist and pulled me down a red-carpeted aisle, until we stood in awe at the foot of the pulpit. Instinctively, again, we fell on our knees; we wept in church; and when the singing went quiet, we were showered with selfless offerings of warm meals, hot showers, extra beds, even a doctor's number to call for methadone. But we were drawn to Genteel, the big-voiced queen angel.

When the crowd shuffled out to their caroling traditions and basted turkeys, Genteel sat us down on pews and put her fists on her hips, like a peeved grade-school disciplinarian. She quizzed us for a while: "Now tell me exactly," she said to Squeaky, "where your teeth gone to?" And to me: "*The heck* you thinkin' movin' down here from sparklin' Gwinnett County, of all places?" I was honest with her again. I lay my pain bare before Genteel and Jesus, and she believed in me this time. Her immense face softened with sympathy. She told us her husband had just passed away from smoking rolled tobacco "since age eleven," and that she had an extra room to rent. On the cheap. Meals and mothering included. With a few strict conditions.

"Now look here, I'll be your shelter, but promise me right now," she said sternly, still donning choir robes: "Y'all ain't leaving my house 'til y'all better. No excuses. No visitors. No goin' back. I'll send you off healed, but 'til then, I'm 'bout to lock you down. I'm-a lock you down in a jail of kindness—and cookies!"

That night we swore to honor her demands, to respect the home she'd made with her husband, and to cause her no strife in our struggles toward sobriety. For several weeks, we slept on bedrolls in the spare room. As morning winter sun warmed the room, I would sit cross-legged in the light, accessing my grief, convulsing with sobs, clutching for those so abruptly gone, the heaven of their cheeks against mine. When Squeaky tried to run away, I'd hold him down, and only once was he forced to return the favor. Eventually, a calmness came, and we burned to be healthy. Genteel fed us orange juice and ham casseroles and hot chocolate and Bible hymns until I peeked through her cottage curtains one morning and saw a dogwood blossom whitely into life. That's when I first walked beyond the porch with Squeaky, when he kept dancing like the "Beat It" video and saying, "I'm reborn, God—I'm reborn!" Maybe it was that general euphoria of spring, or the high pollen count distorting our minds, but I felt just as altered as Squeaky. Within a week I scored a freelance gig on—of all things—the gardening beat for a now-defunct competitor of the *Beacon*'s. I used a chunk of my abused savings to fix Great White's drive-shaft and Squeaky's teeth, and he came home smiling with a cartoon mouth, pronouncing himself Sweetberry's sexiest bachelor. Physical cravings would occasionally creep up, little poltergeists at the windows, but we didn't succumb. We never went back. We contemplated selling weed to the first round of gentrifiers, artistic gay folks, but we couldn't do Genteel like that. For her sake, and to a lesser extent ours, we would not backslide. We would not use. That's not to say we stayed sober. After some experimenting, in fact, I found that libations involving tomato juice make for exquisite poltergeist repellant.

In Genteel's living room now, the scene of so much healing, I sprung up from the couch to check her forehead, feigning concern that she might have a fever, or the vapors.

"I ain't sick," she said, swatting away my hand. "I just know when it's time to sing. And now's the time. This city *need* a song."

"This city needs the National Guard," I said. "But singin's a start."

She fetched a calendar from her desk, as if anything was on it besides sleeping and *The Price Is Right*. "When they layin' the boy to rest?" she said, studying the calendar.

"Not sure. Might be too early for them to know. Or for the forensic examiner to let go."

"Baby, don't with the morbid."

"Sorry," I said. "But you sure you're up to this sort of performance? Have you been practicing?"

"It's been a long minute, honestly," she said. "Maybe two years. But it still in there, right by my heart."

The notion of her not having sung for so long made me sink a little, as if driving a hilly country road. It was a travesty, really. A waste. A beautiful road-worn American classic, rusting in some cluttered backyard. "I'm sure Joey's mother would be honored," I said. "But why now?"

"Because the Lord told me," she said. "And bein' honest, I need it, just as much as this old neighborhood do. Times like this, there's nothing like singin' in groups."

"Sounds reasonable. You want me to approach the family and ask?"

"And another reason," she said, ignoring me, "is because I'd regret it all kinds of ways if I didn't sing again."

"Regret?" I said.

"Yup."

"Didn't think you were capable of regretting anything," I said. "At least not until you inked that real estate deal with Beelzebub."

"You mistaken then, son."

"Really?"

"*Really.*"

"Then tell me your biggest regret in life, Genteel."

"Oh, fwoo!" she said, tossing a drink coaster into my chest. "You nosy!"

"You've got nothing," I said. "I told you. One big charmed existence, that's you."

"You callin' Jim Crow charmed?" she hollered. "You could've passed for White—or at least Middle Eastern—in them times. But not me, honey."

She had me there.

"And what's this you're doin', pryin' in my business?" she huffed. "Some story research? If you quotin' me right now, you gone die!"

Genteel's face dropped as she walked over to a bookcase and fetched a Japanese-style hand fan etched with cherry blossoms. For a moment, she cooled herself in shadows cast by curtains. "How I treated my Charles sometimes," she said. "There, that's my regret. At least my only regret based on my behavior. Only one."

I sat upright in reverence of her departed husband, who stared across the living room from a wooden frame in the corner. He was all mischievous smile, glistening moustache, and oversize disco-era glasses. "I wouldn't sweat it," I said. "Like most men, he probably deserved it."

"Fwoo!" she said. "Probably is the case, in most cases. But look here, my Charles didn't deserve no beatings!"

"Whoa," I said, cocking my head. "You *beat* your husband?"

"You seen pictures of Charles? I mean from the neck down? No? Well, he didn't weigh but a buck twenty-six, and when he come home from them bootleg likuh places... what'd they call them back in the day?"

"The shot houses?"

"Yeah, them! He cash his check from the faucet factory, and instead of getting my stew meat and lard and early peas from Grant Park Grocery, he go to that little window in them shot houses and buy that white moonshine. What'd they call that back then?"

"Happy Water?"

"Yeah, that! Oh, that dang Happy Water! Anyway, I could see the drunk on Charles' face from about three blocks away. He come in, and a couple-a times, I knock my man cold out. The wrongest thing these hands ever done. Except for maybe when I signed that Lotto's paperwork." She fanned herself wildly now, her head swaying. "Day like this, with that poor baby boy, the heat, them reptiles, and these thoughts of my home gettin' all bulldozered... I'm sorry, Johnson, but it's too much to recall for ya anything more. So that's all of my regrets you get."

I thought for a second Genteel was keeling over to weep, but she was untying her black leather loafers. In a great backward sweep, she kicked the shoes off, fell into a cushy recliner, fanned herself twice, and succumbed to snoring sleep. I showed myself out.

CHAPTER 12

Tall Walt's probable cause hearing, to determine whether police had enough evidence to detain him, was set for the next morning. The courts move quickly when public interest is so high, when The People want blood. I couldn't get Becky to return calls, so I had no official assignment. Nonetheless, I grabbed my Canon thirty-five millimeter and set out in the morning for the hearing. Pay or no pay. I had nothing better to do.

Rounding my block onto Boulevard Street, I noticed some Ligustrum bushes shivering, and out popped Carlito with his menacing knife. Beside him was a beefy, benign Sweetberry newbie. A hybrid of fair-haired college boy and lumberjack, this kid had moved in and immediately took a leadership position with the Sweetberry Park Resurgence Association. That group's name was the polite way of not saying, We, the Younger People With Money and Education Who Will Henceforth Take Over. Their ethnic makeup looked like a panel of Norwegian gymnastics judges with a couple of Bangladeshi dudes for flavor, and their main achievement so far had been painting over graffiti on one liquor store fence. Their leadership and clout was ironic, for sure, but deep down they were pretty good kids.

"The hell you fools doing?" I said, rolling down my window.

The big kid perked up. "Oh, hi, Mr. Johnson." His deep voice sounded like a child's record player low on batteries. He was holding a Rambo knife, too. "We're just clearing out bushes for folks, making sure there's no non-native wildlife around here, if you know what I mean."

"Be careful," I said. "They say there's a really potent one around here."

"Yes, sir," said the kid. "But we haven't seen anything."

"You're not alone," I said.

"At the very least," he chirped, "we'll clear out some weeds, increase visibility for these older bungalows. Since the zoo thing, a few legacy owners have been too afraid to come outside."

(And now, kids, a primer on the Sweetberry Park Gentrification Lexicon: "Legacy owner" is code for original or very old-school homeowners, usually widows and almost always Black, who aren't often seen outside and whose houses are viewed by uptight stroller moms as rundown/icky and by developers as succulent. On the topic of houses, a "Teardown" is self-explanatory. But when homes are viewed as salvageable and/or charming, they always need to be expanded with second floors to maximize profits and meet today's living standards, per the gentry; thus they become "Pop Tops." A "Dickface" refers to those White suburban builders who swing through on bulldozers, erect McMansions, and giddy-up with profits spilling from their pleated khakis, usually without so much as shaking a neighbor's hand. A "Family Build," in neo-Sweetberry parlance, refers to a bunch of non-White contractors who work slowly, smoke weed, and are automatically assumed to have no clue what they're doing. A "Legend" is a longtime resident, usually widows and almost always Black, who at some point acted as de facto police officers or contributed majorly to beautification committees. Believe it or not, the Legends have typically welcomed the Caucasian Invasion, if pensively; they view the newcomers as crucial allies whose very presence will mean fatter inheritances for the grand-kids, when it comes time to sell the house or land. Lastly, on the flip side, is what some newcomer punks are calling "Duds"—the vocal resisters to the changes. The longtime residents who decry rising property taxes and $17 bespoke hoagies. This classification is exceedingly rare, because even the most ardent Dud sees little use in speaking up now, at least in a district like Sweetberry. They're mostly resigned to the fact that sweet yesterday, however dangerous, is gone. Ironic as it sounds, it doesn't hurt that all of this is occurring in the Deep South, where folks are used to diversity, and where pride in the bloody past indeed being history is never subtle. The sort of place where Duds, Legends, Dickfaces, and a knife-wielding lumberjack can enthusiastically nod to each other on the street, per custom, and quietly talk shit about each other later.)

"Tell me something, God," said sweaty Carlito, baking beside a wax myrtle. "You think these damn snakes are even real, man? We got all this talk about black mamba sightings and cobras in the shitters, but where's the *proof*? I mean, it's been weeks, and not one bite, not a single casualty, last I heard."

"You sound disappointed," I said.

"Nah, not disappointed," he said. "More like *duped*. Like I'm being fed a line. It's kind of like talking with Paul Bunyan here. All morning he's been trying to tell me we live in a post-racial society, whatever that means."

"Hey!" said the kid, chest puffing. "Don't misconstrue me, man. I said post-racial *relative* to where we came from. I did a term paper on it, for grad-level sociology."

Carlito exploded with laughter. "Huh-ha! Hwoah, man! You *hear* this kid, God?"

"Come on," I said to Carlito. "Ease up."

But he kept pressing: "He's over here calling Sweetberry 'advanced,' like this place has achieved enlightenment or something. Don't get me wrong, I'm glad the poodle kidnappings are over. But this dude is on dope if he thinks we're special."

The kid held up his blade and feigned carving Carlito in half. Then they fist-bumped in a bro truce. I cranked Great White back down into DRIVE.

"Anyhow, on the snake front," I said. "All I know is what I saw in the parking lot, that smashed adder. That thing looked like it'd wiggled up from Hades."

"True, but what about this zookeeper?" said Carlito. "Dude must be a ghost. I mean, how you gonna elude a metro police force for so long in this day and age? How you gonna paralyze a city and disappear?"

"That's my question, too," I said. "I might pose it at work today. I'm due in court, in twenty minutes. Gotta scoot, gents—"

"I'm thinking it's a *cover-up*," Carlito said. "Some kind of complex government distraction. There's your hot tip, newsman."

"That's hilarious," I said.

"No," said Carlito, "it's true."

"So a city government, like, conspires to distract us, as you put it," I said. "They showcase their stupidity in what's become global news. They admit to the world they can't catch a handful of dangerous but slow critters, or the culprit who's come off his meds. That's creative, but absurd."

The kid was hanging his head now, more of a melodramatic softie than I'd expected. "Just a shame about that lady's son, though," he said. "She lives down my street. She's crazy-nosy and anal and all that—but damn, you know."

"On that note," I said, "off to work."

The Brutalist concrete compound that is Fulton County Superior Court had begun life in the eighties as a controversial architectural statement and quickly devolved into an unkempt petri dish of government corruption and minor-offender agony. A place of bribes and one bail-denied injustice after the next. And that's to say nothing of the public bathrooms, which reek like piss troughs at the old Braves stadium. With less than five minutes to spare before Walt's first encounter with a judge, I was hustling through the corridors when I started to recognize faces of older folks—pardon, Legacy Owners—from Sweetberry. We all congealed together in an anxious mass.

After a few moments, a bailiff politely corralled us. He opened doors to a courtroom with nothing on the walls but postmodern sconces, and we filed into smooth wooden pews. All five Atlanta broadcast stations had cameras in position already, their reporters in the prime front rows.

We sat through two hours of dog-and-pony shows involving shoplifting cases and low-level weed deals, in which novice defense attorneys tried to show off for news cameras that weren't even on. Then the judge, a dogged older Black man with studious eyes and a constant scowl, said something to his court reporter about Walter James being on deck, before slipping back into his quarters. That's when a hand reached up from behind me and squeezed my left shoulder. It looked almost mummified, this hand, its skin like a thinly spread gelatin. The ring-finger was missing.

"He's innocent," said the owner, as I craned my head back to him. I knew the face. "That's my grandson, Walter. They're scapegoatin' him."

I unlatched the hand and shook it. "Archie Johnson, sir," I said.

"Pleasure."

"Could you spell your name for me, please?" I pulled notepad and pencil from my pockets.

"Just call me 'the grandfather' in the paper."

"Honestly, sir, not sure this will even be a story that makes the paper," I said. "But I can say you wished to remain anonymous. You live one block over from Genteel Briggs, right?" He didn't respond. "Where is she today? I thought she might catch a ride with one of y'all."

He didn't say a word, apparently wishing to remain extremely anonymous. It seemed like his name was Felix, if memory served. He never said much and hardly visited with The Flank's other antiques, but I recall Genteel talking about him picking guitars on his porch, singing about the pie factory he'd retired from. His thick jaws and sea-green eyes were echoed in Walt's face, as was the smart, sly demeanor. They both had the faces of men who know something you wish you did. "Can I just ask, sir, why you think he's innocent of these charges?"

"For the paper?"

"Hopefully, yes. On the record."

The man flattened his lips and shook his head, the disgusted look of distrust, of frustration. "He's been to jail before, I ain't gone lie."

"I heard that. Walt told me that himself, actually. The night of that church meeting."

"Well, then, he tell you *why*?"

"Nope. I asked, but he wouldn't. And I haven't tried to look it up yet, to be honest."

The man stole a peek at deputies and spoke too quietly for them to hear. "Look, Walter's solid gold, top to bottom," he said. "His charges in the past were the opposite of thuggin' around. He's a good boy and always has been. His arrests were *on purpose*, every single time."

"On purpose?"

"For activism stuff at college."

"Alright," I said, scribbling. "That's a good, fascinating thing to know. Please, go on."

"Back a few years ago, Walter got into Morehouse, just like his hero," he said. "Guess who that is?"

"I bet it rhymes with Carton Sleuther Ring."

"Yup. And what was King all about?"

"Pissing off the FBI?"

"Nope."

"Peace? And love?"

"Yup," he said. "Nonviolence, no matter what."

We were both nodding now. "I see where you're going," I said. "Walt really isn't into guns?"

"Man, that boy never *touched* a firearm," he said. "Didn't believe in 'em, fundamentally speaking. No way in hell he's bringing a pistol to a crazy meeting, in a church no less."

"Have you talked to Walt?"

"Twice."

"So what happened, in his view? Bad detective work? Police profiling?"

"That's part of it." He leaned in now, whispering. He smelled of cigarillos and every cologne with "aqua" in the name. "But it's *deeper*."

"Deeper how?"

"Deeper like Walter got his hands on some plans he shouldn't have," he said. "Some *development* plans."

The connotations of that knocked me back, against the pew in front of me. "What are you suggestin'?"

"I'm suggestin' a set-up, that's what."

This second conspiracy theory in as many hours was deflating, for some reason. "I don't know," I said, shaking my head. "That developer Lotto is a rodent, I'll give you that. But I'm assuming you know that, since you inked a deal with him to sell your property."

"I didn't sign *nothin'*," said the man, nearly shouting, before composing himself. "I'm in the vast minority in The

Flank. I sure as all hell don't want to leave. But my vote doesn't count. Why you think Walter is so motivated? He was goin' to bat like this for his grandad. He wants to save my house, my life. It's the only place I've ever owned. And look where it got him, facin' a gone life."

I reached over and squeezed his left arm, in a gesture, I hoped, of reassurance. "That's noble of Walt, really," I said. "But I don't think Lotto's that cunning. He's too concerned with money and ego to try and take down a protester. That could ruin him, too, like anybody." He wasn't buying a word from my mouth, but I pushed on. "It's especially risky for a fat cat like Lotto with so many enemies. Somebody would snitch—"

"I'm tellin' you, Walter's no ordinary protester. He's *committed.*"

"Plus," I said, "those development plans are available to anybody. They're on Lotto's website."

"I'm not talkin' about blueprints or pretty pictures, man."

He was restraining himself, I could tell, from approaching some dangerous place, divulging too much. "Don't quote me," he said. "Don't you damn quote me."

"I won't."

"Not anonymous or not."

"Sir, you have my word."

He grabbed the back of my head, near the ponytail band, and he pulled my skull so close my ear touched his cold nose. "Walter broke in that developer's office, a few days before the church meeting," he said, barely audible. "He went deep in the computers and things, and he hit the jackpot. Lotto's lyin' to everybody. He's got plans for our shotgun houses in The Flank, alright. But it's got nothin' to do with a museum in the suburbs..."

He leaned back, crossed his arms, and effectively shut down.

"*Expound*, man," I whisper-shouted. "Come on!"

Instead of responding, he stared ahead blank. I kept prodding, verbally at first, and then by writing "Please?" into my notebook and dancing it in his face. "That's all I know, man," he finally said. "You got your clues now. I blabbered too much already."

"All rise!" boomed the bailiff.

In a whoosh, the eclectic assemblage went up to its feet, as that tough, sinister-looking judge lumbered back in. When two deputies pulled Walt in by his chains, I heard a tiny, tortured gasp behind me.

Donning Fulton County orange and looking bedraggled, abused, scared, and about two feet shorter, Walt stole a glance at the gallery; when he spotted his grandfather, his eyes tightened into furious slits, as if to say: *You see this? How'd it come to this?* I turned around, and Walt's grandfather was whimpering, his face smashed with pain. About five rows behind him, in the far right corner of the gallery, I spotted the primped head of none other than Lotto Livingston. He was staring forward with perverse amazement. A few seats to Lotto's left, girded by black-suited security, was Atlanta Mayor Ted Hickson. Clearly, the boy's death and Walt's charges were important news at every stratum. The judge told us to be seated, and I was the last to obey, scanning the crowd.

I was looking for Americana Mama, who was not there.

The hearing lasted maybe twelve minutes. A grizzled veteran detective with a Massachusetts dialect testified about everything everyone who was in the church already knew: The old revolver was either dropped or fired from a low position. But according to the detective, several witnesses, including developer Lotto, who was speaking at the time of the shot, reported seeing Walt stand up and reach into his boot as the audience became rowdy and loud. In the hours following the shooting, Walt, per the testimony, had eluded police and failed to return phone calls until southside beat cops spotted him leaving his mom's house to check the mailbox.

"It'd been more than twelve ow-was," the detective testified, "but still, once Mr. James was booked, our stand-dud, procedural tests showed gunpow-da residue on his right hand."

At this accusation, Walt dipped his head and shook it, as if trying to clear his eardrums of water.

It was doubtful a kempt guy like Walt had failed to shower or wash his hands overnight, so the detective's last damning detail didn't seem particularly relevant; per his grandpa's input, the kid hated firearms anyhow. Nonetheless, I could almost hear public opinion of Walt shift in the gallery, his status as a child-killing villain solidifying.

During a brief cross-examination, Walt's public defender raised that point—"After the gun range, detective, how do you explain that my palms are clean within a few hours, whether I scrub them down or not?"—while squeezing in mention of Walt's Morehouse studies (he was still enrolled, working toward a sociology degree). Lastly, the attorney peppered in document-supported facts about Walt's involvement in various clubs for young Black philanthropists and his time spent volunteering at soup kitchens and with orphaned boys. Saint Walter, basically.

Walt's attorney was a confident, mustachioed thirty-something Hispanic man in a light blue blazer and pinkish bowtie, which he now straightened as a prelude to his finale. The gunpowder, the defense attorney posited, was easily explained: "Walter is a highly vocal activist in the neo-civil rights community, your honor," said the lawyer. "Which makes him, frankly, a potential target."

The prosecution objected, citing conjecture. Sit down, said the judge.

"Anyhow," the defense continued, "Walter had every right to be afraid after leaving a contentious meeting where a White child tragically ended up shot. He was afraid to sleep in his apartment, lest the cops come kicking in the door and booking him in the wee hours. He naturally went to his mother's home and sought advice from her, as well as from her new husband, a former Alabama police officer, in fact. This man, Walter's stepfather, is the most avid gun enthusiast I've ever met. Knowing that Walter has a few convictions to his name—albeit nonviolent offenses—they thought it'd be best to hide all the home's firearms in the attic. Walter lent his stepdad a hand the morning after the shooting. And what'd that hand do? It got contaminated with gunpowder, right before APD took Walter down on his mother's lawn."

That landed like an exculpatory slam dunk for the defense. I saw the Sweetberry contingent nodding, agreeing with the attorney. But in reaching that conclusion, that silent acquittal, they were alone.

The alibi and character-reaffirming details fell on deaf ears at the bench, and the judge found evidence to bind Walt's murder charges over for a possible indictment. I knew that process, with a case of this magnitude, could take about three months. Walt would have to endure every hour behind bars, because the judge declined to set a bond amount. None of this was particularly surprising, given the low standard of proof in such hearings. But as they led Walt through a steel door for the bowels of the jail, he cast a last petrified glimpse back into the crowd, and I'd never heard a row of gallery observers emit such a hopeless moan. The clicking door behind us was the early exit of Walt's grandfather.

I zeroed in on Lotto, hoping for a poignant photo and maybe a quote. But the molasses-like mass of older folks mourning Walt barricaded me from him. Lotto slipped out into the hallway, hustling in a tweed suit.

Once outside the courtroom, in the airy mezzanine, I caught a glimpse of that suit; Lotto had scatted from Superior Court and was beelining for another city building next door. I bounded down the stairs, jogged into the sunshine, and followed him in. I hassled with the metal detector folks, stood back, and watched Lotto waiting at an elevator. The atrium soared for ten stories, and I counted as a glassy capsule lifted him six stories above ground. I caught the next elevator, ignored a receptionist, and blindly started sharking the sixth floor.

I'd entered a realm of municipal minutia, where property records and tax documents gather dust in the afterlife. A different clerk perked up and began to say something but stopped, I think, when he recognized me. I was sweaty and stressed, randomly brandishing a camera. Which is why, I think, he notified security.

As I turned down a corridor of beige walls and suspended ceiling tiles, I heard the high-pitched stutter of Lotto's laugh and followed it to a corner office with the blinds drawn and the door barely cracked open. I announced myself with a tapping fingernail knock that nobody seemed to hear. The door budged open, unveiling Lotto and zoning board president Kim Somethingerother, seated with their knees touching, holding hands like middle-school lovers.

"Hey, Lotto," I said. "How's the wife?"

Kim's face ignited, red as clay under slate. Lotto, meanwhile, looked like he'd swallowed spoiled brie. He said, "What the hell is this?"

"Exactly what I was going to ask you," I said. "About several topics, in fact."

"You can't just walk in these offices," Kim said. "You can't *be* here."

Lotto handed Kim her own desk phone. "Report him for trespassing, right now!"

"I think your clerk up front beat you to that." I could hear the authoritative jangle of nearing security guard keys. "What are you up to, Lotto, with The Flank? What are you really up to down there?"

He didn't mutter a word, just shook his freckled head, until security led me by the elbows not back into court but out to the sidewalk, into the blazing noon.

With no deadline to meet, I pondered grabbing a nice downtown lunch, but the thin-lipped mouth of my remaining folding cash rebutted. The *Beacon* offices, I realized, were but three blocks north on West Central Peachtree Street, a block from Peachtree Street, around the corner from Central Peachtree Avenue. I scatted over there in hopes of apologizing to editor Becky in person—and maybe scoring cold, forgotten pizza in the breakroom fridge.

In the newspaper tower's mezzanine, I must have tapped the scanner with my bar-coded badge and cards a dozen times before I started condescendingly pointing at it, my approach to reasoning with subservient technology. That's when a young security guard in a baggy button-up said, "Apologies, sir, but says here your *Beacon* credentials have been deactivated. It specifically says to deny your entry."

As I drove home, licking fresh wounds again, burly thunderclouds eclipsed the sun and opened a warm flood from the heavens. I bypassed my house and parked, in the rain, in front of the Faux Americana McMansion Deluxe, which swarmed with umbrella-toting mourners. They were surely gathering to feast in there, a means of burying early grief.

I gazed dumbly at the massive structure, with its four dormers and immense walls of cement-board, guessing which room had been Joey's. Probably the one with curtains drawn so tight they were crooked, the better for preserving orphaned toys and scribbly artwork from sunlight. I wondered where his void was being felt the most in there, despite the crowd. Would his mom rue the silence once her grief attendants had gone? Would she pine for the whiz of Joey's automatic wheelchair? Could she bear to enter that house at all?

Delusion took hold, and I envisioned the boy walking, confident and happy, wherever he was. I heard the echoes of advice, back when other mourners had nosed up to me, saying hold with both hands to my memories, that doing so would keep my wife and boy alive. Something about their being cremated, as my wife's family had wished, crippled the part of me that so loved the physical them. They were out of reach. Forever ashen and inhuman, forever gone. I thought of them in my arms. I thought of them in every circumstance I could remember. But no memory is salve for void. The physical vestiges of my wife and boy that were left in our house, my living cage, became teasing lies. A month after the accident, I gathered all of Sage's garments and Wyatt's toys and clothes and even his blankets and drove far out into the Piedmont, to a flat place where the waves of green Georgia relent, and with a gallon of lighter fluid I cremated those things myself.

The rain came harder, so gray and heavy I could hardly see the big house. I went back to my leaky Victorian and took a seat in my side-porch rocking chair. Soon I was entranced by that pecky, persistent lullaby of summer tempests, the final cleansing of May's pollen as the calendar flipped to June. The pleasantness of my trance was shattered by what I saw slither up from the bushes to the porch. It saw me, too. Alarmed by my rocking, it fashioned a horrifically aggressive stance, maybe eight feet of thick, tightening coil, steadily lifting its diamond head upward and backward. I'd found myself *vis-à-vis* with the cocked fist of death that is the fer-de-lance pit viper of Central America—a great damn big one. And all I could whisper was, "Please, please, don't."

CHAPTER 13

In my old wooden chair, I had stopped mid-rock, leaning as far back from the snake as possible. The toes of my beat Adidas sneakers were pointed into the wood of the porch, and my calf muscles began to burn. My ankles felt as if rusted screws in them were infected and hot. I couldn't keep this cowardly pose for much longer, and I feared that even swallowing too quickly, dropping my Adam's apple, would set the pit viper off.

Somehow I could see in her pointed nose, beautiful brown-black scale pattern, and furious stance that she was female. Against the backdrop of old dead leaves beneath my boxwoods, she was all but invisible, if you weren't specifically looking for her; and just behind her coiled intensity, maybe five feet back, I could make out the shape of a dead rat in the lawn. The dinner I'd unwittingly disrupted.

I involuntarily let down my feet, my legs giving up. In seeing this, the blackish tail-tip of her body began to vibrate in warning, mimicking the ominous notifications of her rattler cousins. But no rattlesnake in my *National Geographic* or the corny shows about world's deadliest things was half this hefty. Thicker than a Stromboli, longer than me plus two feet, she was a mighty, magnificent beast. As I dropped my left hand toward my pocket, one hesitant centimeter at a time, that herpetologist's warnings echoed: Her strike-radius is exceptionally wide, her bites are never dry, and she can make your tissue rot within minutes. As if that didn't suck enough, she was stubborn, and patient as a statue. *Why this, why now?* I wondered. *Go on, girl, get your rat.*

Over the course of maybe a minute, I managed to slip my smartphone from my pocket, but its rubber protective casing had caught on my car keys. Straining to move only the joints of my fingers, I tugged on the device—and tugged and tugged again. My elbow bent, and again the pseudo rattle whizzed. So much sweat was draining from my scalp and armpits I could feel my undershirt becoming soaked. At last, the phone popped out of my pocket, but it was upside-down and useless, the face facing my jeans. The fer-de-lance was not retreating, not an inch. It dawned on me that she must have viewed my rocking chair—handcrafted by my bigoted grandpa from felled hickory—as a human weapon, like scythes extending from my elbows. In the instant she lowered her head, perhaps getting tired herself, I quickly twisted my wrist and flipped over the phone. I gently touched 9, 1, and 1.

"Atlanta 911!" a nasally male dispatcher practically screamed. "What's your emergency?"

In the softest voice I could manage, I shushed the man for a second. He became silent, confused. Then I whispered, "Quiet…"

His training must have taught him to hush in such instances, because he said nothing, until I grew brave enough to whisper, with ventriloquist lips: "I cornered, on my horch in Seetwerry Hark, vy one of uh hoo sakes."

My speaker whooshed with the sound of the man's hand covering his receiver. Though he tried to mute himself, I could hear him announce to his officemates: "Y'all! Holy hell. A snake call!" Then he whispered back at me: "Sit tight, sir. Don't move from your location. We have your address. We'll be there within two minutes."

With nothing to do but stare at each other, contemplating the awkwardness of our respective positions, I began to wonder how street cops might possibly be equipped to rectify this situation. I longed for my shovel, an impossible forty yards away in the backyard. But then again, I didn't want that, based on past experiences. I'd watched Grandpa Bigot decapitate a big thick copperhead once, and that manic, bug-eyed, disembodied face haunts me still. I'd stumbled on the snake at Lake Cherokee, up in the scenic chew-spit hinterlands. That was my grandfather's favorite fair-weather respite from urban ills like traffic and diversity. That summer, I was maybe eight. I chased a basketball down a hill and out beside a majestic longleaf pine, and when I bent down to fetch the ball, I damn near put my fingers in the copperhead's mouth. It was sunning its earth-toned chevrons atop a rock. I squealed, and granddaddy bolted to the scene with a shovel. With one thrust he sliced the snake's head clean off.

You'd think that would be a happy memory, but what happened next is the source of my torment. Grandpa pinched the dead head so that the mouth opened wide, revealing whitish flesh, sabers, and a little hole near the tongue like an anus. The body, meanwhile, twisted and writhed and flipped into the grass. Grandpa, reeking of peel-top beer, said, "You'n scrame like a lil' sissy, bwoy!" Then he held out this hideous head and chased me all around the gulley, mumbling about "half-breed wussy"—until I just fell down, curled like an armadillo, and cried. So grandpa went inside with that snake head and nailed it, still twitching, to the knotty-pine wall of my cabin bedroom. The head came loose and fell off that night, landing on the floor, facing me. I cowered beneath my blankets, my own head exposed and watching. In the moonlight, the evil dead eyes and shiny fangs dared me to try and skip away for help, to report my racist kin to child protective services. Instead I drifted off, and in the morning the head, the evidence, was gone.

Something about a fer-de-lance face is more innocent, doe-eyed, and docile than its Southeastern American redneck brethren. Which must be part of the deceit. The allure, even. I was almost becoming entranced by her when the flash of police car lights distracted me.

The first responding officer parked cockeyed at my curb, and he crept onto the walkway of my yard. He took one slow step after another. He said, "Sir?" in a gravelly voice. When I didn't verbally respond or even twitch a facial muscle, I think he knew the score. He switched off his radio, hunched over, and oozed right up to the first step of my porch. And there we stood for a silent minute, a triangle of tense beings, surely the oddest standoff Sweetberry hath ever seen.

When the cop de-holstered his snub-nosed Taser gun, I had to object, albeit quietly: "Hey," I whispered, my lips unmoving. "Hoo can't *hase* his hing."

He was a younger, upbeat, blonde cop with sprightly brown eyes and a broad nose that had obviously once been pierced. The pipes of his forearm muscles heaved and fell with his impassioned grip on the Taser. He didn't turn his head to look at me, but rather flashed his eyes in my direction. Like me, he tried to speak without moving his lips, and he said what I thought was, "Hey, have you seen Peter?"

Now I was furious. "Duh huck you halkin' ahout off-sir?"

Again a flash of eyeballs, and he tried to clarify: "Peter will try to take my badge," I thought he said. "Peter don't play."

"Man, huck Heter!"

He raised a heavy boot and came one step closer, gently lifting himself onto my porch, within surefire range of the Taser. The fer-de-lance shifted her body, zeroing in on the cop, and again her tail-tip vibrated in warning. I saw my chance. Her head was beyond half her body length away from me, so I scooted as far left as my seat would allow, then eased my Adidas to the left of the rocker legs, grabbed the base of a long-broken gas lamp over my head, lifted up, and rocketed myself to the corner of my porch, to relative safety. I climbed atop the banister railing and spat scorn in the officer's direction: "What are you doing, man? One drop of venom from that thing will kill us both!"

Spooked by my voice behind her, the snake inched in his direction, then halted again. Still aiming the Taser, the officer stepped back once and said, "I'd shoot her, but PETA wouldn't stand for it. They'd try to get me fired. This is all being recorded on my chest cam, sir."

"To hell with PETA, brother," I said. "You can't let her get away."

"Stand still, sir. Stop talking."

"Where the hell's backup? Where's animal control?"

"Sir! Quiet!"

At that point, the snake shot like a spear in the officer's direction, and with a crack, a hail of prongs spat from his Taser. I yelped. From my vantage, it appeared that merely one of the Taser's darts had connected with the snake, a direct hit in her white belly, which I knew from police coverage minimized the electrical charge. Nonetheless, she writhed in twisting, twitching, furious loops, biting at the wire that pained her not with quick strikes but menacing, aggressive chomps. I looked above my head, to what seemed a firm piece of wooden molding; I latched upon it with both old hands and lifted my feet into a hanging fern, hoisting my full body far above the chaos.

The officer, suddenly fearless, had snuck up on the preoccupied snake; using a black boot so thick with rubber and leather it looked mechanical, he stepped down and pinned the animal just behind its jaws. The great, irate body began thrashing so violently it whipped him at the knees, thighs, and lower back. He began to shout nonsensical things— "Narrrg!" and "Byoooock!"—in obvious confusion and fear. All the while that faux-rattle hummed.

Then the officer, smooth like a gunslinger, drew his 9 millimeter. He took hesitant aim at her marvelous face, sinister and terrified. In a blink the snake's head exploded redly across my rocker, exterior walls, and stained-glass windows, as the bullet blew a hole into my porch.

The tireless, cagey zoo officials actually beat the backup officers to my yard. Two of them—a man and woman, in matching collared shirts—hopped out of a van and started waving metal snake tongs to get the attention of me and the shooter. I took a seat on my banister and waved back.

"It's OK," the officer shouted into the street. "Threat's eliminated."

The zoo people, apprehensive nonetheless, crept up to my porch and acted like they'd come upon a senseless massacre.

"Didn't want to, but I had to," said the cop. "Don't give me that look. You don't understand."

"Are those *Taser* cords?" said the zoo lady.

"Yes, ma'am," the cop said. "Afraid this thing was too much for Tasers."

"I've never seen anything like this," she said. "This is bad. On every level, this is *bad*."

In the corner I was silently concurring, casting the lion's share of blame upon her team's flawed security practices. When zoo man got a glimpse of the animal's decapitation, he panicked and ordered us to evacuate immediately to the street. We didn't budge, still stunned. "Listen, gentleman, this venom is so potent, it could be dangerous as just airborne chemicals right now, considering the force of this explosion," he said. "You definitely don't want to be walking around in it."

"I'm not paying for cleanup and porch repairs," I said, now tiptoeing. "Y'all are. And this trauma I'm feeling must be worth something, too."

Everyone ignored me. The cop was talking into his shoulder radio, and zoo man couldn't take his eyes off the skull remains, tossed about like bits of bubble gum. "Oh, girl," he said. "You poor, poor girl—"

"You're kidding, right?" I snapped. Finally, they both turned to me. "You understand what I just *survived*? I was cornered like a field mouse for about an hour. And I'm frankly traumatized. So, look, if this porch isn't de-poisoned by my bedtime, I'll add pain and suffering to my lawsuit against the zoo—"

"Enough, Mr. Johnson," said the man, turning away. "Provide your statement to the police. That's the first step."

"No, listen," I said. "I'm willing to forget this ever happened, if you give me the skinny on your zoo colleague. Tell me what you know about Gerald McCaffrey, because nobody's said much, and this terrified city deserves answers."

They said nothing.

"Don't look at me crazy," I said. "I mean, where is he? *Who* is he? Why can't y'all find him?"

Zoo lady looked through me, beyond me, and pointed to my street. "Those would be questions for him," she said. I turned around and saw Atlanta Memorial Zoo public relations head Adam Evans, captain of vagueness, walking cautiously to the scene beside a high-ranking cop. I nodded and started beelining toward these fresh arrivals, but zoo lady gave me pause when she said, "Hey, Mr. Johnson. I knew Gerald for years, and just so you know, he was a great guy not all that long ago. A hardworking man, a church man, a sane man. Off the record?"

"Sure," I said.

"He's been a landlord for decades, properties all across town. Like, *a lot* of rental properties."

"I know. We heard that at a press conference."

"Did you know he's the heir to a small fortune, the son of a building materials magnate?"

"No," I said. "I didn't know *that*."

"It's true," she said.

I clasped my head with both hands, squeezed. "So he's a rich boy moonlighting as a deranged zookeeper?"

"But to your question," she said. "I've been hearing there isn't enough police staff available to keep watch over so many of his properties, not while also keeping the city in order, and the roundup on. They can only do so much surveillance at once. Still, personally, I can't believe they haven't found him either. Gerald's a simple man, hardly a Houdini. I think his going into zoology and working with animals was sort of a revolt, pushing back against the elitist world he came from."

By then, Adam Evans was upon us, asking about the fer-de-lance's well-being.

"She's dead, like I damn well could be, because of your facility's mistakes," I told Adam and the sergeant. "Now give me something, on the record, about your zookeeper. Why'd he *do* this to us?"

"I'm glad you're OK, God," said Adam.

"Don't ignore me."

"I can't discuss that aspect of the investigation yet."

"Just give me *something*," I said. "Something in exchange for all this."

"Given these developments, you can expect a press conference soon," he said. "The important thing is that you're alright."

"No," I said, "the important thing is finding the remainder of the snakes you lost. The important thing is keeping my neighbors fucking alive. And honestly, the important thing to me is doing my job, so I can keep the air conditioner on."

"I'm sorry it's come to that."

"I'm sorry you're so sorry," I said, stomping away, toward my truck. "Give me a call when my home's fit for habitation again."

"Sir," said the sergeant. "We'll need to speak with you…"

I popped the gate latch and stepped onto the sidewalk. "I'll be right back, just doing a bit of work," I said, pointing to my house. "And trying to calm myself down after that shit!"

As they turned around to see the porch, I fled. My laptop computer, I realized, was inside, and no way was I going back in. So I cranked up the truck and chugged toward the nearest open library in East Atlanta.

I called editor Becky's cell phone, but she elected to ignore me again. I left her a brief message describing—or teasing, in a stilted way, like a blockbuster's trailer—the harrowing snake encountered I'd survived so valiantly, hanging upside-down in shameful retreat. At her office, her assistant said Becky had called in sick to handle "unspecified proceedings" which of course meant divorce, and in hearing that, I knew my pitch would have to wait. Only a scoundrel would hassle a woman as she was being lopped off the payroll of a high-earning medical sales rep on the basis of her talent and workaholism. I felt a little panicked, to be honest. It was the feeling of having no money, no ability, nobody to fall back on, and no talent for busking in the streets. While heading down hills, I threw the truck into neutral to conserve gas. Luxuries like non-expired foodstuffs would have to wait. Unless, that is, I could focus enough at the public library computer to pitch and sell—to a *national publication*—my firsthand account of escaping the fangs of Atlanta's snake summer!

"That's it!" I hollered in the cab. "That's it right there!"

Five minutes at the library, facing closing time in an hour, I realized I had no national media contacts. Not a damn one. After five decades in the business. If I went back home, succumbing to laws that discourage the fleeing of crime scenes, soon enough the broadcast news teams would sweep through and bombard *me*, the competition, with questions. And I'd be forced to decline comment—always a bad look on camera. I needed to stay gone. And I needed a fresh angle.

"McCaffrey, you looney bastard," I said quietly, to nobody, near the empty Children's Section. "Where'd you run off to? Macon? Savannah? Ireland?"

A search of the city's online property records database led me to exact addresses for thirty-seven properties associated with one Gerald H. McCaffrey, my guy. I studied the addresses, the street names, the neighborhoods. Beside McCaffrey's name I saw the addresses of tiny Midtown apartment clusters from the sixties, several standalone houses on old streets in Southwest Atlanta, and what I believed to be lofts carved from a former factory on the industrial Westside. Almost no commonalities. No discernible trends. It was clear he wanted to tap different markets, to diversify the portfolio and bleed a variety of tenants, to keep moving. "Quite a collection, McCaffrey," I whispered. "Must be a trust fund."

Now I understood how cops could be overwhelmed trying to surveil so many of these properties across the very specific borders of police zones. But where hadn't they looked? Which place hadn't they mined well enough? I scanned the stack of addresses on the computer screen, up and down, until an outlier shone like light from under a door.

"What were you doing, Mr. McCaffrey, way out on Brennan Drive?" I said. "One of these things is not like the others."

Through the rain-damp dusk I commandeered Great White to the southernmost reaches of Atlanta proper. Down where glorious old pines still tower, the sad country dogs limp, and schlocky gilded mansions cower in the hills.

High atop a kudzu embankment, I spotted the lone home in the area associated with zookeeper McCaffrey's name in property records. It looked like a squatty brick postwar house someone had tried, tragically, to fashion into a contemporary Swiss chalet in the eighties. Not only did it seem unoccupied, it felt forgotten in time, an architectural echo of a confused civilization. I parked near a culvert and searched fruitlessly for a flashlight in the truck. I hoofed quickly up the weedy, gray-gravel driveway in last light. A faint watercolor sunset bled peach and aqua through the hardwoods.

Up close, the house resembled a Frank Lloyd Wright developed by Dali at his most inebriated. A great porcupine of porches and nonsensical windows around a brick core, with Hansel and Gretel flourishes here and there. The work, quite possibly, of a madman contractor. Or the experiment of a home-improvement industry executive's son with an unlimited expense account. I could see through the largest living room window that a portion of the roof had collapsed. The place was too dismal to be a hideout for even the most whacked-out scofflaw. I was convinced detectives had poked around for five minutes and beat feet back to cushier confines like the inner-city slums. Preparing to do the same, to face the interrogatory music back in Sweetberry, I'd turned to the truck and was whistling to ward off predators when a horrid smell seeped out from a window. As I spun back toward the home, the odor whipped around my body and latched ahold of my nostrils. The memories bubbled up, and I nearly puked.

It was the summer of 1993, and I had the bad idea to ride along with a crew of ex-Marines that specialized in urban crime scene cleanups. A real participatory journalism adventure. The first call seemed doable enough: A family near downtown hadn't heard from Grandma in a while, and police had found her dead of natural causes on the second floor of her locked townhome. Nobody warned us this lady had been a hoarder of cats—dozens of barbaric cats. Suffice it to say, when the Whiskas supply had run out, the swarming kitties decided their allegiance to Grandma had expired, like her. Bits of the poor woman where strewn everywhere, left to bake in a tri-story oven with a busted air conditioner. The odor that meandered out of McCaffrey's old house was like that, only with the musty tinge of woods and wetness.

As a breeze streamed through the property, the smell pushed out and became stronger, so thick it deposited a sour taste on my lips. And though I wanted badly to step inside, my inner coward won over, and I walked back to the road. *The dogs*, I told myself, in my head. *All these free-roaming dogs have gathered dead shit and put it in the house. That's all. Forest carcasses. Possums and raccoons and rabbits. Nothing else. Don't go back to that house. Don't go back, man. OK, fine. Go back. Be careful. Maybe after the boy's funeral tomorrow, swing by and have a peek. Bring Squeaky for protection. He's nuts. He's fearless. His ass'll go in.*

CHAPTER 14

The scene back at my Victorian wasn't as painful as I'd anticipated. The broadcast news teams must have had their police scanners turned off for the evening, because nobody was there but the big sergeant, a crime scene documentarian, the two zoo people, and what looked like a disheveled chemistry professor. The sergeant, doing his job, asked me exactly one question: "From the beginning, what happened, sir?" He took minimal notes in his little flip pad as I rambled about my brush with death. I was stressing details that might bolster a lawsuit against the zoo, which, I feared, I'd have to rely on for sustenance soon. I loathed the idea of being the bitchy lawsuit type, but I detested even more the prospects of pulling from unemployment. I'd never gotten around to filling out Social Security paperwork, and I frankly wasn't sure that I qualified yet.

The sergeant jotted a few words, a couple of high points, and memorized the rest of my story for what would turn out to be an exceedingly thorough report. My phone rang, and it was Becky, telling me her reporters would be calling *me* for quotes about what horrible things had happened on my own porch.

"No comment."

"Real funny, Johnson," she said.

"No comments," I amended, "unless I'm writing them."

"Forget it," she said. "No way. Look, I'm sorry. We go way back. But I know for a fact the higher-ups won't let me give you a job. Word travels fast around these offices. Especially when a known contributor does something so colossally stupid as your press conference stunt. And besides, I'm still mad at you, too."

"Please take me back."

"You sound pathetic, Johnson," she said. "Like a hungry little cat. *Mwwrrowwm-mrrwoww.*" Whooshing background sounds intensified. It was wind, and an engine. She was driving, perhaps back to the office, at night. "You know, we're not the only publication left in the world," she said. "You still have name recognition in this market and beyond. Maybe you should quit whimpering and use it."

"This feels like a breakup, like middle school," I said. "Or like a divorce—" I tried to wrangle in the last syllable of that word, to obscure the meaning, to blunt the barb of it. But it had leapt from my mouth and deeply stabbed.

"Very classy, asshole."

"A million apologies, Beck—an accident," I said. "I'm sorry, really. But everything else aside, on a personal level, I hope the proceedings went well in court today. And I mean that."

"Don't go there, God. Not now."

"I apologize."

She paused for a sincere, contemplative quarter-second. "On a personal level, from me to you, I'm happy you weren't killed by a snake this evening. I can't imagine. I just wish you wouldn't have shown up cross-eyed to that presser, because this all sounds like a terribly wonderful story..."

Becky droned on for a while, and though what she said was crucial for my livelihood, I couldn't pay attention; I'd seen Americana Mama being driven past my home in a long, black SUV. In the back seat behind the driver, the mourning mother's face was hanging pale and emotionless, drained of her vitality and fierceness. I muttered something to Becky about keeping her chin up and calling her at work tomorrow as I shuffled out through my gate, past the zoo response vehicles, and straight toward the house of grieving. When unkempt bushes presented obstacles in the sidewalk—doubtless the result of homeowners being too spooked to trim them this summer—I walked down the middle of my street, just like most Legacy Owners still do, for what reason I was never quite sure. Squeaky does it, too, and he blames it on habit, from decades of living with sidewalks so neglected by the city they could trip a man at night.

All the occupants of the big black car emptied out, gathered bags, clothes, and food trays, and filed into Americana Mama's home. Only she stayed inside. Everything about the house, the vehicle, the mood, was even darker than I was prepared for. I needed to know how she was holding up, and what time the funeral had been scheduled, a fact withheld in online news reports.

I rapt on the car window too loudly, which would have startled anyone under normal circumstances. She, however, was stoic, or maybe catatonic. She eyed me briefly and looked back down. Still frazzled, I stood on the truck's running boards to keep my ankles out of the grass. I fashioned a goofy smile and sniffled to make introductory noise.

"I just wanted to say, again, that this is a travesty," I said. "How are you holding up, Shirley?"

In the amber glow of streetlights, I could see her lips were flaky and cracked, likely from screaming. Her haunted, hollow face was that of someone who could not sleep. The straight black hair was tangled, more unkempt than I'd seen before, even during her sweaty, militant summer jogs through Sweetberry. The blank eyes bounced around, as if looking for invisible clues, answers to riddles that didn't exist.

"*What?*" she said sharply. "I'm sorry, but come again?"

"It's me, God Johnson, from down the street."

"Oh," is all she said.

"There anything I can do for you?"

"I'm so sick of people asking that."

"I didn't mean to—"

"Do I look *helpless* now? Like I can't do anything for myself?"

"Absolutely not, ma'am."

"It's starting to piss me off, you people," she said, her voice croaky now. "People aren't asking me, 'How are you?' They're saying, 'You OK?' Or, 'You gonna be alright?' How long will I have to put up with this? A year? Two? All my life? It's aggravating. It's bullshit."

"Believe me, I know."

"It's horrible, really." In the darkness I could see her cheeks tremble. "It's like salt in this bleeding wound, one that won't ever come close to healing. That's obvious to me, already. I might look pathetic now, but I won't let this destroy me."

"You're amazing," I said.

"Excuse me?"

"Listen, I lost my little boy in the eighties. And I didn't talk as strong as you until the nineties."

She glanced up, with the slightest glint of sympathy. "I think I remember reading that," she said. "Sorry to hear it out loud."

"I'll get goin'," I said. "I just wanted you to know that it's possible to overcome, to live with this. It's a scorched road ahead, but it's passable. Give a shout if I can help you get by."

She gave me a quick examination, from chest to eyes, and I had the feeling I'd been verified as an ally again. "Can you convict the asshole who murdered my boy? That would help me. That'd put me at ease."

I reached both hands into the window and gently, warmly squeezed one of her palms. Her hand was hard, like a hand that didn't waste time, a hand that got its way. "I'm just so sorry," is all I could say. "That boy was a light. He really was."

She tossed my hand back out of the window. Her pupils were like toggle switches, controlled by a brain wracked with distress chemicals, with torturous, excessive thinking. "I can't set foot back in that house," she said. "Never will again."

"Can't blame you."

"There's just ghosts in there now," she said.

"I know."

"Ghosts of where he isn't, where we aren't."

"I know."

"You know what I *don't* know?" she said.

I hunched my shoulders.

"I don't know why I moved here exactly. I really don't."

With that, I caught the familiar stench of self-blame. "It's a good place," I said. "A strong community, even still."

"It has soul," she said. "It's real, I guess. Not a damn dull moment."

"It's interesting. It's beautiful. It happened slowly, and you can't replicate that."

"But it's not us."

"Excuse me?"

"Not ours."

"OK," I said. "But who's 'ours'?"

"*Ours.*"

"You mean White folks?"

"No, idiot," she snapped. "My husband and me. Us. The parents. The people who brought our kids down here. We had it fine, out in Cobb County. The grass is greener, though, you know. Everybody's doing it, moving intown. But deep down, I guess, we aren't city people. We're posers. We don't belong."

"You wanna know what I've learned," I said, "after thirty years around here?" She nodded. "Sweetberry belongs to everyone right now and nobody forever," I said. "The only consistent winner is the goddamn highest bidder."

She was straining, I could tell, to not physically lash out. "They finally tracked down David on his Honduran mission trip," she said, referring to her husband. "He was extolling Christ to the locals when they told him Joey, his youngest son, had died from a gunshot to the chest. Of all damn things. How's *that* for God's work?"

We went silent, numb, stunned by the galling shittiness of her predicament. "How is he?" I asked. "Holding up?"

"We'll see. He lands tomorrow morning, a few hours before the funeral."

"About the funeral—"

"*Look* at that house," she erupted, apropos of nothing. "Look at that giant, silly fucking house!"

"Calm down, Shirley."

"We were so misguided. We're so lost."

"It's OK."

"What were we thinking, coming here?"

"It's OK. Just take it easy."

"We were trying to be cooler than we are, I guess." She was rocking now, incognizant of me, all but talking to herself and the back of the black-leather seat. "I was trying to prove my prim-and-proper, Old South mother wrong. She thinks all cities are hellholes. She wants me living at the edge of a golf course, hosting social functions for the PTA—"

With that she squeezed her left hand into a tremoring fist, then the right, and she exploded into a fit of screams and spit, unloading a flurry of punches that rattled the driver's seat. I flung open the door and endured a few punches to my forearm and wrist as I reached in and fell across her, squeezing her arms still like a human straightjacket. We stayed in this weird position until she assured me she'd calmed down, that what needed purging had come out.

"Now," I said, closing the door again. "Listen to me: Don't go pinning any blame on yourself, or your husband. That's nonsense. You hear me, Shirley? We've poked fun at you before, sure. But Sweetberry Park is all the better because of y'all—"

"We're selling the house," she cut in, and her face crinkled with the prospects of that, of dropping her rebellious dreams of intown family-rearing, I suppose. "We can't be here."

"That's understandable."

"I hate to lose."

"I can tell."

"But I can't take it."

"Where to next?"

"Back to the suburbs," she said. "I can prosecute out in the east without even leaving the county. In fact, I can avoid this part of the city entirely. I doubt I'll ever be able to drive down this street again."

My legs straining, I stepped down off the truck, the biters be damned. "I'm sorry to hear," I said. "But I've got something to tell you that might brighten your night, just a bit."

She said nothing. She watched her big house.

"You wanna hear?"

She leaned to the window, and I thought of a starved, lonely prisoner, taking in moonlight. She needed uplifting, something to look forward to. For a moment, she focused on my face. And she was curious.

"Genteel Briggs, the legendary blues singer who lives down in The Flank," I said. "She wants to come out of retirement, so to speak, and sing something poignant at Joey's funeral tomorrow. A way to honor him. The whole thing's got her pretty shook up, too. She was there, in the church basement. She wanted me to ask your permission."

Shirley leaned back into her seat and closed her eyes, as if savoring some sweet taste. "It's five p.m., at Modern Day First Baptist, down the street, on the other side of Sweetberry," she said. "And oh, God, I can't think of a better send-off than that."

An hour before the funeral, I hustled up to Genteel's porch in my lone black suit. She opened the door in an extravagant black gown, dotted with a constellation of faux pearls and frilly seams and these butter-colored streamers that glistened down the back. Her earrings were chunky, glitzy cornucopias, and her makeup was so thick and optimistic it made her cheeks pink and eyelids rainbowed. It looked as if she'd teleported from a 1920s Oscars after-party. She exuded confidence. She was show business again.

Genteel grabbed my cheeks, like a concerned mother, analyzing the clarity of my eyes. "Glad to see you in one piece." The jubilant almonds of her own eyes narrowed with worry. "I read the morning's paper. You got any bite holes in them legs?"

"If I did," I said, "I'd be swelled up like a raft, and probably dead."

She let go of my face and shivered in her gown. "I ain't stepped outside today, and I don't plan to go out alone all summer," she said. "The paper say you got that snake good on your porch, put him down. That right?"

"It's gone."

"How many left?"

"Let's not worry about that now," I said. "Are you ready for this?"

"And why you ain't write the story?" she said. "It happened right at your feet, and some lady name on top of *your* story?"

"Don't worry about that now either," I said. "Come on, get in the truck. Let's get this over with."

Arriving at Modern Day First Baptist—a long flat rectangle of a structure that'd been a Buick showroom in Sweetberry's pre-White flight, monocultural era—I chuckled in remembering the controversy surrounding its founding three years ago. Traditionalist-to-the-nines Baptists and officials from the African Methodist Episcopal Church, the two rulers of the eastside's religious turf, were united in their distaste for the very concept of Modern Day First Baptist. From the beginning, they decried it as a *sacrilegious church*. It was to be a hip, intown, borderline-secular cathedral geared toward younger Atlantans with stronger allegiances to Apple Products than Christ Almighty. It would have Wi-Fi, an organic juice bar, and a vast succulent garden in the bay formerly used for oil changes. Top-flight architects from a downtown firm transformed the old showroom into a towering space with walls of trendy ipe wood and slits of glowing skylights in the ceiling, with modernistic pine pews beneath a dangling forest of luminescent, energy-efficient crosses. Up front, Jesus suffered on a crucifix less like a wooden cross than some metallic Krypton installation. It was all enough to make Genteel clasp her clavicle, fan her face, and declare in the entryway, "Woo, *where* have I come?"

At the front I could see the little white casket. It was topped on one side with a spray of red roses, and it nearly sent me face-first into the stained concrete. Genteel latched ahold of my elbow and pulled me over to the first available seat, farthest from the front. I tried to not look, but I did; I saw two small hands up there, folded atop what looked like a tuxedo jacket, black with playful white trim.

"I'm-a go up and pray for the boy," said Genteel, dabbing her forehead with the back of her hand. "You?"

"Afraid not."

"Understood," she said. "Anything you want me to tell him?"

I snatched a program off the seat as a distraction, to avert my attention from the room's heaviness. "Tell him 'sorry,' I suppose."

She nodded and ushered herself ahead.

"Hey, Genteel," I whispered loudly. "The program says you're going first. The song isn't listed. In case anyone asks, while you're gone, what should I say to expect?"

"Tell 'em an original."

"Your original got a name?"

"Song about a boy," and she frowned. "It don't have a name yet."

She shuffled ahead, and I glanced at all the floral arrangements flanking the casket. All were modest, except the explosion of lilies, tulips, roses, and pageantry banners at far right. I could read the huge condolence card from where I sat, and it clearly said "LOTTO" in writing meant to make a statement. The developer who'd triggered all of this had sent an ostentatious showpiece but lacked the decency to actually show up.

Up front, in a black hat, was Shirley, staring ahead with the same shocked detachment as the previous night. I watched Genteel approach her in the receiving line, both of Genteel's white-gloved hands with a handkerchief at the ready. The women noticed each other, maybe five feet between them, but Shirley merely nodded, maybe smiled just a hint, as a redheaded man to her left patted her back. The miserable procession lurched on. Some took seeing the boy worse than others. A few guys nodded and walked away. An elderly woman wailed. Little girls in fanciful Easter dresses came in a side door, saying nothing but looking stunned and confused by the odd spirit of the place. When Genteel reached the casket, she looked back to Shirley, and I heard her asking in her deep voice, "May I?" before leaning over Joey's body and placing something down beside him. I scanned the crowd for the face of Squeaky, Carlito, or any other neighborhood friend, someone who might offer a smile or lifeline back to normalcy; but there was only the crushed expressions of strangers who'd rather be anywhere else. I'd seen it too many times before, in life and work. A child's funeral. The worst possible reason for coming together.

The church's pastor, who was maybe thirty with a clean-shaven head and lush black beard, slowly took the stage above the casket, signaling for the spoken ceremonies to begin. I recalled my own speech in a room with this heavy air, three decades prior. I walked numb and hungover to a podium with nothing prepared, instead riffing for about five minutes on how fortunate I was to have had them for a while, to have nurtured Wyatt up from a wallowing infant to a wild and wonderful boy, to have enjoyed a sunset horseback ride in Puerto Rico on my weeklong honeymoon, to have lived completely without even knowing it at the time. Genteel hustled back and plopped beside me in the pew, smelling of perspiration and fruity chewing gum. "Woo, this gonna be rough," she quietly said to me. "Rough, baby. *Rough*."

"You'll do great," I said. "You always do. Calm down."

"Honest, now, this rattlin' me. All-a this," she said, flicking her wrist to indicate the entirety of the proceedings. "That baby never caught a break in his life, and now he gone. He look so peaceful. So still."

"What'd you put in there?" I said.

She said nothing.

"In the casket, I mean?"

Her face, serious and sweating, turned to me. "Between me, the boy, and his momma."

As the last standing man went down, the pastor boomed a greeting from the pulpit microphone. He had either known Joey well, or he'd done his homework. He launched into a detailed narrative that painted the boy as a luminous, caring spirit unmarred by the ravages of muscular dystrophy. Joey, turns out, had adored the painter Bob Ross on television as a toddler. He devoured all broccoli and collard greens. He liked Georgia football best, and he could paint sunsets with his toes. In moving from the suburbs, Joey had reacted well, as the pastor put it, "To the embracing spirit and ceaseless stimuli of our city, to the smell of corn dogs at the Varsity, and the brisk autumn air in Reynolds Park. His curiosity was even piqued by the occasional—how should I put this—um, *night sounds* that still go pop, pop, pop around here." That zinger got a laugh. In church.

As the laughter ebbed, the pastor saw his chance to detour into the discomforting climax of his sermon. In a deep, loud way that sounded like a revelation, he said: "A child, it can seem to us now, is not meant to die, because a child has not sufficiently lived." And he tiptoed around the bizarre social circumstances: "At points, throughout the history of man, time and time again, people of different backgrounds and ways have encountered turbulence when they became new neighbors. Our lives in modern Atlanta are no different. Our differences are no different. Our discomfort with the unknown is also no different. Sometimes, in the newness of our lives with each other, mistakes can happen. Sometimes the mistakes are irreversible. Sometimes human nature can be ugly, even if accidentally so." A few moments later, he wrapped up with convincing assurances that Joey was a first-ballot Pearly Gates entrant, because Jesus Himself had said, as the pastor relayed: "'Let the little children come to me, and do not hinder them, for the kingdom of heaven belongs to such as these.'"

The pastor then called Genteel to the front. He introduced her as "terrific" and "world famous" and "as integral to Sweetberry Park as the tallest, shade-casting oaks." He'd done his homework on her, too.

Genteel was praying so hard she didn't hear, breathing so big I feared she might hyperventilate. I nudged her, and toward the pulpit she went, lumbering and apprehensive, humming all the while.

As she went up the stairs, Genteel's pearls caught the natural light that poured in from so many modernistic ceiling slits, and she looked absolutely regal. She nodded and winked down to Shirley, who'd snapped out of her daze. Shirley scooted to the edge of her pew and intently watched Genteel.

After gulping half a glass of water, Genteel peeled a microphone off a stand and cleared her throat a few times. It dawned on me then that there'd be no band arrangement to accompany her, and no backing track of a song she'd implied had not yet been recorded. The show would be her voice alone, naked amongst soft acoustics. *Perfect*, I thought.

Instead of singing, however, Genteel just kept gulping. She reached for a sip of water, and when that went down, she gulped saliva again and again. Her eyes scanned the rows of pews, the windows, the casket, and back to the rows, as if looking for some lost jewel from afar. After that, the poor woman froze in place, shutting down. The entire congregation followed suit, even the children, out of respectful concern. It was the quietest, weirdest silence. A long painful nothing. I tried to catch her attention by waving my head, shaking my silver hair in what I hoped was a mood-lightening way, but it didn't work. Genteel exhaled and dropped her shoulders, moving at long last. She turned off the mic, gingerly placed it atop the lectern, and said down to Shirley, "Ma'am, I am just so sorry," before stomping out the side-stage exit faster than I'd ever seen her move.

Shirley's head collapsed into her hands as she leaned over impossibly far—and then she fell onto the polished concrete. The crowd in the front shot upright; they surged toward the mourning mother in a way that reminded me of the shooting scene. It was chaos, all over again. I hustled to a side aisle and went to the front to help, but as I neared the casket, I felt a sickening sort of hot-stove trigger that pushed me away. I went up the stairs at stage left, aiming for the exit Genteel had taken in hopes of finding her. The pastor nearly knocked me over, rushing to the crowd with a big cup of ice water. Three men were hoisting Shirley, the headstrong prosecutor so worried about seeming weak, back to her seat. Her pale face was staring beyond the lectern, beyond the stained glass and clouds, to somewhere a thousand miles away. I knew then, somehow, it would be the last time I'd ever see her in Sweetberry Park, and it was. As I went through the exit, splashing the stage in the sunshine of a waning summer afternoon, I nodded to the casket—a cowardly, pathetic gesture, maybe, but the best I could muster at the time.

Genteel was sitting straight-legged beneath a crepe myrtle, which was itching to burst purple in flowering summer phases. She looked like she was ready to explode, too. She quivered and hummed and rolled her shoulders.

"You OK out here?" I said.

A blank expression, a strange humming from the ground.

"No shame in that," I said. "There ain't a soul in there who's mad at you, or who doesn't understand. You know that, right?"

The blankness became anger. "*Understand?* Ain't nobody in there understand!"

I took a knee, and the wet grass soaked right through my suit to the skin. At this angle, in the sun, Genteel looked unnervingly old and tired. "What happened?" I said.

Her face softened. "I look out in that crowd," she said, "and I don't know nobody."

"It's OK," I said. "All strangers to me, too."

"No, *listen*," she shot back. "You always askin' why I don't leave the house. That's why. I don't know nobody. This's my neighborhood, but ain't my *community*. Just ain't. Them times is gone. And it all just hit me, up on that stage, at the worst time. I nearly about fainted in there. And I let that boy down—"

"Come on," I said, lifting her up by the hand. "You're sweating bullets. Let's get you some air. Let's drive a while. The truck's AC is shot, but the wind'll do you good."

We whipped west out of the parking lot, and I tried to drive close to the curb, to keep a panting, elderly woman in the shade of the huge sidewalk maples I'd helped plant as saplings. The streets were curiously devoid of pedestrians for a sunny afternoon, albeit it a boiler. Clearly, news of my harrowing snake fight had spread across Sweetberry, reaching each unpeopled porch.

We rounded a corner, and Genteel started giggling, pointing ahead. "*Look* at that fool," she said. "We got us a real Hank Aaron right here."

Besides motorists, the lone person outdoors in Sweetberry Park was a devout jogger carrying a peewee, wooden base-ball bat. It goes without saying that he was White, but it was difficult to tell because he was so thoroughly furry. His wolfman shoulders shuffled beyond a camouflage tank top, which matched his ultra-snug running shorts. The hairy bottoms of his lower buttocks flashed tragically beneath the shorts with each stride. He seemed proud to simply be outside of his house, a rebel in defiance of the reptiles. And with the bat pumping, he stuck precisely to the middle of the street, a few yards from the high, ordinance-violating grasses. "Can you imagine," I said, "if he tried to club an anaconda with a kiddie bat like that?"

"Anna-*who*?"

"Oh, nothin'."

She tossed her head indignantly and clammed up, folding her arms. "It's different this time," she said. "Just *look*! This district really comin' apart, just unfurlin' to awful. Ain't it?"

"You think it's a sort of reckoning for Sweetberry?" I said. "Is this all just a lesson—a weird crucible—for what's happening in our cities right now?"

"Nope."

"You don't believe in that?"

"Nope."

"Sorry," I said. "Didn't mean to scare you with Biblical talk or whatnot."

"What I think is, it's just a natural friction, that's all," Genteel said, sweetly. "Human nature. I think we'll overcome, get through. This here'll pass."

"Why would you care, right?" I said. "You'll be gone, counting your money—"

"Fool, *shush*."

"I'm right, and you know it."

"Look here," she said. "None of this would-a happened, if not for you and these people 'round here you always makin' fun of."

"Whoa, lady," I said. "I thought you welcomed all."

"I *do*." She poked her head out the window, to blow back the sweat. "I'm just statin' facts, bare and simple."

"And I thought you considered me funny?"

"Honey, you got a smart mouth sometimes," she said. "Might try lookin' in a mirror."

"It's just sarcasm," I said. "A way of deflecting pain, I guess."

"It's insensitive."

"Oh, please," I said. "People are people. I don't hate 'em. I don't hate anybody, really, with one exception—"

"You too full-a salt," Genteel cut in. "You swap that salt with sugar, with love, and you'll live a better life. Be somebody by givin' yourself back, like I did with all these kids around here. Sacrifice somethin' to lift up the community. That's how you live full."

Keen advice, but it stung for some reason, as hard new truths tend to do. "Look, ma'am, I've got my reasons for saltiness."

"Nope," she said. "No excuses. Spit out that salt!"

"And besides," I said, "I make fun of myself most of all. Nobody thinks less of me than me."

"Just drive, honey," said Genteel, tossing her fancy glove into my chest. "Just drive."

I rounded the blocks aimlessly for a while to keep the wind going, but I got Genteel home in maybe fifteen minutes total, enough to put the funeral collapse mentally behind us, I thought. I parked in front her bungalow, and I didn't know what else to say. I wanted to joke about that dangerous reptile sanctuary of rose bushes by her mailbox but frankly lacked the energy.

"I could be wrong," she said, opening the passenger door, "but I ain't see that developer in there at the viewin'. Shame on him."

"He sent flowers," I said. "That's for sure."

"They was nice now—"

"Lotto caused this," I said. "He caused a stir that got a boy killed and landed a young, innocent man in jail, likely bound for prison. Lotto not being there in person speaks volumes about him."

Before I could hop out and assist her, Genteel had helped herself out of the truck, bunching up her dress and rapidly straightening it back into place. Proper again, she peeked beneath the truck and scanned the lower branches of a leaning cherry tree. "Somethin' you should know about him," she said. "Mr. Lotto, I mean."

"What now?" I said. "He running a cock-fighting ring behind the gas station?"

"Nope," she said flatly, without getting the joke, because that used to be a real possibility. "He gave us some money."

"Excuse me?"

"Everyone here in The Flank, we just got paid."

"*Excuse* me?"

"In a envelope. Last week. All cash. He called it a 'advance.'"

I clutched my temples. "*What?*" I said. "That's not an advance—that's a damn *bribe!*"

"OK."

"And before a developer closes on real estate, I'm pretty sure it's illegal."

"Really?"

"So is that where you got this fancy dress then?"

"Maybe."

I took a moment to breathe, to lift my bundled suit jacket off the seat beside me and drag it across my wet head. "I can tell you want me to ask, so I will," I said, smiling now. "Where, Genteel, is the money Lotto gave you?"

"Beside the boy, in that coffin, where it belong!"

"*What?*"

"Yep," she said. "Gone!"

"So, ma'am, look: You just gave your money to a pretty wealthy family—"

"Nope, to the Lord!" she said. "As penance for this summer!"

Genteel slammed shut my door, neither waving goodbye nor dishing a simple thanks, as was her custom, and she went inside, locking up Shotgun Three. As I backed away, I glanced into her window. I could see her fanning herself on the couch, shaking her head, rocking side to side. She was trying to sing how she wanted to, how she used to, craning her neck to capture elusive octaves, but instead she was failing, thrashing, and then collapsing into a great sad slump of frilly colors and flesh, like a big sorrowful bird.

PART III

CHAPTER 15

If May was a heat wave, and June a dead, overheated horse, July unfurled across the city like thick, musty carpeting pulled from a flooded funeral home. Suffocating and tinged with death, the weather brought mass unpleasantness. It made your lungs hot to breathe it. It crept up your legs and sucked the sweat right out. A week after Independence Day, we tied the record high for Atlanta's high-temp misery two days in a row: one hundred and five degrees. A week later, it hit *one hundred and seven*, if only for a few dismal hours. They closed the frigid aquarium downtown to visitors in order to house sweltering elderly folks pulled from dilapidated apartments. The big blockbuster hotels welcomed the dying homeless into their lobbies, albeit grudgingly, for lemonade. Rumor had it the Municipal Parks Department was considering closing public pools because of the heat, at least the ones in old-money neighborhoods that were far enough from the snake zone to be open in the first place. Why close the swimming pools? Because kids on bikes kept passing out of heat blindness trying to get there.

Meanwhile, Squeaky and I finally found the time and cojones to organize a mission to McCaffrey's strange southside residence, and we set out determined, like two novice snake sleuths, despite the swelter. "Tell you what," said Squeaky, in my passenger seat, his loose face jiggling in highway wind. "No offense, but you caw-kay-zyin brothers never stop amazin' me. If you don't mind me classifyin' you like that, on account of your Greek-ness."

I was piloting Great White through a tangle of interstate ramps, driving south from downtown. "Call me whatever. But what do you mean?"

The eighteen-lane interstate was so hot in the noon-time sun I was seeing, I thought, the woozy vapors of a desert mirage rise off it. A couple of miles ahead, the minivans and semis had blurred into nonexistent water. Even while pelting us at seventy miles per hour through open windows, the wind was dense and unpleasant, almost tangibly wet. Squeaky was sweating in a Budweiser tank top and dabbing his face with a white towel, wetting the old, duct-taped cloth of my shotgun seat with his back perspiration. He didn't respond. Instead, he shook his head and rubbed the blade of his Samurai sword, polishing it with sweaty cloth.

"Don't get all vaguely racist on me, Squeaks," I said. "And don't get angry and mute either. I need you to stay focused for a mission like this. I need your concentration sharp, like lasers. So purge your head for ultimate focus. Air your grievances."

We passed the brick pillars of the Braves' stadium, which our beloved team had vacated two years before, relocating to a coliseum way out among the cushy cul-de-sacs and disposable income. "I mean, you know," Squeaky finally said, "anyone who watches the news know Black folks do some dumb shit, too." He slipped his sword, sufficiently smeared, back into its sheath. "I'd say the news focuses too much on the bad goings-on in the Black community, because it's easy news, but that's another story—"

"I hear you, but you're getting sidetracked, man. Come on."

We'd be at zookeeper McCaffrey's creepy house on a hill within fifteen minutes, beginning our impromptu and illegal investigation, and I was hoping to coax out a classic Squeaky rant to pass the time and calm our nerves. That morning I'd told him about the horrid smell I'd encountered on the property, and he all but paid me to bring him down there to South Fulton. The last few weeks, since my rendezvous with the fer-de-lance, Squeaky had been more reclusive than usual, hardly spending a minute on his trusted porch, and barely even leaving the house. I thought the man could use some fresh, safe, south suburban air, still fragranced by so many mature pines.

"Right, right, just gatherin' some thoughts," Squeaky finally said. "What I was sayin' was, I just mean that White folks, the way I see it, sometimes they—I mean, y'all—just like to make up problems out of boredom. They get frustrated with the sameness, I think. The sameness of day-to-day that we all put up with. Or they get tired of havin' success, of being spoiled. Because advantages is boring, too. Maybe that's it, yeah? I know there's exceptions, sure, like them poor-ass trailer park White people. And hippie Whites. But I mean, you know, generally, the world leans in they favor. Like the heavy favorite team in college football we all know gone win, and unfortunately that is too rarely them Geeoowwja Bulldogs. But anyway. You know. I just mean. Well, now, God, I ain't sayin' life is easy for nobody. Life ain't nothin' but an ocean of up and down. I'm eatin' cake one day and punched in the damn face the next. Now tell me, what in *the hail* was I talkin' about?"

"Were you working your way to the zookeeper?"

"Yessir, *that!*" he said. "Look, this a perfect case of caw-kay-zyin batty-shit craziness. The city's hummin' like it's the Olympics again. Economy's zoomin', everybody hirin', people gettin' raises. And damn if some mental-ass White boy in safari clothes don't gotta go ruin everything. Am I right?"

I could only nod. I was laughing so hard my belt buckle nearly cleaved out my appendix. South of the airport, we exited onto a forlorn state highway, a dazzling menagerie of taco shacks and Chinese buffets, muffler shops, title salvagers, check cashers, wooded trailer parks, 1950s fleabags, a sprawling Creole market, and the occasional Walmart. We'd entered the Diversifying Inner Suburbs where tens of thousands of lower-earning former city dwellers had been pushed, where hundreds of thousands of immigrants had landed, spooking the timid White-flight expeditioners of decades past farther into exurban hinterlands. It's the sort of place rigid Old South traditionalists might call corroding, or what hip sociology academics describe as culturally blossoming.

"With McCaffrey," I said, "I think you're right about the mental part. That could explain his motivation, as prosecutors say. Or he might just be starved for human attention, having been cooped up with animals forever."

In frustration, Squeaky pulled at his cheeks. "But, God, it's bigger than this one McCafé nut, *way* bigger." He was shouting, pointing toward the windshield. "It's like every time things is going well, that we're finally gettin' along in this country, in this city, everybody doin' their thing, somebody gotta come along and plant the poison. The same old thing, just beneath the surface, makin' us all uneasy. We all know it's there, that poison, but we can't see it. Or at least we think it's there. We need to think *somethin'* is there, some bad thing between us and bein' happy, or else we don't feel right. We get uptight, then we want a developer's blood, and next thing you know it's like hell revisited. I mean, before the boy, when was the last shooting in Sweetberry? Two years ago?"

I paused to consider the question. "It has been a while," I said. "I can't think of the last one, honestly. It's almost weird."

"Exactly," he said. "Now who you think dropped that gun in there, in the church? Walt, like they say?"

"No, not Walt. But maybe one of his allies."

"Then you think Walt'll get off on them charges?"

"I think he needs a miracle at this point."

Squeaky squeezed his hands into gray fists. "The injustice don't *end*."

We passed a gleaming new county jail, an octagonal tower of faux marble; maybe an omen, I thought, that trespassing today was unwise. I saw the right sign and turned down the winding road to McCaffrey's place.

"Man, damn it," Squeaky said. "We need to *do* something about Walt."

"But what?" I said. "Don't even say break him out. It never works in Fulton County."

"Naw, I mean something legal."

I leaned under the tinted strip of my windshield for a better view of the hills. I caught a glimpse of the collapsing hulk through the pines. We'd arrived. "You mean like a fundraiser? To get him some better legal rep? Something like that?"

"Yessir."

"Right on," I said. "But first things first. See that ugly thing on the hill up there? That's the house. Get ready."

At the mouth of the driveway, I parked Great White in the shade. I cracked open my door, with crusty camera in hand, but Squeaky didn't budge.

"You gettin' cold feet, Squeaks?" I said. "Come on, let's move."

"Man," he said, in a long whine.

"What now?"

"You ever get tired of your nickname?" he said. "Of always *goin' by* your nickname?"

I deflated. "How the hell is this relevant to the mission?" I said. "Stop thinking so much. I need you to act on impulse."

"I mean, look, we got, what, about ten good years left of livin'? That'd make me eighty, a decade tacked on to now. Damn, *eighty*! I forget; what about you?"

I'd erred by opening Squeaky's philosophical Pandora's box, and it was my duty, before such a mission, to gently ease it shut. "I'm a year younger. But I'm right there with you, getting flat-out elderly."

"Yep," he said. "It's a shame."

"Honestly," I said. "Yeah, sure, I think it sucks. I wish I had more time. I wish I had a grandchild running around. I wish I had some kids to look after me, to call me on my birthday. I don't have a solid plan in place, for anything. I'm on the verge of falling down completely. Total collapse. My retirement plan is to just pay the power bill on time and keep the walls from sagging with rain. It gets me down sometimes."

"It ain't gonna get better, God. It's just physically down the tube from here."

"You just gotta ride it out, man," I said. "Ride it out with class and dignity and great drugs."

"At least, though, you own your house outright. And I got prime intown land in my name."

"Exactly," I said. "That's the spirit."

"We kind of rich, really. When you think of the equities."

"Worse comes to worse," I said, "we can sell our lots in a weekend. And then, you know, enjoy dementia in dee-luxe retirement condos."

"Squeaky," he said, ignoring me.

"No," I said. "You're Squeaky."

"Exactly."

"What?"

"I am Squeaky. Always have been."

"This is like talkin' to a dog or something."

"Man, I'm gettin' to my point," he said. "All my life I've been Squeaky, since about age seven. And you know how?"

It took me a second to recall the basic, tragic story. "Because your bike with the banana seat was cheap, and it always squeaked?"

"Yes, and no," he snapped. "That's why they called me it. But what they *really* was sayin' is that I'm poor, poor, *poor*!"

Impulsively, I smacked my forehead. "Who cares?" I said. "Own it! Why are we talkin' about this now?"

"Because, if I don't make it back alive and you do," he said, without sarcasm, "you got to know where my heart was, who I really am—"

"Stop!" I said. "Just shut up. We ain't dying here today, buddy. We're armed!"

"I want to be known for somethin' more, somethin' better than a name, or being the village idiot," he said. "That's why I came today. That's why I'm here. I made senior petty officer rank in the Navy, long before that discharge. And I'm capable of doing my city proud, too. I am cape-uh-*bull*!"

I reached over to the passenger-side floorboard and snagged the Samurai sword. "Give me this," I said. "I'll go search the damn property alone."

By the time I'd charged fifty yards up the driveway, Squeaky was ahead of me, acting brave as William Wallace, reckless as Custer, cocky as Super Fly. He was walking with his chest puffed and arms flexed, in the way little boys do when imitating bodybuilders. Above him, a red pileated woodpecker put rapid-fire kisses on a hardwood, excavating a nesting hole, annoying us terrifically. Above the bird, the lush canopy of mature trees shielded us from the blaze. We came to the weird old house. The forest stood quiet, save the occasional rustle of leaves, pushed by a breath of breeze. As we crept into the home's jagged shadows, all went silent.

The collapsing geometry of McCaffrey's residence made Squeaky scratch his head and squint, as if he didn't believe two of his senses. "All my years, I ain't ever seen a home like this," he said, awed. "Jeee-zus, it ugly!"

I moved in closer and squatted, looking inside. "I did some digging on McCaffrey," I said. "He's a complex dude, really. Comes from a rich family that owns a few Dixons Home Improvement stores. He kept rental properties across town, but I'm guessing he built this himself, hopefully not sober."

"I don't smell nothing."

"Just wait," I said. "Let's get in closer."

"I'll be here."

"No, no," I said.

"Give me that sword back, then."

"Fine."

I obliged, and we crept low. From the front, it appeared to me the home's roof—pointed in places, flat in others—had caved a bit more than before. Its cracked plywood pointed down like teeth. Inside were chaise lounges, a toppled armoire, and what appeared to be genuine, high-end midcentury furniture, all sullied with grime, mold, and what looked like deer crap. I squinted through a mud-flecked window and saw the towering nightmare of a stuffed, standing black bear in full snarling attack mode. Its massive, hugging arms were clawing at nonexistent prey.

"What the hell kind of zoo employee keeps taxidermy in his house?" I said, but Squeaky wasn't listening. "Amazing this place hasn't been looted, man. Seriously. Maybe the locals know something and keep their distance?"

I pulled away from the window and found Squeaky lost in Samurai warrior daydreams, working the sword like an oversize paintbrush. I pinched his butt in jest, immediately purging any macho battlefield delusions. He was threatening to cut my head off as we went around the back and spotted a large, rectangular contraption made of steel, half-covered by leaves and branches.

"The hell?" said Squeaky.

"Looks like, I think, a bomb shelter or something."

Behind us, a rustling in a long thicket of rhododendron sent Squeaky upright. "Man, where you *bring* me?" he said. "We ain't solving no case out here. We gonna end up raped."

I kicked off the natural camouflage and unveiled what appeared to be an industrial-grade cellar door, with an immense lock around the handles. I snapped my fingers in aw-shucks frustration, knowing full well there's no chance I'd go down there if we happened to find the keys. "Now that's locked," I said. "Come on, let's get a look inside."

The home's curving backside was a tall stack of calico river stone, the good kind I could never afford for my walkway. We followed it back to a towering glass door that, I thought, had been open on my last visit. I grabbed the long handle; it was unlocked.

"You ready?"

I leaned back and yanked, and the big door fanned open, enveloping us both in a massive belch of sweltering, rancid air. Squeaky jumped away, bent over, and gagged.

"I told you, man," I said, shirt over my nostrils. "Now is that suspicious or what?"

He composed himself, stood up. "It smell like a sewer. In a microwave. With old fish and chicken asses tossed in."

"It's the smell of death," I said, through my shirt. "Big death. I know that odor from the police beat."

"And roadkill," he said. "That too."

"Let's get this over with."

Squeaky slipped off his beer-ad tank top, wrapped it around his lower head like some kind of anarchist, and went shirtless and sweaty toward the unknown, the sword cocked sideways in front of him at arm's length. On his back he sported a jailhouse tattoo: a squirrel in Wayfarer sunglasses holding his grotesquely massive testicles, beneath a speech bubble that said, simply, "Nutty as fuck." Trying to ignore the crude rodent, but pondering whether it was gifted or cursed, I reached out and nudged Squeaky to move beyond the door's threshold, inside. We cautiously entered and stepped lightly on the filthy shag carpet, breathing through our mouths. The stench was so pronounced, the home so hot, my eyes began to weep. Then Squeaky saw the towering stuffed bear, screamed, and swung on the beast with the sword, sending half a paw flying against the brick hearth.

"Thought I mentioned the bear," I said, suppressing laughter. "Sorry about that."

"You said *taxidermy*. I'm thinkin' quail or beaver. Be more goddamn specific!"

I motioned for Squeaky to quickly follow me up the stairs, so that we might search the second story. Those plans faltered when the third step—rain-soaked and muddled with leaves—cracked beneath my foot. I had the distressing feeling that the roof might give in, too, rendering us trapped. I made a beelining for the glass doorway when Squeaky shouted, "Wait, man, there!" He pointed to a door near the kitchen we hadn't yet noticed. Twisting the knob, I opened the door slowly—and was nearly overtaken by the Kraken of household odors, the smell like a vast sulfuric lake, bobbing with whale cadavers, bursting with bull farts.

The door was the entryway to the basement, but the wooden, ladder-style stairs leading down there lay in a dozen pieces, nine feet below us, fallen or chopped to pieces. An impossible distance, with no discernible route of return. I looked at Squeaky. His eyes were coherent but huge and tearing.

"Let's get outta here!" I said, and we fled.

Traumatized and silent we drove away, drinking in the truck's lukewarm ventilation. "Just please get me home," Squeaky said in a sad, small voice.

I was ten miles up the interstate before another word eked from either of us. "I don't really want to talk to 'em, and by that I mean not at all," Squeaky said. "But should we call the police? About that house, I mean?"

"I'm sure they've been there," I said.

"You think?"

"I could call, though, with an update about the stench," I said. "I doubt they would have left that alone, if they'd encountered it. But I've got more important calls to make, like to my boss."

"You mean the one who's single now? The one who's *available*?"

"I mean the one who cuts checks that pay for groceries," I said. "She's mad at me and won't sic me on any stories. And, man, I'm getting desperate. Been eating rice."

"Rice?"

"Yep."

"Just rice?"

"Mustard rice."

"Man, *what*?"

"Not the most nutritious, but not bad," I said. "Beats ketchup rice. Mayonnaise rice was just an insult to—"

"Man, you need *food*?" Squeaky cut in. "Navy don't pay much, but I ain't eatin' damn condiments."

The honor in that sentiment nudged something in my chest. I reached over and punched Squeaky's shoulder in a playful, brotherly way. "I have some money, except it's just enough—almost—for a new roof," I said. "But yeah, I might have to dip into that stash before long."

"Go on den," Squeaky said, pointing to my pocket. "Call that boss. Them idiots can't keep God *Johnson* on the bench for long." He flexed his arms and mimed typing, a superhero journalist riding shotgun.

"Thanks for that," I said. "I'm real low on confidence right now."

I called, and Becky answered on the fourth ring, slacking.

"Can I have some work now?" I said, over the wind. "I promised to call today, and you promised to listen."

"Can you be here within the hour?" she said, in a low voice.

"The *office*? In person?"

"Hell, no," she said. "At that Jamaican coffee shop, across the street. Be there, before two thirty, if you want what I have in mind. And you will want what I have in mind."

Becky hung up before I could utter the first half-question. But the inspired sternness of her directive excited me enough that I boogied a bit behind the steering wheel, like Lionel Richie in his technicolor street as the party unfurled. My stomach growled, excited. I bounced my arms and hips in arhythmical glee.

"Love it," said Squeaky, still flexing and typing on the wind. "Somebody gettin' chicken with that rice. Somebody back in the game!"

CHAPTER 16

I weaved through the early gridlock sludge to make Becky's deadline for the crucial meeting. I found her leaning against a wall toward the back of the Jamaican joint, in slits of shade cast by an open blind. She was sipping a ginger beer, looking all business. My face and forearms were dripping, but I ordered a black coffee anyway, because it was cheap, though I feared the caffeine could make me sick. Becky looked up with mean, tight eyes that instantly softened.

"Oh," she said, "you look like hell."

"Good to see you, too."

"Forgive my bluntness," she smiled. "Haven't seen you this ragged in years."

I was caught for a moment in the spectacular grayness of her eyes, a color like the unfurling edge of an August thunderstorm. In direct sun her eyes were ethereal and wild, punctuated by a bob of blonde knots up top. She gave a firm shake with her perpetually calloused hands. She tried to refasten the armor of her business demeanor. But through the cracks and rivets I could see how Becky was truly feeling: shaken, lopped off, worried, alone.

"It's been an interesting morning," I said, taking a seat in the full shade.

"How so?"

"It just has."

"How *so*?"

"Let's just say that my legwork into this McCaffrey character could be paying dividends."

Immediately the interest drained from Becky's face. She took a slug of ginger beer without wincing and slammed the can on the table, like some kind of Viking.

"Anything about McCaffrey is back burner stuff now, the way I see it," she said. "There are way more pressing topics." A thought jogged loose in her brain, and she perked up, deploying her aha epiphany face. "Speaking of," she said, "did you see the piece Quinton Delano did on the boy's funeral? It was so poignant, so sharp."

Quinton Delano? Really? That sentimental hack? Somehow, years ago, he'd weaseled into a biweekly column called, generically, "Atlanta: My City. My Take." He'd written nothing but purple melodrama since. And now Becky was saying he'd struck narrative gold with funeral coverage? In *my* neighborhood? Was she spoon-feeding me the ashes of what I'd almost been? Was she trying to motivate me to be better? Had my insecurities and utter jealously warped my thoughts? Was I falling in love with editor Becky or just starving?

"That sounds enthralling," I said. "So did I tell you I wrote a book?"

"A book?"

"Yes, ma'am."

"Wow. That's commitment," and she slapped her knee in overblown enthusiasm. "What's it about, Johnson?"

"OK. I didn't write a book."

Becky smirked, victorious. "That sounds more like it."

I could never love her.

"Anyway," she said, "we're lacking coverage on two very specific angles, both associated with this summer's civic mess. Namely in your beloved Sweetberry Park."

"I've noticed," I said, though I'd been too busy not dying and conducting stupid investigations to have read the newspaper lately.

"We've devised a game plan, to a degree," she said. "But nobody else in this city has your connections, with the right sources."

"All ears," I said, "and empty stomach."

"OK, first," she said, quieting her voice. "We need more on this Tall Walt suspect, pronto. His family isn't returning calls. His church won't let us in. And nothing fumbles from the mouth of his dipshit public defender but boilerplate nonsense. *Who* is Walt? *Why* was he so passionate about this Sweetberry Flank cause? And maybe I'm being a tad hyperbolic, but isn't he emblematic of a rush toward justice on the part of these overzealous cops? We're talking about an entire department that hasn't managed to capture a single goddamn snake alive. Hell, God freakin' Johnson has done more to rectify the zoo situation than all of APD. And yet they think they're so smart. They're convinced they have a slam dunk case against a guy like Walt—but why? The court's denying him bond, and I haven't heard a shred of real fact that ties Walt to the killing of that poor boy. Gunpowder residue on his fingers? *Please.* You can't tell me a Morehouse Man like Walt wouldn't have the sense to bleach his damn hands if he dropped a murder weapon in church. It's bullshit. And it's like the tragedies keep mounting—"

"I have an inroad," I said.

"Seriously?" She rose slightly from her chair, perking up. "Who?"

"I know a guy." I tried not to smirk with delight, with the thrill of leverage. "He'll talk to me." Becky leaned over the table, all but licking her pink, muscled lips. "I bet I can score a jailhouse interview with Walt," I said. "Fulton County's granted my requests before, for those type of sit-downs. And it's not like Walt poses any type of threat, you know. Not like he'll take me hostage. Especially since I'll have the blessing of his family. And since I already know Walt a little myself. I'm honestly surprised he hasn't called me from the pokey pay phone yet."

Becky folded her hands and placed the pretty bouquet of fingers beneath her chin, sans wedding ring. "You're sounding more employable again, by the minute. How long will it take?"

"I'll get started today."

"Good."

"But a quick question," I said, gulping. "A pal and I were kicking around the idea of starting an internet fundraiser for Walt, to get him a more qualified attorney. I probably know the answer, but if I'm associated with that, can I still write about Walt's incarceration?"

"Not ever."

"Got it," I said. "Walt's on his own then, poor bastard. What's the second thing?"

"I'm thinking you have inroads on that front, too."

"Lotto?"

"Exactly," she said. "He won't return our calls either. And his secretary pretends she doesn't speak English when my reporters have popped in his office tower." Recalling this made Becky visibly irate. "You realize his plans for The Sweetberry Flank have passed the City Council now, right?"

"*Shit*. No. Really?"

She nodded, proud of having scooped me. Such children, us media.

"The whole neighborhood's been so preoccupied. I guess it got away from us," I said. "That's the last bureaucratic hurdle for Atlanta developers to clear, right?"

"Within a month, I heard," she said. "He wants the bull-dozers and backhoes on site within a month."

"Damn it—that's too soon," I said. "Too much else is going on. This is terrible, Beck."

"What's terrible is that those old folks agreed to this."

I demurred. "Yeah, that's complicated..."

She leaned in, and a tiny pendant danced across her scarlet upper chest. It was a hound dog on the scent, sniffing out corruption and hard-earned Fourth Estate answers, I'm sure. "Obviously, you have a stake in this, but you're the only insider we have on the Lotto front," she said. "I'm still mad at you, keep in mind. But I'm willing to sic you on any good, verifiable Lotto story you can produce. OK? Same goes for the questionably jailed suspect. Maybe it's all related, and the stories could be a series? Maybe a snake update will somehow come of it, too? But keep your first-person ramblings out of this. And work sober. OK? Got it? *Capiche?*"

"Amen!" I said.

"Hallelujah," Becky replied.

"*What?*"

"I don't know!" she said. "I just don't know anymore, Johnson. Everything's just collapsed."

"I don't know either," I said. "But I'll go find out."

Becky clasped the back of my hand, which quaked with excitement, with life. "Look at you," she said. "You're rounding back into form. Like you're that spry, sleuthing, fifty-nine-year-old newsman I used to know."

I regressed into tearful, cheery weeping. And for some reason, I snatched Becky's hand and pressed it against my face.

She gasped. "The fuck you doin', man?"

"I'm just overwhelmed," I said. "It's such an emotional time."

"You're sweating. This is disturbing."

"I've been feeling so lost," I went on, "and I'm so happy to have this back. Your trust. Your jobs. Your touch. Your—"

"Pull yourself together, Johnson." She glanced around the empty café and lowered her voice, wiping her hand on the table. "And if this is some sort of come-on, when the ink on my divorce papers isn't even dry, I'd say you're the most tactless, lowdown dog this side of Athens—"

"It's *not* a come-on," I said. "I haven't flirted since the Reagan Administration. I'm just overheated and wound up. I needed human touch—a hot hand on my face."

"So I'm not *worthy* of your flirting?" And her head slid side to side, a cobra to the flute. "That's insulting."

"I think we just need to reevaluate things."

"Reevaluate what?"

"Everything that's transpired here, after the part about my being a real reporter again," I said. "We're tired, Beck. We're shattered. Our city's a mess. We're better than this. And you deserve better than me."

She thrust out a shoulder. "What if I said I just want to… I don't know, aim low for a while?"

"Then I'd say you're about to shoot yourself in the foot." I sipped the last of the coffee and hook-shot the cup over the trashcan by three feet.

Becky whispered, which I'd never heard her do before: "I'm just lonely," she said. "There. I said it. It's foreign, and it's warping me. I can't stand it."

I hung my head. "Beck, I told ya… I'm spoken for."

"You did," she said. "And that was the most noble, attractive thing you've ever said."

Now it made sense; I'd inadvertently made myself the Unavailable Bachelor, the forbidden, putrid fruit. "I'm sorry to have sent the wrong signals."

"I'm sorry, too."

She pulled a bottle of sanitizer from her purse and disinfected her hand. We were finishing history's strangest editorial meeting.

"Can we get back to talking business?" I said.

"Yes, go."

"So I need to corroborate this a bit more," I said, "with more sources than one, but I have reason to believe Lotto's been dishing illegal bribes to folks who live in The Flank. It's an affront against fair market value, and it's slimy. What's more, I'm convinced he's boinking the city's zoning board president, Kim Somethingerother."

Her face ignited again. "That'd explain Lotto's lightning-fast approvals in the permitting process."

"Exactly."

"We're dealing with snakes of all sorts," she said. "Potentially more dangerous ones."

"Exactly."

"You're on a roll, now *go*," she said, pointing to the door, pushing my shoulder. "I've heard enough. Just do what you do. Go get me answers!"

"I can do it," I said. "I won't let you down."

"The paper needs you. This city needs you right now, God Johnson. Set your ass in motion and make us proud!"

I shot up from my seat, toward Peachtree Street—until a crucial, logistical problem occurred to me. I turned back to the table. "Can I get a little loan?" I said, shamelessly, from across the café. "Just a small something? I'm fine with unreasonable interest rates—"

"Go!"

Becky pointed an angry finger toward the street, shook her head no, and sent me off with an air kiss. But I didn't want that. I didn't want her, or anybody else. No further complications. No messiness. No distractions. I just wanted to do good work, to feel vital, focused, and needed again. As

I beat feet down the sidewalk, I peered up through the shimmering glass valleys of downtown, beyond the crisscrossing contrails, the swollen summer clouds, and I issued a silent apology for all that misguided touching business.

CHAPTER 17

Roaring toward The Flank, I brought the truck around a corner, and the windshield, for an instant, perfectly framed the Faux Americana McMansion Deluxe. It'd been vacant for only a few weeks, but it already radiated vacantness. The fescue was shaggy, the Japanese hollies misshapen, and the crabgrass heaved up like actual crabs. All that remained of the family's elaborate swing set was yellow stripes in long grass. Where an array of flags had flapped brilliantly over the front porch, wires sagged from sad poles. It all looked deceased.

I edged the truck up farther into the shade, still entranced by the big house, and I'll swear on anything that at that moment I felt a *cool breeze*. In defiance of history's hottest summer, it swept through the cab like a benediction, a promise of more pleasant times ahead, and then it was gone, bound for downtown. This breeze even smelled like autumn—the clean, sunny, smoke-tinged air of Southern November. For an instant I was back at the home I'd had to abandon, scooping leaves from the gutter and watching them parachute into the cul-de-sac. I was a family man again. I was young, strong, and optimistic again. I saw Wyatt

in the yard, ankle-deep in auburn foliage, kicking a regula-
tion leather football imprinted with the Bulldogs' "G." In his
loud, squeaky voice he was saying, "Sic 'em, sic 'em, sic 'em"
to nobody but the ball. I shook my head, in the truck, and
punched the gas.

I parked in front of Shotgun Three, leapt out, and in
my haste basically punched Genteel's front door. From that
vantage point, I could tell something was missing. The luxu-
riant rosebushes that had always girded her porch in warmer
months, I noticed, had been sheared to the dirt. Genteel
cracked the door open a half-inch, put a big brown eyeball to
the gap, and said, "What is it?"

"Where's that old friend of yours live?" I said. "I think
his name's Felix."

"*Who* now?"

"Walter's grandpa, the young man charged in Joey's
shooting."

"Why?"

"You want justice or not? Stop being a brick wall."

"Felix stay in Shotgun Twelve, down the road," she said,
still hiding. "He a good man, so be nice. And you probably
should know somethin' else, too: Felix the only one didn't
take that builder's bad money, like I was tellin' you about."

"Good to hear one of you has morals."

"Go on down the street, you scab!"

"What're you hiding in there? You got a boyfriend?"

"Just got out the shower."

"Don't fib."

"Don't call me no liar."

"I can see you shining through that crack," I said. "You
wearin' sequins, lady?"

"Oh, fwoo!" she said. "Fine then. Busted."

The door swung open, unveiling Genteel in a marvelous
lavender lounge dress. She was ludicrously overdone for the
Grammys, let alone a banal weekday afternoon. "Just seein' if

this old thing fits me," she said. "And doin' a little practicin', back in front of my big mirror."

"Love it," I said. "But listen, can you come down the street to Mr. Felix's place with me? Help me get through to him?"

"Why?"

"I met him in court. He's all kinds of skeptical of media."

"Fine. But I ain't walkin'."

Like a five-foot disco ball, Genteel's sequins cast galaxies of sunlight all over Felix's porch. She didn't get the chance to knock before the rascal tore open his front door; he was slaphappy and inspired, shirtless in jeans, like some sort of moonshiner preemptively confronting the authorities. "Oooo-wee! Look-*ee*!" he shouted. "Genteel Briggs, dolled up like it's 1988 again!" And he did a hunched, arm-flailing, leg-tossing, grand-pappy dance out to embrace her at mid-porch. All the while, Genteel was earnestly insisting she didn't look good. With his chin on her shoulder, Felix's eyes caught sight of me. He let her go, shoved hands into his pockets, and said, "Slow news day, Mister Johnson?"

"Hardly," I said. "In fact—"

"You be nice to him, Felix," Genteel cut in. "This man's heart in the right place. He wanna do a story about your grandson. And he know more about Lotto than anyone else. Maybe enough to get our land deal turned around. So you better help him out."

Felix gave me a skeptical, unenthused glare. "I told you enough already," he said. "You want any more, you have to hear it from Walter himself. But so far his lawyer, that knucklehead, ain't letting him talk to the press. Says it can only do harm at this stage. Walter's downtown, caged up and boiling, as he should be."

I stepped onto the porch, in the merciful shade. We all three moved back toward Felix's own rosebushes and a leaning windmill palm, at the side of his house. And then we reflexively stepped back, clear of all that. Felix reached out and nudged Genteel away, as if protecting her, and I noticed again his left ring-finger was missing, gone from the knuckle on. "Fulton County gives you biweekly family visit permissions, right?" I said. "Have you been twice this week?"

"Nope," said Felix. "I'll be going tomorrow evening, though."

"How about, instead," I said, "we hop in my truck and go right now? You can say I'm family. The New York uncle nobody talks about. I'll stop by my house and grab a disguise."

"Man, I don't know." Felix deflated, his face pointed down to ancient floorboards, the lined cheeks and forehead like aerial maps of great rivers. "Not sure about doing anything sneaky, anything that might jeopardize—"

"Jeopardize *what*?" I said. "The fair shake that Walt's getting now? What are *you* risking? I'm the one who could go to jail—for trying to go to jail."

"Don't get sarcastic on me, God."

"Your grandson's doomed, man," I said, patting his shoulder. "At least on the felony manslaughter count. Relatively clean record or not, he's riding the expressway to a twenty-year sentence with no exits."

"If this plan harms Walter's legal representation in any way—"

"It's *cool*," I said. "Relax. We're going to get him a better lawyer anyway. We're going to launch an online fundraiser."

Felix's head snapped sideways. "*Who* is?"

I'd anticipated the question, and now I had to gently answer. "So, look. I can't help because my boss won't let me; it kind of puts me too close to what I'm reporting on. So Squeaky down the street is gonna handle the fundraiser."

Felix leaned back far and fast, as if pushed by tornadic wind. Then he sprung back. "*Squeeeeee-keee*?" he said. "Shit, if that fool knows how to even access the internet, I'll eat my wallet right now."

I stepped toward the street. "Fine," I said. "We'll cross that bridge tomorrow. Let's just go. I'm *starving*."

Felix lifted his head and seemed buoyed by the prospects of my scheme. He reached toward Genteel, and they stood there without talking for a moment, simply holding hands. In my mind I reached a verdict, as I had with Lotto and the zoning czar: THEY FUKN.

"You think you could prove Walter was set up, like I told you?" Felix said, backing me into that corner again.

"Frankly, sir," I said, "I'm not sure I buy that. But I can't know anything until I talk to Walt again. I'll wear a hat and tuck up my hair so that nobody knows it's me. I'll speak with Brooklyn dialect. The risk is very small."

Felix loosened his old neck muscles, dropped his hands. "The Lord is speaking to me, and I don't mean this light-skinned fool on my porch," he said, talking right into Genteel's glowing, embellished face. "Let me get dressed more properly. We'll drop you off on the way, baby."

We stopped by the Victorian, and I found no suitable hats for concealing my telltale silver mane; going in with an exposed head would immediately out me and ruin the plan. But I did have a balaclava—the preferred black garment of vigilantes and McDonald's robbers—and a stick-on porno mustache I'd bought for a *Beacon* Halloween party I didn't attend. In my bedroom, I rolled the face mask into a sort of thick, wooly New England fisherman's cap to capture my hair; immediately my scalp sweated, and I was miserable. I pasted the faux 'stache above my lips, where it sadly drooped but held on. I sprung from the bedroom and out to the foyer, where Felix waited. His eyes bugged out.

"That's the best you got?"

"It's foolproof, Felix."

"Naw, man, it's *proof* you're a fool."

We hadn't made it a mile in the truck before I had to ask: "Not to poke at old scabs, but what happened to your finger, sir?" His facial expression suggested I'd asked for a kiss. "Never mind," I said. "I just noticed, back on the porch, when you were waving your hands around. It's my nature to ask."

"Fine," he said. "I got a tale for you, story-boy."

I merged into molasses freeway traffic as Felix launched into descriptions of his boyhood enterprises around Sweetberry Park. For his most successful venture, he became a weeder of gardens for White folks, before they all White-flighted away. By virtue of his hard work, he'd landed a cushy recurring commission with a regal old dame named Harriett whose family had owned her columned mansion since Sweetberry was but land for pecans, cotton, and virgin heart-pine. One day, Harriet asked Felix to dig her a fashion-able koi pond, and that's when it got messy.

"So you know how they got all those Civil War markers and plaques all over Sweetberry these days?" he said. "Well, they're not shittin'. A lot of fighting and dying happened right there, where all our houses are now—"

"The Battle of Atlanta," I cut in, "started right down the street. About six blocks from my porch."

"Exactly," he said. "The bloodshed this summer is nothin' new. The blood's *deep* in Sweetberry, right under us. And you know what else is under there? Some goddamn Yankee cannonballs, that's what!"

"No!" I said. "Still? I thought the homebuilders and road-builders dug all those up?"

"Not back in '55, when I'z a kid," he said. "Things still went boom back then."

Felix lifted the left side of his T-shirt to reveal a constel-lation of pockmarks across his stomach and ribcage, plus larger scars that reminded me of healed shark bites. "That's what hit me, right here," he said. "I'd got my shovel to make

Miss Harriet's pond. I wasn't down but maybe two feet when I felt metal. I thought I'd struck treasure and kept digging. And then I'm waking up in the ER, at the colored hospital in DeKalb, and they're pulling out the shrapnel from my belly, stitchin' up my hand."

I couldn't believe it. Here was a Civil War *survivor*, living and breathing beside me. "This is amazing, man!" I said, mulling story angles. "You survived a freakin' cannonball."

He tucked in his shirt. "More like a mortar, I guess," he said. "They could tell, from the pieces they pulled out, that it was Yankee. It must have been part of the Union bombardment."

I exited the interstate, kicked the gas, and plunged us into the seedier parts of downtown. "That's kind of ironic, isn't it?"

"Yeah, exactly," said Felix. "Freedom my ass. I can't play my guitar for shit."

In the metal detector line at Fulton County Superior Court, Felix became even chattier in his nervousness, as we toed one step closer and closer and closer to the frontline bailiff. I tried not to smile, thereby not cracking the sun-heated glue on my face. "You see the weather next week, Larry?" he said, deploying subterfuge. "They're predicting a high of 112 on Monday."

"Yo, it doesn't get that hot in Atlanta," I said, in stilted New Yorker. "It literally has never gotten that hot here. This ain't no Phoenix, yo. *Capiche?*"

"It's an all-time record comin', then."

"Oh, cuh-*mon*," I said, flipping my chin with an open palm, hunching shoulders, a real mafia boss. "Look at this mooley over here."

"What, man?"

"Mooley, I said."

"Are you calling me Italian?"

"Yo," I said. "I don't know what I'm *say-in'*."

The bailiff was eyeing my suspicious robbing hat, and Felix couldn't take eyes off him.

"One-hundred and twelve is what I heard," Felix continued. "I'm just sayin' what the weatherman was whining about on Channel 17 Action News..." and he kept rambling, but I was focused on the bailiff, who was staring at my mustache now. With his beady eyes and bulk, he looked like a chaw-chewing country bull. He reached up and patted the top of my head like a game show buzzer. Satisfied, he unsheathed a great wand and circled it around my skull. No beeps. I nodded, scooted by him, and shot back toward the cells. Felix filed in behind me and quipped about how easy that was before I asked him to shush. We went through a dingy corridor, came to a waiting room, and filled out a few pages of paperwork. There was no need to lie about who I actually was; not a soul in the building recognized the name on my ID: Archibald Wesley Johnson. After a few moments and a little more vetting of Felix, we were led by a lady not to the booths divided by thick glass you see in movies, but to a sort of breakroom with three circular tables. Five minutes later, in came towering Walt in county orange, with an equally thick guard beside him. His beard was wild and robust, his wrists and ankles chained together. He recognized me immediately.

"Thank *God*," is all Walt said, before sitting down. His grandfather pulled a paisley handkerchief from his back pocket and dabbed at his eyes.

We had a half hour before Walt would be yanked back to the cage. Quietly, so the guard couldn't hear, I outlined the half-baked online fundraiser plan. And I told him how I'd covered crime for decades and that my gut was seasoned enough to know innocence when I saw it. "During your probable cause hearing, I saw it," I told Walt. "I saw injustice, at its worst. And right now, as we sit here, I see it again."

To the guard's chagrin, Walt scooted a bit closer. And then closer. The guard coughed, his leather creaked, but he stayed put, back against a far wall. Walt leaned in, and he was enormous. The masses of his chest and shoulders were basketballs under blankets. He angled himself so the guard couldn't see us, squeezed my left wrist, and pulled me toward him. "Look at me," he said, in a low growl. "*Look* in my eyes, Mr. Johnson. I didn't shoot that boy. I had nothing to do with that. I'm innocent. For a hundred million dollars, I'd never bring a gun into church."

"I believe you," I said.

"And I believe *you*, when you say that."

"But tell me," I said. "You have an inkling who might have done it, even on accident?"

"Jesus, I wish," said Walt, leaning away. "It was madness in there. I was picking a lady up from the floor when that shot cracked. But I can tell you with absolute certainty that gun wasn't brought by anybody in my group, no sir."

"You mean the splinter militia—"

"Don't, *please*," Walt snapped, tossing aside my wrist. "We never called ourselves that. We were the Preserve Sweetberry Flank Alliance. The PSFA. It said so right on our T-shirts, which grandpa Felix was kind enough to fund. 'Militia' implies violence, and that's the opposite of what we're about. I don't know who started with that 'militia' bullshit. Our weapon was knowledge… intelligence nobody knew I had, and they still don't."

"Intelligence?"

Felix stopped his crying, put down the handkerchief, and leaned in. "See, God," he said. "That's what I was tellin' you, in court."

I shook my head, fighting my disbelief. "I'm sorry," I said. "I can't buy this theory that Lotto set you up somehow."

"Again," said Walt. "I can't say for sure what happened in that basement. But I know for a fact that Lotto's cooking up his biggest lie yet."

"The bribes," I said. "You're talking about the bribes he's paid out, right? To each homeowner in The Flank, except this guy right here."

"It's bigger than those bribes, sir," said Walt. "The bribes are chicken feed."

Maybe it was the woolen skull cocoon, but I suddenly was dripping facial sweat, which wormed into my mustaches. "Come on," I said. "I'll work to prove you're innocent, but you gotta give me some proof here. Stop bread-crumbin' me along, man. I'll need something to stand on, if you want a news story. Something concrete."

Walt nodded, and then he whispered: "Here's what you do: Go to my mom's house, at 58 Praytor Avenue, this evening. She'll be home from her hospital shift then. Take Felix with you, and she'll trust you, as he's her family by marriage. Tell her Bee-Bee sent you... that's our code word for me, so she knows someone's telling the truth, and that I sent them specifically. But then lie after that. Lie your ass off. Tell her you're part of my defense. And, actually, take a shower before you go. Maybe wear a tie, too, if you have it. And then ask mom to point you to my old room, where I was staying, in the back of the house. There's a crusty old bay window with a built-in bench, with one of those lift-up seats. Inside that, you'll see a little locker full of baseball and basketball cards. Under the cards is a manila envelope. And inside that envelope is all the story you'll ever need."

The more Walt spoke, the more I felt that high again, the dopamine of purpose. "A story about what? Can you tell me that, Walt? Just for planning this out?"

Squirming, Walt shuffled his mass around, cracked his knuckles, reluctant and thoughtful. "It's proof our man Lotto is beyond scandalous," Walt said, his whisper deepening back to his speaking voice. "He's lying to the City Council, to The Flank, and to anybody who respects Atlanta history—"

"In your house," I interrupted, "are these the documents you pilfered from Lotto's office? Is that what we're going to find?"

Walt swelled up in his chair, like a Kodiak. "I didn't say that, I'm not admitting to that, so get that theory out of my face." He shot his grandfather a hot, accusatory glare. "All I'll say is that, to my knowledge, nobody knows this paperwork is missing yet. You'll have your exclusive, from an *anonymous* source, if you want it. Cool?"

"Very cool."

"OK, perfect," said Walt. "Now, in exchange, you keep me updated about this fundraiser. My attorney's inept, and y'all just might save my life." He dropped his hands thunderously on the table, stood up, and said to the guard, "I'm ready."

Felix and I both tried to stutter out apologies; Walt cut us off with a wave. His face stiffened in anger, but in his eyes I saw dread, desperation, and fear. All he said was, "58 Praytor Avenue," before ducking back into some dark place.

CHAPTER 18

The last time I'd visited, it was clear that Praytor Avenue was beyond the gentrification influences of more popular CenterTown neighborhoods, where housing prices had become towering, impenetrable walls for poor folks, younger couples, and debt-afflicted recovering students. Praytor Avenue, though, was a stubborn vestige of opportunity for those demographics, which is another way of saying most discerning White people still considered it too sketchy. Enterprising, first-time buyers, for instance, could land a renovated bungalow on Praytor Avenue for a quarter of a million bucks; chump change, that is, for all the transplants flooding in from Jersey and New Haven and Los Gatos. But the relative affordability would be expiring soon, as evidenced by all the Dumpsters dotting the street now—depositories for the roofs and innards of Black family homes—and backhoes in front yards. I'd watched the process play out in Sweetberry about four or five hundred times: a family gathered, mourned for an afternoon, and then hooted out old furniture and great mounds knickknacks and the blouses of elderly deceased. In about a week, with the coast cleared, the frontline demo team would come in with sledgehammers, irrespective of the past, thinking only of tomorrow's profits. In five more days, either the roof was gone to make the house a Pop Top two-story, or it was all a pile of rubble, just busted bricks atop ruined hardwood floors, where tipsy dads had once danced 'til daybreak to Gladys Knight records.

"*Look* at this construction," said Felix, the sun setting over his shoulders. "Is there nowhere safe from it? No place that's gonna just be preserved? It's about to be ruined—"

"Is that too harsh, though?" I said. "There's the argument that no successful place is static."

"Yeah, sure. You sound like Lotto."

"I mean, I bet the Romans were pissed, at some point, about losing their skyline views to richer little busybody Romans," I said. "I'm guessing there was bloodshed, at some point, over rising livestock prices or whatever. Someone probably tried to sell artisanal goats." I took a left. "You ever wonder what this city's gonna look like in twenty years? Or fifty years? I can't even comprehend."

Felix chuckled, but in a somber, empty way. "Hell," he said, "I can't see beyond this time next year, when I'll be livin' on four acres up in Ash County. I'll have a pond, and my own little boat, where I'll fish and play guitar. All damn day, nothin' but bluegill and cold beer."

"That reminds me," I said. "Why didn't you take Lotto's bribe?"

He coughed. "*What?*"

"You're selling your house, yet you don't want money in advance?"

"I took it," he said, dropping his forehead into a palm. "And in fact I spent it all, last weekend. Screw it, Johnson. I am *old*. I got some wing tips. Some golf clubs. I ordered new leather interior for my Cadillac in storage. And I got Genteel a necklace. I guess you can tell she's my new girl, and probably my last girl. I can't get enough of her, really, these past few weeks. She needed some more jewelry, though. It's nothin' too grand, but it does frame that big happy face—"

"She told me you didn't take the money," I said. "She said you're the only one."

"'Cause that's what I told *her*," said Felix. "Tryin' to seem tough. She'll figure it out herself, when that necklace comes in."

"This is bad news," I said.

"Why?"

"It means every single Flank homeowner is complicit in Lotto's scheme. This hurts the idea that contracts can be voided. And it means he has control."

"That's foolish," Felix said, waving a hand. "Every home-owner made a deal with Lotto. It's all inked, and it's all official. A few say they didn't, but they're just too ashamed."

"You're not helping the cause, man."

"Maybe you should let it go," said Felix. "Maybe you should head back up to Gwinnett County, or wherever you came from. I'll be selling my house one way or the other, and won't nothin' stop anybody else from bulldozing it down once I do—"

"You're a profit-monger like everybody else." I flashed up the headlights but had lost track of addresses, and time. "Now what's the number of this damn house? I forgot to take notes, back in jail."

"Slow down," he said. "That's it up on the right, on that hill."

On the stoop of Walt's mother's bungalow, I was pecking the last bits of glue from my moustache when a window went up, to our right. A woman in a nurse's hat thrust out her hands, pointing toward the street. Her head wouldn't fit through the burglar bars. "I gave my testimony already," she said. "Go on back to your precinct."

"Sherry," said Felix. "It's me. Look."

In the peephole I spotted quick movements. As the door opened, I could see where Walt had inherited his extreme proportions. His mother had to be six foot one with the same oaken logs for arms and legs as her boy. Her smile was massive, too, about a half-foot of bright white. She flung aside a door of iron bars and all but inhaled Felix in an embrace.

"*This*," he said, wheezing, "means she trusts us."

I caught her attention and said, "Ma'am, I was told to tell you that Bee-Bee sent us."

"Oh, *shush*," she said. "Y'all good. This skinny old man is family!"

Inside, the home was chilly with air-conditioning and cozy with dog art on the counters and walls. Labradors, collies, a shih tzu, Pomeranian, all arranged in a constellation of porcelain figurines and framed photos and watercolors.

"I'm not obsessed," said this Sherry, watching me as I eyed the canine collective. "I volunteer at the shelter. All of these little guys remind me of dogs I worked with before." She doted on a pit bull statue atop an aquarium. "OK, maybe I'm obsessed."

As we laughed, I could see a flame of recognition alight in her face. "*You*," she said, half-smiling. "You're that old columnist."

I looked at Felix. "Cover's blown, man."

Sherry was staring into me, unblinking. "Hold up," she said. "You're the one that got attacked by that cobra, right?"

"Unfortunately," I said. "But yeah, I took it down."

"Damn, baby," she said. "I saw that on two different news channels. You doin' alright, after all that?" I nodded. She stepped closer, concerned. "So what's the latest news on all these *snakes*, man? These dang reptiles? It's been, what, two months, and we got *two* killed to show for it? With about fifteen more out there, creeping around? I mean, seriously! What are they, *invisible*?" She took a quick breath and relaunched before we could possibly answer. "I feel like people are finally starting to forget, though, or finally moving on, you know. We got kids out playing ball until dark again around here. We got neighbors actually trimming their shaggy-ass bushes again. This whole thing's been scary like nothing ever. But I'm feeling optimistic, and I'll tell you why: It'll be August in two weeks, and then September, and then we're home free into the cool months! Down at the hospital, the doctors are saying none of these snakes will survive the first frost. There's no chance, they're saying. It's evolutionarily impossible for all these breeds, or whatever, to make it through a winter, not even a Georgia one. So come that frost, baby, it'll all be over for sure. We'll all be free of this! Right? Right! And then we can move on to even more fucked-up problems, like my innocent boy, down in the city pen. Now tell me—what are we gonna do about that? And what in the hell are you two fools doing in *my house*?"

I raised my hand, permission to speak. She nodded, granted. "I was there that night, in the church," I said. "It's the worst thing that ever happened. With Felix's help, I'm tryin' to get to the bottom of it. And I mean *all* of it."

Sherry relaxed. "What d'you need then?" she said. "An interview?"

"Yes, but not right now," I said. "I just need you to point me to Walter's old bedroom."

At the back of the house, on the sea-blue walls of the bedroom, an array of plaques and framed certificates was hung like a testament to Walter James' nobility. He'd been a decorated Boy Scout. He'd graduated from a neighborhood police academy for teens. He'd been a "Top Turkey" volunteer at a Thanksgiving drive to feed Atlanta's homeless. His mother was luxuriating in all of this, her face upturned and grinning, as if this gallery of achievement was sunshine in the bleak winter of her emotions. Felix clutched his face and dipped out of the room.

"Now," said Sherry James, nodding to the wall. "Does that sound like a killer to you?"

"No, ma'am."

"Do you look up there, on that wall, and see some punk thug who should be in jail?"

"No, I don't."

"So what did Walter tell you is in this room?"

"Well, ma'am," I said, quietly. "I'm not sure he wants you to know that—"

Before I could finish the thought, before I could flesh out the situation with details about Lotto's secrecy and sordidness and background, Sherry lunged forward and slapped a fast palm across my mouth. It landed with a tremendous, sharp pop. My head jerked with the impact; I felt my ponytail dance across my shoulders. I hadn't been hit in decades. But instantly I remembered it all: the sudden rush of tingling pain, the lips perforated by teeth, the rise of furious blood. Sherry stood silent, but her eyes screamed that I'd crossed a moral boundary, coming into her home and withholding information pertaining to her captive boy.

"Walt told us to look under that window," I said, turning toward it. "He says there's an envelope in a box, beneath some baseball cards. There's some paperwork inside that he says could make all the difference in the world."

Sherry dug through a trough of boyhood junk and emerged with the manila envelope. She balanced it delicately on her fingertips, as if holding the pages of Rome's lost Sibylline Books. I gently lifted it out of her hand. Downstairs, I could hear the front door clack shut. All the drama had obviously been too much for Felix's mild temperament.

"Now get out," Sherry said. "I don't wanna know where Walter got that, or what it even is. I don't want to know what y'all are up to. All I know is, if that's the truth that'll set him free, I better damn well be reading about it in the newspaper."

CHAPTER 19

Felix was leaning out of Great White's passenger-side dorsal as I hustled out into the yard, checking my lips for blood. "What happened to you?" I said, sliding in behind the wheel. "You missed me gettin' my ass kicked in there."

Felix didn't react. "Let's take it to Genteel's place," he said. "We'll open it there, clue her in, too."

We pounded on the door of Shotgun Three until Genteel finally cracked it open. This time she was wearing a shower cap and silky nightgown. At first she said, "Heck, naw," and closed the door; then we explained at length, through her thin window glass, the magical implications of our bounty. She let us in but was fidgety and confused, aching to catch her talk shows and call it a night.

I sat on the plastic-covered couch, which went *rmmp-rmmp* against my sweaty thighs and back, and opened the envelope. I exhumed fifteen different collections of paperwork, each held together by long, strong paperclips. I laid them out on her coffee table.

"Good gracious alive!" Genteel spouted. "It's a buncha resumes. Who cares? Ain't even close to bein' a smokin' gun. Now get on out, y'all. I'm goin'-a sleep."

She was right. The front pages were a bunch of nonsensical numbers and company jargon, little constellations of obscure LLC names and arithmetic. Ditto for the second pages, and third, in each stack. "I don't get it," I said.

"Hold up," said Felix, still standing, not bothering to help me read. "There's fifteen piles there."

"So?" said Genteel.

"There's also fifteen shotgun bungalows here, in The Flank," said Felix.

Genteel gasped as I flipped to the tenth page, and there it was: the meat, the intel, the explanation, the bombshell. It was a detailed graphic of her neighbor's home, bungalow No. 4, only split apart, like diagrams of skinned pigs in butcher shops.

The next page rambled about "RESIDENTIAL RELICS OF DOCTOR KING'S BOYHOOD NEIGHBORHOOD," and I thought for a moment that Lotto had had a change of heart, that he was organizing a petition to have these houses saved and immortalized on the Georgia Historic Register. Felix saw my eyes brightening and picked up his own packet, flipping quickly. My disillusionment died over the course of the final three pages, which I read word-for-word before slamming the packet back down on the coffee table.

Genteel said, "What is it?"

Felix halted his investigation and watched me.

"There isn't going to be a pole-barn museum in the suburbs, and I doubt there ever was," I said. "That's all a diversion. That's all a lie." Felix walked over to Genteel and clasped her hand. "Lotto has no intent to preserve anything," I said, half-shouting. "He's connected, in some way, with a custom furniture business near Savannah. He's going to chop all of your houses up, piecemeal, and sell them as tables and chairs and benches and beds made of reclaimed wood. It's the trendy stuff that all the young professionals are buying now. You take the beams and boards from homes like these, and it becomes stuff with a story, stuff that's *real*, in a world that increasingly isn't."

Felix's right foot started jittering, and he looped his left arm over Genteel's shoulders.

"Lotto's deals are all signed," I said. "It's right there. And Walt found it all. I bet the bill of sale is the last page of every single one of these..." I fingered through to the final page of each pile, and all contained the same sales documents, the death certificates. As I pointed out to Felix and Genteel, the bones and skin of Shotgun Three—all future coffee tables and bookshelves—had alone fetched Lotto another $88,000. That's money he'd pocketed on top of the sale of each forthcoming Sweetberry Lanes home, which could easily total twenty times what he'd paid for the existing homes and land, per my rough math. In hearing that, Genteel flung out her arms and squeezed her boyfriend against her bosom.

"Hold on now," said Felix. "Lotto said all the homes are going to be preserved, man. That they'll live on and on. That was part of the bargain, a huge factor in why I signed—"

"Was it in the contract?" I said. "Was it in writing?"

Felix frowned, searching his memories. "I think it was."

"Nope," said Genteel. "He wrong. It wasn't. I know for a *fact* it wasn't."

Genteel shook her head against painful thoughts, squeezing her man. She said: "But that Lotto promised up and down about it. He was hand-shakin' everybody, talkin' up his shrine to our community, like a temple..." and she trailed off before finishing her thought, realizing as she spoke how little a crooked man's word means.

"I'm sorry, Genteel, but that's all nothing," I said. "He's slick, and he's heartless. He knows nobody will hold him accountable." They stared at me from across the room, increasingly uncomfortable, as if I was slowly cranking a vise around their souls, but I continued. "Lotto's instincts are to crush, not preserve. And he's so well-connected, with so much money in so many pockets, that even lying isn't really illegal in his case, because there are no real consequences—"

"I'm-a shoot Lotto!" said Felix, nodding. "Just as soon as my deal closes, sittin' at the closing table—*pow*!"

That inspired Genteel to adjust her hug into a headlock. Felix choked out apologies, but she held his head a minute longer. It was the wrong summer, clearly, to be cracking jokes about gunplay in her house.

"You wanna hear the worst part?" I said, not waiting for replies. "He's taking your story about MLK being babysat around here and manipulating it. He's capitalizing on it. It says right here he's calling the furniture—get this—the 'Dr. King Bespoke Collection.'"

In hearing that, Genteel expelled Felix from her embrace, tossing him flopping into an occasional chair. We both watched, seated, as she walked over to a wall and hugged its old shiplap instead. She thrust back her head dramatically, like the most overblown cabaret version of herself, and she moaned: "I look right here, and right over there, and right over by the kitchen cupboard, and y'all know what I see? *Huh*? I see Christmas! Nothin' but presents and pretty garlands and my lil' nieces runnin' all over. I see history, all *my* history. I see that nasty ol' spring in the eighties, Johnson, back when I had to nurse you and Mister Squeaky back to yo' right minds! I see Sundays after Easters. I see us when we'd smoke a whole pig at the park, and I'd cook some greens and whip up yams, and we'd eat right in here, with some cloths on card tables we was so many. Oh, we'd *eat*. And I mean *feast*, y'all. Woo! Yes we did!" She paused to catch her breath. "We didn't have much in those times but each other. The whole neighborhood was down, but honey, we felt *up*. At least sometimes we did. There was none of this foolishness of today. None of this whinin' about house colors and homestead taxes and misplaced Fido poop. No! Back then, we knew this community, all of it, all of us. You knew who you was—and *whose* you was!" She dropped her head, stepped from the wall to the window, and deflated completely, from face to diaphragm to bending knees. Felix stood up to comfort her, but she shot out an open hand in warning. "Let me just wallow in this by myself," she said. "It's my doin'. It's all our doin'. The coins started flashin' in my eyes, and I got distracted, God help me. I let sin sneak in and get the best of Genteel Briggs. And now it's my burden, so y'all go on home. Let me soak up the memories as much as I can, with whatever time we've got left until our closin's. I got a bad feelin', Johnson, that you ain't gone find no laws violated about this. I think the evil is too much this time, that this *is* the summer of reckonin'. I just know some lil' punk's gone be eatin' breakfast on my walls, in a dang fancy rowhouse named after me. *Me*! This old crazy lady who's gone be gone like everything else, who cain't even sing no more. A good woman that lost her way, her light, and then her home. *Aww, foo*! We walked right in the devil's hands, y'all. I think we been had. But I *know* I'm goin' to sleep now, right after I un-tape my torlet for a minute, and I'm goin' it alone. So goodnight, men, and don't let them bushes bite."

Genteel thwarted one last Felix advance, drooped her head, and lumbered toward the back of the bungalow, slapping light switches off along the way. I collected the paperwork, with Felix's help, and though neither of us said a word, I knew we both regretted bringing it here. I wanted to make one last point, as a means of warning them both, per Genteel's mention of legality, but I couldn't bring myself to do it; I couldn't potentially leave her tossing in sweaty fits all night. But it had dawned on me, as she spoke, just how good Lotto really is at being horrible. His pre-closings bribes had not only made each member of this elderly flock feel special—he'd lured them into unwittingly committing crimes of illegitimate real estate transactions, which any rookie prosecutor could prove in five minutes. They were all still cogent and independent enough, as Lotto probably knew, that their accepting his payouts didn't quite constitute what Georgia code calls "elder abuse." Should word threaten to get out about Lotto's furniture deals, his affair with the zoning chair, or how the outrageousness of his greed was the impetus for a boy's death, he had fifteen remarkably strong gag orders in his pocket. He had blackmail. He had the leverage. He had their souls.

Felix nodded a sad goodnight, tucked his thumbs into the back pockets of his jeans, and disappeared into the darkness. What a long day he'd had. I could hear the clop of his boots on the busted old road, pattering away, like dying summer rain on a tin roof. What neither of us could hear at that moment, of course, was the immense, coiled, reptilian monster beneath Felix's bungalow, the green anaconda herself, a dark pile of sheer fibrous power and patience.

What us three fogies also didn't know, because we weren't ensnared by the internet at all hours, was that a silent melee was ensuing on the Sweetberry Neighbors Message Portal at that moment. The stolen-snake pandemonium, at least for a few hours, would rage anew that night; it was triggered by a frantic teacher who lived alone in a cottage one street east of Felix's house. She had come home from work that afternoon to find a hole, roughly the diameter of a Frisbee, pushed through a screen of her locked back porch. The basset hound that had resided on the porch for years—an aged home alarm system, Brutus, who had no qualms with lounging in the breeze from two ceiling fans all day—was missing. In Brutus' place were signs of a struggle: toppled planters, claw marks in the green outdoor carpeting, and an inexplicably huge burst of dog-food vomit. On the message board, nearby neighbors who worked from home were recalling how they'd heard brief yelps that day, maybe an hour or two after lunchtime. Others theorized that Brutus had gone sick and senile, bolting off to freedom as delusional dogs sometimes do. A few old-timers, meanwhile, feared the canine thefts and dog ransoms of Sweetberry's lowest days had returned. Just one guy mentioned death by constriction.

We can't know for sure, but judging by the forensics and evidence of nesting patterns, it's a safe bet Felix was the luckiest man in Atlanta that night. And possibly for many nights before that. The original steps of his shotgun had long ago rotted away, and in their place were simple, backless floating stairs he'd built, which left each visitor's ankles exposed to whatever lay beneath the porch. That put Felix within a split-second strike of the great head, which was broad as a toaster, inconspicuous as Midwestern mud, and obviously, finally motivated by hunger.

CHAPTER 20

parked outside my house, all sad and dark. I stepped into the street and fanned the thick night off my skin with a reporter's flip notepad. It had been the longest, hottest day of the summer, and the whole saga had produced nothing but obvious defeat. My spirits were lifted though, for a second, when I squinted to see the blonde visage of a lounging woman beneath my one functional gas lamp, seated at the threshold of my ancient oak door. She called from my porch, in a bemused slur: "A hungred and twenty derrgreeeez thiz weekend, they zay! Can you berweave that shit, God!"

"That you, Becky?"

"Yezzir!"

Given her authority over me, I felt strangely violated by the unsolicited visit, as if Becky was somehow evaluating my lifestyle and work habits, if not outright spying. But I was also excited, naturally. I came through the iron gates smiling. The deep contours of her legs were visible beneath the lamp's soft light, crafting shadows into her stretchy business slacks. Somehow, she looked both defeated and eager. From the first porch step I could smell the sweet, sharp odor of wine coolers. Beside my rocking chair sat her proud collection of empties, huddled up like bowling pins.

"A whole six pack!" I said. "Impressive."

"Yep."

"After all that, though, are you hungry?"

She nodded. "Fuh. Am. *Ished!*"

"Great," I said. "How you take your mustard rice? With ketchup? Mayo?"

"Oh, just shuhzh," she said. "Nobody here'z feelin' zorry for yer azz..." Her face contorted into a clumsy yawn, and she ran the back of her hands along the dirty clapboards of my porch.

"Careful!" I said, clenching up, pointing to the wall. "You see those little red dots? That's radioactive, viper blood-splatter." I reached over, clasped her forearm, and pulled her hand away, back into her lap; what I felt was the hard, thick ropes of cargo ships, only smooth. "Sorry about this," I said. "Haven't gotten around to fixing the bullet hole, or scrubbing that shit off—"

"*Puh!*" said Becky. "Fug it. I gots thick skin. And I been washin' the damn bu-zhes for a hour. Not a damn thing in there movin' tonight."

"You need me to take you somewhere, Beck?"

"Nope."

"You've had enough, I think. Especially for a Tuesday, or whatever the hell day—"

"Thizz a *work* meeting!"

We both laughed for a second.

"We had one of those already today," I said. "The most awkward one in history."

"Yez!" she said. "Buh therez been new developments!"

Without consciously trying to, I learned over, suddenly energized, and put my face near hers, to be closer to the fresh details. The air between us sizzled, at least as I perceived it. "I've got some new stuff, too," I said. "But go on, please."

"Nope," she said. "Yew firz."

I offered her a hand, to aid in standing up, but she declined. Instead she opened her arms wide for an embrace. Heavy eyelids and overdone mascara somehow weaponized her tempestuous eyes, sharpening the blade of them, the sparkling gray magnetism in them. She was drunk and ready, haughty in her numbness. You could see the invitation, the dare, in the way she held her head, cocked back confidently on her shoulders. I stood still, nonetheless. Whether all of this was desperation, or a revenge move against her ex-husband to be, I didn't care; she could use me or adore me all she wanted, until she was infatuated or passed out from disappointment. All I wanted was the warmth of being desired again, however fraudulent or fleeting that was. But when she realized I was not making any sort of physical advance, she emitted a bratty harrumph, stomping her fancy sandals. After that she surrendered her pursuit, I thought, which was uncharacteristic. From her leather purse she produced a few papers, folded neatly in thirds. And she held them in her lap like a stubborn child.

"OK, then, I hope this make sense to you, given your enviable state of mind right now," I said. "In a nutshell, I have certifiable proof that Lotto has lied to all The Flank homeowners. And he's lied to city government. But he's also set a trap. A really *strong* trap, which could land all those old folks in jail, if Lotto feels threatened..."

Becky's head dipped twice, fighting sleep and nodding off.

"Let's take this up tomorrow," I said. "Stand up. I'll call a taxi—"

"No!" she said. "'nuff of that talk. Lookee here..."

And she slowly, seductively peeled back the top of the first paper in her little stack, revealing the letterhead half-inch by half-inch, like a royal flush, until I could make out the crucial words: "City of Atlanta Office of Permitting and Planning."

"Are you trying to seduce me with building permits?" I said.

"Isz Lotto," she grinned, although sadly. "I got theez from that gwuy John, on the zity goverrmet beat. Lotto'z a bad boy, Johnzon. A bad, bad boy. He'z not zhitting this zime, not fwukin 'round..."

I snatched the documents, stepped away, and read them quickly. At that instant, a great consequential clock began to tick. The city had granted Lotto permission—in an *expedited* process, no less—to begin deconstruction of The Flank in late August. Beyond the usual remediation mumbo jumbo, there were no preconditions for Pumpernickel Enterprises to move forward, no mention of historic preservations. Lotto was only restricted by the mandated start date: August 25. That was just a month away.

"This is insane," I said. "I've never seen anything like this. You?"

She hunched her shoulders and gave a squashed, sloshed smile.

"It's really obvious," I said. "It's so blatant, and he doesn't even care at this point."

"What?"

"I mean, is there any better indication that you're screwing an important government official than this? When the city green-lights destruction of things you *don't even own yet*?"

"Let'z take him down!"

"What?"

"Lotto!" she yelled. "We got the proof, in print, to end iz career, man! Iz right *here*!"

"Are you asking for a story about this?"

"Yez," she said, lifting arms up straight, a touchdown. "Tomorrow!"

"I don't know, Beck."

"Pluz," she said, "another idea: I need a rrrighter for the weather. Therszayin' it'll hit a hungred and twenty derr-greeeez thiz weekend!"

Every variation of human emotion besieged me, from glee to paranoia. "I just don't know," I said. "Count me in for the record-breaking heat story. But you sure you wanna spend the time and ink on this one single development? It's just a few houses."

"*Huh*?"

"It's all kind of small, I mean," I said. "And I'm not sure the story's buzzy enough for y'all. I doubt it'd drum up enough interest to meet online click quotas."

Sloppy belligerence overtook Becky, and she rolled over to her hands and knees. Using what looked like barroom yoga, she extended her legs behind her, and with a sort of gravity-defying, superhuman push-up, sprouted to her feet. Then she reared back her leg and, like a punter, kicked her empty bottles in six different directions. Little fruity torpe-does shot off into the bushes. She grabbed the back of my head with one hand and pointed into my face with the other.

"Why you backun down?" she said, her breath a bag of rotten apples. "All zummer you're in my ear about covering thizyit, and now you wanna kill it? You wanna let that boy die in vain? *Huh*? Did Lotto pay yer azz off too?"

"Come on," I said.

"*Did* he?"

"That's a low blow. Let's just get you a cab."

"I'll give the zsories to zomeone else, Johnz-*un*. Don't think I *won't*."

"Look," I said. "Here's the truth: I'm afraid a Lotto exposé would land a whole lot of people in jail. He's trying to pull off the most lucrative deal of his career, by selling every bit of the homes he's slaying now. He'll watch old ladies go to jail and not blink, and then he'll walk. That might sound defeatist. That might not be valiant journalism. But I'm not stirring that pot. He'll win regardless. Do you understand?"

She dropped her hands, obviously confused by how the roles had reversed, how I'd become the knowing, reasonable parent. Despite her intoxication, Becky looked so remarkably healthy, so effervescent in her relative youth, so pink. More than anything, in that moment, I wanted to go fetch Marnie, toast the night with Becky, forget Lotto, dance a hot waltz or ten on the porch, and end up giggling in my bed into the wee hours. We'd commit one regrettable, unholy, fantastic act after the next. And it would be my swan song, because it would not last. I'd be turning seventy years old in a few months. It was inevitable that I'd start to break down before long. Or that I'd enter that utterly elderly stage in which the only guys getting lucky are sitting on oil wealth—not barren refrigerators and unemployment forms. A chance like this would probably never come again in my life. For thirty years I'd been waiting for it, although never actively pursuing it, and yet absolutely dreading it. I deeply missed the physical electricity and sense of pride in having made passionate, carnal love. In my boozy pre-dreams and early morning reminiscences, I'd often try to recall the first years of my relationship with Sage: how that starving guttural zing of youth made us cling to each other, like two licked pieces of candy, and how she'd lay her silken head over my chest—as the sun came up, or as it dipped back down—and never want to leave. It had been so long, my celibacy so thorough, that I'm sure Sage wouldn't have even minded by now. I knew she would grant me permission, if not encourage my straying, in hopes it would buoy me for a while. Nonetheless, I reached into my pocket, produced my phone, and punched the button I had stored for Atlanta Quality Cabs. As I did that, real sadness filled Becky's face. It was the look of fresh hurt, the fear of new loneliness.

"You have to be zo, zo lonely here," she said.

I turned around and pretended to embrace my crooked Victorian. "This old girl keeps me company," I said, through a half-smile.

"They'd *really* go to jail, if we did pubwicizty?"

I nodded. "I'm afraid Lotto's got them, where he wants 'em."

She stomped a sandal and said, "Fine!"

"I'm sorry, Beck, and so is my stomach, but I just can't. We've both gotten to the bottom of this, so we did good work. But there's nothing I can personally do about it now—"

"Then I can't do zyit with *you*," she said, squinting to maximize the gash. "And I'm not giving youz the weather zsory then!"

"That's cool, Beck. I understand."

"You really letting someone elz have this scoop, about your pres-*shuz* neighborhood?"

She was twisting the dagger now. I'd be lying to say my respect for Becky wasn't being tarnished the more we spoke, the more she applied her stinging threats. Thoughts of our beautiful predawn dalliance suddenly died. I only wanted her gone from my porch, that breath out of my face. "When Lotto shows up next month," I said, "with his fleet of bull-dozers, it won't matter a damn bit who had this story first."

"Ahhh, *phfrooooo!*"

With that, Becky tossed the crucial documents into the air and stomped off to the street. I started walking out to accompany her until the cabbie would show up, but she heard my approach and screamed back something blurry about letting the city down, betraying her trust, and being a quitter. I bowed my head, said nothing, and waited until I heard the cab chug away. In that instant I could sense my working relationship with Becky ending; she would awaken tomorrow ashamed, angry, confused, and intent to never speak with me again. At that moment, I knew I'd never see my byline in the *Beacon* again. My bread-and-butter had spoiled. My identity was gone, my poverty all too real. A three-decade tradition had become the summer's latest casualty, and by autumn's first chill, nobody out in the world would really remember or care.

I fetched Marnie, turned off the porch light, and stood there watching my quiet street. In the night the bountiful blooms of pink and white myrtles were black, drooping like sad colonies of tiny grapes in streetlight silhouettes. Maybe "crestfallen" isn't precisely the word, because it's so dramatic, but what I felt was pretty close to having fallen irreparably from a crest, albeit a meager one. In every direction was nothing but lowness. I was convinced that my zenith as a writer—I'd say "artist," but my subsequent laughing could break my concentration—was behind me. I'd been a fraud who spent his career chasing the quick prize, questioning his word choices, and letting editors down. Now I was done, over.

Soon, the chug of heavy construction equipment would be the signal for Genteel and company to scurry away, realize the extent of their financial missteps, and end up crammed into the purgatory of semirural senior living compounds, which is all they'd ultimately be able to afford. Maybe it was time, I thought, that I sold my own house, too. Despite its beauty and inimitable grace, the suffering money pit would be razed, the lot scraped down to bloody mud, cleared of everything but its magnificent magnolia; and within six months, the contrived skeleton of a "rustic-modern triplex" would take shape. But whatever. I shifted to the other side of the porch, took a seat in the rocker, and sipped.

Maybe, I thought, it'd be in my best interest to keep my mouth shut and join the exodus. Give up. Cash out. Move on. Not to sound like an asshole, but I could make stupid money fast. I knew the exact number at which my big corner lot would surely sell in a weekend ($323,000), if it even reached the open market; I could probably lure in cash buyers on sales rumors alone. For my remaining two decades or five years or seven months on earth, I could enjoy the spoils. I'd take a trendy high-rise apartment in Midtown and spend my days embarrassingly drunk on palm-studded pool decks, recounting for bored, bikini-clad millennials the wonders of covering petty burglary cases in places they'd never heard of. I'd be free from the creaky ills of a century-old hole. Free from the perversions of Lotto Livingston. Free from the reach of fangs. Free from the petri dish of civic drama urban America was becoming. I could morph into the old man I'd always wanted to be: that chill cat with a nice watch, a proud belly, and a fuck-you strut, exuding confidence from having sufficiently kicked life's ass. But then again, I thought, becoming that guy could be surrender at its most despicable.

I sat up, fanned my wet face with a seat cushion, and sank into the early stages of inebriated bliss—until, at about midnight, it came to visit me again. That strange, autumn breeze in July streamed through Sweetberry for another glorious ten seconds. It was almost ghostly in its foreignness, yet so real. Oh, it was real. It was a cool bath. It was skin-mint heaven. And this time it shook the oak branches above me and the palm fronds across the street with that smoke-scented, powerful nudge. I came to my feet and lifted my arms and let the wind absolve me of my heavy mind. I drank in the summer reprieve. I worshipped it for each fleeting second. Then it whipped away and dissipated, just as my nearness to the porch-side bushes began to worry me.

I can't imagine what a peculiar, frightening sensation a chilly wind must have been for the green anaconda beneath Felix's porch, that tropical dog-eater. I wonder now what she was thinking then. And I pity her, as she too had been displaced, forced into strange habitats twice. How she must have shivered in the unfamiliar wind, our timid leviathan, coiled in worry, preparing to watch humanity, in all its lunkheaded selfishness, eat itself.

PART IV

CHAPTER 21

The calls came on August 22, midafternoon. Three days before Bulldozer D-Day.

In my foyer, the old beige rotary phone vibrated the antique side table with so much tinny insistence, no matter how long I ignored it. The third call ended, followed by a pause of five seconds, and then came the fourth. Finally I leapt off the couch, brushed aside the empty bottles of dirt beer and my two-pretzel ration for lunch, and swept the receiver off the cradle, shouting into the line: "You're interrupting my third nap. This better be good!"

For a moment, all I could hear was breathing, a younger man's breathing. In my waiting I caught a glimpse of myself in the body-length hallway mirror. Amidst so much depression and societal sadness I hadn't managed to get properly dressed in a few days. The weird summertime hibernation was clearly wreaking havoc, because a slouched, ghostly lunatic was looking back at me. On the bright side, as I was noticing, the combination of sweltering August, the power company's decision to "interrupt" my home's electricity (despite my pending appeal), and general malnutrition had carved a few pounds from my frame. The sickly, orangish tinge of my skin was more disconcerting. "OK, asshole, I'm counting down from five here, and then I'm hang—"

"Johnson. God Johnson?" The voice was muffled, deep as if spoken through cloth.

"Yeah, that's me."

"Listen," he said. "I'm sorry this is last-minute, but are you aware of what's been called for two p.m.?"

"Nope," I said, heart dancing. "Enlighten me."

"Sir, there's a press conference you'll want to know about, happening today," he said, timidly now. "Well, really, you *deserve* to know about it. Despite your fallout with this—I mean, *the*—newspaper, it'd be a travesty if you were kept in the dark."

"A press conference?" I said, rapt. "Called by whom?"

"You sitting down?"

"I'm always sittin' down."

"It's been called, hastily, by Police Chief Montgomery herself—at the Atlanta zoo!"

I dashed across the room, stretching the curly telephone cord dangerously far, and snatched my pen and notepad. "Go on, man," I said. "Where exactly? And when again?" Silence on the other end. "Also," I said, breathing heavy, feeling alive, "I don't exactly have an outlet to report for now. I'm not sure they'll let me into a press conference without active credentials. So is there a possibility we can work together? Could I cover this for you, whoever you are—"

"I can't help you in that regard. But you'll want to be at the zoo's largest public pavilion at ten minutes before two p.m., at the latest. We figured you were left off the invite list, given your recent issues. You might want to wear a hat, or something to mask your face a bit, as some people think you've become a bit... I don't know, unstable. I'm sorry—just being real. Also, I'd suggest you take your old credentials and wave them in front of the youngest PR person you can find, someone who might not recognize you. No offense."

"Someone too green to see the expiration date."

"Exactly," he said. "One other thing: You might want to keep quiet once you're in there. But you definitely don't want to be late. It'd be tragic if you didn't hear this firsthand. We recognize it was your scoop, sir."

"What's the gist?" I said. "Can you give me anything?"

He swallowed, the sound of fear. "Don't write anything until after the conference," he said, a few seconds before promptly hanging up. "But that crazy zookeeper McCaffrey? Well, God, they found him. And that's all we really know at this point."

I dropped the phone. Before it could bounce twice on the lacquered pine, I'd begun hustling around the foyer in hapless circles—a brain blitz. "McCaffrey!" I hollered. "I'm coming! Ya nearly killed me, McCaffrey!" I was talking to my mirrored self, my face, the world's most inglorious mugshot sprung to life. But I was a substitute. What I needed was an editor. A sounding board. A voice of reason. The newsroom equivalent of a wise parent. For the first time in about fifty years, I was electrified by story possibilities but had nobody to talk sense into me, harness that energy, and help create a viable plan. Becky hadn't acknowledged my existence for a month, except to tell colleagues I'd lost my mind. Rumors had spread widely that I was nuts, thoroughly off the deep end this time, and nobody at the Atlanta weeklies or alternative presses or college blogs was returning my pitches. So I changed course and called Squeaky.

He picked up, third ring, with a mouthful of food. "Huwl-woh."

"Squeaks!" I said. "It's me. You sittin' down?"

"Yup."

"The batshit zookeeper—they got him!"

I could hear the awful, slappy crackles of his rapidly spitting out food. "What!" said Squeaky. "They *killed* him?"

"No, no," I said. "At least I don't think so."

"Then *what*?"

"I don't know really. I just got a tip, from the ether, about a press conference in two hours, down at the zoo."

"Day-*um*," he said. "What you need from me?"

"I just needed... I don't know, to break the news to somebody, I guess."

"Well, have fun down there."

"You want to go with me?" I said. "I know that's not protocol, but please?" Squeaky said nothing. "Honestly, man," I continued, "I'm feeling a little rusty, a little weak, and I could use a partner. Plus, you worked on this case, too. You deserve the spoils."

Squeaky blew a long sigh into the phone. "Look, God, I don't want to go in no press conference," he said. "That's too much heat for me, too much bacon."

"Come *on*," I said.

"OK, you right," he said. "I'm dyin' to know. And if they got him in 'cuffs, I got to see this dude goin' down. I ain't slept right for months, on account of him."

"If you're in," I said, "tell me right now. I'll head over there. No sleeveless shirts, and leave the sword behind. We have to slip under the radar. And I need to borrow that detective's hat you have, the blue fedora."

"Man, pick me up!"

Showered, shaved, inspired, starving, dripping with cologne, and wearing a tie, I parked behind Squeaky's two-story flophouse and pounded on the backdoor for a while, trying to keep my hands steady. The rush of excitement—combined with my protracted cocoon of beer on mostly empty stomachs in recent weeks—was taking a toll in the swelter. I could tell by the empty driveway that none of Squeaky's middle-aged slacker roommates were around, so I poked my finger through the tattered screen door, popped up the hook latch, and let myself in. I started to call out to Squeaky and announce myself, but I had a shameful, tremendous idea: Before he could catch me, I'd quickly filch a bit of food, just enough to get me through the stressful day ahead.

The kitchen's general smell nearly cost me my appetite, but I tiptoed on, into a dark pantry. From in there I could hear the sounds of water whooshing through old pipes. I guessed Squeaky must have been obliging my request to clean up. On a low shelf I found a canister with dust on the lid and a few almonds inside; he wouldn't miss those, and down they went. Behind that, beneath a pack of rolled garbage bags, was a box of spaghetti with at least twenty hard strands inside. As they crunched in my mouth, I thought of steamy sauce and mushrooms, and I'll be damned if I didn't slightly taste those things. The water turned off overhead, and as I heard footsteps on creaky hardwoods, I got desperate, hurried, and greedy. I slay a soft apple in about five bites while tossing in a few mini bars of dark chocolate and a gulp of straight honey. Then I scrammed out of the pantry, chewing the evidence away. I noticed a door, cracked open a few inches. It pains me to admit it, but in a quest to pack my trouser pockets with something unperishable and relatively flat, I whipped open the door and rummaged through a closet beside the kitchen's exit. It contained Squeaky's most cherished belongings: his binoculars, camouflage winter coat, sword, and a cache of liquor bottles. Beneath the liquor I discovered a packet of macaroni and two sticks of beef jerky in plastic—jackpot!—and I told myself he owed me as much. All that sustenance, easily four-hundred calories, slipped into my front pockets with hardly a bulge. Barely noticeable.

I stepped out of the closet, checked for the sound of footsteps on stairs, and hearing nothing, took a few bites of splendid, teriyaki beef jerky. I peeked back into the closet, eager for more. Beneath the random stocks of food and cherished flotsam of Squeaky's life, the edge of a gold-trimmed wooden box poked out from a blanket on the closet floor. Curiosity swelled up in me; I could tell the box was vintage and painstakingly crafted, and I had to know more about it, in order to quiz Squeaky on the nefarious way it'd come about being there. I licked the telltale smell of jerky from my fingers and crouched into the closet, pulling back the blanket, admiring the ancient craftsmanship of the box, but finding it locked.

As I re-covered the box and turned to scat away, I saw its little golden key, dangling from a shoestring tacked into a dark corner of the closet's wall. I nearly laughed, the hiding place was so obvious. But upon opening the box, I gasped. My soul swirled down a drain, in such a miserable way I thought I'd never laugh again. Encased in a velvety green rectangle before me was a five-chamber, antique, Lone Ranger-style pistol. It'd been part of a package, a twofer, because the twin indentation next to it was empty. Immediately my thoughts went back to the church basement, to the screaming and blood. Squeaky's other pistol was in APD custody, I knew. With the one that remained in front of me, my instinct was to cock it and shoot him once, maybe in the stomach or leg, a stupid vengeful move for Joey. Instead I locked the box and rewrapped it in cloth, slinked out the backdoor, walked around the house to the front porch, and rang the bell like I'd just driven up. Squeaky pounded down the stairs and answered in a collared shirt and studious-looking spectacles. He handed over his fedora and said something about having had a change of heart and wanting to see the press conference at all costs, but beyond that, his speaking wasn't registering. To my pounding, furious head, it was just murmuring. All I said was, "I'm around back, follow me now." We loaded up and shot off to the zoo.

We parked a couple of blocks away, to not blow my cover with the blatant presence of my big truck. Squeaky was rubbing open palms together and licking his lips, as if preparing for a sumptuous meal, the public skewering of our wayward nemesis. I couldn't manage to speak to him, though. I communicated with nods that the coast was clear, that we should head out. While hustling through the heat, Squeaky told me I looked tired and weird, a little dark yellow. He asked about the prospects of my power being turned back on, adding, "I'll be goddamned if my little thermometer on the porch didn't hit one-hundred-eighteen degrees yesterday. One *eight*-teen!"

That was all I could take. I stopped walking, snatched his shoulder, and before I could catch myself, said, "On second thought, take your dumbass back to the truck. Stay in there, right where you were, head down." His loose face lifted, alighting in fear and confusion. "Crack a window," I said. "And just shut up. I'll be back as soon as possible. Don't try walking home in all those nice clothes, you'll die of dehydration."

"But…"

"But shut up, Squeaky. *Go!*"

Twenty years before all of this, I'd covered the global media fiasco that was the Atlanta Olympics. But I'd never seen a press frenzy in this town remotely as rabid and unorganized as what was happening in the zoo parking lot. News vans, broadcast trucks, military-grade satellite vehicles from the national news teams, storm-chaser trucks, electric bicycles totting bloggers, and the gas-friendly Japanese cars of freelancers clogged the main pavilion parking lot. Neighbors in tank tops and tiny shorts stood around gossiping; they sipped beer from red plastic cups, because this town will party with red cups for any reason; with furrowed brows over big smiles they pointed at the zoo and philosophized, as their friends gathered on high porches across the street. All of their demeanors suggested a great weight had been lifted. Meanwhile, a smoldering and curious mass was huddled at the gates, emitting a low roar. Zoo staff in light clothing distributed bottled water from icy coolers. They issued robotic, practiced warnings about record high temperatures and asphalt. Everyone was soaked with sweat but unfazed, so swept up in the thrill of seismic news. Several television reporters were shooting live pieces from the queues, placing news-less updates for their noontime segments. They chirped about a historic summer, a crime the city would never forget, and a day of answers, answers, *answers* that had finally come.

I pulled down the fedora to my eyebrows and pushed my ponytail up inside it. I straightened the choking necktie. I gulped saliva and sweated and gulped some more. At the far left gate, I caught a glimpse of Adam Evans, so I lined up at right. There we stood for ten or fifteen minutes, unmoving and aggravated. We wondered aloud where McCaffrey might be, and how exactly he had finally slipped up. As the line budged ahead, I saw that a young greenhorn zoo man was checking press credentials at my gate—and diligently so. Panic clutched my neck, as my ID was a month expired and essentially useless. All of that dissipated when I felt a broad sting on my right buttocks, like a duck bite. I whipped around, ready to backhand some escaped animal—and if it wasn't Tabitha Jones, the Channel 8 News ace, smiling devilishly behind me. Beside her was a hulking cameraman, struggling to suppress his giggling.

"That's elder abuse," I teased. "Pinching an old man's ass like that. The hell are you doing?"

Her face dropped. She studied my face, my skin. "Damn, God. You doin' OK?"

In spite of our sweating, Tabitha thrust her arms wide and embraced me in a worried hug. She smelled like straw-berries and youth. "Actually, no, I'm not OK," I said. "I *have* to be in there for this. My credentials went bad earlier this summer, and that kid up there is checking ID dates with passion. I had a falling out with the *Beacon*—"

"I heard," she said, smashing her lips in disappointment. "Listen, honey. Just hold the camera and these bags. We'll flash our badges and then bum-rush right through."

At the gate, when our turn came, I had become very old, wheezing and fearing heatstroke from the mere weight of one news camera. The kid asked us to stop as we tried to scurry in, and he pointed into my chest, asking for my cards. That's when Tabitha attacked.

"Look, kid, this man, Bob, he's won ten regional Emmys for us," she said. "He forgot his badge at the bureau. If you think we're leaving here, heading back to retrieve it, and then facing that line again, let me just say, I've known your boss for about two damn years—"

"Go on!" the kid said, waving. "You're good. I'm sorry."

And we three went in, all silent.

Police and zoo staff shepherded the throng into a vast, cool auditorium that had once shown 3D movies about exotic animals, back when that technology was new. Vines and fake monkeys clung to a huge cruciform lighting rig overhead. All of the technicolor lights were on, and a soft jungle music played, lending the room the aura of a show, not a just-the-facts press conference. I handed the camera back to my coconspirators, shook Tabitha's hand, and then retreated to a dark flank, out of the stage's spotlight. I wanted to be inconspicuous but also felt a strong pull toward being as alone as possible at that moment. On a deeper level, I felt like curling up in a dark cold bedroom and shunning society for a few days or years. I hadn't even brought a notepad because taking notes would be futile, a sadly wistful act, like some boy with a bait-less toy rod at the sea's edge. I slunk lower in my seat. And I thought about Squeaky. The big tricky matter of Squeaky. I wasn't surprised that he'd done something so colossally stupid as bring a loaded pistol to a powder-keg meeting in church. It shocked me, though, that he'd lied to me all summer about it. That he'd let a stewing mother wallow in her own wondering for so long. That he knew an innocent college kid had been branded a criminal for his stupidity. That he'd leave his neighborhood in the dark, with a thousand fingers pointing, rumors churning, bad blood boiling. It all broke my heart.

Suddenly a towering fireman in full regalia, ostensibly the new fire marshal, took the stage and announced that the room had reached maximum capacity. "Sorry, folks," he said, "but shut 'em!" He dispatched two underlings to lock the doors, thwarting a zombie-like rush of reporters clamoring to be the last ones in.

The lights focused and dimmed, warming the stage in rose hues. The anxious crowd fell silent. An army of zoo employees, each in polos with matching rainbowed insignias, flanked the stage in two long lines. Then came a battery of police in formal hats and top-ranking fire personnel, with a couple of ultra-tan dudes who looked like surfers on safari in the middle. They must have been the literal bushwhackers, the fearless snake pros I'd heard about. Between them, a beaming Adam Evans stepped into the light, ready for his glory. It was an immense, sparkling crowd, and if not for their all-business scowls and motley getups, you'd have expected them to start kicking like Rockettes.

And then, like a medal-bedecked monarch, Atlanta police Chief Candice Montgomery marched through the columns of her colleagues and took hold of the lectern. She said, "Good afternoon," and scanned the crowd. The pride she was feeling leapt off her glowing face. This moment, this capture, was clearly the actualization of a thousand girlhood dreams. "I'd like to extend a warm welcome to our local media friends, and to all the new faces from national outlets out there," she said, in her no-nonsense, skeptical, syrupy dialect. "Please relay our apologies to your colleagues who didn't arrive before we reached capacity. This facility has five hundred seats, and frankly, they were claimed faster than we'd anticipated. This, we believe, is the largest press conference in the nearly one-hundred-fifty-year history of this department. Which speaks to the gravity of the situation. A situation we're about to outline for you." She paused, as if waiting for applause, but nobody clapped. "Yes, right," the chief continued. "First, though, I want to point out that our department's motto, like the city's, is *resurgens*. For those who aren't aware, that's translated as, 'to rise again.' And that's precisely what we intend to do—to rise up from a summer of havoc that's cost everyone on this stage innumerable hours of sleep and family time. That's cost many of our citizens their emotional well-being, too. You know, history has shown, time and again, that Atlanta might get knocked down, but she binds together like few other places, and she always emerges stronger. *Resurgens*, ladies and gentlemen. That process begins today..."

With that the chief began a five-minute, congratulatory marathon of praise for anyone on stage who'd been especially devoted to resolving Snakeocalypse, but she curiously mentioned no zoo officials. She was extolling the merits of one lieutenant who'd excelled in providing free lunches for searchers when someone in the crowd, seated far back in the darkened rows, hollered, "Come on, chief, where's McCaffrey?"

Chief Montgomery threw a scowl into the darkness and continued the scripted proceedings for a minute longer. Then she clenched her jaws, cleared her throat, and said, "Regarding the whereabouts of Mr. Gerald McCaffrey..." The newshounds leaned in, preparing to lap from a sparkling stream of delicious information. For once I could sit back and just soak it in, a leisurely observer, as if this was all television and not work. "Mr. McCaffrey, once a decorated employee of Atlanta Memorial Zoo, is not in our custody right now"—a mass, moaning deflation from the crowd. "He is, however, being extradited as we speak, from New

Mexico. That's where he was apprehended at a restaurant last evening." With that revelation, a few hundred heads cocked sideways: *fucking New Mexico?*

"In talking with federal authorities in the Southwest Judicial District," the chief continued, "it's our understanding that Mr. McCaffrey had been in New Mexico for at least several weeks. Mr. McCaffrey was under the impression he was exempt from prosecution, in terms of the many charges he faces here in Atlanta. For reasons we haven't discerned yet"—and the chief bit the side of her lip, holding it with her front teeth, as if thwarting laughter—"Mr. McCaffrey was under the impression he was in Mexico. Not, as it were, *New* Mexico." She let that sink in for a second, a punchline she was proud of. "Per our sources, he'd been living in a motel with a Spanish name. Yesterday, at about eighteen-hundred hours, Mr. McCaffrey was eating a tamale when other restaurant patrons recognized him from national broadcasts about the situation here. He was apprehended by deputies in the parking lot, and he's in transport now, somewhere in Texas."

A bespectacled younger reporter, seated a few rows up to the left, was able to shout the crucial inquiry before the chief resumed her spiel.

"Chief!" called the young woman, now standing. "Rebecca Stewart Kline of *The New York Times*. I understand it's early in the investigation, but could you shed any light, at this point, on where the rest of the snakes might be?"

The chief instantly morphed into someone else: a sadder, softer chief. She was frowning and frustrated. "At the moment, I'm sorry to say that's still hard to answer," she said. "Two of the missing animals have been accounted for, here in the city. Both are deceased. That leaves fifteen more that we're actively pursuing—"

"*Actively?*" shouted a gruff, bearded editor I recognized, up near the stage. "With all due respect, how are you *actively* doing anything when you're in the middle of what looks like a college graduation? I mean, sorry to be blunt, but this months-long fiasco is still keeping people up at night. Atlantans everywhere, especially parents, are still very much on high alert, and—"

"Excuse me!" the chief boomed. She squeezed the wooden lectern. "I appreciate your concern—we all do. What I can tell you is that the situation is more complex than that. We have reason to believe that all of the threatening animals, or *almost* all of them, are no threat any longer. That they, too, are deceased. Now, this goes against our protocol, but we're going to let you hear what I'm referring to from the mouth of Mr. McCaffrey himself. We have one minute of a taped confession, emailed from New Mexico this morning, that we'll play right now. In the interest of transparency and peace in our city, we'll let you hear, in his words, all that we know, regarding the errant zoo animals. Good? Good."

Above the stage, an epic white screen slowly unfurled over the dignified heads. The lights dimmed to near blackness. And without warning, an extreme closeup of McCaffrey's red-bearded, sweaty, berserk face burst into our consciousnesses. The camera panned out, mercifully, revealing a typical interrogation room with a steely desk and beige walls. McCaffrey was younger and fitter than I'd imagined him, his eyeballs teetering back and forth, like turquoise marbles in a kayak. In quick succession, he kept emitting what sounded like cackles wed with grunts—a mix of high and low pitches not dissimilar from mule sounds. He wore a vintage MARTA transit system T-shirt and several Southwestern-style bracelets. He was handcuffed but seemed pretty happy about it, although the darkness around his eyes suggested this interrogation had been hours-long already.

"Now, again," said a very detective voice from behind the camera. "Tell us, with as much detail as possible, why you stole the snakes. And tell us exactly where they are right now."

At that, McCaffrey's eyes bulged, and before he said anything, I felt tremendously sorry for him. I'd seen that thousand-yard stare before, that demeanor of lostness, in a hundred heavy courtroom settings. This was a man, outwardly normal not so long ago, whose mind had simply gotten away from him. It was not his fault. This was usually hereditary, an error in the genes. He was no serpent-freeing terrorist. No trust-fund kid revolting, in boredom, against the easy life. No, McCaffrey was sick. Some dark cousin of schizophrenia, if not the disease itself, was all over his face, that poor bastard.

"Sir, like, I used to be in pop bands, OK, but this was my greatest hits," McCaffrey said into the camera, with a half-smile. "Ha, *ha*! So, listen: Yours, and mine, it's a scared world. It's ruining all of us, the fear of it, the venom of fear. I did my part. I made the extraction. And I executed them. Dead as dirt. Deader than hell. All but the three that slipped away, out the back of my truck, in the night. Happened in the park and, I think, at a stoplight. Real sorry about that. I promise and *promise* it was an accident. They were, you know, a lot to handle. So many bags. *Ha!* But you can handle the three escapees, if y'all haven't already. Beware of the big girl, though. She's a mean old thing, long as a whale shark... and now I can tell by your cop faces you haven't found her yet. Have you? Nope. Nada. But yessir, the others won't hurt you, me, or Atlanta ever again. Their threat is eliminated. You can thank me later. But for now, you are welcome..."

It all clicked right then. The whole fiasco made sense. That wild face was the epiphany. The video ended. The screen was drawn upward again. And as the rosy lights came back, I leapt out of my seat and beelined for a small staircase that led up to the stage, far to the chief's left.

Once sufficiently in the light, I ripped off my fedora, the ponytail fell, and several officers put palms on holstered weapons. "I know exactly where those snakes are," I hollered, my old voice carried long by impressive acoustics. "Call me nuts all you want, a has-been lunatic. Call me whatever. But if you want the evidence—and the answers—you'll have to just follow me. I forget the address, but I'll take y'all down there, right now."

Nobody budged. The auditorium filled with a strange, high-voltage silence.

"I'm serious," I shouted. "Let's end all this. Let's *go!*"

Without fielding questions or awaiting permission, I turned my back and marched toward the emergency exit nearest my seat. I kicked open the door, sounding an alarm and filling the auditorium with a steamy breeze, sudden brightness, and at last, the real prospect of finality.

CHAPTER 22

A block away from my truck, I could see that Squeaky was soaked with sweat, no drier than if he'd just been baptized in the Chattahoochee River. He was panting with his face out the passenger window, and I caught a gleam from his oversize front teeth, the ones I'd bought him so many years ago. He leaned back, looked forward, and his pained smile melted when he saw what was coming right at him.

I was hustling as fast as the heat and atrophied legs would permit, untying my tie, while right behind me was the most bizarre, impatient, curious, and confused parade Atlanta's ever seen. A handful of motorcycle cops led the charge, lights flashing, barking orders for me to stop and submit to interviews, which I roundly ignored, because I didn't care now. Behind them were zoo vehicles piled with all manner of zoologists, PR specialists, security, and curious zoo ticket-takers who'd caught a ride; on the western side of the street, nearest the houses, was a throng of drunk neighbors from the press-conference porch parties, all blindly chasing a sudden flurry of activity; finally, intermingled throughout, regionally famous broadcasters, legacy media writers, and national news personalities jockeyed to get close enough to ask me questions. I could feel the massive, maniacal presence of all that behind me, but I didn't turn back until I'd reached my truck. When I did, the four hundred expectant faces seemed to be under the impression I'd been planning to *walk* them to the answers they sought. I stood atop my crooked front bumper to address the masses, balancing myself with outstretched arms.

"Just follow me," I announced. "It's fifteen minutes down the road, to the edge of city limits."

"If this is a publicity stunt," said one of the cops, "you'll be charged with—"

I leapt down and jumped into the driver's seat. Just then a loud and pushy wave of media suits and inquisitive, drunk locals obscured everything. A hand with manicured mauve nails clutched my forearm, and I looked up to see the famous Natalie Windstrom of CNN in my face. Her sweat was making a heinous Halloween mask of her TV makeup, and I felt bad for inadvertently wincing.

"Our truck is stuck in that logjam, back in the parking lot, never getting out," she pleaded, padding her forehead with a silky kerchief. "Can I hop in there, to wherever you're going, sir? Just me and my camera operator?"

Squeaky clasped my other arm, mouthing into my face, *What the fuuuuuuu...?*, until I shook them both off, feeling caged. "Listen," I said to Windstrom. "Jump in the back. You and whoever else can fit. But let's *roll*, before those motorcycle cops book me for insubordination."

"Look!" she said, pointing back toward the zoo. "More officers are coming. That must be a hundred of them, maybe the whole force for this district. That's insane!" She glared at me with open-mouthed amazement. "Where are you taking us? And who *are* you?"

I worked the truck into reverse, hopped the sidewalk, and nearly clipped the park's ornate stone gates. A huge crescent of folks in the crowd fell away. I shouted out Squeaky's window: "If you're coming, I'm going. Now, now, *now!*"

Windstrom's cameramen tossed her into the truck's bed like a pantsuited sack of oranges. She was quickly joined by two party animals in tank tops who hoisted red cups and cried, "Woo-yeah!" Tabitha Jones hopped in alone, spinning circles in a fruitless search for her own camera operator. Remaining seats on the bed's ledges went to zoo staffers, a security guard, Police Chief Montgomery herself with security detail, another neighbor with two cans of beer, the host of Channel 17's weekend morning broadcasts, a *Beacon* sports writer, and two sweaty teenage boys who'd been playing basketball on a nearby hoop in the street. Pointing a bottle of water, the chief barked orders for everyone to sit down in the bed. As she turned toward me to issue some kind of mandate, I kicked the gas, and off the old truck surged, bound for conclusions, communal peace-of-mind, and one seismic news story for everyone but me.

A swarm of motorcycle police fell in behind me as I took Mayfair Boulevard, the quick route toward the airport. In the rearview, behind my confounded cargo and the motorcycle cops, I could see the roofs of a few news vans; but it wasn't until I swept down a long hill that I could see the cavalcade's true enormity. It stretched for three blocks, at least, consuming all of the three-lane roadway with flashing lights and vehicles, their drivers trying to keep an eye on my truck. The traffic that was headed north, in the opposite direction, was heeding the oncoming flashes and pulling over onto sidewalks and into driveways. To them it must have looked like we were on the run, more than I actually was, a band of psychopaths leading a slow-motion police chase for the ages in a fucked-up truck.

Squeaky, meanwhile, had gone catatonic, his face fallen, his coherent thoughts clearly annihilated. He kept clutching and squeezing his skull, burning the side of my face with his staring but not saying a word. Despite my disdain for him, I couldn't bear torturing the man with silence for another minute.

"I'm taking them to McCaffrey's weird house in the woods," I said. "To the place with the smell."

"*Look*!" he said, leaning forward and pointing up. "Helicopters circling around, way up there. Three of 'em. And there must be fifty cars behind us now. Like we're the Pied Pipers or somethin'. What the hell you *say* at the zoo?"

I squinted into the sky. The news choppers—unfairly unencumbered by traffic jams, as always—had been especially quick to respond to the promise of fresh snake stories today. The telltale numbers of their news stations, painted at the aircrafts' ribs, glinted in sunshine. "That's all news choppers," I said. "We're probably on live television right now, interrupting soap operas. Damn—I should have washed the truck."

"God, what *is* all this?"

For the first time on the drive, I turned to Squeaky and looked at him, subduing the urge to slap. "That god-awful smell we found, coming up from that basement?" I said. "We know for sure it's not McCaffrey's corpse down there, as I'd kind of suspected. But I'd bet the $47 left in my savings account that it's the smell of what he stole."

"Huh?"

"Look at me Squeaky," I said, my hurting heart getting the best of me. But he was still adrift in daydream confusion, his eyes bouncing around the cabin, trying to connect pieces. "Look in my face. *Look* at me!" He complied now; and though I was straining to keep eyes on the road, I could see in his worried, timid face that he knew I knew. "I'm tired of eating rice, and I went into your kitchen for a snack, as you were showering. Can you explain to me where your other old pistol is, the one meant for that fancy storage box—"

"Stop!" he screamed.

"No."

"*Stop!*"

"What have you *done*, man?" I said. "Did you?"

"Ah, God, don't tell 'em. Please don't tell police."

"You fucked up, Squeaks," I shouted. "And frankly, you're fucked. You're gonna pay for this one, man, and I'm worried it might cost you everything—"

"Stop it!"

For five minutes we said nothing, eyes on the road, minds blitzed. Officers in the motorcycle fleet were conversating with each other and making wild hand gestures, which gave the impression they were losing patience with our journey. In the back, the sports reporter, Tabitha, and Natalie Windstrom were trying to interview the chief and zoo officials despite the wind, to little success. The party guys were standing up but crouched low, surfing the bed. And those two boys looked petrified.

In the span of maybe a second, Squeaky regressed from stoic silence to incorrigible weeping. With a shaky voice and runny nostrils, he finally said: "I had that piece on me for the *snakes*, God. To shoot snakes! That's it. That's all. It was tucked in tight and safe, right in the front of my pants. But in all that church chaos, I jumped up, and I felt it kinda tip outta my jeans, right over the belt buckle. Happened too fast for me to catch it or do any damn thing else. Was like slow motion, watching it fall, hit that floor, and explode. And then, all hell. All I could think to do was just kick it, get it away. But just as soon as I heard that boy wailin', I knew I's goin' to hell, no questions asked. I ain't slept a full hour—"

"That's it, right?" I interrupted. "That's the roof of the house, on that hill? It has to be it, a porcupine roof like that."

"Yep."

"Get yourself together, man. Or stay in the truck, I don't care. I'm going to point them all to that basement and get the hell gone."

"You hear what I said? My explanation?"

"I heard you, Squeaky. I'm just not listening to an excuse like that."

"You think I'm goin' to hell?"

"I don't know."

He started to crack again, bending over. He said, "Ah, no, no, no…"

"Stop it," I said. "I believe you that it was an accident. Of course I believe that. Your going quiet afterward about all of this, and allowing Walt to stew in jail, and Joey's mom to go insane—that's what I can't take. That's the lowest you've ever gone. Period. And it's goddamn despicable. I'm shocked they haven't lifted a fingerprint from the gun—"

"And *that's* what keeps me up at four a.m.," he said. "All I can think is that the gun had been in my pants so long, like a full day, my draws must have wiped it clean. That and all the sweat from a summer like this—"

"*Ghah!*" I said, leaning away from him. "Enough of this shit for now. Just keep it together here. OK?"

I held my left arm high out of the cabin to indicate I'd be stopping, and the great parade halted. I slowly pulled into the sloped driveway and parked. The home's wild architecture was almost totally obscured by the full verdure of August. The roof angles and geometric windows that we could see, however, were enough to spook my cargo, including the chief. They all stood up in the truck bed, but none of them budged toward the house. I gave Squeaky a few seconds to clean up his face. Police parked motorcycles, cruisers, and a random paddy wagon behind the truck. They rushed forward in an effort to guide traffic and control a scene they didn't understand. I leaped out and motioned for Squeaky to join me on the driver's side.

Before I could speak a word, the chief pounced down from the truck, thumping the driveway with her thick black boots. "Explain this, Johnson," she said. "Right now!"

Nodding, I pulled a washcloth from a pocket of the door panel and dried my face. "This is my friend Reginald," I told the chief and the rest of those assembled. "He goes by Squeaky. He helped me conduct the journalistic research that initially led us here, a few weeks ago. All we know for sure is that this is one of many properties in our zookeeper's real estate portfolio. I think you're going to find a lot of answers in the basement. We'll point you there from a little distance, but I speak for both of us in saying we'll never go back—"

"A few *weeks* ago?" the chief cut in. "And you're just notifying the authorities today?"

"I'm sorry," I said, genuinely feeling that way. "It just didn't click until I saw McCaffrey's face in the auditorium, during your show."

Natalie Windstrom raised a pen to ask a question, but I shrugged that off, as this was no press conference. My right knee buckled a bit, a strange tic, and I nearly fell down. The chief shot out a hand and set me up straight.

"Now," I said, "let's head up the hill. But please keep me out of your live shots and photos, OK? Squeaky and I aren't heroes." I glanced over the chief's head to the street. "Also, someone will probably wanna grab a ladder from that fire engine."

From fifty yards away, the stench walloped us all. A month of summer baking in the woods had extended its reach. Windstrom, so famously brave in the face of Gulf Coast hurricanes, shook a dainty finger at the home, said "nuh-uh," and beelined back to Great White. The party guys took one glance at each other, shrank with worry, and followed Windstrom's lead. Tabitha coughed, and Squeaky lifted his T-shirt up to his cheekbones. The chief, meanwhile, plunged her face into the stench like a contemplative bloodhound. She nodded to her subordinates, and they all marched toward the main entrance as the boys arrived with an extendable, aluminum ladder. I nudged what appeared to be the zoo leader, a small man with a patchy mustache, and said he'd want to see it all, down there. He was so curious, he accepted my sweaty washcloth to cover his mouth, as he closely followed the police.

"After you enter, immediately on the left, there's a doorway to the basement," I hollered to the search party. "I bet that's where you'll find the slaughter."

Without another word, the boys darted away. We that remained covered our faces, bowed heads in reverence of the unconfirmed carnage, and waited. Until Tabitha slinked up behind me and squeezed my elbow. "Let's hustle behind them and shoot in there, real quick," she said. "I wanna have a peek at the basement before they cordon this whole property off."

"No, you don't," I said.

"Don't make me do this alone."

"Jesus, woman—this is a mistake. You're gonna vomit."

At the doorway, the zoo official popped up from the basement and startled us. But he was so preoccupied with unhinged crying—his face wet with tears—he ignored us. Tabitha buried her face in the crook of her right elbow, and she bent down, steadying herself at the top of the ladder. I pinched my nose and opened my mouth to demand she let me go first, but I had to step back. A thick, fast cloud of flies came over Tabitha, and that was too much; Channel 8's most intrepid news hunter ran out the door, bejeweled flats flapping on her feet. This cleared the way, if only for a few seconds. I grabbed an old flimsy hunting magazine from the living room, near the towering bear. I swatted flies and went two rungs down the ladder, before I was stopped by a combination of sauna heat and rancidness so thick I tasted spoiled meat. Ignoring the chief's orders to get the hell out, I held my breath and took one long, swooping glance around the dirt-floor basement's single room.

The snakes, our unseen tormenters, were little more than deteriorating carcasses down there—moldering, bug-infested clumps. Some were stretched out, as if they'd died by shovel in the process of being measured. Others were curled like sun-scorched earthworms in driveways, their heads crushed flat. What I recognized to be the long, sleek black mamba had barely made it halfway out of her burlap bag before decapitation. A python or boa on a table appeared to have met a shotgun's spray, as evidenced by the blood spatter on the wall behind her. It was a room of rot, the work of lunacy and cowardice. There was never a mamba among us after all; the animal had never been given that chance, or any chance. In the basement, anyone with a soul would have mourned the slain captives. That process had begun in me, until the beef jerky and other lunch started to rise. I pounded up the ladder and out, passing the teary zoologist on the way.

Woozy, I lifted my face at the edge of the woods and inhaled delicious, clean air. Above the treetops, every news chopper in town was hovering low, making a standard spectacle of death, showcasing a scene their crews couldn't yet comprehend. I felt drained of life myself. Maybe "moribund" isn't precisely the word, but aged is. And so is sick. And exhausted. Finished with whatever my life had become, and the unfortunate place it all had led.

The media that'd hitchhiked in my truck began to circle around me, just as my vision showed first speckles of white. Other reporters and zoo people in the street noticed the commotion and rushed toward us, too. "What's in there exactly—and where?" someone yelled, as if I was the scene's predominant authority. "Tell us what you know, God. What'd you *see*, man?"

We all were caught off guard, and distracted from anything involving McCaffrey's execution chamber, by the horrendous, tortured wails of Squeaky. He was still standing beside the truck. He'd simply come undone, melted down, succumbed to his secrets and the heat. He lifted both hands in surrender and rushed toward a cluster of police officers, screaming, "I shot that boy! I shot that boy dead! I shot that boy in church!"

before collapsing at their feet. Two older cops appeared to have understood the confession immediately. They nodded once to each other, pounced on Squeaky's back, handcuffed him, and dragged him weeping to the nearest cruiser. Squeaky's busted tennis shoes zigzagged ravines into the dirt.

No sooner had the cruiser's door shut than the crying zoo man shot out of the home's bowels and rushed to his colleagues beside me. He bent his knees and opened both palms, as if ready to announce some perilous emergency to a village: "We're still missing one, guys," he said. "The biggest one!"

"Martha?" a woman shrieked.

"Yes," said zoo man. "I've counted the corpses a dozen times. Martha's not down there."

My mind shot back to a summer with my niece, when we'd stood in the reptile pavilion for an hour to watch a rat be devoured, from twitchy nose to tail, one millimeter at a time, by the zoo's only green anaconda, Martha. She was, per a sign near her cage, a record size for captivity in America. And then my mind, like my vision, faded to a fuzzy, hauntingly white screen. My tongue and throat felt like scratchy dirt. I was blind. I was done. I went face-first into the gravel. The last sound I heard was a quick chorus of gasps, which registered, for a second, as hissing. I could feel my breath and the freshness of air, however. I could sense a peculiar lifting, a detachment. And then, through the blizzard, I could suddenly see again, even with my eyes clamped tight, but I saw only one distinctive thing: a child's outstretched hand. I tried to clutch the hand but couldn't. I was mute, deaf, numb, and stiff. I wondered if it was Joey, one source of today's chaos, but I'd never known Joey's hand. And this was a hand I knew well. The same pudgy knuckles and skinny fingernails as mine, a hand of my blood. It was the little right hand of Wyatt, a consolation lost so long ago, and now an invitation to shed fear, accept sickness, and join my boy beyond. Or maybe it was just the dehydration, fucking with me.

CHAPTER 23

I snapped awake with tubes in my arms. Gravel dust coated my clothes. For a moment I was terrified and lost. The downtown ER at Grady Memorial Hospital beeped, droned, and hummed. Other patients moaned. Sweaty families, fresh from the street, huddled. Out the windows, the summer sunset was pink and nuclear. I was on a very high floor. "Finally," I whispered, to myself, "the penthouse."

From somewhere beyond the curtains, I thought I heard someone say jaundice. I'm certain that other grumbling involved talk of excessive alcohol consumption. But I kept staring outside, at another evening I'd been granted to live—or cursed to endure. As the sun slid fully down, over Centennial Olympic Park, hot city streets, and expressways lined with taillights, a relative feast arrived on a plastic tray. Before me was a hamburger with four juicy pickle slices and easily three ounces of ketchup, lukewarm greens, ice-cold cottage cheese, and neatly sliced pears in a delicious pool of syrup. I ate it all in two minutes. The feeling of being full and sedentary brought strange euphoria. I talked to the evening nurse about my life choices, about chronic dehydration, about my brush with death. It was a matter of water and stress, what was wrong with me, she said. And then she removed my tubes. I asked which way the bathroom was, took the stairs instead, and slipped out into the street before anyone could inquire about payment.

I searched the parking lots for Great White for a while, in case someone had kindly followed the ambulance with my truck, so that I'd have it. But of course they hadn't. My keys, it turns out, were actually in my pocket, along with insufficient cab money. I cursed the sticky night and the ailments of age. I cursed the scourge of Gerald McCaffrey.

Without options, I walked the four miles east to Sweetberry Park by myself. I felt ravenously hungover, but with more guilt and depression than nausea and headache. All the recent consequences were too real now, having compounded around our lives and exploded like triggered landmines. In the span of one summer, I'd lost my oldest friend, my career, my reputation, and my health. My efforts to preserve our neighborhood's greatest historical assets had backfired so badly that Sweetberry's most decent citizens were destined for a rip-off—and after that, golden years in subpar senior-living communities, out in the boonies. On the sidewalks, I kept instinctively stepping into the street to avoid bushes, though the chances of snake encounters had become miniscule. I began to realize there's a peculiar comfort in being afraid, dreading the unexplored, especially among like-minded cowards. Fear is a cult, a mob. It's difficult to unlearn. The remedy is experience, knowledge, even insouciance. Which is why I started kicking the goddamn bushes, daring Martha to have a bite of my ankle and take me down, to embrace me in a bone-snapping death hug, to end my doomed, cowardly existence for good.

Once home, I opened all of the hotbox Victorian's windows, the anaconda be damned, and slept without budging for sixteen hours. I dreamt of those hospital pickles and the phantom little hand, his fingers curling toward an unseen body, a bright and beautiful realm, taunting.

Around noon, angry banging at the front door startled me awake. The beefy silhouette on the porch, silhouetted through the curtains, could be only one person: Tall Walt. I opened the door and offered a handshake. He declined.

"You got bailed out quick," I said.

Walt glanced down both sides of the street, as if nervous to be seen. "I been out since your boy was booked last night," he said, sounding none too thrilled. "We need to talk."

"You look so much thinner," I said.

He frowned. "About to say the same about you."

"Captivity and jail food… it's true what they say?"

"I cut twenty-five pounds, without trying," said Walt. "Six weeks will do that."

"Just so you know," I said, "Squeaky set up the internet fundraiser we'd talked about, for a new attorney. It generated less than twenty dollars."

"I know," he said.

"People weren't so motivated to chip in, given the nature of the accusations—"

"Don't worry about it. All that's over."

"You want a drink, Walt?"

"No, sir."

"You want to punch me?"

"Not really, sir."

"We tried everything, man. This all came out of nowhere. It hit me like a bus."

"We can talk about this somewhere neutral—"

"I bet you *could* use a drink," I said.

"Naw," he said, "I could use some real food, though."

"Afraid I can't help you there, man."

"I mean, let's go talk somewhere, get some breakfast," he said. "Somewhere cheap but good. I was thinkin' Waffle House. I got my grandpa's car here."

"Let's have a drink first," I said. "You can't go to Waffle House sober. They won't let you in."

Every trace of amusement bled from Walt's substantial face. He reached a great paw across my door's threshold and squeezed my shoulder. "It's time to get serious. It's time to act. Now follow me down to Waffle House, or just get in the 'lac out here."

Without bothering to close the front door, I followed Walt to the pristine leather seats of Felix's 1992 Cadillac DeVille, a two-toned, king-size bed on wheels. Walt didn't say a word until we'd reached what's probably Atlanta's rowdiest Waffle House—a high and honorable distinction among so much competition. Equal parts greasy spoon and dry saloon, this particular location is an after-hours downtown hotspot where college kids like to brawl for reasons they never clearly remember. The occasional parking-lot stabbing, staff rumble, and catfight in the women's bathroom somehow enhances its charms.

"Lord," said Walt, as we walked in, "did I miss this."

We were seated in a booth with a view of homeless encampments along Athens Street. Among the shabby tents, volunteers in city-issued T-shirts distributed water bottles from buckets of ice. A man in bright yellow sneakers, who'd been trying to jog, simply gave up and grabbed a cold water from one volunteer's bucket. Walt ordered two plates of hash browns, Scattered, Smothered, Covered, Chunked, and Topped—a mountain of ham, onions, and more. I opted for the kid's waffle and bacon.

"The hell?" said Walt.

"What, man?"

"A kid's meal?"

"I'm on a diet."

"A bacon diet?"

"OK, shit. I'm broke."

That tightened Walt's face, with what looked like honest concern. "I noticed, in the newspaper they shared in the jail rec room, that your name and little headshot weren't in there," he said. "Why haven't you been working?" When he saw my lips tremble, he backed off. "Sorry," he said. "That's your business, and I hate to think it's gone south. It's just that, I thought for sure we'd be reading about Lotto's *real* plans for my grandfather's house by now. For all The Flank houses, I mean."

"It's complicated."

He leaned his bulky frame across the table toward me, a serious expression: "No offense, but we're running out of time here, and you don't sound very motivated," he said. "Day after tomorrow, Lotto's going to rip those houses apart. They'll be yuppie-ass bookshelves in time for Christmas shopping season. He technically owns them now, every single bungalow. Grandpa said movers are coming tomorrow, to get the last residents out. That's where we stand. And that's terrible."

Mirroring Walt, I leaned forward and spoke quietly. "I understand all of that."

"So what are we going to do about it?" he said. "No offense, but maybe someone else could do the story? I could go down to the *Beacon* offices right after this. People would read the hell out of that—"

"Then they'd also be reading about your grandpa going to jail for being complicit."

"*Say what now?*" he shouted. People from other booths looked our way.

"Nothing," I said. "Long story."

Walt balled two fists, big as beer mugs, and thundered them down atop the shiny, sticky table. "I did all that legwork for y'all. Thieving those documents. Riskin' my ass. And pointing y'all to 'em."

"How is Felix, by the way?" I said, a convenient pivot. "It's been a few weeks since I've seen—"

"He told me what's going on," said Walt. "How his whole crew got greedy and screwed up. How they crawled in the trap, ate the bait."

"*Shhh*," I said. "Keep it down, eh?"

"I thought he was overreacting," said Walt. "You really think the DA would charge a bunch of old duped folks for taking bribes?"

I lowered my voice to a whisper: "Lotto Livingston's family is so well-connected, across several generations, he's probably related to half the assistant district attorneys at City Hall. He's going to make a killing on this deal, from several angles. His plan is ironclad. It's done. Isn't it time we just accept it and move on? It wouldn't be the first irreplaceable little neighborhood to get bulldozed in this town. And it won't be the last."

"Listen to you."

"I am," I said. "And for once, I hear a voice of reason."

"Well listen to this," said Walt, now whispering, too. "I think someone needs to shoot that son-of-a—"

"So how's *your mom*?" I said, changing the subject. "And how's her George Foreman right hook?"

Walt's face lifted with that thought, and his shoulders relaxed. "She sends her apologies for overreacting," he said. "And—oh—she spotted me $20 for our meal. So you might want to catch that waitress and upgrade—"

Within three seconds I had canceled the kid's plate in favor of another horse trough of sloppy hash browns, like Walt had ordered. Back at the table, I got directly to the point: "How you feel about Squeaky?"

Walt leaned back and studied the room for a minute. "You have to understand, and you might not, being so light-skinned and cul-de-sac, what it's like to distrust the police on a very elemental level," he said. "I can't hate Squeaky for not coming forward."

"How long were you stewing downtown?"

The food arrived. We didn't touch it.

"I get all that," said Walt. "But I can't hate him. He's already forgiven in my eyes. That's how it is."

I let that sink in. "I haven't had the time to check what they charged him with."

"Murder."

"No way."

"Yup."

"Goddamn it."

"Plus reckless conduct," Walt said, "and some smaller weapons shit."

I searched my memory for a similar case, some precedent. There was nothing. There were some cases where children had accidentally shot other children. But an adult *accidentally* shooting a kid in a wheelchair? "When he's indicted, I bet he'll be facing something downgraded," I said. "Something like involuntary manslaughter. Don't you think?"

"I think the murder charge is just for show. A PR thing. They know it won't stick, given the circumstances."

"Either way," I said, "Squeaky's going to prison for a long time."

Walt bent over his caloric bonanza, closed his eyes in prayer, and then dug in. We ate like lions in a butcher shop. Outside, EMTs burst from an ambulance and pulled a stiff, overheated man from his clothes-strewn tent. His gone face and blank eyes must have mirrored mine the day before.

Finished, Walt emptied his water glass and became gravely serious, his hands folded under his face. "Have you heard about the ceremony Lotto's planned at The Flank on Saturday?" he said. "It sounds like a circus. And I mean that literally."

"What now?"

"He's calling it an homage. Airplanes and fireworks and shit."

"*Airplanes?*"

"Airplanes."

"Good Lord," I said. "Unreal. When does the actual demo begin?"

"Permits say the Monday following."

"Lotto's famous for wasting no time."

"But he won't be there that night, after the festival."

"Probably not," I said.

"Definitely not."

"What are you sayin', Walter?"

"I mean, it's not like he'll have guards posted at a bunch of empty houses."

"So what?"

"So what if…" Walt said, grinning, and whispering again. "What if there was a sort of… minor conflagration after the festivities?"

"A *what?*"

"A house fire, at The Flank that night," he said. "Starts in one house, spreads to the next, and so on. A real bonfire of—"

"Don't even think like that."

"Look, that'd be a huge blow to Lotto's bottom line, to lose all that valuable material, all that history," he said. "And it'd be kind of, you know, poetic. The Flank going down in flames, right where it was built, ashes scattered where they should be."

"The stupidest idea I've ever heard," I said, louder than intended. "It hasn't rained in, what, two weeks?"

"So?"

"So the city's parched," I said. "It's dangerous. Have you thought of that?"

"I'd be careful."

"Careful?" I said. "Hell, no. That's reckless as hell. And dumb in every way, top to bottom."

"The risk is worth it. Lotto doesn't deserve those houses."

"You wouldn't get away with it."

"I bet I could."

"You're delusional, son."

"Naw, sir," he said. "I'm inspired."

"No, you're out of your damn mind."

"Don't say a word," he said.

"Don't *do* it."

Walt just shrugged.

"We need to hash this out a bit," I said, "consider all the angles."

"It's time to act," he said. "Not hash out. Not think about it. It's time to *do*."

By now my plate was empty, too. There was nothing more to say. I just kept shaking my head. "Why even tell me this, man?"

"I thought you might want in," Walt said. "If you do, leave all your porch lights on that night. No calls to me, no emails, nothing written, no texts, absolutely nothing. Just the lights."

Walt surged out of the booth, slapped the $20 on the table, and rolled out with a marvelous smile.

"Hey, Walt," I called after him. "Can I get a ride back?"

But he was gone.

CHAPTER 24

The Saturday morning we'd all been dreading arrived in
hurry. I could practically hear the fleets of bulldozers
and backhoes grumbling in the distance, eager to chomp
red earth and eradicate history, like Sherman's ranks reborn.
It felt like the eve of something both ordinary—the rudi-
mentary, knee-jerk destruction of history in Atlanta—and
massively awful.

In a way, from my front porch, the strange predawn
morning felt sweet and simple. Bulbous moths bounced
beneath porch beams. A sycamore across the street had
gone crisply orange already, an early autumnal hint in final
streetlights. But as the morning heated, a sad and steamy
lull filled the streets. The few Sweetberry neighbors who
were outdoors, using the sidewalks, wouldn't look at me on
the porch. I guess it was my association with Squeaky, the
notorious child shooter, that repulsed them now. Or maybe
it involved my failing to spare The Flank from destruction
in the end.

To someone who is hungry that shouldn't matter, but
it did. I'd spent my last $40 on canned beans. Save a rotten
lime and half-bottle of simple syrup, the Cubby of Misdeeds

was liquorless and hollow. I planned to visit the unemployment office Monday and ask for an advance. If that failed, I'd raid Squeaky's pantry and take what detectives hadn't confiscated. If that didn't work, I'd scribble, "FOR SALE BY OWNER: $350K CASH FIRM" on a piece of plywood and stake it in my yard. The shameful white flag, waving at last.

I gulped some tap water and walked with aching eyes down to The Flank. Though pleasant, the morning nature sounds were offensively chipper for the dawn of Lotto's Festival Day, the eve of Bulldozer D-Day.

Lines of big strange trailers idled up and down the street. Workers were hoisting metal fencing and shouting directions at each other. At The Flank's entrance, a small team of Lotto's overdressed underlings was crawling up and down four ladders. Each ladder was positioned against flimsy wooden posts. I hung back in the trees, observing. It was still dark enough that they couldn't see me. The power to The Flank's bungalows had clearly been cut off, as not a single interior or porch light shone. It was a shell neighborhood, devoid of life, a series of fifteen brightly colored corpses.

As the sun rose a bit more, I could see clearly what Lotto's employees were up to; they hung two huge, beige banners from the wooden posts, and it was difficult to decide which message was more abhorrent: "Sweetberry Lanes: The Deluxe Urban Lifestyle You Know You've Earned," or its counterpart down the street: "CenterTown®—King's Beloved Community, At Last."

I was watching Shotgun Three in particular, imagining its afterlife as the walls of ramen noodle restaurants and staging tables for $9.50 croissants, when something caught my eye on the porch. It was a great mound of red sequins—with Genteel inside the dress! Fearing that she'd had a medical emergency, or worse, I shot out of the trees and hustled over. That's when one kid in a seersucker blazer at the base of a ladder quipped: "Don't bother her, man. She's fine."

"Huh?" I said.

"She swears she's not homeless, that she's lived there before," he said, as his stylish spectacles reflected blazing daybreak. "It's not worth calling the cops over."

I halted for a second. "If you called the police on that woman—"

"Just let her sleep, man," he butted in. "Or she'll threaten to call your mom, too."

I shot the kid a sarcastic thanks and pounded up Genteel's three steps, onto the porch. I couldn't believe what lay before me. She was sprawled atop a thin sheet, which was draped over a long pool raft with a bubbly pillow at the end. She snored and coughed. Her hair was perfectly coiffed. With every slumbering breath, her sea of sequins swelled up to her neck and drew back.

"What are you *doin'*?"

She tremored awake, her feet dancing, hands grasping at nothing, until her surroundings began to make sense to her. She grinned. Then she frowned.

"Have you lost your head, lady?"

Genteel yawned, twice. "Welcome to my worst day," she said. "The baddest day of all time." She rocked sideways to loosen her old back, unveiling lavish earrings within her hair. In so much regal jewelry she shined.

I clasped her hot hands and helped her sit up. Even her groggy moaning was a bluesy purr. "What is this?" I said. "Felix let you stay out here, alone?"

"Good gracious, no," said Genteel. "He think I'm stayin' at my cousin's place, just over the South Caro-line line. That's where my stuff is, honey, but not me. I stayed behind."

"For what?" I said. "A last-minute protest?"

"Kind of, I guess. In a way."

"You gonna chain yourself to Shotgun Three, in a jazz-lounge dress?"

She gave me a hot glare. "Shoot, no," she said. "I got a hotel, over in Praytor, for a while. I just wanted to spend one more night here, 'mongst this old wood. Charles and I used ta sleep right here, on the porch, durin' cool weather, back in my heavy brandy days. We called it campin'. I don't have the house keys no more, for the first time since about— *shoot*—1958 or somethin'. But guess what I do got?"

"A screw loose?"

"Nope! Money, money, mu-*ney!*"

Her loud bragging caught the attention of dutiful interns, each now sweating. "Go on," I shouted. "Stop eavesdropping." They ignored me and resumed their eternal tweaking of the banners. I turned back to Genteel, looking down. "I've never seen you so proud," I said. "That's kind of disappointing—"

"I'm old, son," said Genteel. "I'm done. And now I'm *rich*, finally!"

She tossed me a high-five, but I retracted my hand.

"How much was the bribe, Genteel?"

"Thirty-thou," she said, beaming. "Boom!"

I nodded, calculating. "And you put most of that in Joey's casket, out of guilt?"

"Oh," she said, caught. "I put a good five-thou in there. But I did tell his momma to take it out, afterwards, to cover expenses."

"So you netted, what, total?" I said. "A hundred and forty-five grand for your property?"

"Mmmrm-hmm."

"And what's that get you now?"

"We done discussed all this—"

"It gets you nothing around here," I said.

"Get on," she said, pointing. "Get on down the street, Johnson!"

"And it probably buys you nothing near your country cousins, either. Not a nice house, at least. You could buy a shoebox city condo, but if you're goin' that route, you might as well buy yourself some quality, built-in living assistance."

"Change the subject, or get out my face," she said. "I'll find me somethin' nice soon enough. And it won't be no old folks' place."

"Why don't you and Felix combine your cash and buy a little cottage or something?" I said. "You thought of that?"

"*Hoo*, that's a hot idea," she said, sarcastically. "For one, it's too early to talk about livin' together. For two, I asked Felix, and he say he don't live under the same roof out of wedlock. And last, I *got* my husband. He dead, but we still married."

"Oh, I can relate."

"Your husband dead, too?"

"Come on," I said. "Let's get you up."

Genteel lumbered to her feet, the tough tendons cracking in her knees. She peeked into the front window, running hands across the exterior boards.

"I take it you heard the news about Squeaky?"

"We not gonna discuss that news," she shot back. "Not on this day."

"Understood," I said. "But did you hear about the discovery, the zookeeper's basement? Very sad but also more positive—"

"*Shoot*," she said. "Positive? You call a missin', thirty-foot snake positive?"

"I call it progress, at least. If you know about her, I'm surprised you slept out here, alone."

"Oh, honey, I got my pepper spray!" she said, cackling.

Genteel leaned over a bit and pulled the top of her lacy bra away from her chest, revealing a small arsenal of pepper spray, a sheathed filet knife, and a rock. It was indecent to stare so long but the storage capacity was incredible.

"Plus, they say she timid, probably scared," said Genteel. "They said on the news that maybe she livin' the high life, down in them sewers, eatin' rats and possums. They say to keep pets locked up but don't fret so much. She probably long gone. She probably scooted off to Florida by now. Said they call her Martha, like some kind of blonde, happy White woman that sells towels."

We laughed on the porch. The banners, at last, were aligned to Lotto's instructions, and the underlings retreated to the shade. I could hear them saying something about cages, clowns, a DJ, and balloons.

"So why the dress?" I said, pointing to so much bright red against the weatherworn wall.

"Oh, this…" and she wilted, bashful.

"What are you up to, lady?" I said. "I can see a devious plan on your face—"

"The dress? Oh, this just a little *oomph* for my performance at the festival, that's all. I came over to spend the night, and I came *pre*-pared."

"Performance? Again?"

"Yes, sir!"

"I thought you couldn't sing anymore, Genteel?"

"I cain't," she said, flatly. "My big buttery notes is all gone, honey. But Mr. Lotto don't know that."

"I'm lost."

Her smile lifted, slow and large, the widest and wickedest I'd ever seen on her. "I got some, uh, alternative plans."

"Stop teasin' me."

"OK, listen," she said. "But don't say nothin' to nobody. We got to hit 'em blind with this."

I couldn't help but chuckle. So many devious plans were percolating I was starting to enjoy it all a little. "Hand to your Bible," I said. "I'm mute."

Genteel peeked around the corner and into her hacked-down bushes, checking for eavesdroppers. "So, Felix's grandson, Walter, he been workin' with me, ever since he got freed," she said. "We doin' a little composition, like in the studio, back in the day. Only it's different. It ain't exactly singin', like I said. And it sure's heck ain't bein' *recorded*. Ain't no way we doin' that! But we got somethin' real good in place, though, for today's festivities. A true original. Don't you miss this, honey."

"Can you give me a hint?"

"Nunt-uh."

"Is Lotto paying you for this?"

"You better be*lieve* he payin'!" said Genteel. "But that little contract say I must 'perform.' Ain't a dang word in there say I must *sing*. And I fully intend, with all the soul left in these bones, to exploit the difference!"

I was riveted, to the point my slight boobs trembled.

"Not to sound melodramatic," I said, "but will this be the swan song for Genteel Briggs? A public encore? The grand finale for the legendary leader of Sweet Genteel and the Gnat Line Players?"

"Hush up now, Johnson. No pressure!"

"The greatest songstress Atlanta's eastside ever knew?"

"*Shoot*," she said. "Whatever, fool."

"I can tell you're excited about doing this," I said.

"I'm excited to be sendin' this place off right—with a big ol' finger up! The bad middle one, too. Which's just right for the devil!"

"I'll be here, lady," I said. "And so will half the eastside. But I'll keep the secret."

"Good, honey," she said. "Now help me get my place in order."

Together we deflated the raft and folded the sheet and left them in a neat pile. She asked if I'd go fetch my truck and take her to breakfast, down at Sweetberry's last remaining greasy spoon, the Bygone Grill. I said I didn't really know where my truck was, because I didn't, and if I did, I didn't have the gas to get too far. Genteel's demeanor changed, her body stooping a bit with pity. She stomped away in her nice flats. We hoofed the eight hot blocks to breakfast. The whole time she harped about my being too skinny, too orange in the skin, too lonely, too irresponsible, too sad, too much for her to fix again. But I was thinking ahead, to the food she'd unfortunately have to buy for me, the toast and exquisite eggs and those free containers of jelly and butter they keep at all the tables. Those little calorie vessels, I realized, would slip easily into all of my pockets. I could whip them into some sort of puree tonight, and I would live at least one more day.

CHAPTER 25

reakfast with Genteel was a feast of buttered breads, real country ham, and free coffee refills. We lingered long, both tired with heavy eyes, nervous to face a monumental day. Lotto being Lotto, he'd scheduled the send-off extravaganza for high noon, amidst the scorching tropics of late August, as if trying to exact one final torture upon Sweetberry's naysayers.

People in light clothing were parking at the Bygone Grill, ordering coffees to go, and walking away without their cars, toward The Flank. I noticed a few of their tags read Gwinnett, Cobb, Clayton counties—suburban culture tourists. The feeling was brewing that a stadium concert or major football game was about to begin nearby. The vibe was thick, the air humming. I shrugged and looked at Genteel. Her hands were trembling. I said it was time to move out, to face the music. She nodded and drank more coffee and rocked her shoulders. About fifteen minutes after noon, she finally called us a cab on the diner's pay phone. She came back to the table, slipped on some long white gloves, and applied makeup from one of those mirrored clams.

"Lotto's had commercials for this on the TV all week," she said. "He talkin' about history being made and free door prizes—and free money." She stared off vacantly, toward the amassing crowds, slowly shaking her tremendous head and cheeks. "You see 'em?"

I nodded. "They're the most repulsive things on basic cable right now."

"Any-*who*," Genteel said grimly. "It is what it is." She fashioned a narrow-eyed grimace, an almost comical meanness that meant business. "Contract say be there and ready by one, on the nose. Guess we got to face it, like you say. Guess it's about time."

"It is, ma'am."

"Let's go say goodbye then, Johnson. And let's make some dang history ourselves."

In the cab, Genteel was a trembling mess, the swells of her exposed arms jiggling like nudged pudding. She reached up and covered her eyes as The Flank's dusty entrance came into view. From three blocks away, I could tell the heat was doing little to keep the crowds away; long, thick rivers of humanity and their baby strollers were pushing ahead, impatient and unruly, hungry for a spectacle and freebies. "Guess the ads is workin'," Genteel moaned, peeking through her fingers. "Not sure why all these folks so happy, though. Feel like a funeral to me."

Ragtag convoys of old, empty semitrailers and horse carriers streamed away from The Flank in the opposite direction, toward the interstates. Porch parties were blossoming on either side of the street, squirming with young people in floral clothing. In one front yard was an inflatable pool that brimmed with shirtless men trying to ride an empty beer keg. Little girls in pink uniforms hawked not lemonade but cups of ice from a makeshift stand; each of those darlings was an unwitting bourbon enabler. Elsewhere, a shabby American Foursquare, owned by an eccentric old gardener I used to know, was decked in a banner advertising use of its bathroom for $2. Indeed, it was like an autumn football Saturday in a Southern college town, with rabid undertones, only hotter. I'd never seen Sweetberry so busy—so alive—than on this day meant for honoring death. The cultural changeover was nearly, utterly complete. None of this, save the blatant substance abuse, resembled my neighborhood of thirty years prior. Genteel put down her window for a second and waved at the girls selling ice. All those little faces opened up and drew back, respectful and astounded, like they'd seen the white-gloved Sweetberry Queen.

At the doorstep of The Flank, which was now Genteel's former district, technically speaking, the commotion ramped up threefold. Everywhere were bobbing heads and balloons and wafting aromas of frying dough and cotton candy and dirt and dung. We were clearly in the midst of a colossal event, a bidding adieu of massive scale, the grandest and oddest carnival Atlanta had ever seen, the Gentrification Woodstock. Gasping, Genteel put a hand to lips that perfectly matched her dress. The cabbie asked if she was going to faint, if she might need a medic from the tent over there with the white cross. She kissed the back of his hand and got out.

A mindboggling transformation had happened since we walked to breakfast, as Lotto's crews were nothing if not efficient. Bookended by two little stages, and punctuated by the offensive banners, a true circus of shoddy security infrastructure and makeshift animal corrals lay across The Flank. The skeletal steel maze covered the district's backyards and nearby railroad properties; several blocks had become one large cage, essentially. Apart from the lucky few huddled in shade beside the bungalows, not a single soul looked particularly comfortable. The Flank's historic core now carried the aura—as best I could remember from the photos I'd seen—of a public execution, a crazed rush to experience what would soon be gone.

As we stood there, a lady who knew Genteel hustled down from her porch across the street, handed over an umbrella for shade, complimented her dress, and shot back toward the air-conditioning. Genteel propped the umbrella over her coif and nodded for us to walk in, deeper into the frenzy of her once-quiet lanes.

Everything was astonishingly random and ill-planned. Although it was summer, children were bobbing for apples in four halved barrels. Beside that stood a stable for pin-the-tail-on-the-donkey with an actual, tailless donkey (kids used duct tape, not tacks), a pony ride, and another station for petting and riding somebody's adolescent camel. Next to that was a small vintage Ferris wheel, which a sorrowful man was operating by hand, reaching up and heaving its buckets downward. To our left, a hot yoga demonstration was beginning, and sweaty, panting kids played flag football on a huge green carpet. Carlito, sans knife, was in the middle of the boys, pulling flags and cackling. "Mr. God has blessed us with his presence!" Carlito cried. He spun closer to me, pointed around the district, and said, "See what you started!" before erupting with laughter. Near the medical facilities, in the millennial Shangri-La section, was a tent for speed-dating, and another for something called a "farm-to-table *hors d'oeuvre* seminar." Next door was the canine psychic. A station with a huge circle of onlookers featured a lumberjack extolling the virtues of the reclaimed wood he was dissecting from old country chairs on the spot. And the clowns! Such an array of clowns! Balloon-pullers, zany bald clowns, classic mutes, French clowns, overweight and skinny clowns, and another that could juggle what I thought were Chinese throwing stars—but were actually sample tiles for future cookie-cutter kitchen backsplashes! Clever Lotto! The commotion paused when, from the far stage, a DJ's enormous bass speakers started thumping like tribal war drums. Overdressed in a white tux and red Ray-Bans, the DJ hollered into the mic: "Ladies and gentlemen of Sweetberry Park, my lovely human beings of Atlanta, and everyone else: *welcome!* Welcome to The Flank's Commemoration Carnival!" The masses hissed and roared—touchdown. "The man of the hour, Mister Lotto Livingston, arrives in five minutes!" said the DJ, pumping his fist. "Time to set this thing off, y'all!"

Suddenly Felix spat out of the crowd, terrifically sloshed and sweating. He hugged and kissed Genteel quickly, so as not to douse her. "I've never seen a more broke-ass send-off for anything," said Felix. "I almost wish they'd just dynamite the damn place, right in front of us!" He stepped back and drank in the sight of his gussied-up patootie; in the shade of her umbrella, Genteel gave a bashful smile. "My, my, *my...*" Felix said. "Now ain't you a rose."

"Oh, *fwoo!*" she said. "Stop that."

"Where your South Carolina cousins, Genteel?" Felix said, cocking his head. "I'm feelin' friendly and wanna meet them country pumpkins."

She froze, caught.

"More importantly," I said, butting in, "where's Walt?"

Felix jolted upright, feigning sobriety. "Not in jail," he said. "Thank the good Lord."

"Seriously. Is he here?"

"Naw," Felix said, gulping the last of a wine spritzer from a small plastic cup. "Walt said he had to rest up, for a big night, whatever that means." He reached over and patted my shoulder, which felt like respect. "Now, Mister God, your hands look too empty. I'm-a be right back with three wines. It's all free, y'all, if you can prove your residency in the neighborhood. Woo-yeah!"

By the time Felix returned, security personnel wearing Pumpernickel Enterprises jumpsuits were parting the crowd for Lotto's entrance. A hush fell over the carnival-goers as the lead black security SUV in his cavalcade entered the property. Genteel reached over and clutched my forearm when she saw what came next: the sandalwood Lincoln Town Car, emblem of my nightmare decades, with a stodgy chauffeur behind the wheel. Lotto waved to folks from the back seat like he thought he was Nelson Mandela. Beside him was a slumped, secretive woman, veiled in an arctic-white dress and hat. Lotto, meanwhile, was wearing a beige seersucker suit, Panama hat, and chunky golden sunglasses.

"Can you *believe* these people?" I said to Genteel. "Instead of bringing his poor, sweet wife, Lotto lugs along his mistress to a massive public event."

"No!"

"Hell yes it is," I said. "Look in the back, at that cowering White lady. That's Kim Somethingerother in there. She heads the zoning board. And she has the gall to show up next to demolition man, like it's the royal wedding."

The despicable automobile lunged ahead, and the masses gave way. The chauffer parked at the largest stage. At this point, the crowd's mood confused me; I couldn't tell if Lotto would be cheered or violently mobbed. As he popped out of the car, used a back tire as a step, and gave a little Pope wave over so many heads, everyone around us joyfully whooped.

"Imagine if this crowd was only Sweetberry locals," I said to Genteel, over the din. "He wouldn't be acting like this. He'd get his ass kicked."

"Yup."

"But again, he's thinking *ahead*," I said. "He's filled the place up with people from someplace else, eager for a party. And now he's gonna play Jesus, with this huge moat of humanity around him, protecting him."

Genteel's head shook wildly, bouncing in all directions—the quaky mountaintop, portending eruption. "He really somethin', ain't he?"

Lotto cheerily skipped and bounded up the stage's steps. At this point, a security guy cuffed my elbow, pulling me toward him. He had the cauliflowered ears of a wrestler and energy drinks on his breath. "Be careful, Mr. Johnson," said the security guard. "And stand way back."

"Stand back from what?"

He leaned in closer. "It sounds crazy, but someone forgot the streamers," said the guard. "So they had to fill the cannons with dirt."

In hearing that, Genteel snatched my other elbow and pulled me between her and the stage, a buffer.

"Ceremonial dirt cannons?" I said. "Are you joking?"

"Not only that," said the guy. "Keep an eye on the sky, too, during the flyover."

"What kind of flyover?"

"Look, they couldn't book a jet in time, or couldn't afford it, I don't know," he said. "What *was* available just might be comin' down, it's so old. Could make for a great story, though—huh, huh!"

Felix returned with three cold wines, smiling. But he tossed them all in the air when—boom, boom, *kaboom!*—a trio of unsynchronized plastic cannons spat geysers of reddish earth behind the stage. This signaled to Lotto it was time to raise his arms, a true champion, and to awkwardly shout, "I love y'all, Atlanta! We are one!" into the dais microphone. A Pumpernickel employee darted onstage with an umbrella and shielded Lotto from the geysers' dusty fallout. He was protected while dirt swept over the crowd like a Deep South sandstorm; a few teenagers ran away as parents squatted in futile attempts to protect their coughing young. We three hid beneath Genteel's umbrella until a horrid scream fell out of the sky. What swooped down dangerously close to treetops was a retro 1930s biplane with rusty patches on the underbelly. In the open cockpit was an octogenarian baron, cackling madly. His engine whined harshly into our ears, louder and louder. As the pilot came within a few hundred yards, pointed directly at us, some overzealous father screamed, "Hit the deck!" and more than a few people dove into the bushes. The pilot corrected at the last instant, lifting upward, sputtering into heaven, and the panic morphed instantly into a thundering cheer. Convulsing with stoked ego, Lotto caressed his microphone and boomed, "How's *that* for an entrance, Sweetberry Park!"

The Lincoln being parked no more than twenty feet away was, of course, an irritant. Salt on a rash. A dirty finger in my eye. But the whooping was the breaking point. As the crowd quieted, Lotto pulled a folded paper from his breast pocket, and I saw my chance. "I won't keep you fine folks standing in the sun too long, not when it's supposed to nip one-hundred and five again," said Lotto. "Keep in mind, though, our hot, *hot* summer is almost over. The summer of the serpents, thank goodness, is almost behind us. And by the grace of God, our fair city was a worldwide laughingstock for just a few short weeks!" The applause drowned out his speaking now, so Lotto took a haughty bow, as if he'd been of any value to Snake Gate's remediation. "But to begin the festivities, and to sufficiently pay homage to this immensely historic Atlanta district, I scribbled down a few thoughts last night, and I'd like to read them in honor—"

"Who's in the car, Lotto?" I shouted, with all the volume my beat lungs could make. "Who's your lady friend?"

"Ex-*cuse* me?" Lotto said. His face twitched with rage, and his eyes scanned the five hundred faces around me for the culprit.

"We were just wondering, you know, if that's the Atlanta Zoning Board Chairwoman in your back seat?" I shouted. "Would you care to comment, sir, on how your affair's been going?"

His nasty little eyes found me.

"This is no press conference, OK?" he said weakly. "It's a one-way speech."

"How's the wife, Lotto?"

He cocked his hips one way and shoulders the other, in what can only be described as sass. "If it isn't God Johnson, ladies and gentlemen," he said. "The failed newspaper columnist."

"We know about the bribes, asshole!"

And there they were. All the chips. Thrust out, onto the felt. Genteel and Felix simultaneously slapped my chest.

Lotto's face melted, his jaw fell, but he filled the void with laughter. "Could security check on Mr. Johnson, please? Maybe get him off to the hydration tent? This heat's gone to his head."

"That boy's blood is on *your* hands!"

The ensuing roar surprised me. Not because it was deafening but because it started from the far corner of the crowd, near Felix's former bungalow. People were rushing toward us, and the amount of dust seemed impossible, until we could see what was behind *them*—three ponies gone mad. Each had been resting in a small stable erected next to Felix's house, but with furious hooves and glistening calico muscles they smashed through barriers. Lotto screamed across the loudspeakers: "Security, three loose horses!"

Maybe it was the bravery of booze, or perhaps his career had included Western horse-whispering at some point, but Felix dumfounded us by charging *toward* the frantic, kicking animals, shouting, "Yah! Yah! Yah!" A wave of red-shirted security joined him, and in about thirty seconds they held the reins of each animal and were petting their great heaving bellies. One pony, though, was still very agitated, its brown eyes huge and darting.

All was beginning to calm down, settling back into festive weirdness, when Felix barked: "Medics! Get the medics! This pony's been bitten! Bitten on the leg. She's bleedin'!"

Now the panicked masses really surged to the east, away from Felix's abode, and Lotto shrieked in fear they all were heading home. "Stop!" Lotto called into the microphone. "My speech, ladies and gentleman! Stop! Stop!"

That achieved almost nothing. A few berserk soccer dads shrugged while booking for the exits. Several spooked clowns scurried away, too. Amidst the outgoing wave of them all, I could suddenly see the towering maleness of Tall Walt, heading against the flow, toward us. I thought Walt was making a beeline for Lotto, possibly to rip him apart publicly, until he stopped and hugged Genteel. He apologized for being late and asked what was going on. Lotto, slapping the podium in an unhinged fit, provided the answer.

"Folks, it's a pony, and it's only a scratch," Lotto pleaded from stage, but nobody listened. He swelled up, more furious than I'd ever seen him, and he screamed: "Fine then! Fine! Run away! But we have a change of programming, right now. You'll want to experience this. Come on! Listen! To! *Me*!" He paused to gulp bottled water and petulantly stomp his fancy sandals. "Folks, we're cutting to the chase. It's time for the grand finale. This is a once-in-a-lifetime opportunity!"

Now he was getting somewhere. The migration didn't stop, exactly, but it noticeably slowed down.

"Good, just like that," Lotto said, wiping a towel over his head. "Since this is a day about history, ladies and gentlemen, we're going to make some history, too. You're going to be part of this history *and* the future! Because it's happening right here, on the site of Sweetberry Lanes, the luxury living accommodations you *all* deserve—" (A groan from the masses). "Anyway, sorry. But yes, just like that. Slow down. Thank you! So now, look here… we're bringing the greatest blues maven this part of Atlanta has ever known to the stage, right now. She's coming out of retirement, just for you, for one last hurrah. Yeah, that's right! You know all her greatest covers, folks. You know that velvety voice. And you've probably heard that she lived right here, in The Flank, since back when MLK was marching up and down these very streets. And here she is, people, in the flesh and so many pretty sequins. Put your hands together, Sweetberry Lanes, for the one and only... Miss Genteel Briggs!"

Now the migration changed course, the ponies be damned, heading back toward the stage. Genteel was incapacitated with nerves, not budging beneath the parasol. I patted her hot shoulder while Walt leaned in from the other side. "Just like we practiced, miss," said Walt, sounding like her father. "With anger. With heart. With *fire!*"

And with that, Genteel swelled up with breath and soldiered onward, onto the stage, a sparkly comet in slow motion. She rebuffed an offered hug from Lotto, who stood for a moment with his arms open anyway, as if trying to take flight.

I reached way up to Walt's thick neck and pulled his ear down to me. "Before you do anything tonight," I said, as quietly as possible. "Come to my house."

He nodded.

"Seriously," I said. "Come over."

"I will, sure," said Walt.

"I'm *serious.*"

"So am I," he said. "But it's on, man. You're not talking me out of it."

"My house. Right before sundown. You hear me?"

"Yes, sir," and he gave a salute.

We turned to the stage. And there, blinking in so much Peach State sunshine, stood that supernova of sass, that star reborn. "Genteel's *back!*" a man's voice blurted from afar. For a moment, she smilingly absorbed the scene, the thrill of so many eager faces waiting to bask in her talents, the glow of what she'd been born to do. But she didn't move—not a twitch—just a grin and silence. The crowd, after a full minute, could sense Genteel's nervous hesitation. A silent pact was reached to help her; what first was scattered clapping amassed into a low, loud, louder chant of her name:

"Gen-teel, Geee-nnn-teel, Geeeeeeeeeee-nnnn-teel!" At last she stepped to the dais, thrusting back her shoulders and whipping her head. The microphone that had looked so significant next to Lotto's head was but a sliver beside the bigness of inspired Genteel. Like her shoulders, her teased hair and jewelry seemed to rise, inflating with bizarre energy, expanding with the moment, the embodiment of *resurgens* before our very eyes.

"Alright, y'alls!" said Genteel, and it echoed across the neighborhood. "You got me feelin' so blessed, like ya have my whole, *whole* life. You really liftin' me up, and I don't wanna bring nobody down, but ya gotta know this: My old voice been croakin' out for a bit. Yeah, sorry, it has. But I signed a deal with that devil over there in seersucker. So I'm gonna perform. And I'm gonna perform like you ain't *never* heard!"

The crowd's response was atomic. Everyone was high-fiving. Cowbells clattered. A small boy was tossed into the air—and caught—in celebration. Again it came, low and rumbling, and then twice as loud as before: "Gen-teel, Geee-nnn-teel, Geeeeeeeeeee-nnnn-teel!"

"Ah-ight, then!" she boomed. "Let's do this!"

"Gen-teel, Geee-nnn-teel, Geeeeeeeeeee-nnnn-teel!"

"OK, OK, *OK*," she said. "I can do it!"

"Gen-teel, Geeeeen-teel—"

"Hey, you, DJ over there," she said. "I need track two, *not* track one. OK, baby? Come on and do it! Do it! Woo-*wee*!"

A simple, chest-kicking beat hit the ground, like a rubber mallet on a huge metal drum, amplified by a billion. It was decidedly not the blues, not *Amazing Grace*, not *Oh Lord Come Down Blessed From thy Mountain*. Genteel closed her eyes and hummed, swaying like seaweed, her hands opening and closing in perfect synchronicity, building the steam within her. She snatched the mic off the stand, stepped to the very lip of the stage, and leaned over the admiring crowd. And then, in a deep, nasty growl, Genteel Briggs launched into the most vile, repugnant, obscene, embarrassing, and all-around inappropriate verses in the history of rap music!

In the first two lines alone, she rhymed "whack off" with "jack off" and "sodomy" with "come on me." Following that was a diatribe on stabbing dogs and "fuckin' grandpas" while shooting developers in "dey fuckin' eyebas."

And then it got worse, which prompted Genteel to clasp her heart and Walt to keep shouting, "That's it, that's it, right *there*! Just like that!"

The crowd's collective gasp was audible as seaside wind. The feeling was that we'd entered an alternate reality, a profane dimension, a real-life opposites day. With twice the haste as before, parents scooped their children and ran from the carnival, as if wolves were nipping at their heels. Spooked, the Lincoln's chauffer slammed that boat of an automobile in reverse and punched the gas; it barreled away from the neighborhood, toward the railroad tracks, barely missing a few guys who kicked and punched the quarter-panels and whacked a lawn chair across the windshield. I caught a glimpse of that poor city official in the back seat—bouncing like blonde popcorn—as the hulking machine splintered posts, crushed trash barrels, and roared backward toward downtown. In the Lincoln's wake, the largest banner sadly fluttered down into the dirt.

"And one more thing for luck," Genteel chanted, as part of the chorus. "Fuckity fuck in the fuckin' fuck!"

Nothing made sense. All was mayhem. The threshold of impossibility was permanently obliterated. Women began sobbing. Men booed. A hail of water bottles and wine cups showered not on Genteel but Lotto, who was rubbing frantically at his chest, his face smashed with anguish, disbelief, and the sting of betrayal.

By the time Genteel finished, having righteously sinned enough for three lifetimes, all but maybe one-hundred drunken fools had fled the carnival grounds. For all involved, that spirit of reverent, gleeful *au revoir* had been annihilated. The day's sacredness, for anyone who saw the spectacle, had been swapped with memories so inappropriate they stung. It was toxic, all of it, an absolute public-relations disaster.

Weeping, Genteel dropped the microphone. Walt carried her off to the shade. Lotto, meanwhile, stepped down from his perch, walked across the tops of my boots, and slogged silently to the fang-bitten pony. He touched the blood and smeared three lines across each of his cheeks. Then he hopped aboard the animal. He tucked his sandals into the saddle stirrups, kissed his necklace crucifix, and rode off to the east, down the railroad tracks, away from the carnage of his busted grand finale.

CHAPTER 26

The carnival medics sequestered Genteel in the hydration tent and wouldn't let her go for two hours. She was in there yammering about the Sweetberry preacher who used to live on that corner over there and the pastor on this one and how they were condemning her mortal soul from heaven as she spoke. The medics only smirked.

Felix, Walt, and I gathered a few chairs and waited outside the tent for Genteel's professional replenishing to finish. This gave us ample time to enjoy the miserable, rushed, hilarious deconstruction of the Commemoration Carnival; it was going away as quickly as it had infected the district. A few dozen Pumpernickel employees and contractors solemnly ripped the arena apart, leaderless, looking as though they feared they wouldn't be paid. Meanwhile, Felix had resumed his one-man wine-spritzer blowout, and he began to glow. He kept popping up, leaning over, and patting Walt's knee. His demeanor suggested he'd never been prouder of his grandson. Or maybe he was just happy to have the kid around again. I didn't ask.

"I knew you was sharp," he said to Walt, finally. "But what I saw today was some General Patton-level shit, man.

And I don't even care that Genteel's gonna scrub her mouth out with mechanic soap!"

Now Walt fidgeted, embarrassed. "Ease back on that wine, maybe," he said. "You're getting intense."

"I hope you got those rap lyrics written down some-where—or maybe I don't!" said Felix. "Anyway, son, jean-*yus!*"

Walt shrugged. "That lady in there's amazing," he said. "She flat out refused to practice with the actual words, earlier this week. Wouldn't even say one little 'shit' or 'dog carcass.' Then she comes out here and nails it."

I went inside the tent to bid Genteel adieu, but she was sleeping, laid out in what looked like an oversize blood-donor's chair. The white line of an IV fanged into her right forearm. The tent's amber lighting, the shimmering dress, and that huge rounded hairdo lent her the appearance of Egyptian royalty, arranged in eternal dignity. I bent down and whispered: "You did good. God forgives you. We'll handle the rest."

She responded only with tiny, stuttered snores.

I walked out and winked to Walt, a gesture he returned. Felix said he'd take care of the dehydrated singer in the tent from here on out, that he'd call a cab or pay one of the medics to drive them to the ritzy Midtown hotel he'd booked for a week. He pulled his wallet from a back pocket, exhumed an impossibly thick stack of large bills, and rubbed the money across his sweaty face.

"How about you do us a favor with that loot, Felix," I said. "Not to be too blunt, too soon, but tomorrow they're gonna start picking these bungalows apart like downed buffaloes. Why don't you keep Genteel far away from all that depressing stuff? Maybe take her off somewhere nice, like to a spa, or a fancy psychiatrist. She'll need both after today."

Felix cast a long look over my shoulder, across The Flank. It was a mess of garbage, settled dust, and yellowing, thirsty foliage. The purples of early evening softened the pocked, weathered folds of Felix's face, but still there was real pain. His boyish, buoyant spirit was starting to sink, nosediving into buzzed sentimentality, or worse. I grabbed a half-full wine cup at the base of Felix's chair and offered a toast. Walt declined and stayed seated.

"A toast to what?" Felix said, lifting his glass. "Gettin' fleeced by the devil?"

"Yes, fine," I said. "To sellin' out!"

"Naw, naw," he said. "I was kiddin'."

"Then how about we toast to winter?" I said. "To all that glorious change, that cleansing, just around the bend?"

"*Hell*, naw," said Felix. "Winter's death." He shot up and raised his wine with militant wobbliness—the stance of proud, drunk men with fantastically bad ideas. "This toast," he said, "is for war!"

I pulled away. "I'm not toastin' freakin' war, man."

He smashed his plastic against mine anyway, splashing sweet bubbly booze down my wrist.

"I mean the damn *internal* war," Felix said, with crazed eyes. "I mean the silent war. The war of heat. The war of friction. The buckin' of a snake-bit pony that nobody hears!"

That evening, the summer sky was grape and cloud-wispy by the time Walt crept into the shadow of my Victorian. He hopped over the fence, bent low to the ground, and met me on the porch. From wrist to ankle his attire was dark green. His face was all business, and his sweating was torrential. I was slunk down low in my rocker, shielded from the street by banisters.

"Where'd you park?" I said.

He sat, crossing his logs of legs and leaning his great back against banisters nearest the palm and tallest bushes. "Around the corner, in an alley, under some trees," he said. "I don't wanna be seen here by all these nosy folks. I'd hate to have you implicated." He spread apart a few branches and fronds and peeked down the street. "Now, sir," he said. "What'd you want to talk about?"

"Where's the gasoline?"

"Are you kidding?"

"No. Why?"

"That's too obvious," he said. "There's no way to covertly get a bunch of gas. It's like begging to be caught by surveillance at the convenience store pumps."

"Makes sense," I said.

"I trust you, and I respect you, so I'll tell you: I have a friend who knows shipping people, from the Savannah ports. I got a half-pallet of lighter fluid that can't possibly be traced to me."

"Jesus, man."

"What?"

"It's just so intense, you talkin' like that," I said. "Like it's the witching hour or something."

"It's going to happen, God."

"I know it is," I said. "It's just, I feel you've done your part already, this afternoon."

"That was the first step," he said. "Now this, it's the climax."

"Oh please."

"I'm for real," he said, perturbed. "All that's left is the finish."

"Yeah," I said, "about that..." I paused for a minute, wanting to ease into my proposal. "You want a tap water, Walt? No? I'd offer you something more interesting, but it's all gone."

"Man..." said Walt, and his thoughts trailed off. "Maybe grandpa can spot you a loan for a bit, until things get going again for you?"

"I'm fine."

"Speaking of him," said Walt. "What'd you make of his pony talk? What'd you think bit that thing today?"

"Another pony, that's what."

"Big bite for a pony."

"Look," I said. "Your grandfather's a bit delusional right now, hopped up on life and cash. Felix is just—"

"This is why you insisted I come over here?" Walt cut in. "To talk Felix? Or what? All due respect, but I got a lot on my mind. I get the feeling you're about to say The Flank should be spared, right?"

"Not at all," I said. "It needs to burn, all of it. Tonight."

"Yes, sir."

"It's just that *I* should be the one burning it."

Walt sprung to his feet, onlookers be damned. He lorded over me like a standing bull, eager to crash down his bulk and hooves at the smallest provocation. "*What?*" he said.

"You heard me, Walt."

"No disrespect, old man, but sounds like the heat's getting to your mind again."

"Hear me out a second, and sit down..." He complied as I fetched the tap water he didn't want and set the glass beside him. "I've thought this through, top to bottom," I said. "I'm about to be seventy years old, Walt. I've got no lineage behind me and no real value to my daily existence at this point. Call me pessimistic, but my ride's basically over. Meanwhile, you don't know it, but you've got everything right where you want it. The whole fruit farm of life is up ahead. You should be back in class, at Morehouse, studying sociology or whatever, instead of plotting shit like this. The burden of risk should be all mine."

"No."

"Yes, son."

"It's my destiny to carry this out, to take it down," he said. "It's my blood in there."

"It's dangerous in there."

"And plus," he said, "the sacrifice was *my* idea."

"Oh, hell," I said, swatting my hands. "It's no time for heroics, man. We're talking about stealing, essentially, a few hundred thousand dollars from a crook, as a means of revenge. We're talking about high-level crime, Walter. Get out my face with this 'destiny' bullshit."

That cast Walt into long, brow-furrowed contemplation, the look of a spurned boy. I was wondering how old he was, because I'd forgotten, if I ever knew. Maybe twenty-three, at most.

"You don't even know what to do," he said, finally.

"Come on," I said. "What's it really take to walk down there and torch some century-old bungalows in a drought? They're all made entirely of wood."

"I've been reading up on this."

"Reading up?" I chuckled. "What, 'The Art of Dousing?'"

Walt ignored me and went silent for a minute, exploring the stockpiled info in his head. "You'd have to start from the core homes, lighting their dry bases, and then work out," he said. "Get through a window and light the interiors, too. I saw some curtains still hanging today, left behind. But damn, you have to be careful, with all the drought we've had—"

"Look at me, Walt," I said. "Just unload the damn fluid in the alley. Two or three cans should do it. Then take side streets to the interstate. Get the hell on the other side of town, and don't come back to Sweetberry for a month, at least."

"How will you get supplies down there, for several blocks?" he said. "You thought of that?"

"I know where the surveillance cameras are, both private and police," I said. "I'll cut west through the woods and come around back, by way of those railroad tracks. The whole time I'll be in the shadows. In and out in five minutes, then I'm back home in bed, acting oblivious if anyone asks."

"Maybe it does make sense," he said.

"It absolutely does."

"Maybe I was wrong."

"Your heart's in the right place," I said. "And now your head is, too."

"Let me ask you something," said Walt.

"Fire away," I said, wincing at the accidental pun. "Ask me anything."

"Why you doin' all this, for a bunch of old Black folks?" he said. "Why do this when you're Nicaraguan?"

"I'm not Nicaraguan—"

"Then what is it, sir?" he said, head cocked sideways. "I've always wanted to ask."

"I'm just a guy, another neighbor," I said. "Maybe one day that'll be enough."

Still, he was unsatisfied, frowning. "But why... why risk everything?"

"Look, man, my 'everything' was gone a long time ago," I said. "Most of my life has felt like biding time. And it's no exaggeration, not at all, to say this place *saved* my life, before it nearly killed me, way back when." I paused for a second, to reflect. "The Flank is the realest thing around here. It's a little cornerstone of real in this fake-ass world. And it deserves to be respected, even if by destruction—"

"Agreed."

"Plus," I said, "something this stupid is right in my wheelhouse."

I hoped Walt might laugh, but he didn't. The heaviness and heat were just too much. We sat without speaking for a while as the shadows deepened, streetlights flickered to life, and the season's last fireflies gave woozy blinks. With no goodbye or handshake or well-wishing, Walt stood up and walked away, toward the alley. "Three cans, by the fence, sir," he whispered back at me. "And I was never here."

CHAPTER 27

I loaded an old downy blanket into a trash bag to thwart the sound of lighter-fluid cans clinking together. I donned all camouflage. Among various paraphernalia from wilder times I found two working lighters and a half-full box of strong wooden matches. I slunk back to the fence, then carefully loaded up the accelerant. With the trash bag over my shoulder—like some nefarious, wartime Kris Kringle—I high-stepped through the shadows of oaks and into the wisp of woods that curled around Sweetberry's northwestern rim.

At the railroad tracks, I crouched so low I was nearly crawling. The rusty industrial emptiness of that land, so close to joyful family homes, made me feel sad and alone, like some hobo cast away on the open rails of America. I shrugged off that nonsense and reached the target area, undetected. And I waited in a poky holly bush, watching for movement, and watching some more.

The Flank's bungalows were so close I could smell their heart-pine walls and floors, cooling and contracting from the day's heat. Two mimosa trees stood sentinel at the district's back entrance, reaching toward me with long floral branches, as if pointing out the interloper with bad intentions. The medical tent was gone. The Ferris wheel had been carted away, too. The Flank's dingy darkness was the only sign that something was amiss. Until, that is, a breeze snuck between the houses, rousing the odors of funnel cakes, cheap summer wine, and urine.

I pulled a tall metal container from the bag and fiddled with its child-resistant spout. The pungent chemicals smelled like finality, like revenge, and my hands began to quiver. My tongue grew furry, and I badly wanted water, or stronger. With the breeze against my perspiring skin, and the prolonged squatting restricting blood flow beneath my knees, I was getting cold feet in every sense. Silhouetted against streetlights up the hill, that huddle of shotgun houses looked both adorable and helpless, immaculate and doomed, like little beings staring defenseless at monstrous, imminent demise. I shook my head and stood up. Backing away and going home would be outright defeat. It was up to me to set the old homes free.

I started with Felix's residence. In thin spray I spelled out "LOTTO BLOWS" in the dust on his front porch. I looped around the entire base, squeezing until my forearms burned, until the lowest boards were all dripping with lighter fluid. Then I zigzagged the accelerant up the sides of all walls, leaving a puddle at the front door's threshold, a real special delivery. I had the eerie sensation on Felix's porch that I wasn't alone, although I heard absolutely nothing. The moonlight was sufficient enough to see that all rooms were empty.

For a few minutes I stood in the darkness, watching and listening. It was Saturday night in the city, and The Flank had already regressed into an afterthought. Everyone had moved on. Beyond the piney ridges, downtown and Midtown hummed. A few dogs yipped in the heart of Sweetberry. Otherwise there was nothing, no life.

I repeated the dousing technique with the seven homes next door to Felix's until the first can was spent. The process was taking too long, and I grew both scared of witnesses and impatient with the mundanity. With trembling hands and limited light, I was having the hardest time removing the cap of the second container, though I could manage to create a gap between the rubber and the can's metal top. I wedged this gap over the front-porch railings of a bungalow painted bright blue, which I thought had belonged to that pastor. I brought my fist down hard upon the can, pounding and pounding until the cap popped off suddenly, which caused me to lose my balance. I fell into a row of gardenias, trying to keep the lighter fluid upright, but it tipped sideways above me, cascading down, wetting my chest and neck and then gushing into my gasping mouth. This caused me to gargle and yell, in fear I'd poisoned myself. I stood up, spit until I gagged, and deflated. I'd managed to make *myself* evidence—and a potential human torch. I found a working hose and washed my face and neck. I drank for a solid minute to dilute the fuel in my belly. But I still reeked. And I'd have to be very careful.

With the cap off, the mission went quicker. I splashed the remaining bungalows while trotting around them, a study in clueless criminal proficiency. Fourteen were sufficiently dripping by the time the second cannister was empty. The entire third can would be committed to Genteel's Shotgun Three, and I set to prepping its violent destruction in the most loving, sympathetic way. I sprayed around the bedroom window where I'd sweated out my narcotic horrors; beneath the main bedroom's windowsill I rubbed the fuel into the wood, which felt to me like a comforting gesture. I reached high and doused the roof and watched as the liquid dripped off where gutters would be on today's homes. The fuel trickled black teardrops into orange dirt. I tried to envision the process as a sort of structural baptism, an entrée to greater glory, but in every conceivable way it seemed the opposite of baptismal, a wicked oiling before hell's inferno. After that I tried my best to stop thinking about it all. Everything about the proceedings was detestable, I realized, but I had to keep moving. Having forgotten gloves, I wiped my fingerprints off the final can and set it next to Genteel's front door. I reached into the sack, buffed fingerprints off the other two cannisters, and left the combustible heap near the facade windows. I touched the door and said goodbye, so long, Godspeed. Somehow it felt right to ignite hers first.

I took a final glance down both sides of the lane and issued a silent apology to the many terrific, historical preservation associations of America. It seemed more reverential and classier to get it all started by way of match, and not cheap plastic lighter. I found the most perfectly formed little wooden stick from the box and held it to my forehead, trying to ignore my panicking heart. A gulp. A deep breath. A single true strike. And now we had flame, which I bent and placed precisely at the threshold of Genteel's door.

And then... *whrooooof!*

It was such an effortless dance, a tragically beautiful parade of yellow waves, the quiet and fast spread of those flames. I was awestruck, immediately. I'd never seen fire so liberated, so big, so without boundaries, and I hadn't considered that before. As the flames climbed up and shot laterally, all at once, a writhing network of sky-blue and orange joined the yellow, and the homey front clapboards were gone, swallowed by an incandescent warpath. At this point, the heat was too much, and I backed away, for my own safety and a more panoramic view. The blaze was driven and heartless. Like fiends in a midnight alley, it snuck around the eaves and windowsills of Shotgun Three with graceful nonchalance. In no more than thirty seconds, the perky front half of Genteel's house was a crackling torch, illuminating its neighbors, showing me the way to mission complete, to the regrettable erasure of a century in five minutes.

I cusped both lighters in either hand and moved my body more quickly than I had in years, racing between yards and leaping over low picketed gates. The more I lighted, the more it became apparent the parched homes might have ignited without a drop of fuel. Each one accepted its demise with almost no fight, as if eager to join the inferno and take this more noble route to nonexistence. At Felix's house, I nodded again in reverence, then put a wide stretch of fire along the backdoor.

By the time I'd circled back to the twelfth target, Shotgun Three was a roaring, angry bonfire, and the lick of flames stretched far over its roof. Light from that blaze showed me the wettest spots on all three remaining homes; with a couple of flicks, I put fire in the center of those targets. I was sweating madly now, feeling woozy, surrounded by open ovens. The firelight was enough to render the moon and stars and city invisible. The Flank had become its own miserable dying realm, a hellscape of human discord at its worst. For a fleeting second I had the feeling that nothing of such importance existed beyond the conflagration, which reached and stabbed up everywhere now like a jagged cage. I realized it was also spotlighting *me*—the proverbial cockroach in the kitchen, the criminal—so I moved faster.

As I hopped the fence of the final unlit home, I dropped the lighter that was in my left hand, which was caked in damning fingerprints. I poked around the mondo grass and kicked the dirt but found nothing. I had to move on. This last home was the least shaded, most sun-exposed of all Flank properties, and it took its burning with enthusiasm. Fire scurried along the exterior walls and curled beneath it, as if sucked by a vacuum. I turned away but was blasted by a quick, thick wall of smoke. The bonfires were so large now the light made me wince; I covered my nose and mouth with my shirt and took in the scene once more, shocked and ashamed. I started to scurry back toward the railroad tracks, to the escape route, but the sound of a shouting man in the last home pegged me in place. I thought it surely had been a trick of my mind, having been besieged with so many toxins, so much smoke. But then I screeched and nearly fainted when I saw the sleep-disheveled head of Lotto Livingston rise from within the last home's living room, groggy and wobbling. I eyed the railroad tracks, yearning for them; I watched Lotto fumble inside the house, clearly disoriented, waving a clear bottle and shouting at the inferno. And then I opted to act just like Lotto would have, turning my back and running the hell away.

Before I reached the railroad tracks, however, my conscience nagged to the point I had to stop. I glanced behind me. The Flank was but ten jagged towers of wrathful orange now; the smoke filling its lanes was like a low, milky October fog. At this point, I could hear the first sirens in the distance, screaming in from several directions. It was already a three-alarm blaze, at least. Multiple fire stations were dispatching help. Soon the area would be squirming with witnesses.

I darted back to the last ignited home, kicked the scalding door handle until it gave way, and shouted into the fogged interior: "Lotto, out! This way! Move, *now!*"

Before I could clearly see his body, I caught a glimpse of what Lotto was holding: a glistening mag of cheap peach vodka. That bewildered me so much I didn't realize the bottle was actually being swung at my face. The assault was more obvious when the glass connected, my head flew backward, and I toppled over railings into the hot yard. My vision speckled, and my temple immediately throbbed, but I got to my feet. My progress was short-lived, however.

As I fled over the front fence, my foot caught, and that sent me crashing face-first into the ground. I was scratching away in the dirt and grass, aiming for the tracks, when the heavy vodka bottle landed again, thudding against the bones of my back shoulder. I flipped over, shielding my face with forearms and legs. From below, Lotto looked like a plump Hephaestus in a golf polo and pleated khakis, the bottle cocked over his head like the hammer of death, his swaying body framed by a burning netherworld. On each of his cheeks the pony blood had cracked and flaked partially away.

"What the *hell?*" said Lotto, with a slurring slowness. His baggy eyes and bunched clothing made it clear he'd just woken up, likely too hammered from five swallows of peach drink to get back to his gilded estate. It's possible, too, he'd been trying to act as his own security guard and failed badly. "You ruin my biggest day," he said. "And now you're trying to *kill* me?"

"I didn't know you were in there!"

"Why do this?"

"I *didn't* do it, Lotto," I said. "I saw flames and came running."

"I smell the gas on you."

"Just run, man."

"You're a lying son-of-a-bitch, God."

"Go!"

"*Why* do this to me? To your sweet fuckin' place?"

"Run!"

Before I could lie more, he swung down fast and connected with my ankle—*thunk*—and again with my knee. I yelped and screamed that we both were going to die. My overturned-tortoise defense wasn't working, and I feared he'd leave me for dead should he really knock me out. As he cocked back the bottle again, I ignored my pacifist leanings and launched a foot into the pit of Lotto's spongy belly. That put him back far enough, coughing and doubled over, that I could stand up and fight.

For a second, Lotto seemed to surrender. He took in his surroundings, the severity of the damage, his draining profits. He looked instantly crushed. His face folded all over itself. And his interest in me ended there.

Lotto yanked on his necklace, pulled the sad Jesus up from his chest, and rubbed it across his cheeks and forehead. He dropped the crucifix back to his chest, closed his eyes, and stood still for a moment, despite the insufferable heat. And then, while crossing his ankles and lifting his arms straight out at the shoulders, Lotto Livingston fully succumbed to his ego and savior complex—until I stepped up and punched him hard across the cheekbone.

My hand exploded with pain. Lotto's clenched face burst open with a panicked, indignant daze, as if he'd been startled awake, pried from the most grandiose dream. He looked me in the face and shouted: "Fucking mongrel!"

"Run, Lotto!" I screamed, hacking with smoke inhalation and trying to mask my face. "Or burn to death. Whatever. But I'm going, now!"

Lotto opted not to run way but to drop the bottle, open his hands like falcon's talons, and charge at me. I bent low, into a sort of jiujitsu stance, with intentions of tripping him and running to safety alone. But Lotto never reached me. Something at ground level made him stop, pivot northward, and dart off toward the railroad tracks at maybe twenty-five miles per hour. In my mind I called him a chump. The sirens were so close now, I could hear them from specific directions, piercing the inferno's moan. It was time to get the hell gone myself.

I started to follow Lotto. I ducked beneath what seemed the thickest layer of smoke and hustled with bent legs. And I nearly stepped on the leviathan's immense black tail.

The anaconda, injured and writhing, was poking its head beneath the engulfed, elevated wood of Felix's front porch, as if seeking cover, trying to get back in. She was confused and desperate, thrashing against burning boards. The latter twenty feet of the snake were punctured and bleeding in places, swinging across The Flank's roadway in gigantic swipes, like a cracking whip with the girth of a telephone pole. I couldn't move or breath, only crouch. I was stuck between a hysterical, gargantuan reptile and a burning civilization. A hell of our own doing. A horror for the ages. The worst Atlanta summer since Yankee bombardment, reaching the true apex of self-inflicted shittiness.

"Let me out, Martha," is all I could say, choking, clinging to dying hope. "Get to the tracks! Get away! We're going to die!"

What happened next is so absurd it can't be true. It couldn't happen. Not even during those absurdly strange months from hell, in this era of utmost urban absurdity. Except it's true. I lived it. And Martha felt it, too.

For the third and final time, that piercing autumn wind came back, whipped across the neighborhood, shocked me to no end. Again it was a cleansing bath, an existential relief, even cooler than July's. Only this time it was more functional and effective—at first in the most glorious way, and then the most apocalyptic.

The strange wind streamed in from the north, pushing across the tracks and over the potentate of lost snakes, and then straight down the scorching gut of The Flank. It blew back my hair, cleared my watery eyes, and permeated my camouflage. In the smoke and flames the wind cleared a sort of tunnel, albeit fickle and dangerous. For an instant, I saw an unblemished path to safety a few hundred feet away, in the heart of Sweetberry. Martha must have sensed the clearing as well, as she dislodged her sleek head from Felix's porch, tasted the smokeless gust, and compressed her extraordinary length, plotting escape. She moved so fast through the dirt and grass—headed toward the rails, trees, and ostensibly the liberating sewers beyond—you would have sworn she was swimming.

I ran in the opposite direction, breathing the air's evanescent purity. I tried not to see the collapsing, ashen clumps the bungalows were becoming. The sirens were very close, but I knew if I could just dive into a nearby backyard, or the right hedge, I could sneak through the neighborhood's verdure all the way home. The getaway route was clear. I'd ditch my evidentiary clothing in a neighbor's trash bin, bleach the evidence off my hands, and take a two-hour shower as fire teams rendered everything under control. That mischievous wind, however, had other plans.

Cooler and stronger than seconds before, the wind pushed deep into the burning bungalow husks and brought out ashes the size of sycamore leaves. Alongside the ashes were infinite, finer molten pieces. A great lifting of heat against the night, these moldering bits seemed to congeal the higher they went, like a million sky-bound cigarettes, all packed together. I ducked behind a row of Italian cypresses and watched the ashes climb. Each gust brought more sparkling orange out of The Flank, toward occupied homes, until the sheer mass of hovering ash must have covered five or six city blocks. It was beautiful, actually, but in a very sinister way. It thickened and compounded, like airborne lava, stealing the stars, reigniting itself, sizzling and popping. Just as I was standing to run, the strange wind weakened, and it all started coming down.

Graceful in its falling, the ash's tiny flames were stubborn. They weren't going to be extinguished by the time they reached very flammable things, like thirsty sheds and parched pines and sunbaked, timeworn rooftops. At this point, I thought I could hear the chatter and yells of neighbors, but I wasn't sure. I wanted to call back through the night: "Are y'all *seein'* this, too?" Either the sky was bringing hell, or I was delirious with smoke.

The sirens had clearly, thankfully arrived. Firefighters shouted directives about wind speeds and structural salvageability; the first two trucks shot geysers across opposite sides of The Flank. But then the wind, as if suddenly shy, halted almost entirely. The danger was amplified. With no updraft, the ashes dropped faster. Dive-bombing, miniscule flames rained across Sweetberry Park. I started jogging blindly, turning circles, preparing to help, anywhere and everywhere, in some small way. My mind filled with visions of those poor, eternal Pompeii bodies.

The first to ignite, we think, was the creaky American Foursquare whose owner had sold use of his toilet during the carnival. His old voice was the first I heard screaming. The roof over his porch was flat, and the ashes had met oak leaves up there, sun-dried for months on the rolled roofing and tar. By the time I arrived, the hysterical owner, Henry, was trying to push an heirloom armoire through the dining room window, screaming for help in catching it. His neighbors did come, and I joined them in pulling out the elderly man, sans furniture, to safety in his front yard, despite his kicks and screams.

I grabbed the shoulder of a younger, athletic guy and pointed to The Flank. "Two blocks, that way," I shouted.

"*What?*"

"Go down and demand a fire truck to save this house," I said, angry. "The Flank's too far gone."

The kid was dazed, his eyes wet. "Mr. Johnson, what *is* this?" he said, catching burning ash with open hands, wincing. "This is real fire—"

"Run, man! *Go!*"

"Jesus, look around," he said, unmoving. "It's Armageddon."

Henry's thrashing knocked me back, and I noticed in the streets that a monumental gathering was afoot, a flood of panicked humanity. Sweetberry Parkers by the hundreds, brought out by the stink of The Flank's cremation, were bearing witness to the fiery skies and smoke. In the blocks beyond Sweetberry Park, on the horizon, you could see clear starry night, and parents were shoving children into cars in hopes of escaping to that, ripping their SUVs and sport wagons through yards only to further clog the jammed streets. Two more Atlanta Fire Department engines honked and growled through the crowd, shooting bursts of water at burning bushes. Hip mailboxes made of contemporary wood slats were ablaze beside the road; angry men kicked them over and stomped them, only to ignite dried-out piles of branches and pine straw.

We all ducked when three thunderous booms came from the west. I feared gunfire and death, a true riot. But a tremendous splash of fireworks above treetops told the truth, that at least one transformer had just exploded; where those sparks landed, black alleys began to glow, as homes and streetlights for two full blocks went dark. A crowd in that direction clamored, the sound of a bad call against the home team in open-air stadiums, only more desperate.

The goateed kid, still standing beside me, screamed, "No!" and pointed southward. Three blocks away, the prized gingerbread Victorian that neighborhood boys used to call a witch's castle was a three-story, lit matchstick. Its grand turret was defiant and intact, a dark pure cone against flames, but within a few minutes it too would bow into coals. So went the neo-Craftsman beside the Victorian and a Colonial reproduction at the rear. We surged with the crowd in that direction in time to see Americana Mama's customized dream go up—a fire so intense it made smoldering orbs of three ancient oaks beside it. Innumerable speeding vehicles smashed into each other in the chaotic streets, and we all screamed as one clunker spewed gasoline, made Oakhurst Drive a river of fire, and caused at least four abandoned, running cars to explode. Already sweltering, the temperature shot up by twenty degrees. Every screaming face glistened.

One by one, we berserk Atlantans pounded on bungalows with their roofs on fire, busting windows with rocks and branches and shouting for occupants to flee. We kicked and stomped bushes and wiped piled embers from parked cars. In one front yard, I watched an old-timer I knew, Fran, valiantly dousing her Queen Anne with a garden hose—until the Escalade in her driveway exploded, kicking her onto the sidewalk and igniting her neighbor's lawn furniture. I pulled Fran into her street by the shoulders of her bathrobe and screamed for medics. The chaos was so thorough nobody cared. Another old lady's hair-sprayed coif had exploded, and I watched as the spray from a stuck fire engine doused her onto her knees, then flat on her back, woozy but extinguished.

With my phone service cancelled, I reached into Fran's pocket, found her cell phone, and called 911. I didn't get a word out before the dispatcher hollered: "All units and fire personnel are en route to Sweetberry Park. Hang up. Flee the area. Seek shelter beyond the fire zone now!"

Guilt threatened to concrete me in place, sobbing in the middle of burning Oakhurst Drive. But I was resolute that my life's most disastrous mistake would not turn deadly, so I joined the roving horde of home-searchers for the next hour, ushering dazed victims to the neighborhood's widest, clearest boulevard. We begged them to just walk toward downtown, into the clear. An army of medics and police and other law enforcement swept in from the non-burning direction. At the commercial village, I saw Carlito standing in the middle of Happy's Pit Stop's little parking lot, preemptively wetting the gas pumps and grounds with the thumb-compressed spray of his garden hose. He was openly crying, a contrast to the musclebound commando he'd always been. I called his name while jogging past. He couldn't hear me over the noise.

As it appeared that firefighters were finally making progress, strategically beating back fires in the core neighborhood and dimming the overall glow, the crowds looked up in amazement to the clearing sky. Three helicopters I recognized from news reports as North Georgia Forestry aircraft unleashed magnificent waterfalls from two hundred feet up, splashing streets and extinguishing smaller homes in seconds. The choppers broke away, toward East Lake Reservoir, and returned within a few minutes with another water show, and then again, eliciting gleeful roars from the displaced populace.

The panic began to subside, making way for early grief. From every direction came the stink of burning plastic and a sad low sizzle. Everyone was exhausted and slouched, the adrenaline ebbing. We all feared what daybreak would unveil. When my band of searchers agreed that all burning or dangerously unstable homes had been cleared, I gritted my teeth and started the five-block slog to my Victorian. One of the helicopter dumps, if my estimates were correct, appeared to have been a direct hit on my block, which was not a good sign.

She was little more than a crooked chimney, a decrepit ancestor to Sherman's Sentinels, a sad stack of brick amongst smoking, naked trees. A small vintage fire engine from a department ten miles away was devoting its entire water supply to her fallen bones and those of the gone cottage next door. The firefighters glistened with overspray, angels all.

The street was eerie and empty otherwise. Everyone had run away. At least four more houses—two Sweetberry originals from the 1890s, the others pricey new-builds—were embers on my block alone. In the flash of fire truck lights, I caught glimpses of gap-toothed blocks farther down the street, where lucky homes looked virtually untouched while neighboring structures just did not exist. My street, like so many others, had been decimated. I'd done all of this. Knowing that was sickening, and my hot skin tingled. What had felt valiant and clever a couple of hours ago seemed like a vortex of shame I'd never escape. I was foolish, misguided, and guilty. What's more, I truly had nothing now, certainly not homeowner's insurance, and I'd dragged good friends and neighbors into the same plight. I didn't bother rummaging. I was too tired to weep. And there'd be ample time for written apologies and repentances in whatever years I had left. I walked to the first police car I could find and lifted a rear door handle in hopes of getting in and surrendering. It was locked, but my efforts drew the ire of a husky officer who asked what the hell I thought I was doing.

Before I could confess and condemn myself forever, his nostrils flared, his face fell, and I could see he'd caught the heavy, telltale scent of lighter fluid all over me. He was instantly enraged. "Officer, what happened was—" is all I managed to say, before he shot a clenched hand onto my jaw, put an extended leg in front of mine, and tripped me forward. My torso landed in the street first, my head bounced, and my breath, like those strange winds of summer, was gone. It would have been the second saddest moment of my long life if not for the singing.

The boot on my skull obscured my vision, but not to the point I couldn't see the towering columns of The Holiness Church of Our Savior up the hill, just down the block. Neighbors were scurrying around its front lawn and streaming inside and generally feeding off the building's good aura in such a time of peril. A hymn I didn't know spilled out of open doors and windows, lifting everything. It must have been a chorus of three hundred voices. I wondered if Genteel knew about the melee yet. I thought that maybe she'd seen it on the news, swooped in, joined her congregation for one last night, and found her singing voice again. I thought that miracles like that could happen, because I wasn't thinking straight. Genteel was at some hotel, miles away. She was on to her new place. The singers were mourning the tattered state of theirs. So in my sulking and miserable guilt I only tried to relax. My life's last moments of uncaged liberty, I knew, would be better spent enjoying the church music than trying to explain idiocy, or entertaining all the stupid thoughts in my head.

CHAPTER 28 (EPILOGUE)

The soupiest summer in history gently bled out and died, as searchers combed the ruins of Sweetberry Park for several weeks. To our great pleasure and shock, not a single human casualty was reported. Hundreds of houses stood unharmed, easily fixable, or rebuildable from solid foundations, which is a cop-out way of saying I'd burned a shitload down. All streets, bike lanes, and train lines were operable, however. No businesses were found to be seriously damaged. The neighborhood's marquee playground was merely half-melted. It was god-awful, but history has shown it can be worse.

Then came an evening of merciful, light-jacket weather. Leaves of oaks, maples, and American beeches began to gracefully wither. It was like a citywide steam valve hissed—humidity escaping, fears dissipating, our tensions lifting. With a slow tumbling of high temperatures, the record summer heat came out of the hundreds, nineties, and soon relented to nippy October evenings and clean November winds, a relative climatological heaven. Meanwhile, what the *Beacon*'s in-house florist Quinton Delano described as Atlanta's "cumulative, communal trauma" and "the lasting delirium from a summer of civic horrors, a localized Civil War"—well, that had transformed by Thanksgiving into a sort of intense calm across intown neighborhoods. Also prevalent was a sense of pride in having persevered, for the most part, as a functioning society, one that would rebuild better than before. A new winter beer gala was declared for February—tentatively called "Ophidians Festival"—that would double as an homage to abused animals and a fundraiser for Sweetberry's resurrection. Nobody mentioned the word "snake" in promotions.

Inspired by her appalling but effective carnival performance, members of the millennial-led Sweetberry Park Resurgence Association proposed a statue in honor of Genteel Briggs. Nobody argued against it, so it was going to happen, eventually. The statue would rise on the former site of Shotgun Three. At its base, Genteel would be described, somewhat hilariously, as a "legendary blueswoman and historical preservation activist." An anonymous donor, rumored to be the owner of a local pro sports franchise, donated $40,000—half of the statue's estimated cost. Final designs for the statue, per neighborhood leaders, would have to be approved by Genteel herself. But that was going to take a while.

Genteel and her boyfriend had left Atlanta in late August for a yearlong series of all-inclusive ocean-liner cruises, destined for ports around the world. Soon after departure, they both went incommunicado. She sent me one single postcard, from Costa Rica, and though it had been mangled by security guards, it smelled like mangoes and rum. On the back was scribbled, "Forgiven," and below that an angel, smiling, above a devil, frowning. At the bottom, she'd written: "We hit the Lotto!"

Lotto Livingston, crestfallen, sold his portion of Sweetberry Park back to the city at his cost. He never stipulated why, at least not in public records. Lotto reportedly told associates he intended to sell off many of his real estate assets and personal properties in the metro area and launch some sort of jewelry business with a Danish broker of gold necklaces. His wife is said to be in the process of divorcing him, citing infidelity and paranoiac tendencies. Rumor has it she doesn't believe Lotto—like nobody believes me—that Martha is still out there, lurking.

Meanwhile, tentative city plans call for The Flank's land to become a public park, according to the most recent Atlanta City Council meeting. It would be a simple lawn girded by trees, with the Genteel statue and maybe a plaque, the type of greenspace where you can do whatever you want, so long as it's peaceful.

Unfortunately, I didn't witness any of the above first-hand, with the exception of the postcard. I read about it all in week-old newspapers floating around the jail's rec room, or I heard it on television in the more spacious dayroom.

Like the general public, Fulton County prosecutors and investigators want my head in a peach basket, pronto. I can't blame them; I only blame me. I refuse to implicate anyone else. I've declined all media jailhouse interviews. My fight's over. My head is theirs, if they want it. It's only a matter of time before I'm a family man again, and I plan to cruise peaceably into those skies—to the extent that prison allows for laidback existential soaring.

As December's nip began to swirl around the city jail, weaving through razor-wire in the rec yard, I settled into the late winter of my days. Letting go brought real comfort. I'd seen and done enough with my life to consider it complete—and to kill my wanderlust for most places beyond the walls. Captivity is terrible but not as bad, at least not yet, as I'd always imagined. The meals are warm, frequent, and comparatively delicious. The heat is free.

By the week of Christmas, I'd developed enough intestinal fortitude to not cry every night on the hard bed of my jail cell in the wee hours. At first, when depression was freshest, I'll admit that I cried constantly for everything: our ravaged neighborhood, our town in general, Joey's life, brokenhearted Becky's life, for the destroyed animals of Atlanta Memorial Zoo, for Martha in her filthy sewers, and, yes, for Great White, impounded and rusting in some municipal vehicle cemetery. But that's all to be expected. Being caged pummels your spirit. And so does turning seventy years old in a place where nobody knows it's your birthday and wouldn't care if you told them.

I did not cry when my home's land was seized and sold—for a drastically reduced $149,000, given the neighborhood's condition—and every dollar went to fire victims as restitution. I hesitate to call that philanthropy. But in a way, it felt like being set free. I became a man of no place, no means, no lasting worries. Just a guy with time—and finally something to say.

Between bouts of weeping, I'd devoted energy all morning, day, and until at least midnight into writing this book. The decades of procrastination were over, the topic obvious. I've scribbled feverishly, in pencil, onto a growing stack of legal pads provided by my attorney. My three cellmates—all younger, nonviolent, and reverent of the frail, vaguely orange septuagenarian among them—admire my perseverance. They've watched in awe as the eraser shavings accumulate and the stacked legal pads climb. They formed a consensus that I was wizened and hip, and that my tome might somehow exonerate them. One accused interstate weed smuggler, Clark, lent me a tiny forbidden flashlight to keep my writing going long after lights-out. All of them have become protectors of the work, too, which I didn't even ask for. During the occasional cell searches, they'll hover near the stacked legal pads, as if the nascent memoir is their own contraband child, barely born and too feeble for rough handling by guards.

Early in the process I gave my book what seemed the only fitting title: "Goodbye, Sweetberry Park."

The outlook is hopeless, but that's OK. Among a binder's worth of ancillary charges, I'm facing 247 counts of criminal recklessness resulting in bodily injury—one for each neighbor treated by medics or hospitalized. Seven counts of animal cruelty for three dogs, two cats, and two exotic birds that succumbed, tragically, to smoke or fire. And the kicker: 320 counts of felony arson, one for every Sweetberry structure destroyed or damaged, including my own home, the fallen heirloom, the attempted curse, my baby. I'm faced with a max sentencing of 1,256 years, give or take. The minimum, per my public defender, is around fifty years.

I've tried to plead guilty already, but my attorney advises otherwise. Let's wait, he says, until next summer, when the mess will be sufficiently sorted out with insurance companies. There's no need, says my attorney, who always smells of mint, to expedite my transfer from the cushy city jail to Georgia's unforgiving prison system. "Plus, there is *zero* chance," the attorney, Sam, often reminds me, "that you'll have those city views in the real-deal pen."

Ah, the views. The long slit of a window in the cell's right corner is a godsend. It's the most inspiring thing, an eighth-floor portal between purgatory and rolling landscapes of possibility, to all that will never be within reach again, to a beautiful city dressed in Christmas. When my hand tires of writing, or my recollections fail, I hop from my bunk and press my face to the window's reinforced glass; I pretend to smell bungalow cookies, backyard fires under towering pines, and wafts of dark beer and Cuban bread in the Sweetberry eateries.

Sometimes, looking across the city, I pretend to hear Squeaky's stuttered laugh. Other times I actually do hear that, because Squeaky has been living on the other side of the open-air jail dorm since transferring in early December. He'll remain there, too, at least until his plea and sentencing. Each morning he greets me pleasantly: "*Damn*, you stupid."

One afternoon this week, Squeaky and I were playing a lunchtime game we call "peas and carrots." It's like tabletop golf only with, yes, peas as golf balls and uncooked carrots as clubs. Nine flat washers Squeaky lifted from the laundry room act as the holes. In this world of wishing time away, our little game is surprisingly enthralling. Neither of us is more talented at peas and carrots than the other, which heightens the drama, especially with such high stakes: After a round of nine holes, he with the lowest score gets five of the loser's sweet potato fries. Sometimes we bet eight fries.

"What's the big plans?" Squeaky asked me this week, whacking a lopsided green orb toward hole three, barely missing.

"I don't have big plans."

"I mean the book," he said. "Them scribbles on legal pads."

A birdie for me on hole three. "It's a long story," I said. "A story about a neighborhood, our neighborhood."

"I mean what's *next*?"

"Not sure," I said. "My lawyer swears I'll have more time to type it out, to get the whole thing organized, when they send me down to Jefferson."

Squeaky raised his hand to drive home a point—likely something about him being paid, should his likeness appear in any book—but instead his throat seized. He dropped his carrot as his eyelids shot open.

"*Ack!*" said Squeaky, pointing across the room.

"What, man?"

"It's McQuackery!"

It sure was. Clad from ankle to neck in Mental Ward Beige, holding a heaping tray of food, Gerald McCaffrey stood across the room, looking confused, sedated, lonely. Seated to his left, a guard was eating a sloppy joe and nodding for McCaffrey to have a seat wherever he wished. The dorm was always locked, of course, and I noticed that McCaffrey's utensils were plastic. But this was liberty he wasn't accustomed to anymore, and he didn't budge. Somehow you could tell he'd gone mute. He stared at the lone wall clock, entranced by the reminder of time's passage. Then his focus inexplicably shifted to us.

"He lookin' over here, ain't he?" said Squeaky.

"I swear that's him," I said.

"Yup."

"There's no doubt."

"That's the nut who made this happen, who did this to us."

"No," I said. "We did this to us."

Squeaky grabbed my wrist. "Can you be-*leave* this, God?" he said. "Let's take him out, right now. Before that guard can stop us."

"No, man."

"This dude has got to *pay!*"

"Shut up."

"Seriously. He sees us. He wants some."

"Relax, Squeaky."

"Is he comin' this way?"

"Looks like it. Oh my God..."

"He is. He comin' over here. *What!*"

"Man, he really is."

"I'm-a hop up and start chokin', God."

"No you're not."

"Yessir. I been dreamin' of this."

"Let him sit down, Squeaky."

"He comin' to us, man!"

"Wow, McCaffrey right here, in the flesh."

"I'm-a hit him with this tray, take him down like that!"

"Stop. Stay seated."

"I'm-a choke him! Yeah! Wait, why he doin' this? Why he comin' to *me*?"

"Holy hell, he is."

"I'm-a get him, God!"

"Stay down, Squeaky. Don't choke this man."

"Argh!"

"Whoa!"

"Arrrrrrrrrrrrrrgh!"

For a second, McCaffrey stood directly over Squeaky, which petrified the seated man, squashing all his toughness. McCaffrey smirked and set his tray on the seat next to Squeaky, so as not to disrupt our golf game. Without warning or invitation, McCaffrey slowly extended his arms and stared at the top of Squeaky's skull, as if amazed by the misguided tempests therein. When he wrapped his arms around Squeaky's head, hugging gently, McCaffrey's guard shot to his feet, and Squeaky hummed in terror.

"Hey, Gerald," I said, trying to diffuse the situation, offering a single carrot and pea. "It's your turn, man, if you'd like to play with us."

ACKNOWLEDGEMENTS

This book is dedicated to my historic, fascinating Atlanta neighborhood, Kirkwood (and past neighborhoods, Inman Park and Old Fourth Ward). To so many neighbors, old pals, brief acquaintances, and journalism interview subjects who've shared stories of triumph and woe over the years. And to anyone struggling to realize their American Dream, that ability to get ahead and stay there, which is disconcertingly elusive today. A special thanks to the Costa Rican tour guide who pulled me away from a dark tangle of jungle foliage like he'd saved my life—he might have—and instantly triggered a fascination for beautiful, potentially lethal snakes. To professors, family, friends, literary agents, publishers, and fellow writers who encouraged me to not give up. And to Martha... may she forever roam free in the sewers of our minds.

ABOUT THE AUTHOR

Josh Green is an award-winning journalist, fiction author, and editor whose work has appeared in *Atlanta*, *Garden & Gun*, *Indianapolis Monthly*, *The Atlanta Journal-Constitution*, *The Los Angeles Review*, *The Baltimore Review*, and several anthologies. His first collection of short stories, *Dirtyville Rhapsodies*, was hailed by *Men's Health* as a "Best Book for the Beach" and was named a top 10 book of the year by *Atlanta*. His first novel, *Secrets of Ash*, garnered a number of accolades, including the Indie Reader Discovery Award for literary fiction and a runner-up placement at the Hollywood Book Festival. He lives in Atlanta with his wife and two daughters. By day, he covers the wild world of Atlanta development and real estate.

ABOUT THE PUBLISHER

The Sager Group was founded in 1984. In 2012 it was chartered as a multimedia content brand, with the intent of empowering those who create art—an umbrella beneath which makers can pursue, and profit from, their craft directly, without gatekeepers. TSG publishes books; ministers to artists and provides modest grants; and produces documentary, feature, and commercial films. By harnessing the means of production, The Sager Group helps artists help themselves. For more information, please see www. TheSagerGroup.net.

MORE FROM THE SAGER GROUP

The Swamp: Deceit and Corruption in the CIA
An Elizabeth Petrov Thriller (Book 1)
by Jeff Grant

Eat Wheaties: A Novel
by Michael Kun

#MeAsWell: A Novel
by Peter Melhlman

Death Came Swiftly: Novel About the Tay Bridge Disaster of 1879
by Bill Abrams

High Tolerance: A Novel of Sex, Race, Celebrity, Murder... and
Marijuana
by Mike Sager

Miss Havilland: A Novel
by Gay Daly

The Orphan's Daughter: A Novel
by Jan Cherubin

Lifeboat No. 8: Surviving the Titanic
by Elizabeth Kaye

Into the River of Angels: A Novel
by George R. Wolfe

See our entire library at TheSagerGroup.net

THE SAGER GROUP
Artifex Te Adiuva